ACCELERATED

ACCELERATED

BRONWEN HRUSKA

PEGASUS BOOKS
NEW YORK LONDON

ACCELERATED

Pegasus Books LLC
80 Broad Street, 5th Floor
New York, NY 10004

First Pegasus Books edition October 2012

Interior design by Maria Fernandez

Library of Congress Cataloging-in-Publication Data is available.

ISBN: 978-1-60598-379-0

10 9 8 7 6 5 4 3 2 1

Printed in the United States of America
Distributed by W. W. Norton & Company

For Will and Nick

CHAPTER ONE

SEAN BENNING HAD PUT IN HIS TIME. HE COULDN'T RISK BEING caught in another conversation about ERB percentiles and after-school activities that cost more than he made in a month. Forty-five minutes was his limit. He downed the dregs of his second gin and tonic before ditching the glass on a mirrored tabletop, all the while clutching his jacket in the other hand. He cast a longing look at the front door, which glowed like a vision through a sudden parting in the overdressed crowd. He allowed himself to be pulled toward it, his pulse slowing with the knowledge that he'd be out soon.

"There you are," a voice growled. A tanned hand grabbed him by the arm, pulling him back. Jolted from his vision of escape, he spun around, almost slamming into a shiny white armoire that was camouflaged in the all-white room. Cheryl Eisner stood too close, her dark eyes softer, drunker, than he'd seen them. "I've been looking for you," she said, her voice rising above the party chitchat.

He panicked. "The Annual Fund donations," he said, stalling. "They're not due yet, are they?" But he knew they'd been due last week. "I lost the form." Not that he was planning on giving the school a cent above the thirty-eight thousand dollars his in-laws were already paying. He couldn't fathom the income you'd need to live decently in New York, pay full freight for even one kid—though who had just one these days?—plus make a big donation to the school every year. But people did it. Lots of people.

Cheryl frowned and shooed away the topic with a graceful swat of the air. "Let's not talk about the Annual Fund. It's too boring." Her son, Marcus, was in Toby's class. Until tonight, Sean had only seen her in tight designer workout clothes at school pickup and drop-off. Now, she wore a fitted gold dress. With the heels, she must have been six-two, almost eye level. Looking a woman in the eye like this was rare, and strangely exciting. She focused on his jacket. "You're not going, are you?" She touched the bare skin just below her clavicle and above the two scoops of cleavage being offered on the gold tray of her dress.

It was almost distracting enough to make him forget the front door.

He tried not to stare as she stroked her own skin. "I was just heading out." Were they real? Fake? Toby's face popped into his head like a censored bar over her breasts. "My . . . the sitter . . . I've got to get back," he stumbled.

She gave him a strange smile and pulled him past the parents of Toby's classmates, who he barely recognized in their party attire, toward a table spread with caviar and blini. "First, you've got to try this," she said. Somehow he'd missed the food on his first sweep of the room. She plunged her index finger into the ornate crystal bowl and held a dripping fingerful of caviar in front of his lips. He was famished, but he pressed them closed instinctively. Marcus had always been a nervous kid. He could see why. "Go ahead," she cooed. "Let me in."

If she hadn't looked so determined, poised with fish eggs on her finger, he would have been sure this was all a joke. At every turn, parents gossiped, laughed, and shrieked at each others' witty anecdotes. He hadn't heard one witty anecdote the entire evening. The good news was that nobody seemed to be watching him. Still, what was he doing? Was she *actually* coming on to him?

Cheryl waited patiently.

Really, what choice did he have? He opened his mouth and she thrust her finger inside. The little black eggs exploded with sickeningly salty pops as he remembered he hated caviar. She ran her finger along the roof of his mouth and around his upper lip and by the time she removed it, he felt like he'd had some kind of internal exam.

She plucked two glasses from the bar. "Now we have to drink champagne."

A waiter had handed him a drink the moment he walked through the door. A second drink had magically appeared shortly after that. He was comfortably numb. Any more alcohol would push him toward drunk. "I'm okay," he said. Besides, why would he drink champagne with Marcus's hot mother? Wasn't that a bad idea?

"Come on." She pressed the champagne glass into his hand. "I have a toast. Please?"

"Sure," he said, charmed by the *please.* "What are we toasting?"

"To Wonder Dad," she said with an ironic smile. "The man who does it all."

"Trust me, I'm not—"

"Drink," she demanded. "It's *my* toast."

He wasn't Wonder Dad. Didn't want to be Wonder Dad. He wasn't sure he wanted to be toasting with Cheryl at all. But he drank nonetheless. The champagne tickled going down. "I'll see you at school," he said with an apologetic smile. "I've got to get back."

He took a few steps toward the door before she dropped the bomb. "You've heard about the new teacher, right?"

He stopped. Turned. "They found a new teacher?"

She nodded in slow motion and didn't let go of his gaze. She waited while he digested the information.

A real teacher could turn everything around for Toby. He retraced his steps on the white shag carpet. "Who is she? When does she start?"

"It's a little loud out here," Cheryl said, and walked away from him. After a moment, she looked back to summon him with a sideways glance. Like a dog chasing a bone, he followed her past a mixed media installation that looked an awful lot like the one he'd seen last year at the Whitney. This wasn't a living room, it was an *Architectural Digest* spread. How could you raise kids in an all-white room? What about crayons, ketchup, barf?

He rounded the corner and when he didn't see her, he panicked that he'd lost his line to the only piece of gossip he cared about.

A stage whisper hit him from the guest bathroom. "In here."

Against his better judgment, he followed her voice into the room that blazed with tiny spotlights suspended from thin wires. She locked the door behind him and propped her ass against the sink. "Much quieter," she said.

He couldn't help laughing at that one. "It is a quiet room." A candle on a glass shelf made the bathroom smell like pumpkin pie. He liked pumpkin pie. Still, it was weird. He leaned against a monogrammed towel. "So." He looked at her and wondered if he was really going to go through with this.

She kicked off her heels and rubbed his calf with her foot. "So what?"

"So what do you know about the new teacher?"

"She's not from New York." Cheryl hooked her finger through his belt loop and tugged. Subtlety was not Cheryl's forte. But she had other qualities.

He took a step toward her. "What's her name?" Turning the banal conversation into something like foreplay was easier than he'd anticipated.

"Jessica Harper." She pushed him away an arm's length and cast her brown eyes down. Not to the ground. "She starts Monday." She pulled him close again, running her hands down his chest and around his back. It had been a long time since someone had touched him like this. Touched him at all. He hadn't realized how much he missed it. Soon, her hands traveled down to his ass, which she began to massage. Almost as soon as she did, it began vibrating.

"Answer it," she said, running both hands down the backs of his thighs. "It might be Toby."

Toby was probably fine. Almost definitely fine. "I can call him back . . ."

She slid the phone out of his back pocket and opened it, holding it to his ear. *Say hello*, she mouthed, and traced her finger down his chest.

"Hello?" he said, locking eyes with her and wondering when his life had become this strange.

"Why aren't you calling me back?" Ellie's voice hit him like a bucket of cold water. He must have backed away from Cheryl, because she tightened her hold on him. Undeterred, she teased her hand under his shirt.

"We need to talk about this medication thing," Ellie was saying.

"I can't talk right now. This isn't a good time—"

"There's never a good time," Ellie snapped. "This is our child's health."

"Look, Ellie, I'm never putting him on that stuff. Never." He'd been louder than he meant to be and made an effort to bring down the volume. "Conversation's over."

"Grow up, Sean." Ellie's voice condescended through the phone from wherever she was. "Dr. Shineman's email said he might need to be on Ritalin. You can't just ignore that. Get him evaluated. Jesus. It's a no-brainer. See what a doctor has to say, then we make the decision."

Cheryl pinched his nipples, which would have felt great if Ellie hadn't been yelling in his ear. "The no-brainer," he said, "is that you have no say in this. You gave that up when you disappeared." Cheryl lifted his shirt and started biting at his abs. The game was kind of fun. He tried to stay on point. "I really have to go. You caught me right in the middle of something."

"Don't you dare hang up on—"

He flipped the phone closed and threw it on the fluffy bathmat.

"Trouble on the ranch?" Cheryl asked between kisses that seemed to be heading south along his abdomen.

He wasn't going to let Ellie mess up whatever this was. She'd messed up too much already. "Wrong number," he said, and Cheryl seemed to appreciate the absurdity of the lie.

"I hate when that happens."

"Very inconvenient," he said, and tried to blot out Ellie's voice, their conversation, the image of her that was now lodged in his mind. "So . . . where were we?"

"The new teacher." Cheryl's smile came off as a challenge.

"Right. The new teacher." He leaned against the basin, his face inches from hers. "So. What kind of credentials does she have?"

"Excellent," Cheryl said, breathily. "They're excellent." He wondered if all parent socials were this social and if it had been a good idea to let Ellie come to these alone for so many years. He now had a clear view down Cheryl's dress. There they were again. He fought the urge to squeeze them.

Then he thought: Why? Ellie had walked out on him. He and Cheryl were adults who happened to be primed for sex and conveniently locked in this fancy bathroom for exactly that reason.

This kind of thing didn't happen every day. In fact, nothing like this had ever happened to him. Not to mention it had been a hell of a long time since he'd had sex. He missed it—craved it. Forget everything else that was messed up with Ellie being gone—not being able to have sex was by far the worst. He deserved this random encounter. He should push away all the doubt and just go with it. Liking Cheryl was not required. And she was making it so easy. There was no room for misinterpretation, just a clear and straightforward invitation—verging on an order—to screw her.

She yanked on his belt buckle and a laser-like flash blinded him. When he got his vision back, he realized that the gumball-size rock on her finger was reflecting the overhead lights into rainbow beams. Kind of like a superhero ring. He'd never seen Cheryl's husband and now he was forced to wonder how big the guy was and if he could throw a punch. Then he remembered she was married to a famous neurosurgeon who traveled around the world saving lives. A guy like that would never risk messing up his hands.

"He doesn't care," she said. She was a mind reader, too, apparently. "We have an understanding."

An understanding sounded complicated. Or very simple. Who was he to argue with an understanding? He helped her undo his jeans and she pressed herself against him. She slid her tongue into his mouth and for the second time in fifteen minutes he felt like he was being probed.

His body wanted to plunge ahead, but his brain kept nagging at him. He could still walk away. He could walk away from this incredibly hot woman who wanted him. But he was a single father now, he reminded himself. It was hard to meet women. Besides, he might not have a chance like this again anytime soon if he didn't jump on it—jump on Cheryl—right now.

It turned out he didn't even need to make the decision. Cheryl was already sinking to her knees. He watched the top of her head tilt as she lowered her glossed lips onto him.

He couldn't help letting out a groan. It had been four months since anyone had touched, much less handled, him with such authority. And to think, he'd almost ditched the party. He'd remembered to prepare Toby's dinner. He'd gotten Toby in the shower early, but he'd completely forgotten about hiring a babysitter.

"Oh well," he'd told Toby only two hours ago. "Guess I'll have to skip it."

"Call Gloria in 6A," he'd countered. "She's always free."

"Why don't we play Monopoly instead? You can win."

"It's how Mom used to get me playdates," Toby said, reasonably. "You have to go."

Life was so unfair when you were a grownup and so simple when you were an eight-year-old kid. Sean had dialed Gloria's number, which Toby had written down for him on a Famiglia Pizza napkin that had come with his dinner. He'd go, but he wouldn't like it. The whole thing had sounded like a gigantic waste of time, not to mention boring.

So he'd been wrong on that last point. Cheryl's mouth was now vibrating with encouraging moans. She really didn't need to be so encouraging. In fact, he realized, panicking, everything was moving too fast. He thought of dead puppies, Toby's tutoring bills. His in-laws. None of it was working. He was dangerously close. He had to stall. He pulled away, hoisted her onto the speckled stone counter that surrounded the sunken basin of the sink and unzipped her dress. He was not going to leave the parent social without knowing if they were real. It would also buy him recovery time. If he was going to make the monumental mistake he was about to make, he was sure as hell going to make it last.

He'd always assumed silicone would be a turnoff. How wrong he'd been. They were dense, fun to play with—a little like water balloons but softer and they stood up all by themselves.

Condoms. It had been years since he'd needed a condom. But he needed one now, and fast. He couldn't imagine anyone keeping condoms in their mansion's guest bathroom. He reached past her toward the medicine cabinet, on the off chance.

"I got it," she said. She put his hand back on the water balloon, then leaned over and grabbed her gold bag from the toilet seat. She pulled out a condom wrapped in matching gold foil that she tore expertly with her teeth and rolled onto him with the speed and precision of a Nascar crew at a pit stop.

He reached between her legs and pushed aside a sliver of silky fabric that counted as her underwear. Her muscular thighs wrapped around his waist and before he knew it, he was in.

Then he remembered his mandate, the reason he was here in the first place. "Does Marcus want to have a playdate with Toby sometime?"

He wasn't sure if the *yes* she gasped had to do with the playdate or the thrusting. Soon, she was clawing his skin with her red nails and arching her double-jointed back. He realized, with a whole new level of respect for Pilates or whatever exercise classes she seemed to take all day, every day, that Cheryl's workouts had even toned her muscles in *there*. There was no doubt about it, he wasn't going to last long.

He tried, futilely, to hang on, but at a certain point it was impossible.

"No," Cheryl ordered, through heavy breathing. "Not yet." She was just gearing up. But there was no turning back. It was all about release. No more than five seconds later, the whole thing was over. He crumpled onto her, spent and relieved. But the relief lasted about as long as he had.

"Don't worry about it," Cheryl said, nudging him off her and snapping her underwear into place. She ran her hand along the side of his face, shook her head with a wistful sigh, and let herself out of the bathroom.

He slid to the floor and thumped his head repeatedly against the shiny tiles. Though most of the blood had left his brain, he was able to focus on the fact that he'd have to see Cheryl every day, twice a day—reliving the mortification of this very moment—until Toby was old enough to take himself to and from school. It would be years. Years of remembering how he'd failed at this basic act. He realized with horror that she might tell the other mothers.

He was deflating quickly, until the condom hung sadly between his legs. He peeled it off. Given a second chance, he'd definitely last longer. He toyed with the idea of getting her back on the sink to prove it to her but soon abandoned the idea. He'd had enough humiliation for one night. It was time to go home.

CHAPTER TWO

HE'D FALLEN, TRIPPED OVER A PIECE OF FURNITURE HE COULDN'T see in the all-white room. The third grade parents circled him. They were throwing canapés and kicking him. "Get up," they shouted. "Get up!" He curled into a fetal position, pulling his knees to his chest.

"Dad, get up!"

It was weird that the third grade parents were calling him Dad. Then he realized: there were no third grade parents. Toby was jabbing him in the ribs and yanking his pillow from under his head. He peeled open his eyes. The light hurt. A dull ache throbbed in his temples.

"It's Thursday." Toby pulled at his arm but couldn't budge him. "We can't be late."

The night rushed back: the disastrous bathroom sex, skulking home, then Toby crawling into his bed sometime around three. Toby never used to wake up at night. But since Ellie left he'd been creeping in four or five times a week and flailing around next to him all night.

"Five more minutes," he mumbled. "Tired."

When Toby pulled the comforter off the bed, letting cold air into the warm cocoon, Sean's reflexes kicked in. His arm shot out to grab it back.

"Ow!" Toby yelped. "Ow!"

Sean sat up, forced his eyes open. Toby was hunched over, clutching his chest. "Jesus. I'm sorry Tobe. I didn't know you were there. I didn't mean to—"

"You hit me!" His eyes were brimming over.

Sean was far from Wonder Dad. He was Hulking Brute Dad. Monster Dad. He rubbed Toby's back. "I didn't mean to, I was just . . ." He rolled up Toby's pajama top. "Let's take a look." It was red. Looked like he'd been hit. "It'll be okay. Really."

Toby nodded and wiped his eyes.

"Okay. Get dressed, I'll meet you in the kitchen for breakfast."

Sean turned up the hot water in the shower until he felt his skin burn. By the time he was out, Toby had poured cereal into two bowls and was rooting around in the fridge.

"Dad," Toby said, drawing out the word into two syllables. "Milk."

Milk was on his list. The list in his head that he never remembered to check. "Do we have half-and-half? You could use that."

"I used that up yesterday."

There were too many things to remember. It was impossible to get it all right. "I'll get some on the way home." He took inventory of what they did have left. "How about some toast?"

"Mom never ran out of milk. Ever."

"Yeah, well *I* never ran out on *you*," he shot back. As soon as he said it, Toby looked stricken. Sean had hit him where it hurt—for the second time this morning. "I didn't mean it, Tobe," he said. "God, I'm sorry."

"Mom's coming back." His voice was small.

"Okay." He wished he could press delete, start the morning over. Toby had been excited about starting the day. Before he'd been beaten physically and emotionally. "Hey," he tried to lighten his tone. "We have an art class to get to. We don't want to be late."

A chocolate croissant from the Hungarian Pastry Shop helped lift the mood for the bus ride. By the time they got to Ninety-sixth and Fifth, Toby was sugared up and ready for the day. He sprinted ahead on the Upper East Side pavement, weaving through the morning migration of well-groomed kids and their parents on the way to school.

Sean had to admit he was looking forward to seeing what went on during a regular school day. Parent-teacher conferences and class parties had nothing to do with Toby's daily life at The Bradley School. Sean was familiar with the black and white checkerboard floor of the lobby that he saw twice daily at drop-off and pickup, but he had no idea what went on beyond that, because according to Toby, he did *stuff* or *nothing* all day. When Toby's teacher quit over a month ago, the school had actually reached out to parents, asking if they would volunteer to teach classes while the search committee found a replacement. In the spirit of covert infiltration, Sean volunteered to lead an art class, and today was the day.

When they turned onto Ninety-third Street, parents and children pooled outside the glass and wrought iron door to the school. Fathers waited impatiently. Mothers chatted. Something was wrong. Drop-off was usually a wham-bam affair with fathers blowing kisses at their offspring while checking Blackberries, and a few malnourished mothers on their way to the gym. It was too early for estrogen and small talk—that came at three thirty during pickup.

Lilly's mom looked up from a conversation with Melanie Drake, the mother of Toby's best friend, Calvin. "You're early today!" she said, looking like she'd been up for hours and already run around the reservoir, worked out with her personal trainer, and cooked a three-course breakfast for the family.

"Am I?" His eyes darted to the entrance. "Why isn't the door open?"

"Five more minutes," Melanie said, holding her wrist out so he could see it was only seven fifty-five.

He took a quick inventory of the scene. Kids and their parents bobbed in place to keep warm as they waited to be let in. Sean froze when he saw Cheryl out of the corner of his eye.

"So have you already started it?" Melanie had returned to a conversation with Lilly's mom. "Susannah's friend did it when she was eight and this girl just aced her verbal SATs."

"We're three weeks in already." Lilly's mom looked at Sean. "Is Toby doing it, too?"

"Doing what?"

"Sight training."

He wasn't sure what she was talking about but guessed it wasn't a class for seeing eye dogs. "Uh, I don't think so."

"Oh, you'd know," she went on. "I bring Lilly to the midtown office three times a week. It's special physical therapy that strengthens the eye muscles."

"The school recommended it for Calvin." He liked Melanie. She was married to one of the biggest developers in Manhattan, but she somehow managed to stay more or less down to earth. "I'm trying to decide if we can fit it all in."

Cheryl was now standing a few feet from him. When she caught his eye, she cocked her head and winked. Maybe he'd been too hard on himself. Maybe his bathroom performance had been okay. Good even.

"When we finish up with the OT for Calvin's pencil grip," Melanie said, "maybe we'll try it. Is Toby doing OT, too?"

"What?" He eyed the door and vowed never to be early again.

"Occupational Therapy," she said. "How's Toby's grip?"

She was waiting for an answer. "Well, the pencil's never flown out of his hand," he said, knowing this couldn't have been the answer she was looking for.

As soon as the front door unlatched, kids streamed into the lobby and their parents peeled off for work.

"Come on, Dad," Toby said, pulling him away from all talk of pencil grips. Sean shot the mothers a look that said *you know how kids are* as he allowed Toby to drag him into the lobby and past the eighth grade Jasper Johns study on display. A few of the pieces weren't bad, especially considering the artists were thirteen. If his own grade school had had a full-time school-museum liaison, everything could be different for him now. He'd had to wait until art school for the kind of exposure Toby had gotten in kindergarten.

Sean tried to keep up, following Toby under the fleet of nine-hundred-ninety-nine origami swans that dangled from an elaborate mobile—the seniors' first semester art project—then up the grand staircase.

At the fourth floor, Sean followed Toby through a fire door and into a hallway that was carpeted in bright blue. The third grade self-portraits that lined the walls smiled out with circle eyes, wobbly red lines for mouths, and an oompa loompa orange for skin. He wondered why the girls' drawings were all about hair and lips, while the boys were obsessed with freckles and teeth. All except Toby's. He'd obviously sketched himself in a mirror and used perspective and shading, like Sean had taught him. It didn't look exactly like Toby, but it captured his sleepy lids and long lashes. In the self-portrait, his bangs fell loosely below his blond eyebrows just like they did now. Sean smiled a self-satisfied, cocky smile of a parent who knows his kid has just blown all the others out of the water. He didn't get to gloat often. Especially at this school. He savored the moment.

"Dad, come on. What are you doing?" Toby was pulling at his arm. "We did those at the beginning of the year. They're dumb."

Inside the classroom, red contact paper covered the walls. Maps and cursive letters and more artwork brought the room to life. He hadn't seen the classroom since the first day of school when Toby had met Ms. Martin. Now, he felt the panic of a tourist trying to see all the sights in a single afternoon.

"Come see my Native American corn project." Toby was practically bouncing as he dragged Sean over to a diorama he'd built in a Merrill shoebox. "These are my artifacts." He handed Sean a belt made of red and yellow and white yarn. "I wove it all by myself." A bell dangled from one of the long strings that hung off both ends.

"You made that?" It was actually pretty well done. Weaving wasn't easy, at least he didn't think so. "No way."

"And this is my wampum." Toby pointed to some marbles and shells. "It's like Native American money."

Before Sean could respond with appropriate amazement, Toby pulled him over to the math corner where he pointed out tricky problems in his workbook that he'd gotten right. What was the school making such a stink about? Toby was doing great.

He wondered which sub they'd throw at the kids today, the fat smelly one Toby and his friends called "El Stinko," or the strict school marm the kids called "She Who Must Not be Named."

But there were no subs in the room. Just the busty assistant, Miss Bix, who was fussing with a map and push pins. With the new teacher starting next week, he figured the school was skipping the subs completely.

When Calvin blustered into the classroom, Toby ran over to him and they plopped down on the rug together to look at a comic book. Calvin made all the special sound effects of guns and lasers. Toby groaned and gurgled death throes of dying bad guys. This was the old Toby, relaxed and happy. The Toby he hadn't seen much of lately.

Sean felt a small finger jab at his thigh. It was Alexis. "Hi Toby's dad," Alexis said. She and Toby had been friends briefly in first grade. The girl was a disaster waiting to happen. Once, Toby had come back from her apartment having played *sturgeon*, in which they fashioned new boobs and lips for her American Girl dolls out of Play-Doh and fed them Tic Tacs that Alexis kept calling Xanax.

"Why are you here?" She gave him the once over, lingering on his extremities. Probably sizing him up for a *procedure*.

He twitched uncomfortably. "I'm going to make collages with your class."

"Representational or abstract?" Alexis asked. Her eyes were squinty and her lips puckered like she'd just sucked on a lemon.

He shrugged. "Up to you."

He ought to sit. It would give him something to do, and maybe Alexis would go away. He lowered himself into a mini chair, but the thing was way too close to the ground. His knees were in his armpits and only half his ass fit on the seat. Suddenly, the chatter in the room stopped. He looked up to see an incredibly attractive sub put a bag down at the teacher's desk. Her hair was brown, almost black, and pale freckles dusted her skin.

Toby was staring at her. They all were. Sean tapped Toby with his foot. "Who's that?" he mouthed.

Toby shrugged, no clue.

The sub smiled at the class, then focused a surprised look directly at Sean. He'd been waiting to be booted. Bradley School rules: no parents in the classroom unless cleared ahead of time.

"Oh. Hi," she said. "Who do you belong to?" She had a great voice. Like she'd spent the weekend screaming her lungs out at a football game.

He looked up at her from the mini chair and wished he hadn't sat in it to begin with. "Oh, I'm . . ." He pushed himself up awkwardly. "Sorry. I . . ." He tried to straighten his knees and hoped the effort didn't show. "I'm Sean Benning. Toby's dad." He extended his hand: *I come in peace.*

"Nice to meet you." She shook it. Her hand was delicate but strong.

Her eyes were blue, but much lighter than blue eyes he'd seen before. They were like blue vapor.

"I'm doing an art project with the kids second period," he said. "I brought some work to do in the hallway until it's time."

"No, stay if you want. It's good to have you." She smiled and went to the board and wrote the name Jessica Harper. She turned to the kids. "Hi." She tucked a strand of hair behind her ear and smiled. "I'm Jessica Harper. Your new teacher."

The kids exchanged looks.

He couldn't believe his good luck. The other parents would kill to be crashing the new teacher's first day.

Alexis, visibly rattled by this departure from the schedule, raised her hand. "You're not supposed to be here until Monday."

"Surprise," Jessica Harper said. "I couldn't wait to get started."

The girls giggled. Toby and Calvin whispered excitedly, then Calvin raised his hand. "What should we call you?"

"You can call me Jess," she said. "That feels more normal to me." This answer prompted more whispering. Until middle school, teachers could choose to be called whatever they wanted. Only a few—the very cool few—opted for first names.

Jess was now focused intently on the class. "Miss Bix tells me you've started some Thanksgiving essays. Why don't you get them out of your binders and we'll get to know each other?"

As the kids rustled around, she carried an adult-size chair over to Sean and placed it next to him. "This should work better." She was twenty-eight, he decided. Maybe thirty.

When the kids settled down, Jess unfolded a piece of notebook paper. "I did one, too. I'll go first." She surveyed the room before starting. "I'm thankful for the Boston Red Sox."

The boys sat forward defensively. He saw Jess stifle a smile and keep going.

"I'm thankful that I don't care about peer pressure and that reading good books is still legal. I'm thankful for my new job at The Bradley School and also for the chance to get to know you guys."

Drew's hand shot up. He had Opie-like ears and a head full of cartoon-grade red hair.

She raised an eyebrow, pretending to be surprised that he had a comment. "What's your name?"

"Drew," he said. His Izod shirt matched the turquoise stripe on his V-neck sweater, a miniature version of an investment banker on a golf outing. "The Yankees rule."

"I'm also thankful for freedom of choice," she said. "And the right to voice one's opinion in a public forum. Drew, why don't you go next?"

He picked up a professionally matted laser printout and straightened his spine. "I'm thankful for my mother and stepfather, my new twin brothers and in-vitro fertilization. I'm thankful for Democracy, technology, and my Xbox."

What eight-year-old was thankful for in-vitro? This kid was going to be pretty surprised down the road when he learned how babies were usually made. Sean got a flash of Drew's mother on Larry King last year talking about her new book, *Liars*. Any woman who claimed she didn't want children, she announced on national TV, was a liar. For six months, news shows featured one angry woman after another debating women's biological imperative to reproduce. During that six months, Drew's mother got divorced and remarried. Not too long after that she was waddling around The Bradley School pregnant with twins at the age that most women were starting to think about grandchildren.

The classroom was a sea of raised hands shaking to get the teacher's attention. Jess called on Kayla, who was wearing a Pepto-Bismol-colored sweat suit with the word "Juicy" emblazoned across her butt. Her Puma sneakers matched exactly. Kayla was just figuring out how to use her talents to get what she wanted from people. Unfortunately, Toby was under her spell.

"My name is Kayla and I'm thankful for my innate gymnastic abilities and for Boris, who fled his country to help me achieve my Olympic dream," she said. "I'm thankful that I am an American and can vote for president when I'm eighteen." She smiled a beauty pageant smile she must have practiced in the mirror and sat down.

A girl he'd never seen before was next. "I'm Emily B," she said, and pushed her glasses up the bridge of her nose. "I'm thankful for J.K. Rowling's magical writing and for Harry, Hermione, and Ron. I've read all the books twice. I like to memorize passages and recite them in a British accent for my mom during dinner."

Toby hated *Harry Potter*. It was way too hard. As it was, Toby refused to read even the simplest chapter books to himself unless strong-armed into it. Getting through an eight-hundred-page *Harry Potter* book would be pure torture—for both of them. He'd get there someday. Maybe.

Calvin stood next. He'd slimmed down a little over the summer and looked very serious. "I'b Calbin." His *ms* and *vs* sounded like *bs*. "I'b thankful for engineers and skyscrapers that bake New York City the bost ibportant city in the world." He stared hard at the paper as if the letters might vanish. His hands were trembling. Sean wondered if Calvin's father, who was responsible for building half of those skyscrapers, had fed him that line. "I'b thankful for Wolberine, Silber Surfer and all the X-Ben super heroes." He sat down and took a deep breath through his mouth.

"Thanks Calvin," Jess said. "Would you like a cup of water?"

He shook his head quickly.

Next she called on Alexis, who batted her dark eyelashes before beginning. "I'm thankful for the new anti-global warming legislation and also for *iCarly*, and the miracle of organ transplants."

"That's a wide spectrum," Jess said. "I like that."

Toby was next. He stood and looked at his paper, then at Sean, then down at his shoes. Sean tried to guess what he'd be thankful for. Saturday morning cartoons? Sour Straws? Christmas presents?

Toby swallowed before starting. "I'm thankful for my dad," he read. "He takes me to school and plays with me and makes me food and stuff while my mommy is away. I really miss her, but I've still got my dad." He smiled shyly, not looking at Sean, then sat down.

Sean blinked back tears. His chest felt like it might cave in as he remembered whacking Toby and telling him his mother had run out on him. Everything else could change, disappear, disappoint. Toby was his constant. The only thing that mattered. He had to be a better father. Tearing up in front of these kids, not to mention the new teacher, was out of the question. For a second, he noticed her eyes dart over to him, trying to figure out what the essay meant. He coughed like he had a tickle in his throat.

"Thanks Toby," she said. "Your dad sounds great. And I'm happy to turn the class over to him for a while." She gestured him up to the board. "Mr. Benning?"

He stood up, which was much easier now that he had the bigger chair. "Uh, thanks. I'm . . . call me Sean." He looked around for the materials, then asked the class if they'd had time to slice up the *Buzz Weekly*s he'd sent with Toby last week.

Kayla marched to the supply closet and emerged with two shopping bags. Sean dumped the pieces onto a table and spread them out, then moved a few onto a sheet of paper and rearranged them until something interesting started to happen. "Just start playing around. Certain shapes and colors are going to call to you. See where it takes you." He recognized the orange and black squares and circles the kids had cut from the "Lapdogs of the Stars" piece that had run last month.

"Can I make a horse?" one girl asked.

"You can do whatever you want. But try it without knowing what you're making before you start. Just see what happens."

They looked suspicious, but gave it a try. Jess pulled up a chair next to Toby and started one too.

Isaac raised an eager hand and fingered his Einstein glasses with the other. "I'd like to do a map of the United States. Can I do that?" The kid was a brown-noser who'd written his first novel the summer before second grade and was currently the reigning ten-and-under New York Regional Chess Champion. Last year, his parents had called a meeting with Mr. Daniels to request a course of independent study because the second-grade work wasn't challenging their brainiac spawn.

"That's going to take a long time, Isaac," Jess said.

"I can take it home and finish it tonight if I'm not done."

"The idea is to let the content drive the form," Sean said, trying not to sound annoyed. "Allow the pieces show *you* what you're making."

"No." Isaac shook his head. "I think I'll make the map."

Jess, who'd stepped deftly out of the conversation, focused on her collage and tamped down an amused smile.

Soon, the kids were busily working. Drew was focusing so hard, Sean thought his tongue might bore a hole through the lining of his cheek. Luke pasted blue squares in a mass at the bottom corner of his page as he scratched absent-mindedly at a patch of red bumps on his neck. They were an intense bunch.

After a double period of working on the collages, Jess looked at the clock. "Who's hungry?" she asked. Toby ran up to her and tugged at her sleeve. "Can my dad have lunch with us? Please?"

"Of course," she said. "I mean, it's fine with me. As long as he doesn't have to get back to work."

"No, I'd love to." He realized, with a rush, he'd never seen lunch. The kids cheered. He was a rock star, at least until someone more interesting came along. As he texted work to cancel his noon meeting, he realized he'd only been in the fifth floor dining room once, on the school tour five years ago. Walking into the room, he remembered Mimsy Roach, the admissions director, in her pastel sweater set and Barbara Bush pearls, boasting about how the same wallpaper hung in the White House. The other parents had oohed and aahed at this tidbit, which struck him as idiotic. It was *wallpaper.* Boring, old-fashioned wallpaper of women in petticoats picnicking on a lawn.

But looking around now, he wondered if the presidential paper had anything to do with how insanely civilized the kids were behaving. They sat at tables, engaged in polite conversation. At least that's how it looked from where he was standing. There wasn't a spitball or mashed potato catapult in sight. Food fights had been a highlight of his grade school experience. Toby was going to miss all that.

He pushed his tray through the cafeteria line. The kitchen bustled with precision movements. A chef in a white hat served him grilled Atlantic salmon with polenta. When Toby came home from school reporting there'd been fish for lunch, he'd imagined fish sticks, overcooked cod. Not this. He followed Toby to the two third-grade tables and watched the kids unfold linen napkins on their laps.

He and Toby sat next to Zack, the only son of the Knicks' once-kickass power forward, Billy Horn. The kid had gotten the height gene from his father and had learned to dribble the ball before he could walk. If all went according to Billy Horn's plan, Zack would carry on his NBA legacy.

Jess put her tray down at the table next to Sean. "How's the lunch here?" she asked. "It looks amazing."

He had no idea how lunch was. "Let's see." He took a bite of the salmon. "Mmmm."

Isaac zoomed in for prime real estate next to Jess, but promptly turned his back on her, pushing away his nutritious gourmet meal.

"Knight to B4," Isaac said to Luke. The red bumps on Luke's neck looked nasty. Even more unappetizing was Isaac's painfully tedious account of a national chess tournament he'd won that weekend in Florida. He paused for dramatic tension. "And check."

"Isaac, eat," Jess said, taking a bite of pork tenderloin. It looked like something you'd order at a restaurant.

He tried to imagine eating like this every day, but that was depressing because unless he came to school with Toby, there was no way it was going to happen.

"I don't eat lunch," Isaac said, and made a face at Jess's food. "Do you know how they raise pigs? It's revolting. The conditions in the slaughterhouses are barbaric."

Sean let his fork drop. "Thanks for that."

"Grab a PB&J or something," Jess suggested.

"The Bradley School is a nut-free zone," he said. "Besides, I'm not hungry."

Calvin pushed his tray away nervously. "Me neither."

"May I please be excused?" Isaac asked.

"Lunch isn't over yet," Jess said. "Why don't you guys tell me about yourselves? Which sports do people like to play? I played lacrosse in college."

"Ivy League?" Drew asked.

"Trinity," she said without missing a beat.

Isaac looked at his Tourneau watch. "I have to go to the nurse."

"I have a pony," Nina said. Her velour top exclaimed STAR! in purple rhinestones. "I ride her in competition."

"I have to go to the nurse, too," Luke said.

"Me too," Marcus said.

They'd each pushed their food around their plates to make it look like they'd eaten something, just like the girls in college used to do.

"You should have our names on the list."

"Oh right. The list." Jess reached into her bag and produced a clipboard and checked it. "Okay, anyone who has permission can go to the nurse now."

Marcus, Luke, Calvin, Isaac, and Kayla got up to leave.

"You sure you all need to go?" she asked, as a few more kids got up from the other third-grade table.

Kayla waved as she followed the boys.

"What's that about?" Sean whispered.

She shrugged and turned back to the remaining kids. "I guess something's going around."

"Knock-knock," Zack said.

"Who's there?" Toby happily obliged.

"Yah."

"Yah who?".

"What are you so excited about?"

The kids howled. The exodus had barely registered with them. Sean made a mental note to buy Toby some Flintstones vitamins. Just to be safe.

"Dad, want to come to computer class?" Toby asked, as Sean scraped his plate. "We're going to make pictures on the Mac to go with our Thanksgiving essays."

"Let's try not to get me fired on my first day," Jess said, winking at Sean.

"Seems fair." He turned to Toby. "I've got to get to work anyway."

When everyone had bussed their trays in an orderly fashion, Miss Bix herded the class out of the dining room.

Jess extended her hand. This was the end of the road. Except for one minor detail. "My coat," he said. "It's still in your classroom."

"Come on," she said. He followed her into the hallway where a pack of teachers waited for the elevators. Something familiar flashed across her features. It was the same look Toby had given him on the first day of kindergarten when he'd been thrown into a room full of strangers.

"Why don't we take the stairs," he suggested. "Work off all that fancy food."

"Sure." He heard a touch of relief in her voice.

"So how's the first day going?" he asked as they entered the stairwell, which was decorated with fifth grade maps of Europe.

"Better than I expected."

"It takes a while to get the hang of this bunch." He paused. "You're doing great."

"It's . . . not like other schools."

"So you didn't go to a Bradley either?"

Her laugh was loud and spontaneous. Like an exhale. "Not by a long shot."

He was looking at her, not at the stairs, when his foot came down on a soft, uneven surface that sent him flying into the facing wall. Jess grabbed the railing just in time to stop herself.

"Oh my God!" she gasped when she saw what it was.

Calvin was lying half on the third floor landing, half on the step. "Calvin," he said. "Are you okay?" Sean's heart raced as he knelt down.

"Calvin!" he screamed. "Calvin!" Screaming at Calvin was ridiculous. The kid needed help, not a hearing aid. He steadied Calvin's head, which was jerking from side to side against one of the sandpaper-lined steps. His body shuddered and flailed and his eyes rolled back in his head. "It's okay, buddy," he said, having no idea if that was true. "It's gonna be okay."

"Call 911," Jess said. She held Calvin's head to free up Sean's hands, and he pulled his phone from his back pocket. In his entire life, he'd never dialed 911, and when the operator answered he stumbled over the information. He told her everything he knew, which, he realized, was very little.

"They'll be here soon," he said. Adrenaline pulsed through him. "What should I do?"

"His medical file." Sean hadn't been able to answer any of the questions the operator was asking. "We should have it for the paramedics."

"I'll get the nurse," she said. "Can you, um . . ." She gestured toward Calvin with her head and Sean traded places with her. "I'll be fast," she said, and sprinted down the stairs.

She was back a minute later, a sheen of sweat on her forehead. "Any change?"

He shook his head. Nurse Astrid lugged her well-padded body up the stairs, a full flight behind Jess. He wondered if Astrid had ever taken the stairs in her life. The nurse getup—white uniform, white stockings, white orthopedic shoes—was out of the fifties. At least she didn't wear the cap.

"No preexisting conditions," she said, reading from the file and gasping for breath. "Nothing. Let me see him." She knelt down awkwardly and took his pulse. "It's fast," she said, almost angry. "Where's the ambulance? We need the ambulance," she screamed. The costume couldn't hide the fact that she was helpless and scared.

Within minutes, the paramedics arrived and strapped Calvin onto a stretcher, carried him downstairs, and loaded him into an idling ambulance.

The air outside sliced through his shirt. Jess hugged her arms across her chest, shivering. Bev Shineman, the school psychologist, barreled onto the sidewalk in a long down coat, her hand gripped in a fist around her cell phone. "I have calls in to his parents and both his nannies." She stared at them. "How are you two holding up?" She added it, almost as an afterthought.

"Fine," he said, even though his heart rate was still way too fast and his knees were rubber.

Shineman's cell phone rang. It must have been Calvin's parents because she lowered her voice and walked quickly away as she spoke.

Jess had a funny look on her face, like she might cry.

"You okay?" he asked.

"Yeah." She tried reassuring him with a smile. "Fine."

"I need an adult," the paramedic barked from the back of the ambulance. She stared at him, then at Jess. "Who's coming?"

CHAPTER THREE

SEAN HAD NEVER ENTERED MOUNT SINAI THROUGH THE AMBULANCE entrance and was disoriented as he raced after Calvin's gurney into pediatric emergency, otherwise known as hell. Inside, he recognized the windowless room from last year when Toby had fallen off of Calvin's bunk bed and hit his head on the way down. He'd turned out to be fine, but the six hours in emergency had traumatized them all. Looking around now, he recognized the terror on the faces of the desperate parents trying to calm screaming babies, cool fevers, and staunch bleeding.

A team of doctors who looked like they were just out of med school circled Calvin, listening to his heart and taking his pulse. The paramedics reported what they knew: no preexisting conditions, no allergies, all in all a healthy eight-year-old boy.

A 12-year-old in a doctor's coat turned to Sean. "Can you tell me what happened today?" Her eyes were huge and dark like in Japanese animé.

"Um . . ." He had no idea what had happened. "I . . . we found him on the stairs. He was unconscious and kind of . . . flailing around."

"Does your son have any known allergies to medicine, food, anything you can think of?"

"I'm not his father." He'd tried to make that clear in the ambulance. "But I don't think Calvin has allergies. According to the file, I mean."

"Have there been any changes to his routine recently? Has he taken any medication or been out of the country? Has this ever happened before?" She stared at him with her cartoon eyes waiting for something. Anything.

"I don't think so. I have no idea," he stammered. "I'm not his . . ."

Shineman rushed in. "There you are," she panted. She reeked of breath mints. "His parents are on their way."

"Let's get him on a monitor and take his vitals." An orderly in teddy bear scrubs began sticking electrodes on Calvin's chest.

Sean heard Cal Drake before he saw him. "Where the hell is my son?" he boomed. His footsteps were heavy but fast. He raced around the corner and stopped short when he saw Calvin lying motionless, hooked up to oxygen, with an IV in his left arm. Melanie trailed a few paces behind. When she caught up, she let out a gasp. "Calvin!" she sobbed and tunneled through the sea of residents and interns to hold her son.

"Jesus Christ." Cal exhaled slowly. He looked around for what he considered to be a real doctor, but finally focused on the girl with cartoon eyes, who was marking information on a chart. "What's wrong with him? Will he be okay?"

"When we finish these tests we'll know more," she said.

He turned angrily to Shineman. "What the hell happened?"

"He collapsed on the stairs," she said. "Sean and the new third grade teacher found him there. They may have saved his life."

Melanie turned her head toward Sean and mouthed *thank you* through a stream of tears. Cal glared at Shineman, concentrating all his fear, helplessness, and hostility into tasers that shot from his eyes. "What the fuck was my son doing in the stairwell by himself?"

Shineman spoke extra quietly to counteract the yelling. "This is a tense time," she said. "For everyone."

"Oh, you're going to feel a lot of tension," Cal spit out. "Believe me! I entrust my son's safety to you and this is how you protect him?" His voice escalated, though it hadn't seemed possible. "I'd like an answer to my question." His nostrils flared. He was waiting—for an answer, for someone to blame. The doctors furiously took readings and looked about as bewildered as Sean felt.

As her husband tore Shineman a new one, Melanie clung to her son, kissing his hand and begging him to wake up. She wouldn't remember the details of any of this. He could see that everything else had fallen away, that she was channeling everything she had into willing Calvin to be all right. Watching her sob over Calvin, he imagined Toby on the gurney. If he didn't slip out now, he would start crying too. He backed away slowly. "I should go," he said, even though no one heard or cared. "I hope Calvin's okay."

As soon as he hit the sidewalk, he broke into a run. He had no destination, just a need to get somewhere fast. It was below freezing and Sean had left his jacket in Toby's classroom. When he saw the sign for Hanratty's, he knew that was where he was going. He plopped himself at the bar, leaving a few empty seats between himself and a middle-aged man whose nose and cheeks blossomed in a web of burst capillaries. The man wore a ridiculous turtleneck covered with lobsters and was sweating alcohol.

The bartender dropped a paper coaster in front of Sean. "What can I get you?"

"Bloody Mary," he said, before he'd made the decision. Drinking in the afternoon was always a bad idea. But he knew there was no way an overpriced cup of Starbucks coffee was going to do the trick. Besides, he reasoned, Bloody Marys were a daytime drink. "House vodka's fine."

Sean drank in silence and pretended to be riveted by a rerun of an old Lakers/Knicks game from the nineties on the flat-screen television behind the bar. He watched a young Billy Horn dribble through the Lakers' best guys over and over to make six easy layups in a row. There was no denying he used to be a basketball god.

When the door opened again, a young, preppy guy bounded in, beaming unguardedly. "Hey man," he said to the bartender. "Can I order some food to go?"

The bartender handed him a menu.

The guy picked it up, but didn't have the patience to read it. "Do you have shrimp cocktail? My wife wants shrimp cocktail and I told her I'd find it for her. You have it, right?"

"We've got shrimp scampi," the bartender said.

The guy considered it for a minute. "Yeah, okay," he said in an annoyingly upbeat tone. "That'll probably be fine. I'll take an order of that to go." He looked at Sean and the alcoholic next to him, and then at their drinks. "And I'll have a beer. You know, while I wait."

He sat at the bar and kicked his feet against his stool and fiddled with the coaster. The energy of the place was suddenly all messed up. The kid was going to want to make conversation. He could feel it.

"I just had a baby," the kid blurted out. "I mean, my wife did."

So his mood was pure joy. Sean decided to cut him some slack. "Congratulations." He saluted with the Bloody Mary. "Boy or girl?"

"She's a girl. Savannah. She's got these little dimples." He pulled his phone from his down jacket and stared scrolling through what seemed like hundreds of photos. He stopped on a picture of his new family. At home in an album somewhere, Sean had an almost identical photo of himself and Toby and Ellie that had been taken eight years ago at Mount Sinai. He loved that photo. In it, Ellie's hospital gown is slipping, her hair is a mess, and she looks like she's been through hell. She'd never looked more beautiful. In the photo they're happy. In love. Hopeful. That first night they'd stared at Toby for hours. "This is it," Ellie had said as they watched their child. "We're in it for the long haul."

The long haul hadn't turned out to be all that long. "I'll have another," Sean said to the bartender.

After his second drink, he looked at his watch. He had five minutes to get back to Bradley. He slapped money on the bar and walked into blinding daylight. The new father carried a Styrofoam box of scampi. Sean didn't have the heart to tell him that if a woman who's just given birth asks for shrimp cocktail and you bring her shrimp covered in garlic and oil, there most certainly will be hell to pay. The kid would find out soon enough.

The vodka only kept him warm for the first block and a half, and as he ran past the Mount Sinai buildings, he thought of Calvin in the ER, Melanie sobbing over his lifeless body. Whatever buzz he'd had was gone now and he felt heavy, slow, sick.

He dragged himself into Bradley just in time to see the kids following their teachers, single file, down the sweeping staircase and across the lobby. A few girls in bellbottoms and sparkly T-shirts giggled. A tousled-looking boy tripped over his feet, but then recovered. Sean winced, remembering how he'd tripped over his own feet all through school.

He watched Toby search the room, find him, and shoot him a toothy grin. He seemed fine. All the kids did. Maybe Jess hadn't told them about Calvin. Sean tried to read their faces, but you couldn't tell with kids. Sometimes information like that took a while to sink in.

Jess had pulled herself together and was talking to the kids like she'd known them forever instead of just eight hours. From a distance it was easier to size her up. She'd said she played lacrosse in college, and now he saw it. She had a great body. Athletic, not sucked-out and bony like so many New York women. Her expression hovered somewhere between authoritarian and conspiratorial and was as intriguing as anything he'd seen in a long time—especially here.

He watched Toby laugh at a joke Zack was telling. Calvin should have been laughing right along with him. The other parents in the room still had no idea how lucky they were to be here picking up their kids while the Drakes prayed to see Calvin's eyes open.

He took a minute to catch his breath, to steady himself before pushing through the wall of mothers.

"You're Sean Benning," a soothing male voice said. A hand descended on his back in a fatherly way. "Walt Renard."

He shook the hand that was extended toward him. "Hi." Walt Renard looked tanned, well-rested, like he'd just stepped off a tropical island.

"I hear you took Calvin to the ER."

Walt was one of the parents who knew everyone, even though he didn't fit The Bradley School's parent profile. In all the years he'd seen Walt at dropoff and pickup, Walt had never once worn a suit and tie. Today he wore blue jeans, a button down shirt, and expensive shoes.

"Word spreads fast," Sean said, keeping Toby in his peripheral vision. "Does everyone know—about Calvin?"

"Not yet. Not most people."

"I have no idea what happened, why it happened."

"There's nothing more terrifying than being a parent." Walt removed his glasses and wiped them with the hem of his untucked shirt. "We do everything we can to protect them. And then something like this happens."

Toby was looking for Sean across the room. "I ought to . . ."

"Yeah, you ought to get your son," Walt said. "You did a good thing today." He clasped Sean's hand again. "Karma points," he said, and gave a wave.

When Toby saw Sean, he stuck his hand in Jess's direction for his formal dismissal handshake. As soon as they'd unclasped hands, Sean scooped Toby into a fierce hug. He hadn't meant to, but there was no fighting it.

"Dad," Toby said, embarrassed.

He hated letting go, but forced himself. "Don't know what came over me," he said. "Sorry."

Jess handed him his jacket. "You might need this."

He thanked her and put it on. She seemed so together. "How are you?"

"Fine," she said, as though they hadn't just saved a kid's life together. Or probably saved it. "Thanks for the art project." Apparently, he *and* Toby had been dismissed.

Toby said nothing as they walked to the bus stop.

"So," he said, when he realized Toby was going to need some prodding. "How was the rest of your day?"

Toby shrugged. "Calvin went to the hospital."

Sean nodded. Wait for it.

"Kayla said Calvin's eclectic," Toby said.

He tried to imagine ways in which Calvin could be eclectic but failed. "He's what?"

"Eclectic," Toby said. "Kayla saw a show on PBS. They get all weird and shaky when there's a lot of bright light."

He should really write this stuff down. "Epileptic?"

"Yeah," Toby said.

Sean was pretty sure Calvin wasn't epileptic. If he was, the doctors would have identified it fairly quickly. The blank looks on their faces had made the whole thing that much more terrifying.

"Drew said it could be a peanut allergy," Toby went on. "Even though Chef Antoine doesn't use peanuts."

"Calvin doesn't have allergies, Tobe." Sean wondered if Toby would ask how he knew this, but he didn't. It was a given that parents knew everything about everything.

"Isaac said school was going to have to pay lots of money if it was their fault."

Perfect. Isaac was working the litigious angle. "So are you worried about Calvin?"

"Remember Patrick?"

Patrick, Patrick. "Uh . . ."

"Remember, he did the Empire State Building set for the second-grade play?"

Sean remembered some kid's parents paying two hundred bucks to have a professional set designer come in and build the set.

"Patrick had a peanut allergy and had to go to the hospital, too. He came back." Toby shrugged. "But then he left school after the summer."

"Calvin doesn't have any allergies." He put his arm around Toby and they walked a while without speaking.

"I hope Calvin comes back."

"Me too," Sean said. "Me too."

CHAPTER FOUR

"WHERE'S THE SEX?!" RICK HOLLINGSWORTH BELLOWED accusatorily through the office. It never failed to make the young *Buzz* staffers tremble in their Vans. But Sean liked Rick—sort of.

"I want flesh on these pages," Rick shouted. The skin under his chin wobbled when he moved his head. Sean routinely photoshopped the same turkey flap out of Harrison Ford's profile. Rick had endured a few too many late-night closes, and the endless supply of pizza and beer had settled into a fifteen-pound tire around his middle. His lids drooped, giving him a heavy, tired look.

"Find me swimsuit shots for Christ's sake," he said. His waddle continued to wobble even after his head came to a complete stop. "Where are the Big Five? Someone's got to be on a beach this month!" He stormed into his office and slammed the door.

The sad fact of the matter was that Rick was a brainy guy. Should have been at *Time* or *Newsweek*. But seven years ago he'd lost his shit and heaved his computer out the window of his eighteenth-story office at *The Economist*. It was a miracle it hadn't hit anyone. Any real career Rick might have had in journalism had flown out the window along with the computer. Now, even though antidepressants had more or less fixed the bugs in his brain chemistry, he was stuck here at this sorry excuse for a tabloid. A lifer. Rick's morose presence served as a constant reminder to Sean to get out while he still could.

The job was supposed to be temporary, a stop-gap after Toby was born while Ellie took time off from the network. He'd given up the freelance work and his painting studio for a steady paycheck and health insurance. But three years had turned into five, then eight. He'd get out somehow, but for the meantime, Sean needed the job. He dialed Gino.

"I'm away from my phone right now," Gino's voice announced. "Leave your number and when I get out of the hot tub I'll ring you back."

Gino never picked up his phone. Sean knew the drill. "Code Blue," he said, and hung up. The sick thing was, Gino might actually *be* in a hot tub. He imagined Gino, flanked by topless Bunnies, their steamy ears askew. His fearlessness, coupled with a total lack of humility, made him one of the best paparazzi in the business. In the middle of Jen and Brad's divorce, he'd left a paper bag full of steaming dog shit on Jen's front step. When she bent down to open it, he caught the whole thing with his foot-long zoom from the mansion next door. The photo—a close-up of Jen's devastated expression—ran on the cover with the caption "Jen on the Verge." Inside, a fabricated story from "sources" revealed she would be checking into a Malibu facility for "treatment."

The phone rang at Sean's desk less than sixty seconds after he placed the call. He picked it up on the first ring. "We need T&A," he said. "ASAP."

"Nice to hear from you, too," Gino said, with a post hot-tub calm. "Tell me."

"Flesh deficit. Big Five only," he said. They'd had the same conversation dozens of times. "So what do you know?"

"Julia is in Aruba with the twins, Brangelina is in Thailand, Britney is in Baja. Any of those work?"

Gino always knew. In a sick way, that impressed Sean. "Just get me the shots by day after tomorrow. I don't care where you have to go."

"Code Blue rules. Code Blue pay, right?"

"Yeah, yeah. Go." Code Blue, the magazine's screw-the-pay scale emergency mode, had made Gino one of the richest slime bags in his slimy business.

If Gino made good on one or two Code Blues a year—and he almost always scored more than that—he was in the black. For the Aniston dog-poop shot alone, the magazine paid him a hundred grand. First class airfare, four star hotels. It was worth it. He was newsstand gold.

Sean, on the other hand, was making seventy thousand dollars a year at the magazine, putting him just barely above the poverty line in New York City. Hand to mouth was pretty accurate. There was never anything left over for a splurge, a vacation, savings. If his in-laws weren't paying, The Bradley School would never have been an option.

He dialed Rick. "Got it covered," he announced. "Gino's on it."

He could hear the sigh of relief through the phone.

But Sean knew even Gino couldn't deliver 100 percent of the time. Just to be safe, he opened his emergency folder. There was a "Separated at Birth" thing he'd put together that played off celebs who looked vaguely similar: Matthew McConnaughey and a young Paul Newman, Kiera Knightley and Wynona Ryder. He also had a "Then and Now" story ready to go that compared high school yearbook photos with current shots of the stars. Then there was the evergreen "Who Wore it Best" story that humiliated two actresses for having generic taste, then went ahead and mortified one of them for not wearing it well enough.

Stories fell out constantly at *Buzz*. Celebrity couples broke up, reconciled, and broke up again so fast, you never knew which story to run with. He knew how to drop in a new story on a dime.

The phone rang again. There were always two or three calls from Gino getting approval to hire assistants, drivers, escorts. The guy had balls. Sean approved it all.

He picked up the phone. "What?"

"Sean Benning?" *Beneeng.* The woman's voice was French and throaty. It brought to mind black underwear.

"Uh, yeah?" How articulate.

"It is Camille Burdot, Burdot Gallery. You dropped off your portfolio last month?"

He'd pushed it out of his mind because nothing would ever come of it. "Right." His voice came out sounding too high. He coughed and lowered it. "Should I come down and pick it up?"

"I think your work is quite interesting," she said. "I would like you to come in for a meeting."

Sean opened his mouth. Nothing came out.

"Mr. Benning? Did I lose you?"

Deed I lose you?

"No. I mean, I'm glad you like my work. When should I . . ."

"Tomorrow. How's three o'clock?"

Three was not good. He and Toby were supposed to be baking an apple pie for Thanksgiving. "Three's great."

"See you then," she said, and hung up.

As the shock wore off, a smile pulled at the corners of his mouth. Next came the victory dance that involved pelvic thrusts and pumping fists.

No way he could do a "Who Wore it Best" story after a conversation with Camille Burdot. It would be just his luck if she were one of those French women with greasy hair, fuzzy armpits, and a two pack a day habit with teeth to match. He shook his head to dislodge the image and tried to get back to the black underwear.

Luckily, it was two forty-five. Time to pack up. No matter how much he hated his job, Sean was well aware that no other boss would let him get away with leaving this early on a regular basis.

"Women are the devil," Rick had told him when Ellie left three months ago. He'd closed the door to his office and poured them each a glass of Johnny Walker Black from a bottle he kept tucked between hanging folders in his filing cabinet. It was 11 a.m. "Maddie dumped me six years ago. Ruined my fucking life," he said. "I see my kids every other weekend." Color rose in his grayish cheeks. He loosened his collar, then took a drink. "You get the work done, you can leave whenever you need to. Don't let her wreck the kid's life, too."

Now, on his way out, Sean stuck his head around the glass door to Rick's office. Rick was slashing copy with a red pencil. Maybe it was the residual effect of the *Economist* episode, but he used the red pencil instead of the computer whenever possible.

"We should have images day after tomorrow." Sean wondered if he was still smiling.

"That's why you earn the big bucks, buddy," Rick said. The gruff act had already passed. "Say hi to your little genius for me."

Sean hightailed it to Grand Central and was on the Lexington subway six-and-a-half minutes later. If he got on the train before two fifty-five, he could make it to school on time. If he missed the train by as little as forty-five seconds, he'd hit a gap in service and he'd suffer the consequences of *tardiness*. Every parent knew that being late to pick up your child from school was mortifying on numerous levels. Not only would your kid glare at you sullenly when you walked into the empty lobby, but the teacher, who'd invariably be checking her watch, would be pissed you were now using her for babysitting.

Today Sean caught the express train and was a full seven minutes early as he rounded the corner toward The Bradley School.

He had never understood the whole walking on air thing, but today he knew exactly what it was all about. He reached for the front door handle. Maybe he'd get his own show, invite Bradley parents, even Cheryl. Sure, he'd still have to work at *Buzz*—for a while—but now it really could be *on the side*. If he had his own show.

The chatter emanating from the mothers and nannies as soon as he got inside didn't even faze him today. The room was already human gridlock, filled with the deafening white noise of women gossiping, bragging, laughing. He liked pickup. He liked watching Toby's face light up when he found Sean in the crowd. Soon Toby would be a teenager and that unselfconscious smile would be buried under acne and angst.

"Sean!" a voice chirped at him. Isaac's mother.

What the hell was her name? Missy? Mousy? She'd been Class Mother for the last three years running and took the job way too seriously. He disliked her more than he thought was normal, but it was what it was.

"You're on my list," she said. Everything about her was precise— her ski jump nose, her lipstick, the demure blond ponytail fastened with a tortoise shell clip. Her teeth were inhumanly white. "I haven't received your thirty dollars for the holiday gifts."

Because he'd been dodging her for weeks. "I totally forgot." He opened his wallet and thumbed through its contents. He handed her a ten, two fives, and four ones. "I owe you six," he said. She accepted it as if it were pocket change and not his lunch money for the rest of the week. Come to think of it, he probably needed it more than the teachers.

He knew she was friendly with Cheryl. Could she have heard about the bathroom sex? He tried to read her but couldn't see much behind the Stepford stare.

She touched his arm with a manicured hand that sparkled with a monster diamond. "No word from Ellie?"

Hearing her say Ellie's name out loud gave him an odd muscle spasm in his intestine. Kind of like gas. He shrugged. The last thing he was going to do was supply her with content for the class website.

"I'm so upset about what she's done to you and Toby." She shook her head disapprovingly. "She was such a hands-on mom. I don't understand it."

"It's pretty simple," he said. "She lost her shit." She could print it if she wanted. Who cared anymore?

But she didn't blink. "It's extremely difficult for successful women to give up lucrative careers to be stay-at-home moms. When their kids get to this age, they feel downsized." Her expression turned optimistic. "I suggested the Parents' Association hire a guest speaker to do a breakfast chat on the topic."

If it were legal to carry a handgun, he would brandish his now and happily pull the trigger. But then he'd get life without parole, and then where would Toby be? Laws were good.

Billy Horn's very blond, very well-proportioned second wife, Deanna, sidled over to him. "Haayyyyy!" she squealed, and punched Sean's shoulder playfully. She was wearing one of her trademark low-cut sweaters that highlighted her best attributes. "How *are* you? Fun party the other night, huh?"

What did she mean by that? Did she know something? "It was pretty good, yeah."

Isaac's mother saw another victim across the room and pounced, leaving him alone with the hottest—and most mind-numbingly boring—woman in the room. Making conversation with Deanna proved difficult on a good day, but he had no choice. "So," he tried. "How's it going?"

"Really super," she said. "I just came from my Zumba class. Have you ever tried it?"

"Uh, no." At the chorus concert earlier in the year, he'd lost an hour of his life listening to her drone on about the bran muffin she ate for breakfast, the new flip tops on toothpaste that "made a big mess on the sink," and the pros and cons of DVR.

"I've already lost five pounds." She patted her hips. Her boobs jiggled in an intriguing way. "Those Latin rhythms really get you going." He scanned the crowd for a way out, but various mom gangs surrounded him, blocking every escape. To the right, the Power Brigade gesticulated madly. They were the Ivy Leaguers who'd quit their law and finance jobs to do the mommy thing but still led their lives with the aggressiveness they'd cultivated over decades of training. They scared the shit out of him. So did the Grannies, the clique-ish post-career mommies whose adopted Chinese, Vietnamese and Romanian children made up a good percentage of the school's *diversity*. The Caribbean nannies clumped together looking disdainful and bored. He'd tried to speak to them a few times, but they always shut up when he got too close. And, near the bust of some hairbrush heiress who founded The Bradley School, were the Chanel-wearing stay-at-home moms in full makeup, who used lunch as a verb and devoted their waking hours to the gods of high-end retail, comparing thousand dollar handbags while they waited.

Then he spotted Cheryl. She was eyeing him as if he were a piece of beef jerky. He'd always wanted the power of invisibility when he was a kid. How could he have known it would prove even more useful as an adult? His stomach clenched. He forced an awkward smile. Maybe if he waved it would make the whole situation less horrible. He waved.

Cheryl flashed him a half smile. She was pretending to decide whether or not to rescue him from Deanna's grasp. Maybe Deanna wasn't so bad after all. For one thing, he'd never had drunken bathroom sex with her at a parent social. He turned back to Deanna. He'd try really hard to make conversation. His mind went blank. "Cold out there, huh?" It was lame, but it was something.

"Oh yeah," Deanna said. "Brrr." She crossed her arms, which squeezed her breasts together. "My dad moved to North Carolina. I like that weather. You know, coat weather, but not gloves and hat weather. Hats just do not work on me. No one from Florida can wear hats. We're just not designed for them." She took a breath. "The other night at the party, my hair was just a smooshed mess because of that darn hat. I felt like I spent the whole night trying to poof it up."

He was glazing over when he realized Cheryl had made her way through the crowd and was heading toward them like a heat-seeking missile. A moment later, she thrust her body against his, pretending to bump him accidentally. "God, what a klutz I am!" she said. Her hand brushed his ass and lingered.

His reaction had to be just right. It would set the tone. "Not a problem," he said, as casually as he could. He put some distance between his ass and her hand. He gestured to Deanna. "You two know each other, right?"

"We sure do!" Deanna said perkily. "We did checkout at the book fair together. All that math!"

"Nice to see you," Cheryl said. Her voice was different when she spoke to women. Less throaty.

"We were just talking about the party," he said, hoping this was the way to go.

"It was super." Deanna nodded vigorously.

"I had a *very* nice time," Cheryl said. She locked eyes with Sean. "It was such an intimate gathering." Cheryl cocked her head, coquettishly. "And I'm sure the next party will be even better."

The next party. If she was talking about a *next* time, then he must've done all right. He stood a little straighter.

Deanna waved vigorously to someone behind him. A moment later, Walt Renard was standing next to her. "And how is everyone on this bitterly cold day?" Walt was rubbing his hands to warm them.

"Fantastic," Deanna said with a wink. "As always."

"What an excellent answer."

"I try." She flashed him a flirtatious smile.

"You'll all be at the auction, right?" Walt looked expectantly at Sean.

"The auction," Sean repeated. He'd gone to the auction once. Ellie had won a family portrait session with Annie Leibovitz for eight hundred dollars, which they'd never used. A weekend on a private island in Greece had gone for ninety grand. "Depends on whether I can get a sitter."

"I'm the emcee this year," Walt said. "Don't know if that makes it more or less appealing."

"Oh I'll be there." Cheryl made it sound like a dare, somehow. "I'm on the committee. I have no choice."

Walt checked his watch, which looked expensive. "Oh boy," he said. "Late again. Gotta go!" He gave a bow and took off into the crowd.

"I just love him," Deanna said. "What a nice guy."

"And loaded," Cheryl added. "He's given more money to the school in the last five years than any other donor. And that's a lot of money."

"Didn't his son graduate last year?" Deanna asked.

Cheryl nodded. "I'm pretty sure he's going to an Ivy League."

"But . . ." Sean couldn't get his mind around this new bit of information. "If his son's graduated, why's he always around?"

Deanna made an expression that indicated she was thinking. He hadn't seen it before. "He's Chairman of the Board, right?"

"I don't think he's the Chairman," Cheryl said. "But I might be wrong. He also does some pro bono work for the school. I know he's got his own environmental law practice."

Sean watched the kids shaking hands with their teachers. "Shall we?" Cheryl said, leading the way.

He retrieved Toby and was almost out the door when he felt a hand on his shoulder.

"Sean," Bev Shineman said. Her down coat was unzipped, revealing a green cardigan that strained at the buttons. "Do you have a minute?"

"Is there news? About Calvin?"

"Can we talk in my office?" She smiled. "I'm sure Toby won't mind waiting in the library."

Shineman's office was tiny and cluttered. There wasn't a clear surface anywhere. "So how's Calvin? What's going on?"

"He's hanging in there."

He waited, expecting more. "Is he conscious?" Pulling teeth would have been easier than getting information from her.

Shineman took a deep breath and let it out ominously. "I should respect the privacy of the family."

He wanted to shake her. "Come on, I was there. Tell me what's going on."

She considered this a moment. "It's touch and go right now. He went into cardiac arrest last night, but they got him going again."

Touch and go. For the first time since it happened, he realized Calvin could die. Really die. "What happened? Why? How?"

She hesitated, as if she wasn't sure whether to confide in him. "It turns out Calvin had developed a severe nut allergy."

"Calvin didn't have any allergies," Sean said.

"He'd never had a reaction until . . . well until the other day." She shook her head again. "Kids grow out of allergies all the time. And sometimes they grow into them. Someone must have brought in a snack made with peanut oil that set it off. It's just unfathomable that this could have happened."

"If the paramedics had known . . ." His head was spinning. "About the allergies . . ."

"It might have made a difference in the way they treated him," she said. "I know . . . It makes you feel so helpless."

Calvin might die because he developed an allergy no one knew about. Talk about life not being fair. This was criminal. How could Calvin die? And how was he going to tell Toby if that happened?

Shineman sighed loudly in an attempt to leave the awful topic behind. "But that's not why I wanted to talk to you." There was a shift in her tone. "I wanted to talk to you about an incident in the classroom today."

"With Toby?" *Incident* could mean anything from a playground tussle to projectile vomiting. Once in preschool it had meant that another child bit Toby on the nose and had drawn blood. "Is he okay? What happened?"

"He's fine. But another student was sent to Nurse Astrid with quite a scratch."

"Toby scratched someone?" Toby liked to play around, but he was not a scratcher. Never had been.

"He didn't scratch the child. He pulled a chair out from under her during social studies."

"Who was it?"

"She scraped her back on the corner of the chair when she fell," Shineman said. They never identified the victim. "I wouldn't ordinarily talk to a parent over one isolated event, but it seems that Toby's behavior is becoming an issue."

"His *behavior*?"

"He's got to stop horsing around." She paused. "What do you think would drive him to do a thing like that?"

"Come on," he said. "Seriously? Why would an eight-year-old boy pull a chair out from under an eight-year-old girl? You don't need a degree to figure it out."

Shineman didn't see the irony and expressed that with an unamused stare.

"You've got a child unconscious in the hospital—a child who might die." He hadn't meant to yell. He tried to reel it in. "And you're giving me grief about a scratch? A stupid prank?"

"Could you please keep your voice down?" Shineman scolded in a strict whisper. "I know Toby didn't *mean* to hurt anybody."

She didn't know anything about his son.

"But this kind of behavior problem is a distraction to the rest of the class."

"Toby does not have a *behavior problem*." He didn't care if everyone in the building heard.

Shineman sat quietly with her hands folded in her lap. Was she waiting for him to calm down? Because that was only infuriating him more. "You're not helping him, you know."

"Everything I do is to help him."

"I've seen a lot of kids, Sean. Toby is easily distracted. It's going to be hard for him to keep up with the other children academically. Which is going to prove to be a major issue for him if we don't do something to help him now."

He pushed himself up from the chair. "I've got to get Toby to tutoring," he said, before she could launch into her medication rant again. She'd hit him with it three weeks ago and then again via Ellie, and he had no desire to go for a third round. "Wouldn't want to be late for that."

CHAPTER FIVE

GETTING DOWNTOWN FOR TUTORING WASN'T SO BAD. EVEN THOUGH the East Village was a different world, the trip only consisted of a handful of stops on the Lexington line. Getting back to the Upper West Side during rush hour was less fun. More than once, he'd considered finding a more geographically desirable tutor, but the uptown tutors charged double Noah's fees. A hundred bucks an hour was pricey enough, plus Toby had liked Noah instantly, and Sean couldn't put a price on that.

Noah had several advanced degrees in education and was probably just a few years younger than Sean, but he exuded that just-out-of-college slack—threadbare jeans that hung off his hips, limp hair smoothed behind his ears. He threw "dude" around for good measure. Unlike the school, Noah had not been *concerned* when Toby was stumbling over his reading last year. "Kids learn this stuff at different speeds," he'd told Sean. "We can crank it up for Bradley's sake, but don't let them get to you. It's all good." As a rule, Sean hated the phrase *it's all good*, but he focused on the fact that it meant Toby was fine.

Now, sitting with Toby on the downtown 6 train, Sean knew he was supposed to bring up the *incident*. Part of him wanted to just let it go. But Shineman had Toby in the crosshairs.

"So I heard about what happened in Social Studies," he said.

Toby took a heavy breath.

"Spill it."

"It was just a joke," Toby said. "Kayla pushed a bouncy ball out from under me at roof-play and everyone laughed. So I did it back to her in the classroom."

Tit for tat. Reasonable. "You can't do that kind of stuff, Tobe."

"I didn't mean for her to get cut," he said. You could tell he felt bad about it. "I took her down to the nurse. I think she's going to be okay."

Sean smiled even though he knew he should use the Serious Dad face he'd practiced for moments like this. He tried frowning a little, hoping that would do the trick.

"We've had this talk, Tobe. You can't be silly in school."

"It's not fair," Toby was whining now. "Kayla never gets in trouble. She pushes in line and the teacher yells at *me*. She makes funny faces in music and I get in trouble for laughing."

Maybe it was time for the Life's Not Fair speech? "Do me a favor," he said. "For the next few weeks—until Christmas vacation—try extra hard to be good. That means no pranks, no giggling, no matter who's making funny faces, and doing whatever the teacher tells you to do."

"But dad—"

"Okay?"

An extra-wide Hasid with perfect ringlets that grazed his shoulders sat in the two seats next to Toby. When Toby had been three, he'd seen a man wearing the same black orthodox-issue hat. "Look dad," he'd exclaimed, happily—and loudly, "a real live cowboy." The memory made Sean smile, in spite of his efforts to keep his Serious Dad face intact.

"Okay." Toby sighed, now sullen and tween-like. He avoided Sean's gaze and started shading in a drawing of a superhero he'd started earlier. It was good. The muscles rippled under the suit and he was fighting some creepy-looking wolf-dogs.

"I hate going to Noah."

"No you don't. You like it," Sean responded, in a brilliant moment of parenting.

"I can read already. Can't we skip it? Just today?"

He shook his head. "Negativo." He couldn't believe now that he was a father he said things like *negativo*.

"Only stupid kids go to tutoring."

"Who said that?"

Toby shrugged. Not telling. But he was sure it was Isaac. Isaac had actually started out okay. He and Toby were buddies that first year, but by the time he was seven, Isaac was rolling his eyes and calling kids morons when they gave the wrong answer in class. Interesting, Sean thought, that if a sweet, intelligent Bradley third grader was at third grade reading level it was a major disaster. But if a malicious, condescending Bradley third grader happened to have a genius IQ the school wrote off the bratty behavior as a personality quirk. In any other school in any other city, this kid would be pummeled on a daily basis. At Bradley, *he's* the bully.

"Hey. You're incredibly smart," he said. "You have a creative mind and you can think for yourself." As soon as he said it, it sounded like a consolation prize. "Besides, everyone can use help with something. I'd like to see Isaac try to draw a superhero like that."

Toby shrugged. Wouldn't look up. "When's Calvin coming back?"

"I don't know, Tobe," he said. "Soon, I hope." Later in life, on the couch, Sean was pretty sure some therapist would refer to this period as The Year Everyone Disappeared. There was nothing he could do about it. Except stick around.

He rested a hand on Toby's shoulder as they emerged from the subway into the East Village. After the buttoned-up, low-density Upper East Side, it was like landing on another planet. It was also the reason Sean didn't mind the schlepp down here: to show Toby that they weren't the only ones who lived in New York without a chauffeur-driven SUV and a fully-staffed townhouse. Down here, New York lifers and art students with pink hair and pierced tongues went about their business as if nothing—or at least nothing important— existed above Fourteenth Street. A six-foot transvestite in full makeup, mini dress, and what looked like size-thirteen heels, strutted back and forth in front of Lucky Chang's. Toby's eyes widened as they passed. He hadn't asked yet, but it was only a matter of time. Sean really should have a good explanation ready to go.

Noah greeted them in front of the door of his fourth floor walk-up with a basketball under his arm. "Toby, dude, what up?"

Toby gave him a half smile and a high five as he entered what Noah called the "Arena."

"Catch," Noah said, and sent him a low bounce pass. Toby caught it, dribbled on the scuffed wood floor, and took a shot on the regulation-size hoop. Sometimes he and Noah shot baskets between reading drills. Three bar stools at the dinette counter constituted the entirety of Noah's home furnishings. Sometimes Noah would make Toby spell vocabulary words as he took free throws. Sometimes he'd have Toby read a story, then ask him comprehension questions while he dribbled.

"I've got some good stuff planned for today," Noah told Toby. "You're gonna like it."

This was Sean's cue to give a quick wave and disappear for an hour while Noah worked his magic. "Do you have a minute?" he asked instead.

They stepped into the fluorescent light of the stairwell and he could hear Toby dribbling inside. The downstairs neighbors had to be deaf not to hear, too.

"You said Toby's doing well, right?" He tried to sound nonchalant. Or at least not like the insane parents Noah was probably used to dealing with.

"He's doing great."

Sean untensed his shoulders. Toby was doing great.

"His reading comprehension is way up," Noah said. "It's all coming together for him. I'm stoked."

If Noah was stoked, how bad could it be? "The school is on him again. They say he's falling behind."

"Those fuckers," Noah said. He was biting the inside of his lip, staring at a smashed cockroach on the wall. "Toby is a smart kid. He's a *very* smart kid. I know he's not into reading on his own yet. That's the key. But you can't force that. He's got to want it. Keep reading to him. Make it fun. The more of a chore it becomes the longer it will take." He ran his fingers through his hair.

It all sounded so reasonable when Noah said it. "Those Bradley kids are reading Proust," Sean said. "Toby can't sit still for Cam Jansen."

"Those perfect Bradley boys—and yeah, I know there are a lot of them—are the exception, not the rule. Back in caveman times they wouldn't have survived five minutes. They'd have been Sabertooth tiger dinner. No joke."

He liked the image of Isaac scratching away at the sand with his spear, discovering calculus or the cure for cancer, not noticing a puma as it leapt on him and ripped out his little jugular.

"Boys need to move around. We're hunters, man. It's genetic. We're wired with quick reflexes for hunting, strength for hauling. Testosterone—we all know what that's for. None of those things make what these schools call a *good student*."

"Tell that to Bev Shineman."

"She knows. They all do. Boys and girls learn differently," Noah said. "It's a scientific fact. But the schools don't want to deal with that. They're treating boys like defective girls. It sucks. It truly sucks."

The whole thing sounded hopeless. "Maybe I should just cut my losses and take him out of Bradley."

"Are you fucking kidding me?" Noah frowned, disapprovingly. "He's at the best school in the city."

SEAN KICKED AROUND THE NEIGHBORHOOD. REGULARS WERE already nursing beers in a dim bar with sawdust on the floor. A hole-in-the-wall boutique was selling underwear made out of recycled rubber, and a pricey new comfort food restaurant advertised mac and cheese for eighteen bucks a plate.

Why was Sean making both their lives miserable? Staying at Bradley meant asking for more abuse from Bev Shineman and subjecting Toby to intellectual bullies like Isaac. But Noah had a point. What were his options, really? Was he really going to move to the suburbs? Every day he woke up and thanked God he didn't have to live in the suburbs.

Not that he could afford to move, even if he wanted to. At nine hundred dollars a month, his apartment was the best deal in the city, and for a pre-war doorman building, it was obscene. A two-bedroom that *wasn't* rent-stabilized went for two or three thousand dollars. And even if he decided to sell his soul and move to the suburbs, there was no way he could afford a down payment. He was staying put.

He walked a few more blocks and found himself in front of P.S. 15. Someone had scrawled *suk my dick* on the building's puke-colored cinderblocks. Mesh wire encased every window. He tried to decide whether it was to keep out the residents of the sketchy neighborhood or to lock the kids in. So it was ugly. Institutional. Kids all over the country went to crappy schools just like this.

And public schools in New York weren't *all* crappy. There were magnet schools and gifted and talented programs. Lots of lower schools were fine. Better than fine. His niece, Kat, seemed to be doing great at P.S. 163. The problem was that there were something like five decent *middle* schools in the entire borough and a zillion kids trying to get into them. Not all private school parents were rich. He knew plenty who were borrowing from their own parents and taking out second mortgages on their apartments. They knew the hundred and eighty thousand dollars it cost for K through five was worth every penny if it meant their kid would be guaranteed a place in private middle school when it came time.

It was the reason he'd finally agreed to let his in-laws pay for Bradley. Ellie had made the lethal argument: "Don't you want Toby to have the best education money can buy?" What could he say to that? Of course he did, even if it meant he would be endlessly humiliated every time he opened a tuition bill that he couldn't pay.

Now Toby had the best education at the best school in the city, maybe even the country, and apparently they didn't know how to teach boys. It was hard to imagine how that could really be true.

What killed Sean was that he knew it was just a matter of time before school clicked for Toby. It had been the same way for him. None of it had made sense in second or third grade. If he pulled Toby out now, it was like giving up on him before it all fell into place. But if he kept Toby at Bradley and there was no magic moment where it all came together, there was a decent chance Toby would fall even further behind—or worse, fail out. And that could shatter his confidence forever. Basically, he was screwed if he did and screwed if he didn't.

CHAPTER SIX

S*EAN HADN'T FULLY OPENED THE DOOR TO HIS APARTMENT* WHEN his sister's voice barreled down the hallway. "Where've you two been?" Nicole's tone was always a little scary. At least he was used to it.

He gave Toby a pat on the back. "Homework. Go." Toby trudged to his room.

Nicole's pumps lay where she'd kicked them off. She was reclining on the couch reading *The New York Law Journal*.

"You, too," he said to his sister. "Go, you'll be late." Thursdays were insane. As soon as he got Toby home from tutoring, Nicole went back to work and left Kat with them.

"I'm off tonight," she said. "They had to wait until the last minute to tell me, those assholes."

Over the years, Nicole's thighs had thickened and gray strands had crowded out the brown in her short haircut. She'd always been a tomboy, and now, as an adult, she'd embraced a butch look that worked for her. Her official orientation was heterosexual, but nonsexual seemed more fitting.

"And my class is canceled next week," he said. "Don't forget." The gig at the Art Students League paid him just enough to cover one-sixth of a shared painting studio downtown. Without Ellie around to stay with Toby, he hardly used it anymore. But he refused to give it up.

"Mommy!" Kat was sobbing as she ran out of Toby's bedroom. Her bony little legs looked like they might crumple from the exertion. Kat embodied everything her mother lacked in girliness. She played with dolls, wore pink daily, and wanted to be a ballerina when she grew up. Nicole would shrug her shoulders. "She must get it from her father."

Nicole got knocked up during a one-night stand around the same time Ellie got pregnant. He and Ellie used to call it the immaculate conception because neither of them could imagine Nicole having sex or anything approaching a relationship. She was far more comfortable in a prosecutorial role.

"Kiddo, what is it?" Nicole reached out and pulled in her daughter. "Calm down. What's wrong?" Kat tried to catch her breath. Her face was a streaky mess. "He called me . . . he called me a COOL."

"Well that doesn't sound so bad." Nicole smoothed back a strand of her hair.

"Not cool," Kat said. "A COOL."

Nicole and Sean eyed each other. What were they missing?

Toby skulked guiltily out of his room.

"Toby says a C-C-COOL," Kat stuttered, "is a Constipated, Overweight, Out-of-style Loser." She burst into tears.

He had to admit the insults had gotten more creative since he'd been in school. "Toby," he said. "Over here. Now."

Toby let out a defeated sigh. "What?"

Sean raised his eyebrows. No need for more.

"Sorry Kat," Toby said. "You're not a COOL."

Kat's lower lip was still trembling. "Really?"

"Yeah, you're a JERK."

"Mom!" Kat was ready to unleash another flood.

"Toby," he now used the Ultra Serious Dad voice he reserved for serious infractions. "Go to your room."

"No dad, a JERK is a good thing," Toby said defensively. "It's a Junior Educated Rich Kid. There's also PERK, which is a Perfectly Educated Rich Kid. That's what I am."

Sean stared at his offspring, unable to control his jaw, which had gone slack. Forget the fact that Toby was not rich. If he was going to go around telling people outside of Bradley that he was rich and perfectly educated, well, he was going to get the crap kicked out of him. But this probably wasn't the moment to get into that.

Nicole rocked Kat. Her glare screamed disapproval.

"Enough with the acronyms," he said to Toby. "Apologize."

"But . . ." Toby started. He looked at Sean, then at Nicole, and decided not to push it. "Sorry Kat," he said. It was less than convincing. But it would have to do.

"And no more name calling," he said. "Last warning."

They dragged their feet down the hallway. Before they turned the corner into Toby's room, Kat stuck out her tongue. "Told you you'd get in trouble," she taunted. Toby just shook his head and rolled his eyes.

"Bradley kids—future leaders of the free world," Nicole mumbled. "Nice."

Obviously Bradley had its drawbacks. He'd never planned on sending his kid to private school. And Ellie—always up for rejecting her past—had been fine with the idea of public school. They were all set to do it. Somehow Ellie's mother had convinced them to take a look.

"Bradley has changed," Maureen had said. She was your classic volunteer lady—the thing Ellie was most afraid of turning into.

"You'll see. It's very *with it*. They have minorities now—scholarship students from Queens and the *Bronx*." To Maureen and Ellie's father, Dick, the outer boroughs were exotic and volatile, much like third world countries. Sean couldn't remember now why they'd agreed to take the tour.

"At Bradley we focus on the *whole child*," Mimsy Roach had said with feeling as she guided prospective parents from the gymnasium to the black box theater. "Each child's differences make her unique." The use of *her* had thrown him, but he tried to stay with Mimsy's spiel. "Different ethnicities, socio-economic backgrounds, learning styles, we welcome it all," she went on. "That's what makes this place stand out from all the other independent schools. We don't only *accept* diversity. We *crave* it."

Mimsy was a walking billboard for the place. With casual asides like, "There's no challenge we don't love," and "our primary goal is to teach children to give back to the community," everything that came out of her mouth was exactly what you wanted to hear. She let it slide toward the end of the tour that she'd graduated from Bradley and rushed back to work at the school after matriculating to Wellesley.

By the end of the tour, every parent was sold on the place. Suddenly, neither Sean nor Ellie could imagine sending Toby to a school that *didn't* have a state-of-the-art computer room, cutting-edge science labs, a competition pool, and a professional art studio. Ignoring, for the moment, the joy they knew it would bring Maureen and Dick (who never tired of wearing his Bradley '53 varsity sweater), they found themselves being swept up in the excitement. They decided to go for it. When they got Toby's acceptance letter, they jumped up and down and shrieked with joy. They couldn't help feeling like they'd won the lottery.

"You're spending tens of thousands of dollars," Nicole said now, "or should I say tens of thousands of dollars are being spent—so Toby can learn to be a snob."

"I could send him somewhere I could afford," Sean said. "But you of all people know you get what you pay for." This hit her where he knew it would hurt.

Nicole had decided to save on student loans by choosing an affordable law school. At eight thousand dollars a year, University of Buffalo seemed like the perfect choice. "Suckers," she'd say, when her friends graduated from Yale and Harvard strapped with one hundred and fifty thousand dollars of debt.

When it came time to apply for jobs, it turned out that Nicole was, in fact, the sucker. The big New York law firms—and the six-figure salary she'd been counting on—dried up when they saw SUNY Buffalo on her resume. Maybe if she'd been on *Law Review* or at the top of her class or something it would have been different, but Nicole had had to work two jobs just to pay the discounted tuition plus room and board.

Her job as an Assistant District Attorney wasn't bad, but the pay was. She lived on 155th Street and was barely getting by. Luckily, Kat had gotten into the G&T program at P.S. 163—New York-speak for "Gifted and Talented." In theory, it was an "enriched" curriculum available free to any four-year-old who scored high enough on a standardized kindergarten exam, but it was still public school, which meant money was always tight. As a result, music and art—anything extra—flew out the window in lieu of things like lunch and toilet paper.

Sean was breaking his one rule with Nicole: do not under any circumstances get her started on school. Not only did she have a gigantic chip on her shoulder, but she was also an excellent litigator, not to mention she'd been trained to go for the jugular by the D.A., and by their parents before that.

"At least I'm not taking handouts from my in-laws," she said.

"Nice," he said. "What's up with you tonight?"

"I'm on the rag."

"Well back off. I've had a hard day."

Nicole's body language changed. "What happened?"

Sean shrugged away the question.

Nicole narrowed her eyes and lowered her voice. "Did you hear from Ellie again?"

"No." He said it defensively.

Ellie had been sending postcards to Toby from all over the country as she got progressively farther away from home. The last one had come from Santa Fe. But she'd only bothered to call Sean three times since she'd been gone. Once to say she was okay—that she'd gone off the Prozac and was no longer staying up all night and dropping a thousand dollars a day (that he was still paying off) on Internet purchases. But she didn't want to come home. Not yet. She told him not to worry. But not to call either. It was temporary, she said. "I'm not sure I want to leave you." The statement had been as reassuring as a two by four to the solar plexus.

The second time she'd called she was crying hysterically and slurring her words. "I'm a bad mother," she'd said.

"So come home," he said and hung up. It seemed to have completely escaped her that she'd abandoned him, too. The third time had been the other night at the parent social.

The last miscarriage had pushed Ellie over the edge. He hadn't been convinced another kid was even a good idea—the cost, for one thing—but when Ellie realized how hard it would be to get back into network television at an executive level, she decided to bag the job search and throw herself into another six years of the super-mom thing. It would be great for Toby to have a sibling, she'd argued, until he agreed. She waged a highly orchestrated attack involving ovulation kits, waiting thirty-six hours between "tries" as the doctor called what had become of their sex life, and elevating her legs in the air for twenty minutes afterwards. It took almost a year to get pregnant. Ellie was devastated when she lost the baby ten weeks in. It took another year to get pregnant again. When she had another miscarriage, she sunk even deeper. He'd tried to stop the "trying" then. But when he suggested that maybe a second child wasn't in the cards, that they were good the way they were, Ellie became even more focused on success. "I'm not giving up," she'd said, as if sheer will and hard work were going to make the difference. "We can do this." The two other pregnancies ended almost before they started. She managed to take Toby to school in the mornings before crawling back into bed for the rest of the day. She stopped shaving her legs and shopping for groceries. He told her he loved her, that they didn't need another baby. He kept telling her that their family was perfect the way it was. He cooked her dinner and combed her hair, but Ellie couldn't shake it. She was depressed.

He took her to a shrink. The Prozac helped her get out of bed. Three months later, she left him.

"So if it's not Ellie, what is it?" Nicole had tossed the *Law Journal* on the table and was gearing up to hound him. "Is it work? Wait, don't tell me. You have to do a layout of Brad Pitt's colonoscopy."

"Funny." Sean went into the kitchen and grabbed a couple of beers from the fridge.

"So it's school. Let me guess . . ."

This was not a fun game. "Just drop it, okay?"

But Nicole didn't drop things unless she wanted to. "Let's see, they want Toby to start training now for the SATs."

He handed her a beer.

"They're worried because he's not in AP physics yet and he's falling behind the 11th graders."

"Okay. I get it."

"He's in too many after school activities." She was on a roll now. "He's not in enough after school activities."

He took a drink, and tried to ignore her.

Nicole plowed ahead. "His advanced artwork is taking time from his advanced math so they'd like to give him extra help and maybe throw in some study drugs to get him up to speed."

He stared at her, annoyed but slightly impressed. She took a sip of beer and raised her eyebrows as if to say, *Am I close?*

CHAPTER SEVEN

BACK WHEN HE'D BEEN AT THE SCHOOL OF VISUAL ARTS, GAS stations, warehouses, and questionable middle-eastern fast food joints littered the far-west section of Chelsea. Now, art collectors and dealers came from everywhere to see Manhattan's newest gallery mecca. It was impossible to believe the Burdot space had once been a condemned factory where underpaid Chinese workers sewed potholders or underwear or something equally wretched.

A wash of southern exposure streamed through oversized windows, bathing white walls and blond wood floors. Edgy photographs of dark and light that looked more like angry drawings, lined the walls. He spotted a woman at an immaculate desk at the back of the huge space. She wore a black skirt that hit just above the knee, a cropped jacket, pearls, and an aloof smirk.

She walked slowly across the room to him, sizing him up. "Camille Burdot," she said, shaking his hand.

"Nice to meet you." No question, he'd been right about the black underwear. He stood about a linebacker-and-a-half from her as she studied his work, arms crossed, eyes squinted. Camille Burdot was gorgeous. Her bedside manner, however, left something to be desired.

"Your drawings are . . . *eh*," she said, tepidly. Sean shifted and bit the inside of his cheek. Obviously she knew nothing about art.

"But these," she said, gesturing to the collages. *Zees*. "These are . . . good. Very good. You have captured something absolutely unique."

Of course the work she liked had been a fluke, inspired by Toby's food pyramid project. The assignment had entailed cutting pictures of food from magazines. Slicing up back issues of *Buzz* with Toby had not only been therapeutic, it had been a blast. So much so that he continued to mutilate the magazine and explore the form long after Toby had gone to bed that night. When he ran out of magazines, he'd found a box of awful family photos buried in the coat closet and sliced up the ones of him and Ellie. In one, his eyes were half-closed, making him look like a heroin addict. In another, Ellie's stomach hung over her bathing suit, even though he'd never seen it do that in real life. Each one was worse than the next. It was cathartic, satisfying. He couldn't remember how he got the idea to paste the sliced-up photos, mosaic-style, into old charcoal sketches he'd done of Ellie. The pieces Camille liked so much were kind of weird—Ellie's breasts, thighs, and stomach were crammed with deconstructed photos of their old life together. He'd liked them, but he wasn't sure if it was because it was a way to vandalize his memories.

"It took me a while to figure it out," Camille was saying. At first, I thought it was too sentimental. But then I saw the anger. You've destroyed the relationship, and the way to get rid of the memories is to stick them inside the woman you no longer love." She nodded her approval. "Very nice."

"Thanks," he said.

"Where have you shown before?"

"I had a show . . . upstate. A few years ago." He wondered if he needed to mention that the show had been in a café his friend Herb owned in Woodstock.

"Nothing in the city? This surprises me," Camille said. "We have a show in February. Martin Vols and Tina Crowe. You will be the third."

Vols and Crowe were known artists who sold actual work to actual art collectors. Vols specialized in detached photojournalistic views of crashes and carcasses. Crowe worked in mixed media that inevitably involved women being tortured.

"Yes!" he said, trying not to seem too enthusiastic, but not too blasé either. "Great. Thanks. Thank you."

Camille turned on her kitten heels (he remembered an article about Drew Barrymore called "Getting Catty in Kitten Heels" they'd run last year) and walked to the back of the gallery and sat delicately at her desk, crossed her legs to the best possible effect and opened a huge date book. "I'll need the work as soon as possible."

The work. So this could be a problem. Over the past three years Sean had stolen hours here and there—after Toby went to bed or on weekends at his studio painting or sketching. But the collages were an experiment. He only had the three he'd sent Camille. "So, how many pieces will you need for the show? Five, six?"

"I'll need at least twenty. We'll edit that down to ten or fifteen. You will deliver them fully framed, yes? It's a fifty-fifty cut. We charge two thousand apiece. Good?"

"Uh, yeah, very good." *Twenty new pieces.* That meant seventeen pieces by . . . "When do you need them?"

"Beginning of January. Latest."

"But . . . that's . . ."

"Is this a problem?" Camille eyed him coolly.

"No. No, of course not." He shook her hand, bestowed what he hoped was a grateful—but not groveling—smile, and hurried out the door before she could change her mind.

He took the steps two at a time. When he emerged from the gallery, walking wasn't fast enough and he started to run. It was happening. He'd gotten a real show. This could be the beginning of everything. A new life, new work, some real money. It could mean recognition as an artist. A life apart from Ellie.

His face muscles felt strange. He realized he was sporting an all-out, shit-eating grin and there was nothing he could do about it. He'd gotten exactly what he'd always wanted. He stopped running to contemplate it.

"Yesss," he shouted. It exploded from deep inside him, a booming celebration of the moment. He unclenched his fist and stopped pumping the air when an older black lady cut a wide berth around him, keeping him in her peripheral vision.

A man walking toward him caught his eye and squinted in recognition. As he got closer, he realized it was Walt Renard.

"You okay?"

"Yeah," he said, the shit-eating grin persisting. "I'm good. Very good."

Now Walt was smiling, too. "You look like the cat who swallowed the canary. Spit it out."

"I just got some good news." He tried to make it sound like no big deal, like this wasn't the most important thing that had ever happened to him.

"Don't leave me hanging," Walt said. "Come on. Spill it."

He opened his mouth to tell Walt, which would make it real. "I just came from Burdot."

"The Burdot Gallery. It's one of the best in the city. I've known Camille for years."

"Camille . . . she just gave me a show, in February, with Martin Vols and Tina Crowe." He loved the way it sounded coming out of his mouth.

"Whoa! That *is* good news. Fantastic news!" Walt slapped his back. "Congratulations."

"Thanks," he said, suddenly self-conscious about sharing this deeply personal news with someone he hardly knew. "So do you work around here?"

"Not too far." Walt swiveled to reveal the nylon gym bag on his shoulder. "I've got a regular game twice a week at Chelsea Piers." He sized up Sean. "You play ball?"

"Basketball? Not for a while, but yeah, a little." He'd played intramural basketball. At art school. Nicole had always been the jock in the family.

"You should play with us." Walt's eyes lit up. "It's not a killer game, but you'll get a workout."

Basketball could be fun. "Why not? Let me know next time you play."

"Sure thing. Got a card?"

Sean dug a business card from his wallet and wished it didn't say *Buzz Weekly* on it.

"I'll email you." Walt looked at his watch. "I better run or they'll start without me."

"Have a good game."

"I will," he said. "And Sean, congratulations on Burdot. That is phenomenal news. Phenomenal."

Walt jogged toward Chelsea Piers and Sean hauled ass to Thirty-eigth and Tenth, where he doubled over and gasped for breath. Taxis, commuter busses, and limos raced past him toward the Lincoln Tunnel. The wind kicked up off the Hudson and he tightened his jacket against it.

Reality began to set in. How the hell was he going to pull off seventeen new pieces by January while keeping his job and entertaining

Toby over Christmas break? His mind, now cold and clear from the wind, turned the impossible math problem over and over like a giant Rubik's cube. No matter how he twisted it, he couldn't make it work out. There simply weren't enough hours in the day to get it all done.

He fought to stave off the panic. He'd figure it out. He'd have to. This opportunity was not going to get lost in the insanity that had become his day-to-day. This show was going to happen. Period. He checked his watch.

He was supposed to be making an apple pie with Toby. The apple pie that Ellie should have been making. Sean was responsible for it all now—taking care of Toby, earning a living, making the fucking apple pie.

Worst of all, he'd finally gotten the show he'd been waiting for and there was no one to tell. No one who knew how desperately he'd wanted it. Except Ellie. He should call Ellie just to prove he'd done it. That he was good enough. But he knew he wouldn't call her.

He'd pick up Toby from Nicole's house, tell him the news, then they'd figure out how to cook an apple pie.

His apartment hadn't felt so warm since before Ellie left. Way before she left, when she was still the real Ellie with a job and a staff to boss around and meetings to run and endless energy that kept their family humming along happily.

Now, a young Mick Jagger belted "Ruby Tuesday" while he and Toby air-guitared around the living room, jumping on furniture, squeezing their eyes shut in musical ecstasy and thrashing invisible instruments. When they were sweaty and tired, they collapsed on the couch, breathing heavily.

"Dad, you should have been a rock star," Toby said, without irony. "You've got some good moves."

"You too. What was that hip thing you were doing? Kinda racy for eight, don't you think?"

"Da-ad!" Toby said and hit him with a pillow.

"So did you think about what you want to do during Christmas break? Should I see if there's some kind of art camp you can go to or something?"

"I can be your assistant."

"Boring. Trust me. We'll find something good for you."

"Zack is going to Vail with his mom. Why don't we ski, Dad?"

Where to begin? Skis, lifts, resorts, gear? Next to polo and scuba diving, it was probably the most expensive sport ever created. "Cold," he said. "Too cold."

"Dylan is going to South Africa. It's not cold there."

"South Africa?" Sean tried to imagine a life where he could jet his family to Africa for a getaway. "Wow."

"Maybe we can go someplace during spring break. I don't care where. Just anywhere would be good."

If everything went according to plan, he could have some cash by March. He could take Toby to Miami or Puerto Rico and they could have a family vacation. Just the two of them. "It's a deal."

They shook on it.

"Dad, you realize we still haven't done the pie," Toby said. "I think we better get on it."

Toby pulled a cookbook off the coffee table. "I did a little research. It doesn't sound too hard." He opened to a dog-eared page. "It says here the secret to a perfect pie crust is lard."

"No, Toby," he said, walking to the freezer and removing a pie crust he'd picked up on the way home. "The secret to a perfect pie crust is the frozen food section."

"Isn't that cheating?"

"Only if you tell Grandma."

Toby nodded seriously. "Deal." Then he started jumping up and down. "Come on, let's get this puppy started!"

Sean wished it could be just the two of them tomorrow, sitting at their little, round kitchen table, watching football, hanging out.

But Maureen had called on Monday. She called periodically for Toby, to ask about his schoolwork and to find out what size he wore now.

"Sean," she'd said, with an exuberance she usually saved for company, "You *are* coming on Thursday." It was a statement.

"Oh, I thought. I mean, since Ellie—"

"It's a family tradition," she said.

Sean was no longer clear on the definition of family. But it was the only Thanksgiving tradition Toby had ever known. He loved the holiday. "Thanks Maureen."

"We'll expect you at three-thirty. I hope you'll bring Nicole and Kat as well." She hung up and that had been that.

Ellie's parents were not warm, and they weren't particularly doting. But they did love Toby. He wouldn't be the one to deprive Toby of the only set of grandparents he had. It wasn't simply because they were paying for Bradley, either. Sean wanted his son to have some sense of an extended family, some continuity. His own parents had died before Toby was born—his mom from a two-pack a day habit and his dad a couple of years later from "who knows," as the doctor had told him. Thanksgiving at his house as a child had been loud and messy and fun. Maureen and Dick were none of those things.

It turned out that the only tricky thing about frozen piecrust was that it didn't stay together when you stretched it over the apples. As Toby was trying to patch the deadly fault lines with water and extra dough, the phone rang.

Sean picked it up with a sticky hand. "Benning Bakery, piecrusts are us."

"Sean?"

"Ellie." He felt like a ball of raw dough had lodged in his trachea.

Toby looked up. His eyes got wide and he started yelling, "Hi Mommy! Hi!"

"I'm not talking about the medication anymore, so if that's why you're calling—"

"It's not why I'm calling."

"What's wrong?"

"I'm fine." Her voice sounded far away. "Well, Happy Thanksgiving, I guess."

"Can I talk, can I talk?" Toby was grabbing at the phone.

"I'll put Toby on," he said to the disembodied voice filtering through fiber optic cables from God knows where. He handed the phone to Toby.

"Hi Mommy!" Toby's face lit up when he heard her voice. "Where are you? We're baking a pie." Toby listened for a while. Sean could hear Ellie's voice telling him how much she loved him. "I love you, too. Are you coming home soon?"

The look of disappointment on Toby's face was almost unbearable. "Okay," he said, and handed him the phone. "She wants to talk to you."

He braced himself and put the receiver to his ear.

"I have a favor to ask."

"You've got to be kidding." He walked toward the bedroom, gesturing for Toby to wait a minute. He shut the door behind him. "What?"

He waited. She was there, but she wasn't there, this person he was supposed to know inside and out.

"What's Toby doing for break?" she finally asked.

"Art camp."

"Which one?"

"There are a few I'm thinking of."

"You haven't signed him up yet? And aren't they something like a thousand bucks?"

"You seem awfully interested in Toby's schedule for someone who dropped the ball on everything three months ago."

"You must hate me."

He did. He hated her. But hearing her voice was confusing. Maybe he didn't hate her quite as much as he'd hoped. Why the hell was she calling?

"I'd hate me, too," she said.

"I got a show." It was out before he knew it. He wished he could take it back.

"Oh my God," she screamed. "You got a show! Where is it? When?"

"Burdot. In February."

She paused. "Well, then maybe this won't be such a favor after all."

•—•

"Please dad? Please, please?" Toby's eyes were red. His pillow was wet. His mouth was a horrible quivering line. "I want to see Mommy."

Sean should have told her to call back after Toby went to bed. But there was no way he could have known she wanted Toby to stay with her for the entire two weeks of Christmas break. He had to admit she sounded more sane than she had in years. But the request itself was insane. Could she have really thought he'd say yes?

Toby's chin was shaking and he couldn't catch his breath. "Please Dad," Toby sobbed.

He shook his head. "Tobe, it's not going to happen. Maybe she can come down and see you for a day or two. But you can't go stay with her."

Toby was taking deep breaths, trying to stop crying. It looked painful. Sean wished there was some way to make him see it was for his own good—without telling him his mother had had some sort of breakdown.

"Dad," he said, focusing hard on not crying. "It's what I want for Christmas. It can be instead of *all* my presents."

It was impressive, and horrible, to realize that Toby had become so adept at torturing him. Though his stomach was one big knot, he managed a sad smile and reached over to mess up Toby's hair. But Toby rolled toward the wall and out of reach, twisting the knife slowly. His son hated him at the moment. He could feel it radiating from him. Parents were supposed to let their children's hatred roll off them the way water wicks off Under Armour. He was just no good at wicking.

"It'll be okay," he said, as much for his sake as for Toby's. "I love you."

He shut the door behind him and sprawled on the living room couch where he let himself sink into the spongy cushions and replay the bizarre conversation with Ellie. Over the past few weeks she'd let them believe she was on some far-flung adventure.

"There's no way I'm going to put him on an airplane to God knows where," he'd started.

That was when she dropped the bomb that she was only a few hours away on Long Island.

"It just felt right," she said, describing the place she'd found. "My pulse slowed down, my shoulders relaxed. I could think again. I knew I was home."

She'd said *home*. "So you're staying?"

"For now."

CHAPTER EIGHT

Sean skimmed the surface of sleep, replaying Ellie's chorus of "It's not fair" until the morning light pulled him out of it. He rolled over and squinted in the bright living room, wishing, like he did whenever he woke up on the couch, that they'd gotten around to installing window shades. Now, without Ellie to orchestrate it, there was no way it would ever happen.

He'd been mad at her when he went to bed. Furious. Now he wondered if he'd gone too far. Maybe he shouldn't have told her to go to hell. She was Toby's mother. She could see him, *should* see him. Spring vacation wasn't so far off. Maybe Presidents' Day. He'd see how it went until then and they could talk about it. After New Year's.

He was shaky and everything looked fuzzy and unfocused. He was bad without sleep. But he made out the time on the kitchen clock.

Nine o'clock. Why wasn't Toby jumping on him demanding cartoons? Toby hadn't slept past seven-thirty since he could walk. He plucked a pillow from the floor and sandwiched his head to shut out the light. He exhaled deeply and tried to relax. He should use the extra time to rest.

He threw off the pillows. Why wasn't Toby insisting on waffles? Something had to be wrong. He sat up and listened, but there was nothing. His heart sped up as he approached Toby's room. The door was closed, just like he'd left it last night with Toby sobbing on the other side. Now, Sean turned the knob and pushed it open.

The blinds were still drawn and it took a minute for the amorphous shapes to become the bed, the dresser, the papier maché totem pole he'd made for Toby's fourth birthday. He saw Toby curled on top of the covers wearing his jeans and sneakers. He put his hand on Toby's back to make sure he was breathing. A moment of relief was chased quickly by a sinking feeling. He'd helped Toby into his pajamas last night.

Toby's face nestled against a piece of white, flimsy fabric. Sean tugged on it gently, but Toby had it in a vice grip. Luckily, Toby could sleep through just about anything and didn't wake up while Sean worked the thing free. He held up the ratty T-shirt and got a flash of Ellie crawling into bed, the T-shirt grazing her mid-thigh. It was big enough for a sumo wrestler, but it was also, somehow, sexier than any lingerie she owned. She'd worn it to bed every night.

Toby had taken the T-shirt as a memento, the only piece of Ellie he could hold on to.

He sat on the ground cross-legged and held the T-shirt to his face. He breathed it in. Impossibly, it still smelled like her. Toby must have stolen it from the hamper after she left. Before it went into the wash. Smelling Ellie was not what Sean had expected, not what he'd wanted. But he sniffed it greedily, breathing in the smell of his wife until he couldn't smell her anymore.

He wasn't sure where the tears came from. They'd been shut off for months now, shoved down under all the reasons he didn't need her anyway. He stayed like that, on the floor next to Toby's bed for as long as it took for him to cry them all out. He did it quietly, even though he knew it would take a fleet of sirens to wake Toby if he wasn't ready. When the tears dried up, he was almost disappointed. He wiped his face with the T-shirt and studied his son.

He was so small. How could he let Toby go off to Long Island for two weeks? Yes, she was his mother, but who knew what condition she was in? It was true, she'd sounded more like herself than she had for a long time. He hadn't heard that speedy, manic tone that had fueled all their conversations in the months before she left.

The Spiderman suitcase Nicole had given Toby for Christmas lay next to the bed. He unzipped it. Inside were T-shirts, socks, underwear, and a pile of bite-sized candy bars. Toby had packed a bag. Sean didn't even know he was capable of packing a bag. And he'd done it, no doubt, to go see his mom. To run away.

That's when he noticed a piece of notebook paper on the floor. It was folded in half and on the front Toby had written "DAD." He opened it slowly, prolonging the moment before he had tangible proof of Toby's unhappiness. "Dear Dad," the note said. The handwriting was neat and even. He'd put some work into it. "Don't be mad or worry. I'm going see Mommy in Momtalk. I'll call you when I get their. Love, Toby."

It was so matter of fact. So reasonable. *Don't be mad.* What about devastated, terrified, desperate? Sean truly sucked at this father thing. What if Toby hadn't fallen asleep before sneaking out? What if he'd really done it?

He watched Toby sleeping peacefully, looking calm and angelic, not like a kid who'd almost walked out the door into New York City in the middle of the night. Anything could have happened to him out there alone. Anything. He reached out to touch Toby's hair, but stopped himself. He didn't want to risk waking Toby and catapulting him back to his shitty waking life. All he wanted was to grab on to Toby and squeeze hard—hard enough to show how much he loved him.

As if awakened by the mere suggestion of the squeezing, Toby stirred. He stretched his arms and legs. He rolled his head from side to side. His eyes opened slowly.

"Morning," Sean said. It sounded so benign. So normal. Not at all right for a day he'd almost lost everything.

"Hi," Toby said. It took him a few seconds to realize he was dressed and a few more to remember his escape plan. When he did, his eyes darted away from Sean's like a trapped animal. Finally, Toby just looked up at him, guiltily.

He knew he'd cry if he told Toby what a great kid he was, that he loved him, that even though everything sucked now it would get better. Instead, Sean reached out and hugged him—not the super-human squeeze, which would certainly have freaked him out—but a good long hug. "I know you want to see your mom." He coughed, so his voice wouldn't break. "I'm just trying to protect you, Tobe. Trust me on this."

Toby nodded.

"No more running away, okay?"

Toby nodded again.

"Promise? Because I don't know what I'd do if something happened to you." It was something people said, but he meant it more than anybody had ever meant it.

Toby nodded seriously, then noticed Sean was holding Ellie's T-shirt. There was nothing to say. Everything and nothing. Sean handed over the shirt. An offering. Toby reached for it and tucked it under the covers.

"Come on." He'd try to salvage the morning with an upbeat tone. "I'm going to make waffles, then we'll get ready to see your grandparents."

Toby unpacked the suitcase on his own and crumpled the note and threw it in the trash. He didn't say much over breakfast, but doodled a picture of a dragon coming out of an apple pie. "Dad," he said, finally, "I think Mom's going to come to Thanksgiving."

"No Tobe." He shook his head. "She's not."

He didn't look up from the drawing. "But she might surprise us."

He couldn't blame Toby for wishing it, expecting it. "Mommy's not coming. But everyone else will be there. Just like always."

Nicole and Kat picked them up in a taxi right on time and they made the annual trip across town to Dick and Maureen's with a gaping hole where Ellie would have been. The trip only took twenty minutes, but as Toby and Kat argued over who'd find more chocolate turkeys, he replayed every Thanksgiving they'd been to over the past decade.

"It'll be okay," Nicole said.

"What?"

"Today," she said. "It'll be weird, but okay."

"I know." He'd never appreciated the fact that Maureen and Dick packed their place with family friends on Thanksgiving. All those bodies would fill the emptiness. There would be funny anecdotes and holiday banter. It would be fine. Or at least he thought he could get through it.

Nicole patted his leg as the taxi pulled up in front of their apartment building. "Family is good on holidays," she said. "Even if it's Dick and Maureen."

He took deep breaths as the elevator pinged with every passing floor.

"I call we play Life first," Toby said to Kat.

"No fair, I want to play the Gnome game." They had games at home, but there was something about the ripped, dusty boxes from the seventies that lent Dick and Maureen's board games an exotic flair.

"Okay, but then we play Life."

"Deal."

At the front door, he wasn't sure what to do. Ellie always just let herself in. He rang the bell. Being here without her was all wrong. He felt like he was missing a leg or a hand, something crucial you never think about until it's gone. When Maureen opened the door for them, she greeted them warmly, hugging Toby and Kat. "There are some turkeys hiding around the place, waiting for some hungry children to find them," she announced, and they scattered. "Come in, let me take your coats."

The apartment was quiet except for the sound of the kids finding chocolate turkeys. "I guess we're the first to arrive." He snuck a peek at his watch. He'd made sure to arrive fifteen minutes late so this wouldn't happen.

"I thought we'd keep it intimate this year," Maureen said. "Just us for a change."

"Oh . . . great," he said. At least there would be booze. He watched Nicole's stunned expression and knew she was having the same thought.

After cocktails, they moved into the dining room, which was covered in a somber mauve on mauve wallpaper that matched the upholstery on the dark wood furniture. The chunky crystal chandelier loomed over them ominously. They sat at their seats, leaving Ellie's chair empty. Maybe Maureen secretly hoped Ellie would show up, too.

Sean nodded enthusiastically to a waiter in a white shirt and bowtie who was offering to refill his wine. The guy came to the apartment every year to cater the event. Ten years and Sean had no idea what his name was or what he did with the rest of his Thanksgiving. The waiter felt Ellie's absence, too, Sean was sure of it.

He thought about the Thanksgivings growing up in Troy. Their dad used to chase them around the yard with a loaded hockey stick playing shoot the turkey. That was the only Thanksgiving ritual Sean could remember. After a few years, his mother got bored with turkey. One year she made a Thanksgiving curried goat and another year she made something she called Thanksgiving Surprise, which made everyone gag, so they ordered pizza. They sat around the TV eating pizza and laughing, saying they were thankful for playing cards, toothpaste, and Wacky Packs.

"Come on," he called to the kids who were playing Life in the hallway. "Dinner."

He watched Toby get up, look toward the front door expectantly, then come to the table, shoulders slumped. Across the table, he caught Nicole sucking down her third gin and tonic. If she started on a fourth, all bets were off.

"So, Sean, how are you and Toby getting along?" Dick asked. "We haven't seen you boys in a while." Dick wore his white hair combed slickly to the side like a boy on his way to church.

"Great," he said. Dick probably didn't want to hear about how Toby had almost disappeared into the night with his Spiderman suitcase and a pound of Halloween candy, or that he missed his mom so much he was sleeping with her old night shirt. He didn't want to know that Sean had no idea how to deal with whatever Toby was going through at school. "Everything's great," he said again, this time with a presidential tilt of his head he'd seen Bush use on TV once.

"Splendid," Dick said jovially. He sported a blue blazer with brass buttons and suspenders embroidered with wild turkeys. "I think you'll enjoy the bird this year." Dick puffed his chest. "It's a fine specimen. Chased this guy a quarter mile before I finally nabbed him."

Dick fancied himself a hunter and had joined a private Millbrook club to prove it. Twice a month throughout the fall, he drove out to the Mashomack Preserve to shoot at quail and pheasant that had been raised specifically for the purpose of being killed by Dick and other members of his tax bracket.

"And what about you, young man?" Dick turned to face his grandson. Toby pulled at the neck of last year's button-down.

"Good," Toby said.

"That's not too convincing, son," Dick said. "Tell me about school. What wonderful things is my alma mater filling your head with?"

Toby shrugged. "Nothing."

"Nothing?" he exclaimed.

Why couldn't kids just play along? Sean had prepped Toby on easy answers to questions just like this. "We're doing money in math class" or "I'm learning how to make découpage in art" could have gotten him off the hook with minimal effort.

"Well I happen to know *that* is a lie, young man," Dick said. "If there's one thing we know for sure, it's that you are being pumped full of fascinating facts and skills that will serve you throughout your lifetime. You're a lucky young man to be at a school like Bradley."

Across the table, Nicole narrowed her eyes. Had anyone else heard the snort? It was subtle, but audible.

Sean slurped his pea soup as loudly as possible. "Wow this is good, Maureen. Bacon, right?"

"Tastes more like ham hocks, actually." Maureen turned to Nicole. "Everything all right, dear?" She poised the silver spoon at her lips.

Sean glared at his sister. She knew better. But that rarely stopped her.

Nicole grabbed a breadstick and crunched it aggressively. "Mmm." It was more of a grunt than anything.

This was when Ellie would swoop in with a Topic. He wracked his brain. All he could come up with was P. Diddy's love child, Lindsay Lohan's latest arrest, and the top ten celebrity divorces of the year. He had nothing.

"Toby has a new teacher," he blurted out. "She seems good, right Tobe?" He realized a moment too late he'd made a tactical error. He was supposed to steer the conversation *away* from school.

"I'm sure she's wonderful," Maureen said. "Bradley has its pick of the litter."

"Only the best," Dick said, smugly.

Nicole's nostrils flared.

Sean had to think of something benign, landmine-free. And quickly. "Crazy weather, huh?" He wished there were a hurricane or a tsunami somewhere to keep the conversation going.

"Even though the teachers are excellent, I've always felt that Bradley's academic excellence comes from the exceptional children they admit." Maureen smiled at Toby.

Nicole rolled her eyes and sat back heavily.

Everyone turned to look at her.

"Is something wrong?" Maureen's eyebrows furrowed. She was oblivious.

"No," Nicole said. "Of course not. It's just impressive that we've already started talking about how *exceptional* Bradley is and we haven't even had the salad course yet."

"You disagree?"

"Not everyone here goes to Bradley," she said, modulating her voice. "Remember?"

Maureen looked confused, then caught on. "Oh, well I'm sure Kat's school is just fine."

Kat smiled, unfamiliar with the concept of the backhanded compliment.

"Really? *Fine?*"

"We think Kat is a lovely girl," Maureen said. "Public school is just so . . . fraught."

"Public school is the only option some of us have. Most people in the country go to public school. It's a great, democratic education."

"Of course it is," Dick chimed in. "Some wonderful minds have made it through the public system."

"Oh come on, you know I wasn't saying that Kat isn't smart," Maureen said. "It's just, well I read the stories in the paper every day. I was just reading about the rubber room. Have you heard about that?" She turned to Sean. "The school isn't allowed to fire the teachers because they're unionized, but they don't want them near the kids, so they keep them locked in the rubber room all day." She snorted. "Bureaucracy. That's what you get when New York City runs anything."

"Public schools have a lot going for them. I would have sent Toby to—"

"And the money. New York City schools are always cutting programs. Art, music, gym . . . the city has decided they're luxuries. It's madness."

"You're talking about Kat's education," Nicole reminded her.

Maureen turned to Kat, who sat primly at her seat. "Sweetheart, how many teachers do you have in your classroom?"

If she was doing what Sean thought she was doing, it was ill-advised.

"We have Ms. Herbst."

"So just one." Maureen nodded. "And how many children in a class?"

"Twenty-eight."

"Wow," Maureen said with a *see-I-told-you-so* tilt of her head. "That's a lot of kids for one teacher to handle."

"At least they're not snotty Bradley kids who go around bragging that they're perfectly educated." The drinks were fueling the true Nicole, who didn't put up with anyone's bullshit. She might have gotten away with it on those grounds, but she'd called Bradley kids snotty. Which was going to be a problem.

"Why the name calling?" Dick said, disapprovingly.

"She's talking about Kat like she's one of the unwashed."

"Kat is an extremely bright child," Maureen said.

"Yeah," Nicole said. "*I* know that."

"She's going to be able to rise above the twenty-eight to one student-teacher ratio," Maureen said. "And the funding problems."

Nicole put down the plaid napkin that, he now saw, matched Maureen's dress. "Maybe we should go."

A pang of jealousy hit Sean. It wasn't fair. He wanted to go, too.

"But Mommy, I want to have stuffing." Kat pouted and tears welled in her big brown eyes. Nicole sat back down with a sigh.

But Maureen wouldn't stop. She couldn't. It was a pathology. "The thing that makes Bradley exceptional is its *screening* process."

"Ha!" Nicole exclaimed, and rolled her eyes. "The idea of basing admission on an interview with a four-year-old is pure insanity."

"Oh, I disagree," Maureen continued, in an upbeat tone as if she were discussing the benefit of insulated drapes or cooking with canola oil. "It weeds out the hyperactive children and the slow children."

It hit him then. Ellie had grown up with Maureen for a mother, a role model. It put everything into perspective. Ellie had done well—fantastically well—given the circumstances of her childhood. He really should cut her some slack.

Instead of thrashing back, Nicole channeled her frustration into a long exhale. Unfortunately, her lips were pressed into a snarl and they slapped against one another, hurtling specks of saliva onto the tablecloth.

"Jake jumps on the table during reading and imitates the teacher," Kat said to no one in particular. "Ms. Herbst calls him "Wild Child." He poked Chloe with a sharp pencil and her hand was bleeding."

Nicole frowned at her daughter, who was not helping her case.

Sean's mind raced. He needed a topic that would get Maureen and Nicole to disengage. He tried to channel Ellie. He reached for his wine glass and the idea hit him. He remembered drinking himself into oblivion one year when Maureen went on endlessly about her volunteer work. Since then, there had been an implicit pact among the family to avoid the subject at all cost. He realized now it was the only way. "Maureen," he ventured, throwing caution to the wind. "What's happening with the volunteering?"

She looked surprised and, he thought, suspicious. But she took the bait. "Lots of exciting things."

He polished off his wine and signaled for a refill. "Start at the beginning. Tell us everything."

Dick glared at him from the head of the table.

"I'm focusing most of my time these days on Bright Future," she said. "They're doing such important work." Maureen leaned forward, eagerly. "I just helped coordinate a huge mailing about peanut allergy awareness. We'll save dozens of lives this year."

"My friend Calvin might die from a peanut allergy," Toby said. "He's my best friend." The entire table went quiet. Toby looked around trying to figure out what to do next.

"Oh no," Maureen said, looking genuinely upset. She grabbed Toby's hand and held it. "I'm so sorry, Toby. How awful." She shook her head and clucked her tongue. "These allergies are getting worse all the time. Terrifying."

Toby broke the substantial silence that followed with another bomb. "Mom called last night," he said.

The news was enough to jolt Nicole out of her funk. She tried to catch Sean's eye across the marzipan Pilgrims and Indians.

"She called you?" Maureen looked almost hurt. She leaned toward Toby. "What did she say?"

"She's in Momtalk now. She says Happy Thanksgiving to everybody."

"Did she say what she's doing? When she's—"

"She sounded good," Sean said. "Much, much better."

"She wants me to visit her for Christmas break."

Maureen's eyebrows shot up defensively, then her mouth spread into a grandmotherly smile. "Of course she does. She loves you. We all do."

"Dad won't let me." He avoided eye contact with Sean.

Maureen's face softened when she looked at Toby. "Well your dad knows best. And I think he's right, it's probably not a great idea." Ordinarily, having Maureen take his side was helpful. Why did it make him squirm today?

"It *is* a good idea," Toby whined.

"I know you miss her," Maureen said. "But Mommy's still tired. She needs to rest."

Toby protruded his lower lip into an impressive pout.

"And besides, what would we do on Christmas without you?"

"It won't be Christmas without Mommy. I always see her on Christmas."

"Well if she wants to see you, she can just come here." Maureen didn't try to hide the edge in her voice, then set her mouth in the same way Ellie did.

Toby looked at Sean, confused. He sensed something was going on, but had no idea what it was. "I want to visit Mommy."

Maureen shook her head. "Not after . . . not after the way she left you all." Under her breath, she added, "That is not what a good mother does."

Toby's face fell and he looked like he might cry. Sean opened his mouth to tell Maureen to stop, but Nicole gave her one cutting look, which did the trick.

"She was a good mother," Sean said, wondering where this deep-seated reflex to defend his wife came from. "*Is* a good mother." The words caught in his throat as he said them. The last thing Toby needed to hear on Thanksgiving, from his grandmother, was that his mother was a fuckup. His rescue of Ellie's reputation, he realized, had much less to do with Ellie than it did with Toby. "In fact," he went on, taking a deep breath before jumping into the abyss, "I've decided to let Toby go to Montauk." His heart pounded as he said it.

Toby stared at him, his mouth gaping slightly. "Really?"

Now it was Maureen's turn to be indignant. "You can't do that!"

"I can," he said, as Maureen's face flushed with agitation. "If Ellie continues to sound as good as she did last night, I'm going to let him go for the whole two weeks."

"Yes!" Toby jumped out of his seat and threw his arms around Sean. "Thank you Dad! Thank you!"

He hugged Toby hard. Allowing him to visit his mother was more difficult than anyone at the table could have known, but it was the right thing for so many reasons. He was sure of it.

CHAPTER NINE

TOBY WAS HAPPY AND CAREFREE THE REST OF THE WEEKEND, AND Monday morning he literally skipped to school. But by the time he got home that afternoon, he was anxious and grumpy. "I can't do it," he whined over his math homework.

Sean didn't look up from the bills that covered the kitchen table. "Yes you can." He added up the rent and the tutoring bills but didn't have enough to cover both. Noah would probably be fine with half of what he was owed as long as he got the other half in a couple of weeks. The cable bill was also going to have to wait. He looked up when he heard Toby whimpering. "What's the matter?"

"I'm stupid," he said, pulling his hair. "I can't do word problems."

"Come on Toby, calm down and read it again." He was going to need some extra cash this month for Christmas presents. And framing supplies for the Burdot pieces. He could pay the minimum on the credit card for a few months. But there was no way he could put Toby in the after school art class he wanted to take next semester.

Toby rolled his forehead back and forth on the coffee table, a death groan emanating from deep inside him.

"Cut it out and do your work." He hadn't meant to yell at Toby, but the drama was over the top.

"I told you I'm stupid," he yelled back. "I can't do it!" Toby hurled himself face down on the couch.

Sean pushed away the bills, took a deep breath, and let it out slowly. Yelling was only making it worse. It always did. "Come on, Tobe. I'm sure we can figure it out." Actually, he wasn't sure about that at all. Helping with math always ended badly.

"Sit up," he said, as he lowered himself to the ground next to Toby. Toby grudgingly sat up, his face red and streaky. Sean held up the worksheet. "Jane has pennies, nickels, and dimes in her purse." He started to glaze over. He hated word problems. Maybe reading it with more expression would make it less deadly. "She has eight coins altogether," he said, stressing the eight. "Including more dimes than nickels, more nickels than pennies, and fewer pennies than nickels. What are the two different amounts of money she could have?" Sean's stomach contracted with that sick feeling he used to get in math class when he didn't know or care.

"Um, huh. Okay." He had no idea where to start. This had to be high school math. Or at least middle school.

"So how do you do it?" There was a challenge in Toby's voice.

Sean stalled, hoping something would come to him. "I have no idea," he said, finally. While there were many wrong answers he could have given, this was probably the most wrong. He tried to rally. "Let's try to work it out."

He picked up Toby's pencil. "Uh, okay, Jane has how many coins? Eight? Okay. So . . . if she has the most dimes, which it says, then, um, huh. Should we just start trying out combinations and see what happens?"

Toby's forehead was back on the table. "I hate math." He raised his head. His eyes were full of anger. "I hate myself."

"Come on." He tried to sound encouraging. "At least we can try."

Maybe Toby's bullshit meter was more developed than Sean had given him credit for. "No!" Toby shouted. He picked up the math packet and tore it in half. Sean ducked as Toby hurled the pieces in his direction.

"What the hell are you doing?" Sean yelled before he could stop himself. He'd let Toby get a rise out of him, which was bad. And he'd said hell, which was also bad. Once you said hell in front of a kid this age, you couldn't take it back, and it would, without fail, be trotted out later, usually in front of company.

But Toby wasn't even focusing on the slip. "I'm the dumbest kid in my class," he screamed. "I can't do it." He ran into his room and slammed the door hard behind him.

His inclination was to run after Toby. But Toby needed time to cool down, and Sean needed time to form a plan.

He wondered how Ellie would handle the early-onset teenage outburst, but this was virgin territory. He dialed Noah, who picked up on the first ring.

"Hey man, how's Toby?" Noah asked. "Everything all right?"

Sean described the math problem and the response it had elicited.

"Yeah, it's too hard for most kids this age," Noah said, which was a huge relief. "And no, I'm not surprised they assigned it."

"But I don't get it. Why would they—"

"Do you want to know how to do it?"

Noah walked Sean through the problem and explained how to help Toby figure it out on his own. As he hung up the phone, he knew West Side Tae Kwon Do would have to wait another month. He would pay Noah's tutoring bill in full.

Sean took his time pouring orange juice into a SpongeBob cup then knocked on Toby's door. No answer. He opened it a crack. Toby's head was buried under the pillow. "Can I come in?"

Sean put the cup on the night table and sat on the edge of the bed. "Hey," he said. "You all right?"

Toby took the pillow off his head. "Everyone can do word problems except me."

"I bet that's not true, Tobe. That was a hard problem," he said. "I talked to Noah and I think we can handle it now."

Toby looked skeptical.

"And I can talk to Jess about it. Ask why she's assigning such hard math. Okay?"

Toby nodded and eyed the SpongeBob cup suspiciously. "Pulp?"

Sean shook his head. Thank God he'd bought the right juice this time.

By the time Toby had downed the juice, the storm was a mere memory. They worked through the problem, which took about thirty seconds, Sean read him a chapter from *Prince Caspian* and tucked him in before eight o'clock. Then he emailed Jess. Now that there was a head teacher, he figured he might as well use her.

He set up a meeting for two thirty the next day while Toby would be in science.

Being back at Bradley the next afternoon gave him a bad case of déjà vu. As he climbed the stairs, he remembered the soft thud of his foot making contact with Calvin's torso. The memory set off a wave of nausea that forced him to sit for a minute. He thought about the tubes running into Calvin's arm and nose and about the machines that beeped when his heart beat. Was Calvin better? Was he worse? Shineman had told parents not to call, to give the Drakes some space, some privacy. But she'd also said she'd send an email with an update, which she hadn't. The silence was ominous and ate at him the longer it went on.

Someone trotted down the stairs toward him, then stopped abruptly. "Hey!" Walt Renard said, jolting Sean from the depressing reverie. "What's going on?"

"Just taking a moment."

"Mind if I join you? I just came from a maddening meeting. I need to decompress a little or I might blow." When he'd plopped himself a few steps above where Sean was sitting, he looked around. "There a reason for the moment?"

"It's where I found Calvin."

"Shit," he said, staring at the spot where Calvin had been. "Allergies," he said, wistfully, and trailed off. "Unbelievable."

"I still don't get how Calvin could have been so allergic—so suddenly."

"My upstairs neighbor's daughter is so allergic to strawberries," Walt said, "that a knife that had been used for strawberry jam a *month* before—and washed many times since—sent her into a life-threatening episode. The family is at the ER at least three times a year."

"It's so unfair," Sean said.

"It's terrifying," Walt said. Kids squealed on the other side of the fire doors. "You going to be okay?"

"Me? Yeah, I'll be fine." He stood and checked his phone. "I'm late though."

Walt started down the stairs. "I'm counting on you for basketball one of these days. Don't disappoint me."

"You got it," Sean called down after him.

When he got to Toby's classroom, the wild-haired computer teacher who did all of The Bradley School's tech stuff was giving Jess a Smart Board tutorial. Sean couldn't remember the guy's name, but Toby had him every year for computer class. "Have a seat," Jess said when she saw Sean. He'd been hoping for a slightly warmer greeting. "We're just finishing up."

He sat as instructed. The computer geek was perched too close to Jess, nodding eagerly when she pushed the right button.

"Great!" he said. "You must have had a Smart Board where you taught before."

"I had a blackboard."

"Oh," the guy said. Adoring was the only word to describe the way he was looking at her. "How about if I come by sometime and show you some tricky stuff you can do on here? Advanced stuff."

"Sure," Jess said, tentatively. "Okay."

"I mean, like I pull all-nighters sometimes," the guy went on eagerly. "So anytime really works for me."

Jess was looking at him as if he were slightly crazy. Which he may have been.

Sean cleared his throat. "Do you think you'll be much longer?"

"I think we're done," Jess said to the computer teacher, with a smile that softened the blow somewhat.

"Oh. Okay," he said, the disappointment tugging at his face. "I'll check back tomorrow."

"Looks like you have an admirer," Sean said, when he was out of earshot.

"I'm hoping he's just excited about the technology." She pulled up a chair. "Are you here about the extra credit?"

That would explain everything. If it was extra credit Toby wouldn't have had to do the problem. "I hadn't realized it was extra credit," he said. "No wonder it was so hard."

"What was so hard?"

"The math problem. Jane and the pennies."

"Oh. No, that wasn't extra credit." Jess waved her hands in the air as if to delete everything they'd said so far. "Let's start again. Tell me what's on your mind."

Sean described Toby's meltdown. Jess nodded seriously. "I was worried about that."

"You were worried about Toby?"

"No, no," she shook her head. "Just in general."

"So why'd you assign it?"

"Last year my third grade ran a bake sale during lunch period. That's how I taught them about money. But Bradley wanted me to teach *conceptually*."

"But if the kids are going to freak out because they can't do it, what's the point?"

She opened a file and spread out the homework packets. "Fifteen out of the eighteen kids got the problem right."

"Or their parents did."

Her sigh was barely audible. "I'll work it through with Toby," she said. "It's hard at first, but he'll get it, don't worry."

He sat, trying not to worry. "That wasn't actually why I came in," he started. "I mean, it's not the only reason I wanted to talk to you."

Now that he was here, he wondered where to begin. Jess knew something was going on—she'd heard Toby's Thanksgiving essay. He wanted her to know the whole thing. "In September his mother left." It sounded terrible when he said it. She probably thought he was a shitty husband, a shitty guy. "She was having some . . . she was depressed, I guess. Toby and his mom were close, so, well, it's been a big adjustment. He's having a hard year."

"I'm really sorry," she said. "That's got to be hard for everyone. It would explain why he'd be having self-esteem issues, though. It could be why he was so down on himself not being able to do that math homework." She put her hand to her chest. "I'm glad you told me. I'll think of some ways to help him in the classroom. If you have any ideas, let me know."

"Thanks," he said, oozing gratitude. "I appreciate it." To her left he saw a sign that read: The Show: Music, Dance, Art. "Sounds interesting," he said.

Jess pointed to it with Vanna-White hands. "*That* is the extra credit."

"An extra credit *show*?" Toby had brought home puzzles and problems over the years, but this was new.

"Almost every parent has called or come in asking for extra credit for their child," she said. "I don't get it, honestly. My fiancé thinks it's because I gave back some gifts." He looked at her ring finger. The diamond was so small he wondered why the guy had even bothered. Sean had been living on a freelancer's salary, but he'd managed to get Ellie a nice ring. A ring you could see without a magnifying glass.

"That's off the record," she said.

"That parents were trying to bribe you?"

"Your words, not mine."

"So what did you give back?"

She waved away the question. "Nothing, it's not important." When she blushed her whole face—and the scoop of chest not covered by her top—turned red.

"Tell me."

She looked toward the door, to see if anyone was around. "Promise you won't say anything?"

"Promise."

"Season tickets to the Knicks, a Prada purse," she said, then took a black velvet box out of her desk drawer. "And these." She pushed it toward him. "I'm giving them back today." He snapped open the box. Inside was a pair of diamond earrings. Each one was ten times bigger than her ring. "Holy shit," he said. "I mean, they're nice. Really . . . nice."

He'd heard some of the parents did stuff like this.

"I don't get it," Jess said. "Who gives a third grade teacher diamonds from Tiffany's?"

"Now I feel bad I didn't bring you anything."

She laughed. Her whole face lit up when she did. "I'll let it go this time." She put the diamonds back in the drawer. "Forget I showed you those."

"Showed me what?"

Jess smiled again. "Good."

Just then, Bev Shineman let herself into the classroom.

"Hope you don't mind my crashing," she said. He couldn't remember minding anything more.

"Oh." It was pretty clear Jess was as surprised as he was.

Shineman pulled a chair next to his. "Don't let me interrupt."

It was creepy that Shineman was always right there, waiting to pounce.

"We were just finishing up, actually." Jess held out her hand formally to Sean. He shook it. "Thanks for coming in."

"I'll walk down with you," Shineman said. "There's something I wanted to talk to you about."

He checked his watch.

"This won't take long," she said, and started to walk. "I've been observing Toby and some other children in the classroom. He seems to be focused at certain points of the day and very unfocused at others, especially during music, PE, and transitions between classes." She popped a breath mint in her mouth.

Toby had been coming home on music days complaining that the teacher made him sit out while the other kids played the recorder. "I'm worried that every time his teachers reprimand him—and they have been reprimanding him recently—it's going to negatively impact his confidence." Impact was not a verb, Sean thought, and should not be used as one. Math had never been his strong suit, but he'd always been oddly attached to grammar.

"It seems pretty obvious to me," he said, "that making Toby sit out in music is not the way to get him motivated."

But Shineman wasn't done. "At the beginning of the day he starts playing with his friends right away instead of hanging up his jacket and checking in like he's supposed to. And he forgets things. He's forgotten his spelling book twice this week."

This woman was out of her mind. "He cannot be the only kid forgetting to sign in." *Signing in!* Who cared? "And he can't be the only kid who's excited to see his friends in the morning. At least I hope not." Why was this being billed as a major catastrophe? And were other parents getting the same lecture? "This can't be that unusual for a kid his age." He tried not to sound defensive. "Boys, especially."

"That may be true in the larger population, but here, we need to get all the children on the same page," she said. "Many of our children are very capable of these basics."

"You're a shri—a psychologist," he said. "Why are you refusing to acknowledge that an eight-year-old boy might be upset that his mother is MIA? That his best friend might die? Why do I have to convince you?"

She cleared her throat. "My concern is that we don't overlook something more serious because *we're* distracted by a coincidental occurrence."

They stood in front of the library. "Okay, so I'll make sure he brings his spelling book. I'll remind him to sign in."

"I know you've rejected this option in the past, Sean," she said. A vague Long Island accent slipped out when she said his name. *Shawan.* "But medication might work wonders with Toby. Even a tiny bit of it. If he can break out of this cycle—and it is a dangerous cycle—he could get some confidence in school. Positive feedback from teachers will make Toby want to get more of it. We've seen it a million times. In the end he'll stop goofing around. If that's the problem."

She made it sound so neat and clean. So easy. But what she didn't seem to get was that his kid was not one of those hyper brats who bounced off the walls. He wasn't an ADD kid. "I just don't get why you think Toby needs to be on Ritalin."

"Of course we couldn't tell you to put him on medication." Shineman was now backpedaling. "We're not even *allowed by law* to mention that. Just think about an outside evaluation. It can never hurt."

"I took him to Dr. Hess, remember? He did three days of testing. I'm not putting Toby through that again. It was a waste of time."

"Dr. Hess tests for different learning styles, academic and emotional strengths and weaknesses. And it was *inconclusive*. Not a waste of time." She gave him a smug smile as if she'd won that round. Which she hadn't. "I'm recommending you see a psychiatrist to determine whether Toby has any type of Attention Deficit. I'm happy to recommend someone if you like."

"He does not have Attention Deficit. Trust me."

She put her hand on his arm in a motherly gesture. "Maybe it's *not* a neurological disorder. Maybe it's some other fixable problem." This comment was obviously supposed to make Sean feel relieved, but instead it gave him heartburn.

She removed her granny glasses dramatically for effect. He noticed now that her eyes were bloodshot and the pouches under her eyes had been covered with skin-colored spackle. "And Sean, just so you know, third grade is a bitch. Kids start to notice who's ahead and who's behind. I'll be honest—they can be cruel. If we can save Toby that kind of humiliation, I'm all for it. Aren't you?"

NICOLE LEANED BACK ON SEAN'S COUCH, HANDS BEHIND HER HEAD. "So, wanna hear about my date?" she slurred. The bottle of tequila, full when the kids had gone to bed, was now half empty.

"You had a date?" As far as he knew, she hadn't had a date since she got pregnant with Kat.

"I have dates."

"Really?" He poured a shot.

"You don't have to act so surprised, okay?"

He tried briefly and unpleasantly to imagine Nicole having sex. He downed the tequila and waited for the burning to stop.

"You can be such a jackass," Nicole said. "All right forget it. So what else you got?"

This was Nicole's way of asking how his day had been. He imagined the assistant district attorneys sitting around asking each other *what they got*. She was used to answers like extortion, rape, murder.

"The school shrink is riding me to get Toby evaluated. She thinks he has ADD."

She squinted her eyes and tried to focus on Sean. "I *am* officially fucked up," Nicole said. "I thought you just said Toby has ADD."

"I have to get him out of that school," he said. "You were right, it's not worth it." He'd called six other schools that afternoon—schools he couldn't afford, that Maureen and Dick wouldn't pay for—to discover it was already too late to apply for next year. "Maybe I should put him in school with Kat. He'd love that."

"If you repeat what I'm about to say, I swear I'll disown you as a brother." She rubbed lime on the webbing between her thumb and pointer finger and shook on salt: "Public school in this city is a train wreck. It's free. And as I've learned the hard way, you get what you pay for. Kat's school is only slightly more educational than day care."

Sean stared at his sister. Her endless arguments about the evils of private school education were just for show.

"If he can survive Bradley," Nicole said reasonably, licking her hand and taking another shot, "you've got to keep him there. I know kids can do it without the fancy school. But your kid got into *the* fancy school. It's free—for you, anyway. You can't flush that down the toilet."

"What about the Thanksgiving war? That was all bullshit?" It was so typical of his sister. Arguing for argument's sake. She was such a lawyer.

"Kat's been to the principal's office five times," Nicole said. *"Behavior issues.* Fucking school."

"No way." Sean poured a shot even though he'd decided he was done a few shots ago. From what he'd seen, Kat didn't bat an eyelash without Nicole's approval. She'd always been a pleaser.

"It took me a while to figure it out," Nicole said. "Bored. She's bored. She's trying to keep herself entertained."

"I thought the curriculum was enriched," he said. He was unraveling the arguments Nicole had masterfully made in favor of public school. "Gifted. And talented."

"They've been doing multiplication tables in her class all year. Kat knew those going into third grade. They're reading *Junie B. Jones*, for Christ sake. She's reading *Trumpet of the Swans* at home." Nicole snorted. "They have gym once a week. Once. And they only have art if a parent volunteers to teach it." She looked at him with a *so there* expression. "At this point, she's just showing up. She's getting in trouble." Nicole hesitated before dropping the bombshell. "Sometimes she pees in her pants."

Sean's jaw went slack.

"Don't fucking tell anyone. Or I'll kill you."

Sean crossed his heart, like he'd done when he promised not to tell that Nicole had taken twenty dollars from their dad's wallet to buy weed for the high school prom.

"Can you get her out of there?" He thought Toby had it bad. Kat must be miserable.

"I've applied to private schools for the last three years."

She was a master at conversation-stopping bits of information.

"The worst part is she's gotten in every year and the fuckers won't give me financial aid."

"Shit, Nicole." Now he felt like an ass. "You make a crappy salary. All these schools have money for financial aid."

"Oh, I make the cut for need. But just my luck I'm a white lawyer with a white child. Now, if I were a struggling performance artist living in the far Bronx with a half-Puerto-Rican child, they'd be all over me. Apparently I'm not diverse enough." She shook it off with a wave of a salty hand. "Toby's going to get through this," Nicole said. "This is a glitch. He's going to shine, that kid."

He wanted that to be true. And having Nicole say it made him believe it might be. "Kat, too," he said.

Nicole smiled weakly. "Get him tested. Maybe if a professional tells the school he's suffering from Mother Deficit Disorder—not some neurological disaster—that will calm them down. Rule it out."

"I'm not telling Ellie." *Tellingellie* slurred into one word.

"Screw her." Nicole lay back on the couch and closed her eyes. "You don't need to tell her shit." Within seconds she was snoring.

CHAPTER TEN

"So is he going to give me shots?" Toby couldn't seem to get his mind around the concept of a shrink. Granted, Sean wasn't explaining it well. He was trying not to lie, only to remain suitably opaque. Kind of like whenever Toby asked about sex.

"No shots. And um, it's a her." A co-worker of Nicole's had gone through the same ordeal earlier in the year with his kid and recommended a psychiatrist named Angela Altherra. He liked the idea that Bradley hadn't referred her. And he liked the idea that someone from the D.A.'s office thought she was all right. "She's just going to ask you some questions. About school, I think. All you have to do is sit there and answer."

"And then what does she do?"

"I don't know, I guess you leave."

"I don't have to take off my clothes?"

"No. Tobe, it's not that kind of . . . she's a psychiatrist. Remember? She takes care of people's brains and, you know, emotions."

Toby scrunched up his face into what was clearly a comment on how his father had lost *his* mind and was the one who needed the shrink. "Why do I have to go to her? My brain isn't sick. Is it?"

"No. I mean . . . look don't worry about it. Just talk to her. Ask her anything you want about it. She can probably answer better than me."

This was a scene he'd never imagined. Him, Sean Benning from Troy, New York, walking along Park Avenue on the way to his son's psychiatric appointment. He knew this wasn't unusual in Manhattan, where everyone seemed to have a shrink. Last year at a dinner party he'd gone to with Ellie, everyone was telling therapy stories. He realized he was the only one who had nothing to contribute and decided to make up something. Luckily, before he'd gotten a chance, the bipolar woman to his right started to choke on a wild mushroom canapé. After the manic landscape architect performed the Heimlich, the conversation turned to life-saving techniques and Sean was able to riff about a CPR class he'd taken in college.

"Okay," Toby said. "I'll do it. But afterwards we go to Cyber Zone so I can kill you in Ghost Recon."

"We'll see who kills who," he said. "I think today's my day."

Toby shook his head wearily. "If you don't practice, Dad, you're never going to beat me. You've got to put in the time."

An Irish doorman with ruddy cheeks and salt and pepper hair stood bolt upright at the front door of the Park Avenue apartment building. He wore his gray cap and uniform with brass buttons as if it were a general's. East side doormen called you Sir, and if it rained they held a golf umbrella over you while you climbed into your taxi. West side doormen wore their uniforms if they felt like it, called you by your first name, and had no problem whatsoever getting up into your business. Manny had been the first one to notice—or dare to mention—Ellie's pregnant belly.

"Ay, congratulations!" he'd said, patting his own belly, and the cat was out of the bag.

The General would never risk that kind of intimacy. There was something to that.

"May I help you?" he asked, sizing them up. This guy opened doors for a living but he probably earned more than Sean did. Plus he had a killer union and a nice fat 401 K, too. His kid was probably doing fine at a good public school in Jersey.

Sean muttered Dr. Altherra's name.

"One B. On the right," the doorman said. Sean was sure he saw a smirk on the guy's face as he pointed to a glossy door past a mammoth flower arrangement that glowed under a spotlight.

The door opened into a closet-like waiting room, and they sat in uncomfortable straight-backed chairs. At exactly three thirty, an attractive woman in her early forties emerged from an office.

"Hi, I'm Dr. Altherra," she said. "Come in."

Dr. Altherra's office, as if compensating for the waiting room, was spacious, with warm tapestries on the walls and an oriental carpet on the floor. Sean and Toby sunk into the velvet couch.

He'd expected another Shineman, but this woman was in another league. She was slim, fashionable, and wore her dark hair pulled loosely back. A few wavy strands crept out around her face, giving her a soft, Renaissance look. She was much more attractive than she'd sounded on the phone. Nicole's friend from the D.A.'s office might have mentioned it.

"So Toby, your dad's told me a lot about you," Dr. Altherra said. Toby didn't respond. He stared at a patch of carpet a few feet in front of him. "I'm looking forward to talking to you about school and home and whatever else you want to talk about." She smiled kindly even though Toby had given her nothing to smile about. "First, though, I'd like to talk to your dad alone. Just for a little while, then I'll bring you in. How does that sound?"

Toby looked at Sean nervously.

"It's okay."

"Should I just sit out there?" Toby had never waited alone in a waiting room before. Sean or Ellie had always stayed with him. It was a strangely poignant milestone you don't log in your baby book.

"That would be great, Toby," Dr. Altherra said. "It won't be too long."

Toby remained on the couch like a deer in the headlights.

"I'll get you settled," Sean said. He led Toby to a seat in the waiting room and handed him a *National Geographic*. He pointed at the wall. "I'm just through there."

Back in Dr. Altherra's office, Sean tried not to worry about Toby sitting out there alone. He'd be fine, obviously. But if Sean had prepped him beforehand—if he'd stopped to think this could even come up—Toby might feel less betrayed at the moment.

"I asked you some questions on the phone the other night," Dr. Altherra said. "But there are quite a few more on the Conners scale. We should get through them all today. Will your wife be joining us?"

"No." He hesitated, not sure how to explain the status of him and Ellie. "She's been . . . she's been out of the picture since September. She's living on Long Island."

Dr. Altherra nodded in a professionally interested way. Was she wondering what hellish thing he'd done to make her go? "I think it's having an effect on his schoolwork and his behavior."

"Does he seem withdrawn?"

"No, not really. Not usually."

"Is he more irritable than usual? Is he eating more or less than he usually does?"

"I don't know. He's just himself. But a little sadder. And the school keeps telling me he's disrupting music class."

"Encourage him to talk about her," she suggested. "He might be waiting for a signal from you that it's okay to do that." She paused. "Are you seeing someone else?"

He shook his head.

She gave him a sad sort of smile he didn't appreciate. "Well, let's finish these," she said, gesturing to the questionnaire that would determine whether Toby had ADD—or ADHD, as she kept calling it. "It's important to get a full history from the parents—or parent—when it comes to this type of neurological disorder."

Disorder. It was a word he'd use to describe a piece of defective equipment you bring back to the store for a refund. "My answers tell you whether he has ADD?"

"I also talk to Toby," she explained. "And I'll send a shorter version of the Conners scale over to school." She handed him a sheet of paper. On the left was a list of behaviors: Restless in the "squirmy" sense, Demands must be met immediately, Distractibility or poor attention span, Disturbs other children, Restless, always up and on the go, Excitable and impulsive, Fails to finish things started, Childish and immature, Easily frustrated in efforts, Difficulty in learning. To the right were four choices for each: Not at all, Very Little, Pretty much, Very much.

"That's it?"

"That usually tells us everything we need to know."

"And then you prescribe drugs?"

"If I've made a diagnosis of ADHD," she said, as if clarifying a rule for a three-year-old. "Otherwise, no."

He chose to ignore the condescending tone. She was *that* good looking. "So you'd prescribe Ritalin?"

"I like to start with short-acting methylphenidate—that's the generic name for Ritalin. There are several options we can talk about if we get to that point."

The research he'd done online had only confused him. He'd read as many impassioned rants, both pro and con, conflicting studies and medical horror stories as he could stand before signing off at two a.m.

"But isn't that pretty risky?"

"Five decades' worth of research have proven it's safe."

"But it's speed, right? That can't be good for a child."

"Speed is a street drug. Ritalin is a pharmaceutical," she said. "In children with Attention Deficit Disorder, the stimulant in the drug usually has a reverse effect, calming them down. Nobody knows why exactly. It's absolutely counterintuitive."

"So how often would he have to take it?"

"We're jumping ahead of ourselves. Why don't we get a diagnosis first, then we can discuss what to do about it."

"I'm just curious." He knew not to believe half the stuff on the Internet. He just didn't know which half. He was sitting across from a qualified professional and he was going to get his money's worth. "I know there are extended-release pills, right?"

She uncrossed her legs, then recrossed them. "Okay, let's talk about it now." At whatever she was charging an hour, she should really lose the annoyed tone. "I never give extended-release in the beginning. I start with half a pill to make sure there's no negative reaction. Then I raise the dose slowly until it gets to a therapeutic level. And even then, if there's any problem, methylphenidate is metabolized completely after four hours."

"So after four hours what happens?"

"He'd have to take another dose." She sat back.

He digested the information. "That means he'd have to take the medication during the school day. Everyone will know."

"Not necessarily. But I understand your concern. Does Toby have a problem sitting down at home and focusing on homework?"

"Not usually," he said.

"If he's not hyperactive . . ." she started.

"He's not hyperactive." He sounded defensive.

"So then he might have inattentive-type ADHD."

As if he was supposed to know what she was talking about.

"It means that he's unable to focus in distracting situations, like school. But at home, without his friends and all the visual stimuli of the classroom, he wouldn't need the medication. I wouldn't want to have him on medication more than he needed to be."

"Even though it's safe." Sean was being bratty, but she deserved it.

"I'm quite conservative when it comes to medicating children," she said, unfazed by the brattiness. "So yes, that's right."

He liked that she'd called herself conservative.

"Why don't we finish the questionnaire so I can get Toby in here."

"Right. Sure." He'd almost forgotten about Toby sitting out there alone.

She wanted to know if Toby tended to misplace his shoes or his jacket and if his room was messy. He chuckled, assuming it was a joke.

It turned out she wasn't the joking type. She simply stared at him with an impenetrable expression until he stopped laughing.

Despite the unsettling combination of attraction to the doctor and a generalized queasiness about what he was doing in her office, he did his best over the next fifteen minutes to answer her questions. Did Toby forget his backpack at home, did he hand his schoolwork in on time, was he squirmy or restless, was he impulsive, did he fail to finish what he started, was he easily frustrated? The hardest questions were about the tantrums. Yes, he had them, he said. No, it wasn't typical. He mentioned the math packet and Jane's pennies.

Dr. Altherra—he wondered if he could call her Angela—was scribbling notes on her pad, nodding in encouragement.

When she finished with him, she opened the door to the waiting room and told Toby to come in. He shot Sean a look of disgust as if to say, *You left me there all alone. What is wrong with you?*

"Do you know why you're here, Toby?" She focused only on Toby, as if Sean weren't there at all.

Toby shrugged. He was still in his down jacket, still wearing his backpack.

"You must be boiling," Sean said, unzipping him.

Angela waited patiently for him to get comfortable. "Your dad wants to make sure you're able to pay close enough attention at school. I'm going to ask him to step outside, if it's all right with you. And we can talk for a few minutes."

Toby's eyes widened. Sean nodded reassuringly. Toby looked at the ground and responded with a less than enthusiastic, "K."

"I'll be right outside." He gave Toby a pat on the back and took his turn in the waiting room. But sitting patiently was not easy. He moved his chair away from the wall and pressed his ear against it. He strained to hear, but an annoying contraption on the floor that looked like a smoke detector was emitting a fuzzy noise that made it impossible. He reached down and unplugged it, then pressed his ear against the wall again. The damn pre-war walls were too thick, Angela's voice was so muffled he could only make out every third word: *Toby . . . year . . . school . . . on.* He couldn't hear Toby's response at all. It was more frustrating than enlightening. He picked up *Newsweek*. The cover type read, "The Boy Crisis: At Every Level of Education They're Falling Behind. What To Do?"

"Fabulous," he said out loud and started reading.

Finally, Dr. Altherra opened the door and ushered Toby out. "We had a nice talk about school and about home. Then Toby drew me a picture."

Toby held up an excellent drawing of Jess that somehow captured her toughness and vulnerability. "He had a lot of nice things to say about his new teacher," Angela said. "But he said some of his other teachers consider him a troublemaker. He was very engaged and focused in the room with me, though." She turned to Toby. "You're a very bright young man."

He couldn't tell what to make of the report. "So . . ."

She handed him a bill. "I'll need a check for $325," she said.

He took the bill and put it in his jacket pocket. She had an expectant look on her face. Then he realized. "Oh, you want that now?"

"That would be great, thanks." He wrote out the check and thought about the fact that they'd be eating ramen noodles for the next month. On the way out, he stuffed the *Newsweek* in his jacket and proceeded to Cyber Zone, where Toby destroyed him in Ghost Recon, as predicted.

THE NEXT DAY TOBY'S CLASSROOM WAS PACKED WITH PARENTS who had arrived early to stake out prime real estate. The room was impossibly loud as they talked over each other. How did this many parents manage to get away from work at two o'clock in the afternoon? Especially in December, when parents were "invited" to attend holiday presentations, performances, or parties every other day. There was no way he could make it to everything. He'd already chosen to keep his job over hearing Toby try to squeak out "Twinkle Twinkle" on the recorder.

He snaked his way through the parents, many of whom were typing furiously into Blackberries. He propped himself against a bookshelf in the back and eavesdropped on Cheryl and Lilly's mom. "Don's back here for a Board meeting tonight." Cheryl faked a yawn. "Boring."

"Come by my place," Lilly's mom said. "We have lots of wine left over from the party."

Cheryl noticed Sean and winked. He looked away, wondering if anyone had seen. Luckily Jess was busy trying to quiet the group. "I'd like to welcome you to 3 B's first annual extra-credit performance," she said. Her dress wrapped around and tied at her waist. The engineering was so simple. Untie the belt, give her one good twirl and she'd be out of it. He pushed the thought from his mind when he saw how she smiled nervously at the roomful of power parents. "The assignment was to tell or show something that says something about who you are. Just so you know, I've never given this assignment with such a huge turnout. Every single student in the class wanted to join in. So I'll stop talking now. We have a lot to get to."

She gestured to Kayla, who sprung up as if propelled by a trampoline. She handed her iPod to Jess. Glittery stars dotted its pink case. Jess hooked up the iPod to the Mac and Kayla flashed a prim smile. "This song describes me best because I have such an optimistic personality." She gave a theatrical nod and Jess pressed the play button. Soon, Annie was belting out: *The sun'll come out tomorrow.* Sean shuddered. *Bet your bottom dollar that tomorrow, there'll be sun.* Kayla started doing cartwheels and flips in the tiny space at the front of the room. She had a shit-eating grin on her face as she hurled her body through the air. At one point she picked up a long baton with streamers on the end and made some figure eights with it. Sean looked over at Kayla's mother, whose plumped lips silently counted out the beats. She couldn't have been more intent on the performance if she'd been up there herself.

Next was Alexis. She passed out flyers from the "Bodies" exhibit at South Street Seaport and took great joy in describing exactly how each organ had been preserved for the show. Someone really ought to watch that kid. She was the type to put the cat in the microwave just to see what happened.

Lilly tapped for her life in shiny tap shoes. Zack dribbled and twirled a basketball like a Harlem Globetrotter. Marcus illustrated how to use a solar oven he'd made from a shoebox and tin foil and Isaac displayed a scale recreation of the Acropolis he'd made out of Legos.

Drew carried up an electric keyboard. "This is *Für Elise* by Beethoven," he said, then played it flawlessly. "Can you tell us what *Für Elise* says about you?" Jess asked.

His cheeks flushed and his eyes darted around the room. "Um, I . . . um . . ." he stuttered. "I forget." Drew rushed back to his seat, mortified. Drew's mother pressed her lips into a tight line of disapproval.

"Well, you played it beautifully," Jess said. She turned to address the whole class, making sure to avoid the glare Drew's mother was aiming at her son. "Don't forget, extra credit is just like any other work. It's for you to do on your own. I can give your parents extra work, too, if they need more to do."

The parents laughed, uncomfortably.

Finally, Toby stood up. Not only hadn't Sean helped him, he had no idea what Toby had done for the show. He unrolled a truly impressive drawing of Calvin and pinned it to the bulletin board. In the picture, Calvin was dressed as a super hero with a super hero's expression, body language, attitude. "I think who your friends are says a lot about you," he said. "Calvin is my best friend, and I wanted him to be here today."

The room was quiet. Some of the parents dabbed the corners of their eyes with tissues. He was so proud of Toby just then, and thought about Melanie and Cal and what they must be going through. He decided to call them. He had to, no matter what Shineman said.

CHAPTER ELEVEN

RICK HAD BEEN STRUTTING AROUND *BUZZ'S* BEIGE-ON-BEIGE offices ever since the Reese Witherspoon cover had sold out on every newsstand across the country. Somehow, just before Gino was arrested in the south of France for shooting Jessica Simpson sunbathing topless, he'd managed to snap Reese topless and propped on her elbows, a studly unidentified Mediterranean man rubbing her back.

It turned out that Gino had spent a total of three nights, not the standard one, in the Cap D'Antibes jail, for which he charged the magazine heavily. Gino's trying tale of incarceration—which Rick conveniently leaked to *E!*—coupled with the money shots of Reese, had become the story of the moment. Now everyone was chasing *Buzz*, which made Rick immeasurably happy. Reese was planning to sue, but Rick wasn't worried. That went with the territory when you were a sleazy tabloid.

Rick floated across the industrial carpeting in presidential mode, one hand thrust into the pocket of his Dockers, the other administering gentle slaps of encouragement to underlings as he passed. He stopped at Sean's cubicle and contorted his face with benevolence. Rick never truly smiled. Even now, what amounted to virtual beaming from Rick took the form of an athletic frown, the corners of his mouth pointing down, his eyes lit up with glee.

"Life is good," Rick said, enigmatically.

Life was never good if you were Rick Hollingsworth. Life was depressing, unjust, unpleasant. It was something you endured. No matter how bad his own life seemed, he was always better off/happier/less suicidal than Rick.

"The company's still high on us, huh?"

"Understatement of the year." Rick puffed his chest. "They are thrilled. *Crandall's* thrilled. So thrilled," he went on, "he's invited us to dinner on Saturday. At the Townhouse."

"No shit?"

"No shit," Rick replied. Their hands met in a slow motion high five. He'd never met Art Crandall. Crandall was a *Page Six* staple. He owned three television stations and twelve magazines besides *Buzz* and was always in the middle of an affair, divorce, or hostile takeover and was known in the media world as a "colorful character." One of Bradley's most well-known alumni, he was a media mogul who people in the industry feared and courted simultaneously. Plus, if the write-ups were accurate, everyone from Mick Jagger to Obama to Bill Gates had stopped by the Townhouse in the past two months.

"Seven thirty." Rick winked. "Bring a date."

On his way home that afternoon, the streets were clogged with masses of humanity. The main thing was to maintain forward momentum. A wiry little guy with glasses tried to squeeze between him and a woman wearing running shoes and nylons, like a car trying to weave in and out of bumper-to-bumper traffic. Sean nailed him "accidentally" with his elbow. The guy tried from different angles, but ultimately gave up. Sean smiled. A small victory.

His phone rang as he got to Grand Central. It was Dr. Altherra.

"Do you have a moment to talk?" she asked in her soothing voice. He imagined the loose wisps of hair framing her face.

"Sure," he said, and tucked into a spot by the information booth. The wiry guy darted past.

"I've spoken with the school about Toby and I've also read through their Conners scales. It seems that his behavior in school—and occasionally at home from what you and I discussed—is in keeping with a diagnosis of Attention Deficit Disorder, Inattentive Type. Though from what some of his teachers are saying—the music teacher in particular—it sounds like he may have some hyperactivity as well."

She had to be wrong. That could happen, he was sure of it.

"Did I lose you?"

"You said he was focused and engaged when you met him."

"Yes," she said. "But that's not counter-indicative for the diagnosis. For Toby and other children with Inattentive Type ADHD, they're perfectly fine one-on-one and in small groups. They're usually fine at home. But in distracting environments like school they find it hard to pay attention. That's why the school's reports are so important for the diagnosis."

The *diagnosis*. Altherra had had a few conversations, administered a questionnaire, and boom, Toby was diagnosed.

"We live in New York. Everyone's distracted."

"I'm not," she said. Of course she wasn't. She was perfect. "And I'm afraid Toby is more distractible than other children."

This diagnosis struck him as overly vague. Unscientific. What about lab results? A blood test? Empirical proof? "What about his mother leaving? You need to factor that into all this."

"I haven't forgotten that."

Could the diagnosis be accurate? Could it be a result of something he'd done? Had some rogue gene from his screwed-up family snuck in and messed up Toby's brain? His uncle Hutch had always struck him as overly antsy.

"The good news is that there are proven ways to treat the problem," Dr. Altherra said. "I think we talked about this in my office."

His head was spinning and there was nowhere to sit, just hoards of people rushing past him.

"If you're nervous about giving Toby Ritalin, I can tell you I've had a lot of success with another methylphenidate-based medication specifically designed for children, called Metattent Junior."

"Are you sure this is the right way to go?"

"In my medical opinion? Definitely."

"I'm going to have to talk to Toby's pediatrician about this." He'd put in a call to Dr. Jon, Toby's pediatrician, three weeks ago, but Jon was getting harder and harder to reach. He was an Upper West Side liberal who hated private school, privilege, and parents who overreacted. Sean trusted him completely and always got a straight answer from the guy. If there was anyone who was going to tell him not to medicate his eight-year-old—to take it slow and explore less extreme options—it was going to be Jon.

Unfortunately, Dr. Jon had overextended himself. In a city where the best doctors had virtually stopped taking insurance, Jon took any insurance card you dug out of your wallet. As a result it took weeks for him to return a call.

"Great. You should do all the research you can. Not necessarily online, though. There's a lot of misinformation out there." She paused. "I can't call in a prescription for a controlled substance, so I'll pop it in the mail. Call if you have more questions."

He snapped the phone shut and stood in the middle of the craziness. The panic started somewhere in his chest and spread through his body like a swarm of red ants. He had no idea what to do. None of it was supposed to be this way. Major decisions like this required two parents. For the first time he realized how utterly alone he was.

He flipped open the phone and scrolled down to Ellie's number. His thumb hovered over the call button. His heart was racing and he squeegeed the sweat from his forehead with his forearm. No, he decided. He'd rather throw himself in front of a speeding Metro-North train than call Ellie and ask for her help.

He called Dr. Jon's office again. "No I do not want to leave a message." His voice was loud, but none of the people around him seemed to notice. You had to blow a foghorn in Grand Central to get anyone's attention. "I've left five. I need to speak to Jon today. Now."

The sheepish girl at the desk told him Jon was with patients and that the office closed at six. He left another message.

He called twice more on his way to Madison Square Garden. He'd just keep calling until Jon was finished reattaching a severed digit or surgically removing an M&M from a four-year-old's nostril or whatever pediatricians did.

When he got to the Garden, the place was eerily empty. He didn't know it could get so empty. The last time he'd been here was over the summer. He and Ellie had fought their way through packs of aging Dylan fans. But the venue was so big, the real Dylan had looked like a tiny spec on the stage. They had to watch him on a screen mounted above his head.

Now, Sean had the run of the place. He stopped in front of a poster of Billy Horn from his glory days, charging the hoop, biceps bulging, a look of utter determination on his dripping face. He'd passed by it a million times, but he'd never stopped and just looked— there were always too many people rushing past. It had been five or six years since Billy Horn was winning games. Still, he was a fixture in New York. A decent guy—or at least that was his reputation. The Knicks would never trade him. But they weren't going to start him anymore, either.

He wondered what it was like to have your ninth birthday party at Madison Square Garden. Toby must think this was how kids all over the country celebrated turning nine. Sean hated to admit that it was cool as hell, being here in the middle of the day, his name on the guest list.

The jowly guard directed him to center court.

Remnants of cake and pizza littered the bench as Zack and his friends dribbled and flailed under the house lights and the glow of the scoreboard. They were dressed in miniature Knicks uniforms that were, no doubt, party favors. Toby's friends had taken home super balls and Mexican jumping beans from his party. He really should remember to buy a present for Zack.

Billy took the ball down the court with some between-the-leg dribbling designed to entertain the kids. He passed dramatically to Charlie Wilkins, the team's power forward, who found Zack and passed to him. Zack went up for a long shot and nailed it. The boys on his team whooped and chest bumped. Zack could already shoot three pointers like clockwork.

Sean watched for a few minutes from the aisle. Billy passed to Toby. Somehow Toby caught it, dribbled twice and shot. Sean held his breath as he watched the ball arc up and swish cleanly through the hoop. Toby stared, slack-jawed at his basket. The megawatt sound system exploded with Knicks cheers. The LED screen flashed GO KNICKS! A huge grin spread over Toby's face.

Right now, no one would know Toby was missing his mother or having trouble in school or suffering from some scary deficit. He was a basketball star, a hero.

Billy jogged over to Toby and gave him a high five. "We could've used that shot last night against the Mavs."

When Billy saw Sean, he summoned him with big, overblown motions. "Come on down." As in down to the Knicks' court where every great basketball player had played.

The court was huge and hot from the lights. The floor had a bounce to it.

"Can we talk for a minute?" Billy asked.

He led Sean to a seat in the first row, away from the others. "I've got a situation." It turned out that a *Buzz* photographer had snapped Billy at the Hustler Club on Twelfth Avenue. "It's pretty tame," Billy said. "But it doesn't look good. Deanna's going to be pissed."

He knew exactly where this was going. "That sucks," Sean said, shaking his head.

"Yeah. It does." He looked at his size fifteen shoes. "I hate asking, but is there anything you can do about it?"

"Billy, I don't know . . ."

"I hate asking for favors," he said. "I don't know what to say to Zack."

Sean had never destroyed film. Not on purpose, anyway. There had to be a line. Then again, *Buzz* was a crappy publication. It existed to make the lives of celebrities miserable. This wasn't Watergate or The Pentagon Papers. It was a once-great basketball player in a tittie bar. He might be able to misplace the file for a few weeks. Just until it was old news.

"I'll see what I can do," he said.

"I owe you, man," Billy said, slapping him on the back. "I owe you."

BY THE TIME THEY LEFT THE GARDEN, IT WAS FIVE THIRTY. SEAN took out his phone to dial Dr. Jon one more time, then reconsidered. Instead of taking the train all the way to 110th, they got off at Eighty-sixth and walked the extra block to Jon's office.

"I'm sorry, if you don't have an appointment he can't see you today," the receptionist said when they got to the office. She looked like she'd had a long day dealing with screaming children and their screaming parents and was counting down the seconds until she could get out of there.

"I'm not leaving until I see him." He crossed his arms over his chest and settled in.

"I don't know what to tell you," she said. "The office is closing in a few minutes."

"You're not going to tell him I'm here?"

"Without an appointment, I really can't."

"Wait here a minute," he told Toby. "I'll be right back." He stepped over a plastic bead-counting toy in the middle of the floor that could have been used to culture every strain of strep and flu on the west side of Manhattan. "Don't touch anything."

"Where are you going?" The receptionist stood up. "Get back here!"

He walked to the back of the office past the empty examining rooms. He hung a right into the cramped room where Dr. Jon was filling out paperwork.

Jon looked up blearily. "Do we have an appointment?" His long face sagged at the jawline and his hair had thinned significantly since Toby's physical five months before.

"I've left ten messages. I have an emergency."

Jon sighed, pushed his chair back, and clasped his hands over his stomach.

"So," Sean asked, "do you have a few minutes?"

"I'm waiting. What's the emergency?"

"Oh, okay. Well, Toby has been . . ." He lowered his voice, even though the place was empty. "He's been diagnosed with Attention Deficit Disorder. Inattentive type. We went to a psychiatrist. And . . . she prescribed something called Metattent Junior. I was wondering what you thought about that. I mean, I've been online and it seems extremely dangerous to give children this kind of . . ."

"Don't research this online."

"In 2005, the Canadians recalled ADD medication because studies showed that children were dying from it."

"Look, if he has ADD, there's no other way to treat it. You can do behavioral modifications, which is a good idea anyway. But if you want to give him any real relief, medication is the way to go."

"But the studies I found online . . ."

Dr. Jon let out a weary sigh. "The Canadians put Adderall back on the market within two months. They were using American studies they hadn't analyzed properly." He paused. "Whatever negative information you're finding online is garbage."

Garbage was not what Sean had expected to hear from Jon. "So you think I should give him the drugs?"

"Who did the testing?"

When he mentioned Dr. Altherra's name, John looked impressed. "She's good." He considered it for a moment. "She had the school fill out Conners scales?"

Sean nodded.

"If Angela thinks he needs it, I would try it."

"But . . ."

"There are only a few things to monitor. We'll make sure it's not affecting his blood pressure, and we'll weigh and measure him twice a year to make sure he's gaining at a reasonable rate."

"Gaining?"

"Yeah, these drugs can suppress the appetite. We want to make sure he's eating enough so his development isn't impacted."

"So there are risks."

"It's just my opinion, but I'd say the risk of failure and low self-esteem from poor school performance is a lot greater. He's in third grade, right? It starts in third, but fourth is even worse." He shook his head. "Especially at private school. The work is harder, plus kids are extremely aware of how they're doing compared to their peers. It's not pretty."

Jon talked to him for a full twenty minutes. He was impossible to pin down, but once you got him, he was full of information.

"I've got to go," Jon said. "My wife is dragging me to a benefit for kidney disease." He switched off his desk lamp and put a fat folder into his bag. "Get the prescription filled, give him half a pill on a day he'll be home to see how he reacts to it. If all goes well, see for yourself if it makes a difference at school. Then go from there. And call me."

CHAPTER TWELVE

HE PULLED THE ZIPPER AROUND THE CORNERS OF TOBY'S SPIDERMAN suitcase, cataloguing the myriad reasons why this visit was a huge mistake. What if Ellie sunk into another depression and freaked Toby out? How would Toby fend for himself? Or worse, maybe she was fine. Maybe Toby would realize how much he'd missed her and decide to live with her full-time. Why hadn't he considered this until now?

"If Mom seems tired, or if she's acting, you know, not like herself," he said, "just call me, okay?" Could he reneg at the eleventh hour? Probably not without major damage to his credibility.

"She's better, Dad. I can tell when I talk to her on the phone." Toby knew more than Sean gave him credit for. "But if she starts acting like an alien clone again I'll call," he said. "Don't worry. I'll be fine."

Sean remembered Toby's running away note. It had also told him not to worry. Didn't Toby realize that was 99 percent of what parents did all the time? He couldn't imagine the world without worrying about Toby. Why the hell had he agreed to this?

"Can you pack me snacks and stuff to draw with?"

Snacks. Right. There must be something in the kitchen. Ellie had been good with snacks. He was not. He rifled through the cabinets and found some crackers. They were old, but they hadn't been opened. They were probably fine. Buried behind a can of chicken noodle soup, he found a flattened fruit roll-up.

He offered up the scavenged treats. "Okay?"

"Yeah." Toby wasn't thrilled, but he seemed to appreciate the effort.

It was still dark when he and Toby arrived at the Jitney. In summertime, the Jitney was a mob scene. December was a different story. Now, a few die-hard Hamptonites shivered at the bus stop.

He handed Toby a present he'd wrapped in a *Buzz* story on celebrity pugs.

"Merry Christmas," he said. "I thought you might be able to use these on the trip."

"Can I open it?" Toby was already tearing at the paper.

"Go ahead."

"Wow," he said, with just the right level of awe. When Sean had seen the old X-Men comics in a store in the Village, he'd hoped for a reaction just like this.

"These are so cool," Toby said, flipping through the stack. "I hope Calvin comes back after break so he can see these."

"Me too."

"Your present is at school," Toby said. "I made you a lamp in woodworking. It looks like a dice. It had to dry, so I couldn't bring it home."

"I can't wait to see it." Woodworking had sounded like such a good idea when he'd seen it listed in the afterschool catalog. He'd had no idea Toby would be so prolific. No surface in the apartment had been spared. "I can really use a lamp."

When the bus pulled up, he got Toby settled in a seat next to the driver. The seat looked so big, and Toby looked small. He'd expected saying goodbye to be hard, but not quite this hard.

Toby had pushed to do the trip alone. "Zack did it over the summer," he'd argued. "Please dad? It's totally safe. You can ask his mom." Maybe Sean would have fought it more if he'd been able to stomach the idea of a face-to-face with Ellie. He wasn't ready for that yet. Not on her turf in her new life. So he'd filled out forms and signed the waivers and now it was really happening.

"You sure you want to do this?" he asked. "You don't have to."

"I'm fine, Dad. Really." He worked his grown-up look. "Thanks for letting me go."

"I'm gonna miss you, Tobe. Call when you get there, okay?"

"I will." Toby smiled. "I'll be home in two weeks. It'll go by fast. I promise."

He waved as the bus pulled away, then dialed Ellie's number. "He's on the way," he said, when she picked up.

"Great," she said. "Okay."

"Okay." It turned out that this was all they had to say to each other. He hung up, clutching the closed cell phone in his fist as he made his way uptown.

Back home, he had nothing but time to work. The house was too quiet. The kitchen was a mess, which he usually couldn't care less about. Today he decided to clean. He washed the dirty plates and scoured the pots. He took out the trash and scrubbed the inside of the garbage cans with Clorox.

He lay down on the couch to close his eyes for five minutes. By noon, he'd wasted exactly four hours of the work time he'd been counting on. Maybe a quick run to the deli to stock up on supplies, then he could come back and start fresh.

He took the elevator to the lobby. In 1906 when it had been built, this had been billed as a "luxury building." If you looked closely, you could tell the detail work on the moldings must have been pretty amazing at one time, before fuzzy dirt had taken up residence in the grooves and contours.

"Hey Sean, how's it going?" Manny was a slight guy. He always had way too much energy. "Great day today. Great day," Manny said, as if he were responsible for creating the weather instead of just reporting it. "Mail's here," Manny said, and went back to his Sudoku book.

Sean plucked his mail from the box that still had Ellie's name on it and flipped through the letters as he walked around the corner to the deli. Mixed in with a fistful of bills was a small envelope from Dr. Altherra that held Toby's prescription. *Benning, Tobias. Take 1 tablet every four hours as needed. Metattent, Junior. 10 mg. Tab 100s.*

Fill it, he thought. Decide later. The Rite Aid pharmacist asked for the patient's birthday and gave Sean a judgmental once-over as he wrote it down. *Bad father,* his arched eyebrows scolded. *Shame on you.*

What he actually said was: "Come back in twenty minutes."

Back at his desk, Sean stared at the bottle. Orange stickers on the bottle read: "Controlled substance. Dangerous unless used as directed."

He rolled the bottle between his hands, then struggled with the childproof cap and shook the pills onto his desk. They looked like lavender Tic Tacs. He realized now that there was only one way he could ever give this medication to Toby.

He funneled the pills back into the bottle, leaving one on his desk. He popped it in his mouth and downed it with a gulp of water from the bathroom sink.

He'd never been big on drugs. After his sophomore-year roommate dropped acid and tried to jump off the clock tower. Sean decided to skip the experimentation that kept most of his friends high through art school. Taking the Metattent was different. It was his responsibility to try it. He sat at his desk waiting for something to happen.

Half an hour later, Sean felt exactly the same. Then again, he weighed almost three times as much as Toby. He popped another two pills. Twenty minutes later, he realized he was working steadily. He didn't feel speedy or shaky. He felt clear-headed and tuned-in. He didn't want to clean dishes or take a nap. He felt great. All he had was this moment, and it was devoted to the work he was doing.

Exactly four hours and ten minutes later, Sean slammed back to earth. He was tired, and the sandwich he'd made was still sitting next to him. He felt slightly queasy, as if he'd been driving a curvy coastline road for an hour. He looked at the collage he'd been working on. Ellie's profile was shaded with a ghoulish mosaic of sliced up photos. It was the best work day he'd had in months, possibly ever.

It was only six o'clock. If he took a few more pills, he might finish before midnight. It was in the name of medical research, after all.

At ten o'clock, his body felt tired. His eyes burned. The piece was close to done. He rubbed his eyes and decided that the perfect end to this day involved a beer and a good night's sleep. He padded across the dark apartment. He hadn't left his desk all day—not even to turn on the lights.

He opened the fridge and light poured out. He'd been sure there was one last Budweiser in there. He should just skip the beer and go to bed, but now he had his mind set on it. He stepped into his shoes, pulled on his jacket and grabbed his keys on the way out.

He never went to the market this late. The night time shoppers represented a different demographic altogether. Lonely-looking men carried plastic trays of sushi and frozen meals. Students, who made up the remainder of the shoppers, carried economy-size bags of chips and boxes of Entenmann's donuts. They loitered in the beer section. Sean reached for a six-pack of Bud, but stopped mid-reach. He'd had a good work day. A great one, actually. He took a few steps to his right to the imported section. As he was trying to decide between Pilsner Urquel and Bass, he heard a familiar voice.

"Pilsner Urquel is without a doubt the superior beer," the voice said.

He turned to see Jess. Her cheeks were flushed from the cold and her eyes looked a little bloodshot, like she'd been crying.

"It's what the Czech Republic does," Jess said. "It makes beer."

"Excellent point." He picked up the Pilsner. "You on a beer run, too?"

"After the day I've had, I thought I better stick to Oreos." Jess held up a giant package. In faded jeans and a sweatshirt, she looked like a college student out for munchies. "If I turn to the bottle, there may be no turning back."

"That doesn't sound good," he said. "Is everything okay?"

"Not really." Her eyes teared up easily as though they'd been doing it all day. "Sorry," she said, not bothering to wipe them away.

"No, don't be sorry." Great. He'd made Toby's teacher cry in the beer section of D'Agostino. "Can I ask?"

She was taking deep breaths and blowing them out her mouth slowly, trying to get a hold of herself. "I just found out. You'll probably get a notice about it in the next few days."

"A notice about what?"

"About Calvin."

"What happened?" He didn't need to ask. Her face said it all.

"He's . . . he died. Earlier today."

"But," he fumbled. "What happened? I thought . . ." He had a sickening image of Calvin's parents holding their dead child, knowing they'd never see him run around again, never get to tuck him into bed at night. They'd never know how his life was supposed to turn out, where he'd go to college, who he'd marry or what his children would be like. He couldn't help himself: Sean thought about Toby and everything that lay ahead of him. An entire life still to be lived. His future was open, limitless. If Toby died . . . no, he couldn't think about it. Wouldn't think about it. He pushed the idea as far from his mind as he could.

The devastating fact remained that Calvin was dead. He didn't exist anymore. How was he going to tell Toby? A metallic taste filled his mouth. The oxygen level in the market was dropping fast.

"I keep thinking about the day we found him," she said. "I was sure he was going to pull through. I mean, he was just a kid."

She'd said was. *Calvin was.* He flashed on a playdate the kids had at the beginning of the year. They'd criss-crossed packing string throughout the apartment, and tied it in surprisingly tight knots to chairs, tables, light fixtures, creating a huge, impenetrable web. They'd called it Spiderman's Lair. It had taken half an hour for them to put it up. Sean spent the better part of the night breaking it down.

He put the beer back on the shelf. "I don't know about you, but I need a drink. Something stronger than beer. What do you say? A drink for Calvin?"

She nodded. "Okay."

They went around the corner to a dive-y bar where old men drank in the mornings and college kids joined them at night. Scotch seemed like the only drink serious enough for what had happened. He ordered two.

"To Calvin," he said, raising his glass. "He was a good kid. A really good kid."

Jess raised her glass. She looked exhausted. "To Calvin."

After they drank, there was an awkward silence. "So . . . what happened?" he asked.

"He never came out of the coma." She shook her head and took another sip.

"All because of a peanut allergy." The idea of it chilled him.

"I keep thinking about that day. If I'd gotten the Epi Pen, maybe Calvin would still be alive."

"Without the information about the allergy, there was no reason for it. This wasn't your fault."

"But I found him. It was my responsibility to get him help."

"*We* found him. And we did get him help. We did everything we could."

She squeezed her eyes shut and nodded, like she was trying to believe it. "I have to tell the kids."

"What are you going to say?"

"We're meeting with the grief counselors over break," she said. "There are specific ways you're supposed to talk to kids about death."

"I could use some tips," he said. Toby's world was far from perfect, but he'd never had anyone die on him.

"You're supposed to avoid euphemisms. Don't say Calvin passed away. Say he died. Use words like *forever*. Say he's not coming back."

The words stung. "That's so harsh."

"I know, but you want him to understand. You're supposed to answer his questions, then not bring it up again unless he wants to talk about it. That's what we learned in teacher training, anyway." She paused, then added, "And he's going to be afraid you're going to die."

He hadn't even thought about that one. Poor Toby. "I guess I'm not allowed to tell him I'll live forever."

"It would be so much easier," she said. "Say you're young and healthy and you won't die for a long time. That's the best you can do."

"He was Toby's best friend," he said.

She reached over and touched his hand. It was a sympathy touch, obviously, but he couldn't help noticing that her skin was the exact same temperature as his. It was nice, something he'd never thought about before.

"My mother died earlier this year," she said. "I'm thirty-years-old and I didn't think I could survive without her, and sometimes I still think I can't. How do you deal with death when you're eight?"

"I'm sorry."

She smiled sadly. "I'll say from personal experience, give Toby some time to process the news before school starts again."

That was a problem. Toby was scheduled to get home the Friday before school. He signaled to the bartender for another round.

She took the drink skeptically. "For the record, I'm not sure what happens to me after two Scotches." She raised her glass and took another sip.

For the next half hour, they talked about death.

"We've gotten ridiculously heavy."

The bartender watched Jess sway slightly and slid a wooden bowl down the bar. It stopped in front of them and they stared at its contents.

Jess picked up an unshelled peanut as if it were a piece of plutonium. "You've got to be kidding."

So what if it was morbid? Laughing was a relief. "Maybe we should take it as a sign and change the subject," Sean said. "So we don't have to slit our wrists when we get out of here."

"Deal," she said, pushing the peanuts out of the way. She reached into the D'Agostino bag on the floor and produced the package of Oreos. "They're the perfect bar food," she said, tearing open the package and offering him one.

The Oreos went surprisingly well with the Scotch. "Do you have far to stumble home?" he asked.

Jess twisted open the cookies and ate the halves individually, the way Toby did. "Oh, uh, I'm not actually staying at home."

"So, where are you staying?"

"With my godmother," she said. "She lives near here. My place is farther uptown."

"So you have relatives in the city? That helps."

She scraped the white stuff off the cookie with her teeth. "I have a confession."

If they were confessing, the evening must be going well.

"So you know Bev Shineman?" she asked.

"Sure," he said, willing his face not to be expressive.

She let her shoulders drop in defeat. "She's my godmother. I don't know if you knew that already."

"No," he said. He hated the idea that Jess was related in any way to Bev Shineman. "Are you two . . . close?"

"She and my mom were college roommates," Jess said. "And since my mom died, she's been right there for me. So yeah, I guess we are."

"That's how they found you? Through Bev?"

"It's kind of embarrassing. Nepotism."

"It's only nepotism if you're unqualified. I don't think that's an issue."

She accepted the compliment with a grateful nod. "Still . . . weird."

"Yeah, a little," he admitted. "And you're . . . staying with her?"

Jess picked at something that had hardened on the bar decades ago. "Yeah. It's kind of complicated."

"Roommate drama?"

"You could say that. Except my roommate is my fiancé."

So there was trouble in paradise. "Want to talk about it?"

She considered it and looked like she was about to say no. "We're on a break," she said, twisting open another Oreo. The miniscule diamond was still on her finger.

He watched her chew. Her jawline curved perfectly up to her earlobe. If it didn't sound like a come-on he'd ask if he could draw her. "What happened?"

She shrugged. "Complicated."

"What does he do?"

"He drives a FedEx truck. For now." She said it a little defensively. "He was just rejected by Columbia Business School for the second time."

So the guy was a fuck-up. "It's a tough school to get into," he said.

"He was always the one who wanted to come to New York and get a great job. Only I got it."

He nodded, sympathetically. "That can be tough on a relationship."

"Yeah," she said with a sarcastic smile. "Tell me about it."

"So . . . and tell me if I'm out of line, but don't breaks usually lead to break *ups*?"

"I don't know," she said. "You tell me. Are *you* on a break or have you broken up?"

"Touché." The truth was, he thought about taking off his own ring every day, but he couldn't do it. It wasn't so much because of Ellie. It felt like a lie walking around without it. "Legally I'm still married." He tugged at his ring distractedly. "I haven't seen Ellie for almost four months."

"So what are you going to do? About being married, I mean?"

He'd been wondering the same thing, but no one had asked him the question point-blank, not even Nicole. "I have no idea."

"I mean, what if your wife walked in tomorrow and said she wanted you back, wanted to go back to the way it had been. What would you do?" She took a sip of her drink and watched him with interest.

What *would* he do? He wanted to say he'd never take her back, but the idea of throwing in the towel once and for all was too grim. "It's hard to imagine going back to the way it was," he told her. "Things were pretty messed up by the end."

She nodded like she understood exactly what he was talking about. He wondered if she did. "Sometimes I'm not sure humans are meant to mate for life," she said. "From where I'm standing it doesn't seem to work out so well."

Perversely, he felt the need to be optimistic. "Some people manage to figure it out," he said. "I bet you will."

There was a pause, during which he thought about what it would be like to mate with Jess. He cleared his throat. If he didn't change the subject, walking out of here was going to be humiliating. "Have you tamed the extra-credit parents yet?"

"They're kind of intense," she said. "I gave back all the loot, if that's what you're asking."

"So you have the moral high ground. Excellent."

"It's all I can have with this crowd. Most of these kids are living lives I didn't think really existed."

"When Toby started at Bradley it was like we'd landed on an alien planet," he said. "I understood the life form there was scientifically significant, but I was completely freaked out. To tell you the truth, until this year I pretty much stayed away from the other parents." He thought back to last year and all the years before it when he'd let Ellie handle everything. He hadn't realized then how much of Toby's life he'd been missing.

She laughed. It was a nice laugh. "So you're not from around these parts."

"God no. I went to public school in Troy, New York. This is all . . . very different."

"Westerly, Rhode Island for me," Jess said. "Public school all the way. Then I taught at the school I went to."

She looked at her watch. "Whoa." She motioned for the check. "I had no idea how late it was."

He wasn't tired anymore. He picked up the check. "Let me get this."

She was shaking her head and reaching into her bag. "No. Really. Here." She handed him ten bucks.

"Moral high ground," he said. "I forgot."

"Exactly." She got up and put on her down jacket. "I feel significantly better than I did a few hours ago. Thanks."

"Me too." Would it be tacky, he wondered, to ask her out, given the circumstances?

"See you back at school," she said, and turned to go.

The idea hit him just in time. "What are you doing tomorrow night?"

"Oh, I've . . . I've got a bunch of things to do tomorrow."

"Because I've been invited to a dinner party at Art Crandall's," he said. "You'd really be helping me out if you'd come as my plus-one." Did it sound like he was inviting her on a date? Was he inviting her on a date? "As friends."

By the expression on her face, he knew he had her. But he might as well put the icing on the cake. "It's at the Townhouse."

"Seriously?" she said.

A nod was all it took for her other plans to evaporate.

CHAPTER THIRTEEN

ELEVEN YEARS IN NEW YORK AND SEAN HAD NEVER ONCE BEEN TO Sutton Place. Probably because there was nothing here except private cul de sacs, private mansions, private signs, private everything. He was sure someone was going to stop him and ask what he was doing here. But there was no one around. No through traffic, no noise. Only a thin layer of snow and the crunch of his footsteps. On this block, right now, it was impossible to imagine the noisy, crowded New York everyone else had to live in. He found the right building, looked once more at the killer view of the East River, and pulled at the brass claw mounted on Art Crandall's front door. It cracked once against the backplate and a truck of a man in a dark suit pulled it open.

"Welcome to the Townhouse," he rumbled. "Name please?"

"Benning. Sean Benning." The guy was so pumped his seams looked like they were about to burst.

"Someone's looking for you." The man pointed into the foyer with his chin.

Jess was leaning against the curved wooden banister that led up to the main floor. He almost didn't recognize her. The woman standing in front of him—sleek, elegant, and totally hot—looked nothing like a third grade teacher. Her hair was twisted loosely and pinned above her neck, revealing a deep V of pale skin where her dress dipped in the back.

"You look amazing," he said. You could compliment a friend. He was sure that was okay.

"I never wear stuff like this. But I figured . . ." Her hand went nervously to her dress.

"The *Townhouse*, I know." He pulled at his tie. He hated them in general and made it a point never to wear one unless absolutely necessary. "Shall we?" he gestured up the stairs.

"Hold up," the doorman said, and pulled two sheets from the back of his clipboard. He handed Sean a pen. "I need you both to sign these. They say you promise not to repeat anything that happens here tonight. In other words, it's all off the record. Makes people more comfortable letting their hair down, if you know what I mean."

Signing things always made Sean nervous. "I don't know . . ."

"House rules," the guy said. "Sign or see ya later."

Sean looked to Jess. She shrugged and took the pen. "Why not?" she said.

Why not seemed like it might work for tonight. He took the pen and signed.

"Enjoy," the guy said with a wink.

Sean let Jess lead the way upstairs and wondered how bad it would be if he did, say, brush his hand along her back accidentally.

The party in progress upstairs gave him a queasy flashback to the parent social. The room was filled with grownups. What would he say to them? He'd been an idiot to think this party would be any different. Art Crandall was a rich guy with rich friends. What was fun about that?

Then he noticed the Picasso hanging a foot away from him. Jess was already standing in front of it, mouth gaping slightly.

He'd never been this close to one and fought the urge to reach out and trace the form with his finger. The old woman in the painting looked into the distance with tired eyes. Her life had been drained away like the color in the monochromatic palette. He thought he'd seen most of Picasso's work from the Blue Period—not only had he studied Picasso in art school, he'd gone through an embarrassing copycat period in his early twenties—but he'd never seen this one. It was spectacular. Apparently Crandall knew something about art, and that fact, though Sean was loathe to admit it, raised the man at least a little bit in his esteem. "I could stand here all night," Jess said.

"Do you think it would be considered anti-social?"

A cute waitress with a pixie cut slid over to them carrying a tray of champagne. "Dom?"

He took two glasses and handed one to Jess, who accepted it as if someone handed her expensive champagne all the time. When the waitress moved on, Jess turned to him and mouthed *Dom*.

"Shall we?" He led her through the crowd. The crystal chandelier threw off an inhumanly flattering glow. Then again, this group would look just as beautiful and successful in flickering fluorescent.

A big, ruddy-faced man wearing an ascot and velvet smoking jacket blustered into the room. He threw up his hands in greeting. "Welcome, welcome!! Thank you all for coming to my little soirée!" He zeroed in on Sean. "Art Crandall," he announced, aiming his outstretched hand in Sean's direction. "You must be Sean Benning. Glad to meet you. Brilliant stuff! Brilliant!" Art Crandall had that polished look of success and an overall glow of wealth Sean wasn't used to seeing in person except at Bradley. He was also unprepared for Crandall's aggressive graciousness.

"Mr. Crandall." Sean offered his hand. "Nice to meet you."

"Mr. Crandall! Hah! You're a guest in my house tonight. It's Art! All my friends call me Art. And I think we're going to be good friends." He turned to Jess and gave an approving nod. "And who might this lovely peach be?"

In a million years, Sean would never describe anyone, much less Jess, as a peach. Peaches were sweet and fuzzy. Jess was sexy and sharp.

"Art Crandall," he said, "meet Jess Harper."

Art looked at her as if she were a dessert smothered in whipped cream, then took her hand and kissed it with a dramatic flourish. "A pleasure."

"Uh, same here." Her eyes darted nervously to Sean. In a seamless recovery, she withdrew her hand as if nothing out of the ordinary had happened. "I love your home," she said, using that same hand to take in the room.

"Ah yes, the Townhouse." Art sighed for emphasis. "Lots of good times here. Come, let me introduce you two around."

He steered them through the sitting room, slapping Sean on the back, his new best friend. The room was a blur of conversations and introductions to people Sean would never see again. He shook their hands. Their names slid by him. Nothing was sticking except for the fact that Jess was inches from him. He was lightheaded and he was sure it had nothing to do with the Dom. No one had made him feel this way in years, since the early days with Ellie. Just being near Jess triggered an onslaught of what felt like tiny geothermal events inside him—tremors, eruptions, floods—nothing as tame as the butterflies people talked about.

When a waiter passed with a tray of lettuce leaves, Art got excited. "You've got to try these," he said. "Endive boats. I dream about them." He popped one in his mouth. "Mmmm," he groaned.

Jess tried one and before she was finished chewing, she was talking. "Oh my God, this is the best thing I've ever tasted." Art gestured to the tray, encouraging her to take another before he walked across the room with his arms outstretched to greet another guest.

Sean wasn't going to dream about the boats, but they *were* good. "As Toby would say, these *rock*."

"They rock hard," Jess said in pitch-perfect eight-year-old. "I can't believe we're here." Not only could she pull off licking her fingers in a cocktail dress, she looked amazing doing it.

"Sorry, I thought it would be more, you know, fun."

"Think of it as an anthropological study," she said, looking around the room. "We'll compare notes afterward."

He was elated at the concept of *afterward*. This might be the moment to touch her back. But she was pulling him toward the bay window where an Indian woman wearing something that looked like see-through sequined drapes had set up a fortune-telling table.

Before they reached their destination, though, Rick Hollingsworth had spotted them, and Sean re-routed them to say hello. Rick spread his arms in greeting. "Benning," he said, beaming as he took in the surroundings. "I do believe we've arrived." He was wearing one of his trademark bland beige suits. Tonight, though, it had been pressed and his shirt was buttoned to his flabby neck. The bright red tie clashed with his usually morose personality.

"Rick," he said. "I'd like to introduce you to Jess Harper." He knew more explanation was required. "A friend of mine."

"A pleasure," he said, shaking Jess's hand but not removing his other one from the waist of the gorgeous woman he'd brought along. Sean wondered how much she was charging for the evening.

"Hi." He extended his hand to Rick's date. "Sean."

"Sammi." She nuzzled closer to Rick. "With an *i*. Rick says you work together."

"Best boss ever," Sean said, knowing the compliment would embarrass Rick.

"Aw come on," Rick said modestly. "Sean makes my job easy."

Jess snuck a peak at the fortune teller. "Have you had your fortune told yet?" she asked Sammi.

Sammi's eyes widened. "It's freaky." *Freeeky*. She pretended to shudder. "She *knew* things."

Rick gave a discreet eye-roll. "I'm going to be rich beyond my wildest dreams."

Sammi swatted at him like a real girlfriend might. "What about that thing she said about your son?"

"Okay, it was a little freaky," he admitted.

"I can't help it," Jess said. "I'm curious."

"You guys should go," Sammi said, eagerly. "But come back and tell us what she says."

Sean let Jess lead him to the fortune-teller as Rick mouthed *You dog*.

"You first," Jess said, when they were standing in front of the purple velvet tablecloth.

"No way." He pulled out the chair for her. "I mean, ladies first."

She sat and the woman took her hand. "Do you read palms?"

"Not exactly," the woman said, and closed her eyes. Despite the perky body he could make out under the getup, her expression made her seemed older. She sat with her eyes closed holding Jess's hands for a long time. Sean stood next to them, waiting for something to happen. He watched the woman hold Jess's hands. Then he realized: Jess wasn't wearing her engagement ring. Maybe she knew the ring was crap and was embarrassed to wear it to the Townhouse. Or maybe they'd broken up for good.

Trying not to move her head too much, Jess found Sean with her eyes. It did seem like the fortune-teller had fallen asleep.

He opened his mouth to speak, but the fortune-teller beat him to it.

"There's someone here. A woman. Your mother."

Jess stared at the woman. "My mother?"

"She died this year." The woman nodded to herself. "You miss her."

This caught Jess off guard. "Is there . . . what's she . . . what else . . ."

"She wants to tell you she's proud of you."

Jess opened her mouth to say something but nothing came out.

"She's getting fainter. She's gone now. But she seemed at peace."

Jess looked dazed. She sat, waiting for more. But there wasn't more. "What did she look like? I mean, did she seem lonely? Is there anything else you can you tell me?"

The woman shook her head. She had nothing. Then, almost as an afterthought added, "You will have a long life. Despite many hardships you will find truth." She let go of Jess's hand, now finished with her, and beckoned a twitchy guy in Gucci shoes to sit next.

"Weird," Jess said. She was a little shaky, which gave Sean the opportunity he'd been waiting for. He put his arm around her shoulder.

"Dinner is served," Art was bellowing.

MELISSA MORRISSEY SAT TO SEAN'S RIGHT, BUT FOR SOME REASON he didn't care. So what if he'd seen her naked in half a dozen movies? Or that he'd had a phase after college during which she'd starred in a disproportionate percentage of his sexual fantasies? Jess was all the way across the table charming Bill Clinton, who'd sauntered in during the appetizer course. "I was just in the neighborhood and thought I'd stop by," he'd said, with that Yale-edged Arkansas thing he did. He'd pulled up a chair at Art's urging.

Now, he was directing his election-winning charisma at Jess. "I'm impressed with your knowledge of education policy," he was saying. "For someone so young, you really get it."

Sean stabbed at his filet mignon. There was no way to compete with the former president of the United States. He slouched in his seat. Melissa Morrissey turned to face him. Her eyes didn't seem to be able to focus very well. She tilted her head to one side, like she did in the movies. "You remind me of Jude Law," she said. "I just finished shooting a film with him. What a sweetheart."

"What movie?"

"It's a thriller where I play a prostitute who stumbles across a top-level government secret. It's gritty." Her bosom heaved as she said *gritty*. He wondered if that was part of her method.

"You're wondering if they're real."

"What?"

Melissa Morrissey took his hand and placed it on one of the most viewed breasts in the history of non-porn cinema. She held it there, waiting. "So?"

"I . . . uh . . ."

From across the table, Jess was staring. Great. *Now* he had her attention.

He gave a thoughtful nod. "Real," he said, freeing his hand. "Definitely real."

Melissa Morrissey smiled. "No one believes it until they've felt for themselves."

On her right, Art was describing an orgy he'd been to a few nights before at some hedge fund guy's house. "Don't get me wrong, I took full advantage of the situation." He laughed like a dirty old man. "But if I'd been thirty years younger, well, let's just say there was a lot I didn't get to."

Sean snuck a peek at Jess. The waitress was filling Clinton's glass with red wine. "Chateaux Palmer." Clinton nodded. "Very nice." Then he leaned toward Jess, chummily. "It's good to have friends who drink good wine." Clinton raised his glass. "A pleasure to meet you, Jess."

"Likewise." She toasted with him.

From across the table, Sean studied the former president. There was something about him that was both appealing and unusual. The guy looked happy. Like he enjoyed his life. Why wouldn't he? He'd been president of the United States. Twice over. His ease stood in stark contrast to the twitchy guy who sat a few seats away. He turned out to be a billionaire Google geek and chewed nervously like a bunny under surveillance.

Sean tried eavesdropping on their conversation, but Melissa Morrissey was reciting a monologue from *Cat on a Hot Tin Roof* and it was hard to hear.

"So Jess," Clinton said. "What do you do for a living?"

"I teach third grade."

"Good teachers are the key to the future." He delivered the line with a flourish Sean thought was over the top. "Where do you teach?"

When she told him she taught at Bradley, his eyes lit up. "No!" She nodded.

"Art," Clinton exclaimed. Art looked up from fondling Melissa Morrissey's boa. "This young lady teaches at your Alma Mater."

"How spectacular," Art said.

"Sean's son is in my class," Jess said. "That's why I'm here."

Art looked at Sean. "I knew you were good people!" His expression expanded. "You must have a hell of a bright son."

"Toby's a great kid," Sean said. He sat up taller and hated himself for doing it. "I didn't know you went to—"

"Ah, Bradley. Some of my best memories are from there."

"Childhood memories are always the strongest," Clinton mused. "The good ones and the bad ones."

Sean thought about Calvin, who would never get to look back on his childhood memories. While he was sitting at Art Crandall's rich-people party, Calvin's parents were mourning their son. A flush of guilt and of missing Toby took hold of him.

Clinton turned to Jess. "But let's talk more about you. Tell me about what you do. What are your dreams, what makes you happy?"

"I teach handwriting to eight-year-olds." Her delivery was dry. Perfect. "I love it." There was something about the way she was with him. It wasn't flirtatious exactly. Or maybe it was. Which was driving Sean slightly crazy.

"Jess is a great teacher," Sean said, lamely. If he could get into their conversation, maybe she'd remember who she came with.

Next to Clinton, a Swiss diplomat was slurring as he told the president of EMI about his high school garage band.

Clinton glanced across the table at Sean, then back at Jess. "That does not surprise me one bit," he said. "I bet all the boys have crushes on you."

She ignored the compliment. "I'd love to hear about what *you're* doing now." She turned to Sean. "Wouldn't you?"

Almost as much as he wanted to have his fingernails plucked out one by one. "Absolutely."

"Okay." Clinton's body language said *I'm all yours.* "Ask away."

Rick, who'd been debating the relevance of pop culture throughout history with the head of the New York Public Library, suddenly noticed the progressively intimate dynamic between Jess and her seatmate. Sean watched him spring to action.

"I actually have a question," he said, loudly enough so Clinton would know this was directed at him. "If I'm not butting in."

Clinton grudgingly turned away from Jess. "Not at all," he said. "I don't believe we've met."

"Rick Hollingsworth. I used to be a senior editor at *The Economist.* There are some things I've always wanted to ask you about your economic policy."

There was no doubt about it, Rick was a good friend. Jess caught Sean's eye across the table and shook her head as if to say *I cannot believe you two.* He shrugged innocently: *no idea what you're talking about.*

Rick turned to the woman who sat on Clinton's other side. "You don't mind, do you?" He gestured to her seat. "It might be easier." The woman got up and actually changed places with him.

After they'd finished dinner, Art threw down his napkin. "It's time to start the dancing." He led everyone through a secret door that had been cut into one of the deep red walls. On the other side, ten small tables, each glowing with a single votive candle, framed a dance floor. A buff male model posed behind a full bar. Onstage, the champagne waitress was slapping a bass guitar and bouncing around with an equally young, beautiful band. The music was loud and whatever they were playing was catchy. Sean hadn't wanted to dance in years, but now he wanted to dance. With Jess. He turned to ask her, but she wasn't there. He scanned the room desperately.

It seemed like another twenty people had piled in. Art was grinding with an ingenue. The Swiss diplomat, who was by far the most wasted of the guests, gyrated alone, eyes closed, in the center of the dance floor.

The lights swirled and the bass shook Sean's kidneys. He spotted Jess across the room and windshield-wipered his arms, stopping only when Clinton, the bastard, appeared next to her and held out his hand, an offer to dance. She hesitated, then smiled and followed him to the dance floor.

Sean took up residence at the bar as Clinton, or *Bill*, as he'd asked Jess to call him, spun her around the floor for two interminable songs. They looked like they were having a good old time.

Sean drank a vodka tonic, then another. When he saw Jess beg off the dance floor, he took her a glass of water.

"You're psychic," she said, taking a long drink. "Thanks."

"You looked great out there." He tried not to sound pathetic. It was all going wrong, and he wasn't sure how to turn it around.

"She's a great dancer," Clinton said. He touched the arm Sean had no claim on. Then Jess did an amazing thing. She took a step away from Clinton and slipped her arm through Sean's. Not in an intimate way. Maybe in solidarity as the two most out-of-place people at this thing. Still, he couldn't help the smile that crept onto his face. What had he been worried about, anyway?

"Bill's giving a lecture at the NYU law school next week," Jess said.

"It's on the moral imperative of lawmakers," Clinton said. "You should check it out. If you want."

Sean shrugged. "Why not?" It was the motto for the evening, but he could think of a million reasons why not.

"Great," Clinton said. "Next Wednesday at seven." He winked at them. "Enjoy the rest of the party."

When he was gone, Jess said, "That was weird," and led Sean to the dance floor.

Almost as soon as they joined the pack of sweaty people dancing, the music stopped. There was some commotion, and when things settled he saw what all the fuss was about.

Jess gaped. "No fucking way."

She was adorable when she said fuck.

"Way," he said, not taking his eyes off Bruce Springsteen, who was tuning his guitar.

Soon, Bruce was rocking out on Art's small stage, unleashing that classic Springsteen sound. He was so close, Sean could almost reach out and touch him. Bruce Springsteen. The Boss. It was crazy. Stuff like this didn't happen. He tried to take it all in, how the room shook with the big guitar sound, the voice he'd listened to all through high school and college. The bodies around them jumped and grooved, on fire in the presence of the Boss. Jess was no exception. She knew all the words and was singing them at the top of her lungs. The crowd fed off itself and the Boss fed off the energy of the crowd. He played for over an hour without coming up for air. When it was over, Sean was dripping, exhausted, and exhilarated.

"Water," Jess gasped. On the way to the bar, they brushed past the tech nerd. He was pressing his body up against Melissa Morrissey in a corner, his tongue shoved down her throat, his hands creeping up under her evening dress as she clawed at his back.

"*They're* glad everyone had to sign a release," Jess said.

"Yeah. I'm *sure* that's what they're thinking right now."

It was four in the morning by the time the guests stumbled down the stairs to the foyer. Art kissed Jess's cheek, saying "Beautiful, beautiful!"

Jess pulled a black wrap around her shoulders. It was flimsy and sexy and when they stepped out into the cold morning, he realized it was nowhere near warm enough.

"Where to?" the cabbie asked, after they'd climbed into the idling taxi.

"Um," he turned to Jess. "Where do you live?"

"Can you drop me at 103rd and Riverside? I'm still staying with Bev."

"Or you could come back to my place." It was worth a shot, wasn't it? "To compare notes."

She hesitated, which he took as a good sign. "It's kind of late."

Late was so relative. "The sun's not up yet."

She gave him a grateful, tipsy smile, then shook her head. "I should get back."

"You have fifty blocks to change your mind."

She collapsed back on the leather seat. "That was an amazing night." She touched his leg for emphasis. "I'm so glad you asked me."

Her hand lingered on his leg in a way that could have been platonic. Or not.

"It wouldn't have been any fun without you." He put his hand over hers. To see what that would be like. Her skin was perfect, completely smooth and still the same temperature as his. He'd never noticed someone's skin temperature before. Maybe because no one else's skin had ever been exactly the same temperature. And then there was something like humming when his skin came in contact with hers. He fought the impulse to run his hand up her arm, to kiss her neck. He should remove his hand and try to stop imagining her out of that dress.

Before he could move, he felt something. He waited to make sure. Then she did it again. Jess had started to stroke the side of his thigh with her thumb. It was subtle, but unmistakable.

He moved his hand up her arm slowly, feeling every inch he'd been fantasizing about, continuing over the graceful curve of her shoulder and up her neck. When his hand stroked her hair, she turned to face him. She wanted him. He was pretty sure. He should kiss her. Right now. Give her a light kiss on the mouth, almost a brushing of lips, and she could decide. But what if he was wrong? What if she was simply being, what, friendly? It was a moment of crisis. And try as he might, he couldn't forget the inconvenient fact that in addition to being a gorgeous woman who happened to be caressing his thigh, Jess *was* also Toby's teacher. Nevertheless, his desire had progressed into a powerful ache that was traveling from his groin to his chest.

He couldn't think. The next moment, her hand was on the side of his face, pulling him toward her. Then they were kissing—more like devouring—each other and pulling at each others' clothes.

Her tongue was in his ear, but somehow she managed to say, "Your house. Hurry."

When they got to 110th Street, he threw some money at the driver. They tried to keep their hands off of each other as they passed the obese night doorman Sean almost never saw.

He dropped the keys at least three times before managing to open the front door. His legs were weak. His body was shaking. It had one directive and luckily for him, Jess's body seemed happy to oblige. Ferociously so. They'd generated a decent amount of heat on the ride uptown, and now that they were inside, he had no intention of waiting another second. He kicked Toby's scooter out of the way, pressed her against the hall closet and set to work getting her out of her dress. Zipper? Tie? Hooks? The detail work was frustrating. He hiked up her skirt, slid off her underwear and tossed them aside. She pulled at the buttons on his shirt but it was taking too long. Her hands aimed lower and unbuckled his belt.

There was no time to think, to decide, to choose. He knew he was supposed to care about school and the fiancé, but he didn't. Not in the least. Everything else but this exact moment had dropped away. He wanted Jess—all of her—as quickly as humanly possible.

Walking the extra steps to the bedroom, or even the living room, seemed an extravagant waste of time and effort when everything in his universe was pointing toward Jess. He hoisted her up before he'd settled on a plan. Not only didn't she seem to mind, the spontaneity and weird vertical position seemed to excite her even more. She worked his boxers down, though he couldn't tell if she'd used her hands or feet or both, before wrapping her legs around him. It wasn't as logistically difficult as he'd imagined it would be once they got into a rhythm. Jess had figured out how to raise and lower herself using just the strength of her legs. She weighed nothing. Either gravity had disappeared or he had superhuman strength. Tonight, he decided, anything was possible. This moment was a clear example of that.

In his wildest dreams he couldn't have imagined the heat and intensity that was coming off of her. It couldn't have been more different from screwing Cheryl in the bathroom.

Nothing had felt this urgent in years. Maybe ever. Had it been this way with Ellie at the beginning? He couldn't remember and didn't want to. All he wanted to do was focus on the way Jess smelled, the way her body was moving, and the sounds she was making. He was blurry with desire and the overload of sensation and almost fell over when Jess's body began to shake. He tried to spread his legs wider for a better foundation, even though his ankles were still shackled by his boxers. The shaking set off a reaction in him that involved his entire body seizing up and releasing. Without warning, his legs went wobbly and staying upright became much harder. And though his problem-solving skills were impaired, he managed to anchor himself against the closet doors to keep from falling over.

He held on to her tightly, tasting the salt on her neck as they caught their breath. Dropping her would definitely be a deal breaker and putting her down was not something he wanted to do.

By the time they made it to the bedroom, they'd had sex twice, stopping on the living room couch for an encore.

"I can't believe we're doing this," she said, sprawled next to him on the bed. The glow of daylight was pushing at the dark sky outside.

"You're not feeling bad about this, are you?" His hand traveled from the curve of her hip up to the curve of her shoulder. "Because I'm not at all."

"That feels so good," she said, closing her eyes.

He looked at her body, trying to burn the image into his brain. "What about . . . what's his name?" It was stupid, inane, to conjure the fiancé at this particular moment. What made him so self-destructive?

She hesitated. "I don't know."

He should keep touching her but stop talking. It was only going to get him in trouble.

"Something changed. It's hard to explain."

Change sounded bad. Which, of course, was good for him. "Mmm," he said, running his hand back down from her shoulder to her thigh.

"Have you ever had sex with someone and, suddenly they're not, well, themselves?" She didn't seem to want an answer, which was good, because he had no idea what she was talking about except that it involved sex with someone other than him. "There was one night right after summer, when Chris and I were, you know. He looked like Chris, smelled like Chris, he *was* Chris—but something about him was just essentially different. Like in *Invasion of the Bodysnatchers*. It was über-Chris. God, do you want to hear about this, I mean, maybe I should just . . ." She cut herself off.

What was he going to say? He wished he could rewind and delete, but he'd brought it up. "No. Go on. You can tell me."

She sighed deeply. "It was like I wasn't even there. I remember thinking that as far as he was concerned I could have been anyone, or anything—a blow-up doll from a sex shop. He didn't hear me or feel me or see me."

This forced Sean to imagine the guy on top of her pounding away, which stirred up an unaccountable possessiveness.

"It was a really shitty feeling."

"For the record, I feel you, and you feel extremely good." He kissed the crook of her elbow, the back of her kneecaps, inside her thigh.

"I do," she said. "I feel really good."

He explored her ankle bone and her toes. It seemed that over the course of the night, her entire body had been transformed into one giant erogenous zone. The third time they had sex was slow and sweet and possibly more exciting than the first two times. When she climbed on top of him, everything started to slip away. The last coherent thought he had was that there was no blowup doll anywhere that could even come close.

The next morning, he was smiling before he opened his eyes. He hadn't smelled sex on his sheets in a long time. He rolled over and muscle groups he hadn't used in months cramped up. Flashes from the night before, his own personal porn flick, were getting him worked up all over again. He reached out for Jess, but she wasn't there. He opened his eyes and saw the sheets on her side of the bed peeled away. How could she leave after the night of mind-blowing sex they'd had? It was dumb to think she'd been interested in him, that she'd want to stick around for coffee and who knew what else. When he heard the water running in the bathroom, he calmed down. Everything was going to be okay. She was still here. He got up, grabbed a pair of boxers from the dresser and knocked at the bathroom door.

"Just a minute." Her voice was tighter, more formal than it had been a few hours ago. She opened the door wearing her backless dress. She'd pulled her hair, which he'd helped work into a sex-induced tangle, into a ponytail. "I should go," she said, avoiding his eyes.

She definitely should not go. "Why?" He sat on the bed and patted it for her to sit, too.

She sighed and sat next to him. "It was amazing last night," she said. A smile flicked across her features and was gone. "But . . . I can't. It was a mistake. A big, huge mistake."

"No," he said. "It was one of the three best things to ever happen to me."

"One of three?"

"I thought it would sound too pathetic to say it was the best thing."

"I woke up this morning to a nightmare of Chris—my fiancé—and the Bradley Ethics Committee stoning me in the auditorium during morning assembly."

"What were you wearing?" He used his most lascivious voice, which he thought would have to make her smile.

Without missing a beat, Jess made a fist and hit him in the arm, harder than necessary.

"I promise I won't tell. Just stay."

She shook her head sadly, then started rooting through the sheets.

"What are you doing?"

"Looking for my underwear."

He had to imagine her not wearing any under the dress. He got down on his knees and looked under the bed with her when he had a flash from the night before.

"Front hall," he said.

They stepped over shoes, pants, socks to get there. He picked up her panties from the handlebar of Toby's scooter and handed them to her. "Will you have dinner with me tonight?"

She shook her head.

"How about tomorrow?"

She balled up her panties and tucked them into her evening purse. He wasn't sure, but she seemed to be tearing up. Making her cry was the last thing he'd wanted to do.

"I can't," she said. "I'm really sorry." She gave him a quick kiss on the cheek, opened the front door, and was gone.

CHAPTER FOURTEEN

THE ARCH OF CAMILLE BURDOT'S EYEBROWS RAISED AND LOWERED as she made a slow tour of his work. Each of his new pieces was clamped to its own easel along one wall of the gallery. As the damp patches under his arms spread, he concentrated on breathing. It was a bad day to forget deodorant.

He tried to see his work with an objective eye, which was hard, given everything he'd put into it since Toby'd been away. Since his night with Jess. Camille emitted occasional noises of what he hoped were approval but could just as easily have been disappointment. The pieces were interesting, at least he thought so. But if Camille didn't, he'd wasted his time—and a lot of energy.

His mind wandered to Christmas morning, the heat banging against the radiator, the absence of Toby drowning out even that. Looking at the old Christmas albums had been masochistic. No matter how many more Christmases they'd have, he'd never get this one back. He'd been gloomy, self-indulgent, as he snipped up the worst Christmas photos—and the ones of Ellie—and used them in the piece Camille was now looking at.

"Very nice," Camille announced, finally. "I will take all," she said. Her smile was a twisted pout. "You will frame them."

"You want all of them?" Maybe he'd misunderstood, with the accent and English being her second language. "All twenty?"

"So modest," she said, with a wink that only a French woman could get away with. "Now go away. Back to work!"

When he hit the sidewalk, he ran west toward Chelsea Piers, not quite believing what was happening. He wasn't used to feeling elated.

He dialed Ellie's number and thankfully Toby answered.

"You're just who I wanted to talk to. Guess what? The gallery lady liked all my work. She's taking it all."

"You rule, Dad," Toby said. "Hey, Mommy and me are painting snow later. But I'm not going to use white."

Ellie had given him a set of acrylic paints and an easel. "That's a great idea, Tobe."

Sean had decided that telling Toby about Calvin would wreck Christmas. He didn't need to do that. He'd wait until Toby was home, where Sean could keep an eye on him and help him understand. It could take days, weeks, months for something like this to sink in.

"I just got to the basketball courts," he told Toby. "I've got to go. I'll see you in a few days." He felt good as he strutted onto the court.

"Sean!" Walt and his buddies were warming up. "Get out here. We need your height."

The other players didn't look too intimidating. They were all a good ten or fifteen years older, most had guts, and fewer than half had full heads of hair.

"Meet the guys," Walt said, and introduced Sean to an elite splinter group from *Who's Who* that included the chief counsel for the *New York Times*, the minister of The First Presbyterian Church, the head of Orthopedics at the Hospital for Special Surgery, a bigwig at the ACLU, and a couple of hedge-fund guys.

The aging, overweight group wasn't as pathetic as it looked. What they lacked in stamina and basic cardiovascular health, they made up in ball handling, fakes, and excellent use of all that extra body weight. Sean's team squeaked out a victory, but he was going to be sore for days. At least he'd avoided injuries. The others hadn't been so lucky. Bobby, the orthopedic surgeon, sat out with a bloody nose for the last twenty minutes, compliments of Gunther, one of the hedge-fund guys. Gunther was wiry and feral and his elbows flew around like Samurai swords. It was a miracle there'd been so few casualties.

"Who's up for a drink?" Walt was sweaty, cheerful. "There's a place just up the block."

The others begged off with excuses ranging from board meetings to wives to a conference call with Japan.

"I'm in," Sean said. Drinking afterwards was the best part of playing sports, as far as he was concerned.

The bar was designed to look like a roadside joint, but was packed with ambitious twenty-five-year-olds all trying to catch each others' attention with a studied and animated avoidance. If this was the singles scene, Sean wanted no part of it.

He followed Walt into a booth and ordered an Anchor Steam. With twenty pieces in the Burdot show, Anchor Steam was now in his budget. Or would be soon. From now on, only the good stuff.

"Good game," Sean said. "Those guys know what they're doing."

"In just about every way," Walt said with a wink.

"Kind of a successful group," he agreed.

"Compliments of Bradley."

"Why doesn't that surprise me?" He tried to imagine Kayla, Dylan, even Toby, as the future decision-makers of the country, the world, but that was still a ways away.

"When I got to Bradley in sixth grade, it freaked me out." Walt took a sip of his beer. The happy hour white noise surrounding them was deafening. "All that money and power. I constituted the school's token middle-class child."

"Yeah right."

"I didn't say I was poor. But my family didn't own islands and run corporations."

Walt was getting more interesting by the minute. They had some things in common after all.

"In high school I finally figured out it was all about attitude. If you acted like you belonged, you did." He raised his glass. "Good life lesson, actually."

"Yeah, well I don't know if Toby'll be at Bradley for high school." He hadn't meant to drop that bomb.

Walt screwed his face into a question mark. "Of course he will be."

Sean shrugged so it didn't seem like such a big deal. "I don't know if Bradley's the right place for Toby. He's a great kid and all they're doing is giving him a hard time. I'm sick of every little thing being a major crisis."

Walt was nodding. "You know they do that on purpose, right? It's part of their thing."

Sean shook his head. "Bradley has a thing?"

"It's maddening," Walt went on. "But I guess I understand why they do it."

"Why they do what?"

"Okay, so people pay ridiculous sums of money to send their kids there, right?" He was hunched forward intently. "Why do they do that?"

"The education. Obviously."

Walt was shaking his head. "So their kids don't fall through the cracks. That's the whole thing. People can send their kids to P.S.

Bumfuck down the street for free. Will they get a decent education? Maybe. It's hard to know. What we do know is that at Bumfuck, their child is simply one of the pack. There's no way to keep track of who stinks at math, who can't really read, who's dyslexic. For thirty-five grand a year—no, thirty-eight this year—Bradley watches so closely they're bound to find a problem. From what I've heard, parents get nervous if the school *doesn't* find something."

Yeah, he thought, they're watching so hard they let a kid die.

"Personally, I think they're just trying to get a feel for which parents are committed to making their kids the best they can be." Walt allowed a self-conscious smile. "I guess that's the cheerleader in me talking."

"You really think I'm overreacting?" Had he misread the messages? Was Bradley's crisis-mode bullshit just their *thing*? He went over the most annoying conversations with Shineman. Did every parent go through some version of the same thing? And if so, why the hell didn't he know that before? Maybe Walt was wrong. But if he was right . . .

"When Mikey was in third grade," Walt said, "we had him evaluated. The teachers recommended it."

"No shit." Hearing that it was par for the course helped. A little. "Same thing happened to Toby."

"I think third grade is the sweet spot for catching whatever's going on with kids. That's what they told us, anyway."

"So . . . what happened? With Mikey?"

"I love my son, but there's no other way to say it: Mikey was a space cadet. The doctor suggested we try Ritalin. Said it helped kids like Mikey do better in school."

"Did you do it?"

Walt's expression said it for him: *duh*. "Mikey went from a severely average student to Dean's list practically overnight. He was on Ritalin until he graduated last year. I'm convinced he never would have gotten into Harvard without it. Honest to God."

"So he had ADD?"

Walt shrugged. "Whatever he had or didn't have, the medication helped him."

"But—"

"I know that look. You thinking about it, too? For Toby."

"It's a hard one."

"Welcome to parenthood," Walt said. "You need to decide for yourself what to do. All I know is that for Mikey it worked. Turned him into an A student, which affected the entire trajectory of his life. It's a powerful little pill."

Walt downed the rest of his beer and opened his wallet. "I should head back. I've got a brief to write tonight."

"Here, let me." Sean reached for his back pocket.

Walt shooed it away. "My treat. You'll get me next time."

ON THE SUBWAY RIDE UPTOWN, HE WONDERED IF WHAT WALT had said was true. Jess would be interested to hear his theory. Soon, though, all he could think about was Jess's legs wrapped around his waist and the way her body responded to his. And then, ultimately, he had to think about Jess walking out the door near tears. He hated the fact that he couldn't even email her. Then he realized that was ridiculous. Of course he could email her.

As soon as Sean got home, he sat down at the computer. All he had was her school account. It would have to do. *Dear Jess.* Dear was too formal. *Jess,* he wrote. Then he stared at the computer. What did he want to say? That he couldn't stop thinking about her? That he needed to see her? Way too desperate.

Jess, he wrote. *Hope you're having a great break. Looking forward to seeing you. I've been having a craving for Oreos and Scotch, but it wouldn't be the same without you. Any interest? Sean.*

It wasn't perfect, but it was something. He pressed send and as soon as he did he started waiting for a response.

Lucky for him, there was prep work to do for Toby's arrival. He'd gotten way too used to the quiet, to forgetting to turn on the lights, to never having milk in the fridge. He went to the market and stocked up on frozen waffles, apple juice, and other staples. He even splurged for the chocolate chip granola bars.

Toby had sounded good when he called every night—if not like Ellie's personal flack. "Mom started running again," he said, when he called the first night. "Mom baked a cake," he reported the next. It sounded like Ellie had pulled herself together, which was both a relief and also a little annoying.

That night he couldn't sleep. Partly because he was excited to see Toby, partly because he was dreading having to break the news about Calvin.

The next day Toby was back and the apartment was happy chaos again.

"I had fun, Dad," Toby said. He was smiling, relaxed. He was as close to the old Toby as he'd been in a while. "But it wasn't like being home." As long as Toby knew where home was, everything was okay.

Toby put on the Rolling Stones and as he rocked out to "Shattered," his hair caught air then flopped back down again in true rocker form. Maybe it was time for a haircut. He wondered if Ellie had indulged Toby's air guitar habit. As he tried to imagine her doing Chrissy Hynde, the miraculous happened. Toby stopped mid-guitar solo to volunteer information.

"So there was this girl named Delia," he said, looking Sean in the eye with an older-than-eight expression. "She can grind."

He pictured the kids on a dance floor in some seedy club, this girl rubbing her pelvis against Toby's ass. There had to be something he was missing. "Huh?"

"On her skateboard."

This visual was so much better.

"Plus she can do a half-pipe. She was really cool."

So they both had crushes. He wondered if Toby's had turned out better than his. "So what's Delia like?"

"I don't know. She's nice."

"Yeah? Great. So . . . what does she look like?"

"I don't know. She's pretty," he said with a shrug, to show he didn't care too much. "She has long hair, kinda brown, and her eyes were happy. Oh yeah, and she wore tie-dyed T-shirts and stuff."

"So, is she . . . did you . . . are you just friends?" What was he asking?

"I have her email address. And I sort of, well, I kind of kissed her good-bye," Toby said, twisting his mouth to cover up a smile.

"Wow." Wasn't Toby a little young for kissing girls? "So you must really like her."

Toby squirmed a bit. "Yeah, I guess. I don't know. She told me she had a boyfriend already. But I think she liked me back."

Atta boy, he thought. Confidence. "Who wouldn't, Tobe? You're the best." He elbowed Toby in the ribs. "I missed you like crazy."

"I missed you, too, Dad."

Sean knew he had to tell Toby about Calvin, but did he have to do it instantly? Toby took a shower, and Sean heated up a frozen pizza. While they ate, Toby told him about Ellie's cottage and how they'd made fires in the fireplace at night and walked on the beach in the snow. He was almost jealous.

He nodded at the right places as Toby recounted Ellie stories, but his mind was on Calvin. He couldn't send Toby back to school without enough time to process it all. When Toby was brushing his teeth, Sean re-read the mass email he'd received from Bev Shineman:

To the Bradley Community:

It is with great sadness that I'm writing to you today. Calvin Drake passed away last night at Mount Sinai Hospital, a result of complications from a peanut allergy.

Parents, you should discuss this sad loss with your children. I've enclosed a helpful article about talking to children about death. And of course, please contact me if you have

*any questions or need to discuss your feelings. When school
resumes we'll have discussion groups in homeroom and grief
counselors will be available for the children and anyone else
who would like to speak with them.*

*We are newly committed to our efforts to keep Bradley
a nut-free zone. This terrible occurrence was an unfortunate
result of a snack that was brought in from the outside. With
all of us working together, we can make sure nothing like this
happens again.*

*Sincerely,
Dr. Bev Shineman
School Psychologist*

He'd practiced a million times, but now nothing seemed right.
How to start? One of the "helpful" articles he'd read stressed that
there was never a good time to break the news.

Toby stood in the doorway of Sean's bedroom, traces of toothpaste foam still in the corners of his mouth.

"What is it, Dad?" He seemed grown-up despite the superheroes
that crawled all over his pajamas. "You look funny."

"Let's sit." He patted his bed slowly. The motion was as much to
regulate his own heart rate as it was to summon Toby.

He hopped onto the bed. "You're freaking me out, Dad."

"There was an email from school." He laid his hand on Toby's
back. Maybe he should have read some more articles before having
this conversation. He felt entirely unprepared. "Tobe, Calvin
died."

Toby looked at him like he hadn't heard right.

"Do you understand? Calvin is dead. I'm so sorry."

"Yeah, but . . ."

Sean bit his tongue and waited for the rest of the question. He
wasn't supposed to tell him more than he wanted to hear.

A dark cloud passed over Toby's face. Then a flicker of hope. "In the SpongeBob video game you get three lives. In Ratchet & Clank, too."

"Tobe, those are just games. In real life you only get one."

Toby's eyes started to fill. "He should get more lives."

"I know," he said. "This is so sad. I'm so sad, too." He reached around Toby and gave him a hug. Toby buried his head in Sean's shoulder.

"It's not fair." Toby was sobbing now, his breathing was ragged and his body shook.

Kids cried all the time because you wouldn't let them watch *Scooby Doo* or have seconds on dessert or because they fell in the park and tore the skin off of their knee. But watching your child cry because he was filled with profound sadness was worse than awful.

Toby looked up with sad eyes. "You're supposed to be old when you die," he said. "Calvin wasn't old."

"I know." Sean wiped his face with his sleeve. "I know."

"Am I going to die?" Toby's brain was in overdrive now. Sean could see the questions percolating.

"No, Tobe. Calvin was allergic to peanuts and somehow he ate something with peanuts in it. Most kids don't die. Almost none." He could finesse the facts slightly, couldn't he?

"Are you going to die?"

He was ready for this one, thanks to Jess.

"No, Tobe," he said. "Not for a long time. I'm not going any-where." He swallowed. "Neither is your mom."

"Is Calvin in heaven?"

He hadn't thought about that one. He was hoping Toby wouldn't even know to bring it up. "I don't know."

"If he's not in heaven where is he?"

Toby wanted answers, and Sean wanted to give him some. *Don't lie.* It kept running through his head. Exactly how far was he supposed to take this not lying thing? Because while he was at it, he might as well throw in that there was no tooth fairy or Santa Claus. "Lots of people believe in heaven, Tobe. If you believe in heaven, then Calvin is definitely there."

"Is that where your mom and dad are?"

He thought about his parents. About how loud and abrasive they'd been when they were alive and about how empty everything seemed without them. Toby had never even known them. "I don't know. Nobody really knows what happens when you die."

"Mom says people are reincarcerated."

"Reincarnated."

"Yeah," Toby said. "They come back as grasshoppers and butterflies."

"She said that?" Was Ellie out of her fucking mind telling this stuff to Toby? Not that he was faring much better here, but still. "I mean, it *could* be true. But . . . I don't . . . probably not."

Toby was quiet for a few minutes. "So where *is* Calvin?"

"Like I said, nobody really knows."

"No, Dad. I mean where *is* he? Right now."

He was pretty sure Toby was asking about Calvin's earthly remains, but if he was wrong he didn't want to be volunteering information like that. "Calvin will always be here because we'll remember him." It sounded like a lame Hallmark greeting card and he wished he could take it back as soon as he said it.

Toby was getting annoyed now. "Dad, where's his *body*?"

"It's probably in a cemetery."

"Under ground? Buried?"

He nodded. It wasn't necessary to go into specifics about cremation. That fell into a gray area somewhere between the *don't lie* and *don't give too much information* instructions outlined in the article.

"But when he wakes up how will he get out?" Toby looked panicked. "He'll be trapped."

This was obviously going to take some time to sink in. "He's not going to wake up, remember?"

"Oh, right," Toby said and got quiet. "So I never get to see Calvin again?"

Sean shook his head slowly. "You can remember him, though, and see him in your mind."

"It's not fair," Toby said. He was crying again. "He didn't get to see my comics. It's not fair."

"I know." He pulled him in, hugged him and rocked him until they both fell asleep. When he woke up at six a.m. with a stiff neck, they were still huddled together.

He tried to sit up without waking Toby, but the pain in his neck made him groan.

"Dad?" Toby said, groggily. "Will you make pancakes?"

As he was mixing and pouring, Sean realized he hadn't cooked a thing while Toby was away. The routine was comforting. Maybe Toby would feel the same way.

Toby padded into the kitchen. "Can I help?"

"Absolutely."

Toby dragged a cast iron skillet from the cupboard to the stovetop and gave a serious look. "Stand back," he said, before turning the dial. A ring of fire leapt up to the pan. Toby had always been good in the kitchen. Responsible, careful. How could he have ADD? Then he thought about what Walt had said. They were watching him all day, much more closely than Sean could. Maybe all he needed was to get the new semester off to a good solid start and they'd lay off him, let him relax. It was worth giving the drugs a shot if it gave Toby some breathing room. Toby deserved that.

"Did you sleep okay?" he asked.

"Yeah," Toby said. "I'm still sad about Calvin."

"Yeah, it's okay to be sad about it for a long time." Like probably forever. "Remembering him is good, though, and you can do that anytime you want."

Toby didn't bring him up again for the rest of the day. As they moved into their second hour of an endless Monopoly game at the kitchen table, Sean noticed that Toby seemed to have filed the whole thing away. He was sure it would come up again, but for now a break was a happy relief, for both of them.

It seemed like as good a time as any to bring up the other huge topic that had been on his mind all vacation. "I talked to Dr. Altherra the other day."

"Who?" No name recognition whatsoever.

"You know, the lady—the psychiatrist—we went to. She asked you about school?"

"Yeah?"

"She thinks it might help you pay attention in school if you take some medicine in the morning."

"Okay."

"You have to tell me if it makes you feel at all funny—like funny bad."

Toby shrugged. "Okay."

And that was that. Sean had been sure there would be more questions, concerns, apprehension. But that had all been Sean's to deal with. Toby didn't have to think about the risks or question the decision. If his father told him to take medicine, he needed medicine. It was all so blissfully simple.

The next morning, his hand shook as he tried to cut the pill in half with a dull knife. Toby was so calm right now, so completely himself, so completely non-ADD, it seemed crazy to be doing this. But what did he know about inattentive ADD? He was no psychiatrist. The knife split the pill too quickly and half of it flew across the kitchen. He saved one half, though, and handed it to Toby. "Here you go, try this," he said, going for a nonchalance he did not feel.

Toby looked at Sean like he'd asked him to eat a sharp piece of glass. "What is that?"

Then he realized. Toby had never taken a pill. All medicine— Tylenol, Motrin, even the antibiotics from the pharmacy—always came in liquid form. He explained how to put the pill on the back of his tongue and wash it down with water. Toby looked skeptical.

"Want to give it a try?"

Toby shrugged and took the pill between his fingers. He gagged a few times trying. Finally, he took a big swallow of water and smiled. "Hey, I'm pretty good at that."

For the next four hours, Sean asked Toby if he was feeling racy, tired, more focused. No, was all he said.

"I wouldn't expect half a pill to have any therapeutic effect at all," Dr. Altherra said on the phone. The half pill was a test to make sure Toby didn't have any bad reactions. She told Sean to give Toby a whole pill the next day, and to give him some reading or math problems to see if his focus was any sharper.

The next day Sean gave Toby a whole pill, which he swallowed on the first try. "Yes!" Toby said when it went down. Again, no bad reactions. No change at all. When Sean presented him with math problems, Toby flat-out refused. Asking a kid to do schoolwork on his last day of Christmas break amounted to cruel and inhuman punishment. To make matters worse, he couldn't tell if Toby's attention was any better, because at home, for the most part, Toby was fine focusing on his homework. He decided he was going to have to send another email to Jess, even though he was still waiting to hear back from the last one, to let her know what was going on. If Toby's problems were happening at school, then the school was going to have to tell him if things were improving.

He composed an email to Jess that night. *Hi Jess—Could you give me a call when you get this? It's about Toby. Look forward to seeing you at school, Sean.*

But she didn't respond to that email either.

The next morning, the first day of the new semester, he handed Toby the lavender pill with a glass of water and watched him swallow it. "I'm going to bring some of these to the nurse. You need to go down after lunch and she'll give you another one, okay?"

"Whatever," he said, spooning more Cheerios into his mouth.

If Toby had a fever, Sean would give him Tylenol. For strep, he'd give him Zithromax. But this was different. He blamed the Ringling Brothers.

Back when Toby was five, he and Ellie had taken Toby to the circus. Outside Madison Square Garden, animal rights people had set up a massive campaign with poster-size photos of drugged elephants and doped-out tigers to show how barbaric the circus really was. The animals were kept nicely stoned at all times, the protestors said, robbing the fierce animals of their fierceness, making them docile, easier to train. Every time an elephant balanced on a ball or a tiger jumped through a flaming hoop, Sean had gotten a sick, sinking feeling. It was kind of like the feeling he had now as he drugged Toby for school so he could learn loftier circus tricks like advanced math and reading.

"What?" Toby was looking at him strangely.

"Nothing," he said. "We don't want to be late the first day back. Hey, how do you . . ."

"Dad, if you ask me how I feel one more time, I'm going to have to do something drastic."

Sean pressed his lips together dramatically to show there would be no further questions. He opened the front door and gestured for Toby to walk through. Toby smiled, slung his backpack over his shoulder, and obliged.

CHAPTER FIFTEEN

THE BRADLEY LOBBY VIBRATED WITH POST-VACATION ENERGY OF tanned people explaining how they got that way. But the knot in Sean's stomach distracted him from the spectacle. He'd been up all night wondering how it would be to see Jess again and now, tunneling through the crowd, he tried to form an expression that didn't reveal how devastated he'd been by the blowoff. He was just a father picking up his son. He needed to untense his shoulders and pretend he'd never ripped off her clothes. "I can do this," he said to himself like a mantra. He wondered if any of the tanned parents could tell he was a nervous wreck.

From across the room, he watched Jess dismiss the kids one at a time. Walking toward them, he saw her pale skin glow next to the orange-brown skin of Kayla's mom. Toby waved and Sean slipped into line next to him. "Hey Buddy. How was your first day back?"

He shrugged. "Okay."

The cloud of vanilla and musk coming off Kayla's mom caught in Sean's throat and he coughed, causing Jess to look up and notice him. When her eyes met his, he could have sworn she blushed for a second. He smiled at her, which he hadn't exactly planned. She looked away.

"How was your break?" Kayla's mom was asking Jess, in a voice far too deep to be coming from her skeletal body.

"I was in Rhode Island with my dad and my fiancé," Jess said. "We had a nice New England Christmas." So the *Invasion of the Bodysnatchers* guy was back in the picture. His eyes flashed to the ring on her finger. It was all making nauseating sense.

"St. Maarten's was ninety degrees," Kayla's mom said. "Not Christmas-y at all. But we had a nice time."

Not that he knew what he'd say when he and Toby reached Jess, but the waiting was killing him. Now Dylan was giving her a presidential handshake, looking her right in the eye. When Dylan's Caribbean sitter whisked him away, it was Toby's turn. They were last in line.

"Bye Jess," Toby said, giving her a perfunctory handshake. Jess shook his hand then flashed Sean a fleeting smile that packed a lot in: regret, wistfulness, kindness, and even, he thought, a hint of longing. It was possible he was reading too much into it.

"How've you been?" He tried to sound like a regular parent. One who hadn't explored every inch of her naked body.

"Fine," she said. Her eyes darted away briefly. "How was your break?"

The chitchat was practically unbearable. "It started out well, but the rest of it was just so-so."

She took a breath and held it before letting it out slowly.

"I sent you a couple of emails."

"Sorry, I'm pretty backlogged."

"It's about Toby," he said, enjoying the small pleasure of being able to play the parent card. "It's kind of important."

"Oh." This had taken her off guard. It would derail her from whatever script she'd prepared. "Okay." She looked at her watch. "I have about ten minutes."

Toby waited in the library while Sean followed Jess to her classroom.

She pulled an adult-size chair next to her desk, and he sat on it. Her eyes looked everywhere but at him. Finally she focused on him, business-like. "We should probably deal with . . . what happened."

"What happened was great," he said. She was so close he could reach out and touch her. Except, of course, he couldn't.

"This relationship," she started, "our relationship—has to be strictly parent-teacher."

He knew it had been coming, but it sucked hearing it, nonetheless. "Okay." He nodded. "So . . . you two are back together?"

She fiddled with the ring. "I feel awful. This whole mess is completely my fault."

Fault was a tough word. It implied a deep crack that couldn't be mended. "I don't know about that. I'd like to think we can both take credit for what happened. And for the record, I don't see it as a mess."

"Still . . ." she said.

"I do have a parent-teacher thing to discuss."

"Oh." She clasped her hands in her lap. "Okay."

He told her about giving Toby the Metattent Junior. Her mouth gaped slightly. "The doctor suggested that?" Her tone was strange.

"Why?" he said. "You don't think he needs it?"

"No." She said it quickly. Emphatically. Then she backed off. "I mean, look. I'm not a doctor. I can't make a diagnosis. But Toby's . . . he's not what I'd call ADD."

"But . . ." It was what he'd wanted to hear all along. "They're calling it inattentive-type ADD. Because he gets distracted in class."

"Yeah, well I call that being a kid." She sighed. "Sorry, this is just one of those things that drives me crazy."

"No, I want to hear what you think. I need to hear it."

"I can see medicating kids who need it—kids who jump off walls and kick and scream during class. I've seen drugs help kids like that. It's amazing, actually. But in general . . ." She trailed off. "Look, a lot of boys can have trouble sitting and listening. They get there, though."

Maybe Altherra had been wrong. Toby *would* get there.

"Do you think I should stop giving him the pills?"

"God, don't ask me that." She looked nervous. "I'm not a doctor. I don't have a clue what the right thing to do is."

He'd made this decision already. And it hadn't been easy. "Will you keep an eye on him? Tell me if the medication is helping at all?"

"Of course." She wrote her number on a piece of paper and handed it to him. "Let's talk in the afternoons. I'm here until five."

He folded the paper and put it in his wallet, then tried to see what was going on behind her eyes. "How are you doing?"

The smile looked more sad than happy. "I'm okay. I'm good." She got up and held out her hand. "I'll be in touch. About Toby."

CHAPTER SIXTEEN

EVERY DAY FOR THE NEXT FIVE DAYS, HE GAVE TOBY A PILL BEFORE school. Every afternoon he called Jess at four forty-five to check in about Toby. Every afternoon Jess told him there was no change, nothing to report.

When he talked to Dr. Altherra, she upped him half a pill. "Relax," she said on the phone. "This is how we get the dosage right. We'll know when we've hit it." The stab in the dark strategy seemed to lack scientific specificity.

On Monday he dialed Jess, but hung up before it rang. He wanted to hear her voice. But not at school, not in the middle of a workday. He wanted to hear her voice the way it had been the night of Art's party. He decided to wait and call later—after Toby had gone to bed. He wondered if the fiancé would be there, if he'd answer her cell phone. The guy probably had one of those my-dick's-bigger-than-yours voices, too. If Sean could just talk to her, she'd have to remember why she attacked him in the taxi. At the very least she might remember she liked him.

That night, he stretched out on his bed. She'd been lying on this exact spot just a few weeks ago. He dialed the phone.

"Sean?" She sounded surprised and possibly annoyed.

"Yeah. Hi."

"Is everything okay?" Her voice was full of concern. "Is Toby okay?"

"He's fine. I just . . . I hope it's not too late to call." Obviously it was too late to call. "I had some meetings at work that went over and I wanted to make sure I talked to you today. About Toby."

"Oh . . ." He heard a man's voice in the background. He couldn't make out the words, but the guy didn't sound pleased. "Hold on," she said into the receiver. Her voice was muffled as she said something about work.

So this had been a bad idea. But he couldn't hang up now. What would she wear at home on a weeknight? He pictured her in her oversized sweatshirt and jeans from the Scotch and Oreo night. He remembered how her eyes had been pink from crying.

"Sorry," she said. The business-like tone was back. It was the exact thing he'd been trying to avoid.

"So what's the report from today?" He tried to sound parent-like.

"He was adorable, as always," she said. "But no change. Mrs. Looning made him sit out again in music."

He didn't want anything to be wrong with Toby, but somewhere along the way he'd found himself hoping this would be the easy fix Shineman said it would be. Dr. Altherra would most likely tell him to up the dose again.

"Sean?" she said. There was just a hint of panic in her voice. "You there?"

"Yeah." It was all so futile. Trying to make Toby fit Bradley's expectations. Being stuck on a woman who was engaged to be

married. "Thanks. Sorry to bother you at home like this. It won't
happen again." He started to hang up.

"It's okay," she said. "I know this is a hard time. How are you
holding up?"

"Honestly," he said, "it sucks."

"Just trust your instincts."

How could he trust his instincts? They were obviously untrust-
worthy because they were telling him to pursue Jess. "Can I ask you
a kind of personal question?"

"I don't know." The wariness was creeping back into her voice.
"Maybe."

"Have you set a date?"

A pause. "For what?"

"The wedding." He was officially pathetic.

"You know, I should go. Let's be in touch tomorrow," she said.
"About Toby."

He rested the phone on his chest after he'd hung up. He had to
get a grip. He'd heard the muffled voice of Jess's future through the
phone. She was taken.

Toby knocked and pushed open the door to his bedroom.

"Hey Tobe. Aren't you supposed to be asleep?"

"Can't sleep." Toby had a funny look on his face, somewhere
between puzzled and sheepish.

"Hop up."

Toby climbed onto the bed and faced him, seriously.

"What's on your mind?"

"I heard a word today. Can you tell me what it means?"

So maybe Bradley was paying off after all. Toby was
interested in expanding his vocabulary. "I'll try. What's the
word?"

"Master . . . master bashun."

Sean opened his mouth. Then closed it. Not what he'd expected.
"Where'd you hear that word?"

"Kayla said her brothers do master bashun. But I'm not exactly sure . . ."

"Her teenage brothers," he nodded, thoughtfully. Trust his instincts. Maybe the advice was the same as it had been in the death article: be honest. But where did you start with a kid this age?

"So do you know what it means?" Toby was getting impatient.

"Uh, yeah, I do. It's just . . ."

"So what is it?"

Why had Sean been so keen on Toby learning vocabulary? "Okay. Uh, so you know what sex is, right?"

"Sure," he said, way too quickly. "Yeah. Of course."

Toby was eight. He didn't know what sex was. At least they'd never had that conversation. It was idiotic to start the conversation that way. Whatever Toby knew, he'd probably learned from Kayla and Lord knows what she was telling them. "You know what, scratch that. Never mind. Okay. So masturbation . . ." It was like in a spelling bee—you had to say the word out loud before spelling it. "So . . . it's when you, uh, touch your private parts. Do you understand?"

Toby was nodding yes but his eyes said no. "Why?"

"Because, you know, it feels good."

"And does stuff come out? Kayla says stuff comes out."

What was an eight-year-old girl doing with this kind of information? "Yeah, that can happen. It's totally normal." He was sure this was the part of the conversation where he was supposed to make his son comfortable with his own sexuality, like when Toby had finally gotten out of diapers and discovered he could yank on his penis all day long unencumbered by bulky absorbent plastic. Ellie'd reminded Sean that men of an entire generation were in therapy because their mothers told them they'd go blind if they jerked off too much. "And, just so you know," he went on, ". . . masturbating is fine. As long as you do it in private, it's, you know, totally fine." This conversation would be so much easier if Toby were thirteen or sixteen, or maybe twenty-one. But at this point, his main objective was to walk a fine line. Sean had to send Toby from this conversation knowing it was okay to jerk off and yet not make it sound so appealing that he'd decide it was the best invention ever and that his dad was totally into it.

"So boys do this?" Toby was still trying to wrap his mind around the concept.

"Well . . . not *only* boys," he said, before remembering the other crucial part of the death articles: *don't give too much information.* Why had he felt the need to share that gem?

Toby's eyes went wide. "*Mom* does that?"

Toby might have been able to deal with all of it up to that moment. But now his little head was spinning. Sean had to backpedal, and yes, maybe even lie. "No," he said. "No, I didn't say that." He hadn't actually said Ellie *didn't* masturbate, but he hoped it would be taken that way. "Maybe you ought to get back to bed."

"But . . ."

"It's pretty late." Sean helped him off the bed and walked him back to his own room. Bedtime was such a useful excuse. What would he do when Toby was too old for bedtime? "We can talk about it more tomorrow if you want." He would invent better answers in case the subject came up again, but he was banking on the fact that Toby would move on to something more age appropriate like Pokemon or temporary tattoos.

ON FRIDAY, DR. ALTHERRA UPPED TOBY'S DOSE AS PREDICTED, to two pills twice a day.

"There's news," Jess said that afternoon when he called her. "The kids took the ERB today."

"How'd he do?"

"We won't get the results for a few weeks," she said. "But he sat through the whole thing and filled in answers for all the questions."

"That's good, right?"

"Yeah." Her voice was full of energy. "It's good."

On Friday, Toby came home with a grin on his face. "I got a gold star." He held up a piece of sheet music with a sticker on it.

"In recorder?" He hadn't meant to sound so shocked.

"I know, it's weird. But I didn't laugh when Kayla made faces. I forgot to even look at her. And I played "Mary Had A Little Lamb" with only about five mistakes. Or maybe ten."

Sean stuck the piece of music on the fridge with the Liberace magnet he and Ellie had bought in Las Vegas before they were married.

Later that afternoon, Shineman called him at work. "I wanted to say how pleased I am with Toby's results," she said. "You must be thrilled."

Relieved, cautiously optimistic, worried, maybe. But *thrilled*? "He seems good," Sean said.

"I was in the classroom today observing Toby," she said. "He's definitely heading in the right direction." Her tone was shifting almost seamlessly into something else. "But I think there's still room for improvement."

"But . . ." She had an uncanny ability to blindside him. "You just said—"

"He's doing much, much better." But her tone wasn't mirroring her news. "When I was in the classroom, though, I noticed he was looking out the window. And he was tapping his foot against the leg of the table. He's still fidgety. If he can settle down even more, I bet we'll really see some results," she said.

"You just said you *did* see results."

"Calm down, Sean. We're just having a conversation about Toby's progress. This is good news. He's responding very well."

"Are you saying the other kids don't look out the window? No one's looking out the window except Toby?"

"This is what you asked the school to do. To keep an eye out. And Jess and I have been doing that. It's my professional opinion as an educator and psychologist that I don't think Toby is getting the maximum benefit from the medication yet."

"You've got to be kidding me."

"Call your doctor. Talk it over with her."

Before he could even hang up, Dr. Altherra was calling to check in. "Are we seeing results yet?" she asked.

He told her about Jess's report and wondered if she noticed that his voice was shaking. Admitting Toby was responding to the medication was the same as admitting something had been wrong.

"So we're making progress." Dr. Altherra sounded happier than he'd heard her. "Is Toby feeling good about it?"

He told her about the gold star.

"We're getting close. Now we figure out if this is the right dose. This is when I like to send a new Conners scale to the school."

Gathering more information sounded at least sort of scientific.

"So do I have your permission to send that over today?"

"Okay." He allowed his shoulders to untense for the first time in weeks. "Sure."

CHAPTER SEVENTEEN

"Meeting!" Rick bellowed through the morose *Buzz* offices. "Now!"

The shit had hit the fan. Somehow, *Buzz* missed Owen Wilson shoving his tongue down the throat of a nineteen-year-old model at Liquid. And while stories like that usually constituted a blip on the slime-covered celebrity radar, this affair seemed to have stuck, rendering *Buzz* disastrously behind the other tabs. Ideally, this would be the moment Sean would save the day with a quick call to Gino, who in turn would stalk the star until he or she acted like a moron, looked like shit, stripped naked, or ended up in another compromising position.

But today Gino wasn't answering. A little research revealed that a run-in with one of Katie Holmes's bodyguards had laid him up in a fifteen hundred dollar per night room at New York Hospital.

Sean picked up the phone at his desk and put in a call to Lauren Ropa, the photographer who broke the Madonna thing for *Star* last year.

"Let's go!" Rick was still yelling. Sean joined the staffers who were trudging toward the conference room heavily. He refused to take Rick's theatrics too seriously, but he seemed to be the only one.

"How the fuck do we turn this around?" Rick's face was red and the circles under his eyes were darker than Sean had seen them. "Hey, I'm talking to all of you. Wake up!"

"I've got Ropa on this thing," Sean offered. *On it* may have been an overstatement, but it was what Rick needed to hear. "If Owen Wilson so much as brushes the ass of a woman on line at Starbucks, we'll get it on film." He knew he should care more about the botched coverage. But he'd gotten an email from Camille that morning telling him the top reviewer from the *Times* was coming to his opening. Things were looking up. Finally.

"My very best clients will be coming," she had said. "I guarantee the specialty collectors will take home a couple each." *A couple each.* It was less than a month away.

"What are you smiling about, Benning?" Rick glared at him.

The whole room turned to look at him. "Nothing," he said, trying to look like he cared. "Not smiling. We'll fix this, but you've got to let us get to work."

Rick shooed them out with a disgusted wave of his hand.

When Sean got back to his desk, the message light was flashing. He prayed it was Ropa telling him she'd already gotten some money shots. He put the phone on speaker and pressed play.

"Mr. Benning, this is Patty from Bradley," the voice said. "I'm afraid there's been a . . . well, there's been an accident at school. A serious accident. Toby is at Mount Sinai, and you should go there as soon as you get this message. The address of the hospital is—"

As soon as he heard the word *hospital,* he couldn't think straight. Somehow, his body went through the motions of getting him out of there fast. *Don't worry* was what the school always said when they called during the day. *Toby's fine.* But they hadn't said that. Patty had used the word *serious*. Sean shoved his arms into his coat as he ran toward the elevator bank and punched the button. For strep or a fever it was a call from the nurse. The school had never told him to go to the hospital. He imagined stitches. Lots of them. A concussion. Broken arm. How long would it take to climb down forty-two flights? He punched the button again.

"Where the fuck do you think you're going?" Rick was still flushed from the meeting.

"Hospital," he spat out. "School just called, I—"

Rick's expression softened a little. "What's a matter? Toby okay?"

He had no idea. "Yeah, I'm sure he's . . ." Sean trailed off, not knowing what to hope for, what to imagine. The elevator made a binging sound before it opened. He was already inside and jabbing at the button when Rick told him to go. The doors closed on Rick's solemn, single-father nod that was supposed to be supportive but instead terrified him.

It was surreal, pulling up to Mount Sinai and pushing through the heavy doors to the pediatric emergency room. The scene was just as chaotic as it had been when he'd come with Calvin, but now every crying child and bloody bandage shot him full of such dread that he thought he might pass out. His eyes darted to the gurneys lining the walls. No Toby.

The attendant pointed Sean to a small room sectioned off by a curtain. Bev Shineman stood in front of it, frowning, waving her cell phone around to find a signal.

"Sean," she said when she saw him. Her voice was maddeningly calm. "Toby's unconscious, but he's stable."

"Unconscious?" Could he go back and change his wish to a broken arm or stitches? His heart raced as he parted the curtain. Toby lay still on the white sheets, an oxygen tube running into his nose and an IV taped to his left arm. His stomach twisted and he felt light-headed. This wasn't happening. This was not the way you were supposed to see your child.

It was cold in the room. Too cold. He reached out to touch Toby, who looked so delicate, so fragile, in his non-sleep. He ran his hand gently through Toby's hair. "Tobe, buddy. You're gonna be okay. I'm here and I'm not going anywhere."

Toby had been alone in the scary cold room. How could they just leave him there like that? He called to Shineman who was still outside the curtain.

She peered in, then stepped over the threshold delicately. "Are you okay? This must be very hard for you."

"What the hell happened?" He was livid, terrified, helpless. "What's wrong with him?"

"Let's wait and talk to the doctor," Shineman said. "He knows much more than I do."

"What the hell happened to Toby?" He wasn't a screamer, but now he couldn't stop. "Where's the fucking doctor?"

Fast footsteps stopped outside the room and Jess pulled back the curtain. Her face was red and she was out of breath. "How is he?" she asked.

"Do *you* know what happened?" He was desperate for answers. Why was nobody giving him any?

She nodded and tried to catch her breath. "Mr. Trencher said they were doing a relay race and halfway around the track Toby went down." She was talking fast and her eyes looked scared.

"Neither of us saw this firsthand," Shineman interrupted.

Jess kept talking as if Shineman weren't there. "When he saw Toby shaking and grabbing his chest, he performed CPR and had one of the kids call 911."

Then it hit him. This was *his* fault. He'd done this. Despite the temperature in the room, he was covered in a panicky sweat.

"I have a hunch we're very close," Dr. Altherra had said when she got the new Conners scales. "This is how we do it."

"Do what?" he'd asked.

"Find the right amount for Toby. We keep going up 'til it hits, slowly and carefully." And we watch closely to make sure we haven't gone over. I've done this hundreds of times," she assured him. "Don't worry."

Worry was now the tamest emotion he felt. Then he thought: Ellie. He had to call Ellie. She would never forgive him. And she'd be right. His fault. This was all his fault. There was no one else who could share the blame—or the guilt.

He turned to Shineman. "It's the medication." He was afraid if he moved, his legs would give out, his body would crumple. "This is just like those stories I read online . . ." He turned to Jess. "But he seemed fine, right? You said he was fine." His mind raced as he tried to remember something, anything he might have missed, a clue that Toby wasn't responding as well as everyone said he was. It didn't matter. He was Toby's father, he should have known. Then a wave of nausea washed over him. Because on some level he must have known. And he'd done it anyway. He'd been an idiot, agreeing to raise the dosage, to give him the medication in the first place. What had been the point? To turn Toby into a super-student, some robot that could keep up with the other overachieving children at this Ivy-League factory? When had he decided that Toby's academic performance was more important than his health? What had he been thinking?

Jess opened her mouth to speak, but Shineman cut her off. "Sean, you should try to calm down."

"My son is unconscious," he yelled. "I'm not going to fucking calm down."

"For Toby's sake. You'll talk to the doctor when he comes in, but I don't believe this could have been caused by the medication. It just doesn't add up."

"Where the *hell* is the doctor?" It came out louder than he'd thought it would, but it didn't feel loud enough. He pulled back the curtain. "We need a doctor in here," he yelled into the hallway. "Hello?"

"We should give Sean some space," Shineman said.

"I don't want space. I want to talk to a goddamn doctor!"

"I'll get one," Jess said, and looked at Sean with an unguarded openness he hadn't seen since The Night. She was gone a second later. He wished Shineman had gone instead.

"Don't jump to conclusions, Sean," Shineman said. "That's not useful now."

His head spun with the horror stories Altherra and Dr. Jon had told him to disregard. "There was a story online about a boy on Ritalin who dropped dead while he was riding his skateboard." *Dropped dead.* God it was a horrible expression. He fought the tears burning behind his eyes.

"You have no idea what caused that boy's death." Shineman was trying to be reasonable. He wanted to strangle her. "Who knows if he had a preexisting condition? There are a million things that could have hurt that child that had nothing to do with the Ritalin he was taking to treat his ADD. You're a good father, Sean. You did not hurt Toby."

He wanted to hurt *her.* "Can you just stop talking," he snapped. Why was she here, anyway? "Where's the fucking doctor?"

Jess ushered the doctor into the room. He was unshaven and looked like he hadn't slept in a week.

"This is Dr. Schwartz," she said.

It looked like it took a lot of effort for Schwartz to extend his hand and shake Sean's. "Your son had an arrhythmia—an irregular rhythm of his heart," he said. "Which deprived his brain of oxygen for a short time."

"His heart stopped beating?" Sean couldn't believe he was standing here having this conversation, that this whole thing was really happening. "For how long? What does that mean?"

Schwartz rubbed his eyes. "No one knows," he said. "We have to wait." He wasn't in a coma, Schwartz said. He kept calling Toby's condition a persistent vegetative state. *Vegetative.* Like vegetable. For a moment, it was as if all the molecules that made up Sean's body, his brain, the universe, had come undone. He wasn't sure what the purpose of anything was.

Schwartz said Toby's organs were functioning on their own but that there was no way of knowing how extensive the damage was—especially to his brain—until Toby regained consciousness. *If* he regained consciousness.

Sean took deep breaths to avoid vomiting. "This is my fault," he said, shaking. He told the doctor about the Metattent Junior. "That's what this is from, right?"

Dr. Schwartz crossed his arms in front of his chest. He wore a thermal T-shirt under his green scrubs. He pursed his lips in thought. "I don't know," he said, finally. "What I do know is methylphenidate is an amphetamine. Amphetamines accelerate the heart rate, and if someone is exercising and it increases to a dangerous level yes, that can cause problems."

"So . . . but . . ." The room was starting to sway. "It's from the pills, right?"

"Look," he said, running his hand through his hair. "Not that this has much to do with your son's case, but I took Ritalin all through med school as a study drug. Everyone I know did. This kind of reaction is extremely rare."

Sean assumed this piece of information was supposed to make him feel better. He wanted to take the guy by the shoulders and shake him as hard as he could. "So why is this happening? Why is my son unconscious?"

"I wish I could tell you more. All I can say is that in healthy children with no preexisting condition, this kind of thing is very rare. Very." He paused. "Does he have any kind of heart condition that you know of?"

"No, of course not." Toby's heart was fine. At least he thought it was. He did a quick mental inventory of his dead relatives, cataloguing how they died. His father's father died of a heart attack. Did that count? Maybe there was something buried in his genes that Sean should have known about, told someone about.

"He's going to be okay, right?" Sean asked, focusing all his mental powers on the doctor's brain and willing him to say yes. *Yes.* It was such a simple word.

"You have to understand," the doctor said, "in any given population of children, there are always a few instances of sudden death whether they're taking medication or not." The word *death* hung in the air. This guy was brutal. Had he ever heard of bedside manner?

Dr. Schwartz tried to gloss over the ominous report he'd just given. "The good news is he's still alive and he's breathing on his own. Let's hope he wakes up in the next forty-eight hours." The doctor paused. "Because if he doesn't, the chances that he will, get slimmer and slimmer. Mr. Benning, you should be prepared. This kind of thing can go either way."

The doctor might as well have told him to prepare himself for the end of the world. Sean collapsed into the chair next to Toby's bed and listened to the monitor's hypnotic beeps. He wasn't at all prepared, much less remotely willing to entertain the idea that Toby might . . . He couldn't even think the word. He couldn't bear it.

He had to call Ellie. And Nicole. Dick and Maureen. He had to get everyone on board so that Toby would not be alone for a second. He had a surge of energy when he realized there was something he could do. It wasn't much, but it changed everything. He took out his cell phone but he couldn't get reception.

"Fuck, fuck, fuck!"

"Go," Jess said. "I'll stay."

Gratitude surged through him. "I'll be right back," he said to Toby. "I'm going to call Mommy."

He left Ellie a message telling her to get into the city and come to Mount Sinai as soon as humanly possible. He told her that Toby was unconscious, but he didn't tell her why. Why should he? At least not on her voice mail, not like this. That conversation could wait. Besides, the doctor didn't say for sure it was the pills.

Sean also left a message for Ellie's parents. Their machine said they were on a Queen Elizabeth cruise. Since they didn't believe in cell phones, they wouldn't get the message until they came home. Nicole was on her way.

When he got back to the ER, Shineman was gone, thank God. Jess watched Toby silently. She looked like she might cry.

"Thank you," he said.

"Can I talk to you?"

A nod was all he could manage.

"I don't know how to . . ." And then she was crying. "I noticed something earlier today at school. I don't know how to describe it exactly, but Toby was acting, well, kind of *off*. I started to email you, but . . ." She took a deep breath, trying to stop crying, but the tears came in another wave. "I wanted to give it 'til the end of the day, to make sure Toby wasn't just . . . coming down with a cold or something."

His lungs quivered. "Off how?"

"There were no jokes, no smiles, no goofing around."

Another surge of anger, no, hatred as he remembered Shineman's constant nagging about Toby's behavior. "That's what the school wanted," he said bitterly.

"He just didn't seem like himself, is the only way to say it. He didn't eat lunch again today. And I'm not sure about this, but . . . I think his left hand was twitching a little during reading."

Sean closed his eyes, trying to imagine what it must have been like for Toby at school, before it happened.

"I didn't want to jump the gun."

"So you just let him suffer?" Jumping the gun could have prevented this. An easy phone call. An email. Toby's life had been in her hands. He could never have imagined Jess would be the target of the kind of anger building in him.

"I made the wrong choice," she said. "I'm so sorry."

"Sorry? You're sorry?" Screaming at her wasn't going to change anything, but he couldn't help it. "Look at him."

He stared at Toby, rehashing every moment, every wrong decision along the way, wishing he could go back and do it all again. He was mad at Jess—furious—but not as mad as he was at himself.

She touched his arm, an offer of solace. But he didn't want solace. He wanted Toby back.

"Get out," he said, shaking.

"I'm so sorry." She looked stricken, miserable.

"Could you just get the *fuck* out?!"

CHAPTER EIGHTEEN

SEAN'S EYES BURNED. HE RUBBED THE BRILLO SPROUTING FROM his cheeks. Somewhere around three a.m. they'd moved Toby into the Pediatric Intensive Care Unit, or *pick-you* as everyone kept calling it, like Toby had been specially selected, chosen as the sickest of the sick kids. The PICU, which circled back on itself in an endless loop, existed outside the parameters of the real world where time, space, life, and death were clear-cut concepts. Here, even the basics seemed surreal. The sound was muted, the light unnatural. Nurses padded around the hallways to incessant beeps. They seemed unaware of day and night as they tended to patients who, though not dead, were not fully alive either. Definitions were blurred. Sean's head hurt.

He kept checking his cell phone, but it had died at some point. He sat and watched Toby, waiting for something to happen while the math circled through his brain: Toby hadn't moved in twenty-six hours. He had another twenty-two hours left—just under a day—to pull himself out of it.

The throbbing lodged in the fleshy base of his skull. Had Ellie called him back on his dead cell? Why the hell wasn't she here? He'd tried one more time, but again the call went straight into voice mail. Maybe she'd lost her phone, or it had been stolen and she hadn't gotten his messages. That thought was better than the alternative— that she simply didn't give a shit.

Seeing Nicole and Kat in the doorway caused something inside him to crumble. "God I'm glad you're here."

When Kat saw Toby, she buried her head in her mother's fleshy stomach.

"We talked about this," she told Kat. "It's okay."

Kat nodded, looking at the floor. This would probably traumatize poor Kat, but right now he didn't care. He needed family. He needed not to be alone.

"How you holding up?" Nicole asked.

He shrugged to show he wasn't holding up at all.

"Sean," a voice whispered from the doorway. Dr. Altherra had slipped into the room. He vaguely remembered leaving her a message in the middle of the night.

"I'm so sorry," she said. "I thought I'd come by to see how he was doing. I hope you don't mind."

She'd been the one to diagnose Toby, turning all the school's bullshit into reality. She was to blame, at least as much as he was, and she was going to have to answer some basic questions. "We need to talk."

He led her around the loop of the hallway and into the lounge, a hodgepodge of chairs and couches upholstered in purple and turquoise, while Nicole kept watch over Toby. Now, face to face with the doctor, his rage had drained away and he was left with a profound sadness. What was it about shrinks? One look at them and all you wanted to do was cry.

"I'm terribly upset by this," she said. "But there's a very good chance this is all completely unrelated to the medication. I've given his doctor the pertinent information."

"Come on, just admit you were wrong," he said. He wanted to sound more angry, but desperation was winning out. "He never needed those drugs."

"Sean, I understand your desire to reinterpret the facts." She paused to show she was human. "I do." She leaned forward in her chair. "But here's how I saw it and still do see it. Toby was acting out because his lack of attention in class was causing him to fall behind. Three separate teachers filled out Conners scale questionnaires that without a doubt pointed to ADHD behavior. The medication focused him in class. His teachers saw results—that was clear from the questionnaires they completed. He was doing better. As for my part diagnosing the disorder, it was open and shut. I prescribe Ritalin and Metattent Junior frequently for ADHD and negative reactions are extremely rare. Extremely. Toby's collapsing in gym class is very disturbing, and I'm honestly not sure what to make of it."

The teacher questionnaires had factored heavily into the diagnosis and he realized he had no idea what they said. "I need to see the Conner things."

"They're in my office. I—"

"I need to see them."

"I'll send them to you this afternoon," she said. "You'll see that Toby—"

"Toby didn't need those drugs."

She set her mouth and stared at him impenetrably.

He didn't know what to believe, and it didn't matter anyway. Toby needed him and he was wasting his time with Dr. Altherra. "I need to get back." There was nothing else to say. He pushed his chair away and headed into the hallway, which was unnaturally quiet for housing sixteen children. He tried not to look at the sick kids on his walk to Toby's room, but the walls were made of glass so the nurses could see their delicate charges at every moment, from every possible location on the floor. These kids were not only sick, they were hanging on by a thread. He wondered how many of them would leave the floor alive. He wondered whether Toby would be one of them.

When he reached Toby's room, Kat was sitting on the bed reading him a *Magic Treehouse* book about ninjas. She was good at reading. Better than Toby, despite her supposedly sub-par public school education. He realized now it made absolutely no difference. Reading was nothing. It didn't mean anything. Nicole looked up from marking a brief.

"Any change?" he asked, even though it was pretty clear there'd been no change.

Nicole shook her head wearily. She'd been at the hospital with him until late last night and then at work all day. He hadn't seen her this wrecked since their dad had died.

"You should go," he said. "Take Kat home. This is no place for a healthy kid."

Kat put the book next to Toby's bed. "I'll finish the story tomorrow," she said to Toby. She paused, then gave him a kiss on the cheek. "Love you."

"I'll bring her to the neighbor's and come back." Nicole reached out and wrapped her arms around him. Nicole wasn't a hugger, but she held on to him for a long time. Tears started to leak out of his eyes. There was no way to stop them so he didn't even try.

When she let go, he saw she'd been crying, too. He picked up a Kleenex box and they both wiped their eyes.

When Nicole and Kat left, the room was achingly lonely. He'd brought a paper to read, but all he could do was stare at Toby. If he kept watching, Toby couldn't stop living.

He stayed that way for what could have been fifteen minutes or an hour before he heard a tentative knock at the door. "Do you want me to leave?" Jess looked cold and red and alive, in stark contrast to everything else here.

He shook his head. "No." He motioned her in.

She pulled off her hat. "Any news?"

He shook his head grimly, trying to fend off the leaking.

"I'm so sorry," she said. "I should have called you yesterday as soon as I noticed Toby was acting funny. This is all my fault."

"No, it's my fault." He stared at Toby. At the floor. "I shouldn't have taken it out on you."

They breathed together in the quiet. "Can I ask you a question?"

He nodded.

"Why were you so eager to have Toby evaluated? I'm just wondering."

He laughed, but it wasn't funny. "I was practically forced at gunpoint."

"Bev said you insisted."

"She made it pretty clear that if I didn't do it, Toby's Bradley tenure would be short."

"But . . ." Jess was filtering everything through this new bit of information. "Bev said . . . I thought you . . ." She let out a long, sad sigh and stared at Toby. "I'm so sorry this happened. It's the worst thing I can imagine."

He put his hand on hers and held on to it. "I needed to blame someone. But this isn't your fault." Comforting Jess diffused his own misery. It gave him something useful to do. Before he realized he was doing it, he'd wrapped his arm around her and kissed the top of her head. "Thanks for being here," he whispered.

She rested her head on his shoulder and he thought about Bradley and why Bev Shineman would tell Jess he'd wanted to get Toby evaluated. None of it made sense.

Jess's body was warm and comforting and a new wave of exhaustion swept over him. He closed his eyes.

CHAPTER NINETEEN

"SEAN!?" THE VOICE BARGED IN FROM THE OPEN DOORWAY, jolting him and Jess awake. It was unmistakable: throaty but delicate, with a hint of disdain. Ellie.

He wasn't sure which one of them tensed first, but he and Jess were putting distance between themselves quickly.

Ellie burst into the room like a banshee. "Oh my God," she wailed. "Oh my God."

She rushed to Toby's side and started pawing him, touching him to make sure he was warm, then for some inexplicable reason she started rubbing his arms, his chest, his legs. "Wake up, sweetie," she pleaded. "Wake up Toby." Ellie climbed into bed next to Toby and, navigating tubes and the IV, took him in her arms. "My sweet boy," she said, resting her head next to his.

"I'm here. I'm not going anywhere." She kissed him on the temple three times like she always did before bed. "I love you, sweetie. Mommy loves you."

"Ellie," he said awkwardly from across the room. "He's unconscious."

"I know that, Sean," she said, coming out of her misery long enough to glare at him with all the blame in the world. "I talked to the doctor on my way in."

Suddenly, the room was claustrophobic. He didn't know how to hold his body. He'd been caught. But he wasn't sure what he'd been caught doing. He realized he hadn't introduced Jess, which made it worse. "Uh, this is Toby's teacher."

Ellie was rocking Toby and couldn't have cared less.

"I should get going," Jess said. He thought he heard her sigh as she hurried out of Toby's room.

Ellie was unreachable for over an hour as she sobbed into Toby's pillow. He hadn't thought he could absorb another drop of guilt. Still, sitting there with blame radiating off Ellie, he managed to take in even more.

Despite being in agony, Ellie looked amazing. She always looked amazing. But there was something different about her now. Dressed in jeans and a bulky sweater, with her hair tied in a loose knot, her usual New York veneer had been replaced with a wholly un-Ellie-like earthiness. She looked like she'd discovered some secret he would never be allowed to know.

She finally dislodged herself from Toby's side, blew her nose, and faced Sean full-on for the first time, fury in her eyes. "What did you do to him?"

His first instinct was to deny that he'd done anything. But that wasn't a viable position. He *had* done this and they both knew it. "I did what the doctors told me to do." He despised himself for passing the buck. "I did what *you* wanted me to do."

"What I wanted you to do?" Every word was a dagger. "I wanted you to have him evaluated. Not put him on dangerous drugs without consulting me first."

"You wanted consultation rights?" Sarcasm dripped from the words. "You should have stuck around."

She took a deep, hostile breath and swallowed it. "This is my fault," she said. He wasn't sure where she was going with this. Ellie never accepted blame without putting up more of a fight. "I'm an idiot," she said. "A complete idiot for thinking you could handle this. That you could make adult decisions on your own."

She was un*fucking*believable. "Where the hell were you, Ellie?" he screamed. "No one fucking knows. You took off. Vanished. And this is *my* fault? Guess again."

"*You* put him on drugs, Sean," she spat out.

"*You* abandoned him."

"I'm his mother." She enunciated *mother* in a menacing way.

"I called you almost two days ago," he said. "You sure took your time getting here." The clean, deep cut did the trick.

She bowed her head and squeezed her eyes shut. "Fucking retreat didn't allow cell phones." She tried to explain that she'd been at a chakra cleansing seminar in Arizona, but he had no interest in hearing it.

"Look," he warned. "I'm doing my best here. Which is more than you've done for months."

"I know." She stared at her hands miserably and bit her lip.

He was all yelled out and barely had the energy to produce sounds or form words. "I was trying to help him. I was . . . I screwed up."

The admission took the wind out of her sails. "You were trying to help him." She breathed. She didn't want to fight, either. That was good. "So this is a reaction to the drugs? You're sure?"

"Not a hundred percent . . . but I don't know what else it could be."

She nodded, looked at Toby, and was overcome with another wave of tears. A nurse walked past them as if they weren't there and fiddled with Toby's monitors. He and Ellie could fight all they wanted, they could blame each other and cry and wish it had turned out differently, but nothing they could do was going to change what had happened. Nothing they could do would make Toby better. This was the definition of torture: sitting and watching, waiting, unable to do a goddamn thing.

"Sean can you stop that?" Ellie was glaring at him.

He hadn't realized he'd been kicking the leg of the chair, but forcing his foot to stop was almost painful. He walked to the window. He turned and walked back to the door. He turned back to the window again.

"Can you do that somewhere else?" He was driving Ellie crazy.

"Where am I supposed to go?"

"Go home," she said. "Lie down. You look like shit."

Sean shook his head. "I've got to be here when Toby wakes up."

Without looking at them, the nurse said, "There are no signs anything is going to change soon."

"I'm here," Ellie said.

Sean shook his head. "No way. I'm not leaving."

"Bring back Teddy," Ellie said. "He needs Teddy."

Sean thought about it for a second. Toby loved that ratty bear. What if it would help? He could get Toby's bear and charge his phone. And maybe if he slept for a few hours and took a shower he could think straight.

He pulled on his coat. "I'll be back soon."

Before he was out the door, Ellie twisted to face him. "That was Toby's teacher?"

He nodded and she turned back to Toby. As soon as he'd slipped out the door, he broke into a run and didn't stop until he'd crossed the park and arrived at his apartment.

CHAPTER TWENTY

THE APARTMENT WAS GRAY AND STILL AND LIFELESS. WAY TOO QUIET. So much worse than it had been over Christmas. He flicked on the Wolverine lamp and sat on Toby's tangled dinosaur sheets. His chest ached thinking about all the times he'd yelled at Toby to make his bed. Making his bed was so unimportant, so meaningless. He swore to whomever you swear to that if given the chance, he'd never yell at Toby again. Not for anything.

He scooped up the teddy bear and stroked the fake, matted fur. He should bring Toby some pajamas and his toothbrush. He grabbed everything he thought Toby might want or need. Then he saw the Spiderman suitcase in the corner. If Toby woke up, *when* he woke up, he'd love seeing it in that drab, sterile room. But when Sean unzipped the suitcase, it wasn't empty. Dozens of letters filled it, each one folded in half and addressed to "Mommy." Sean slumped to the ground, dropping everything he'd gathered and stared at the pile of letters. He picked one up and opened it. "Dear Mommy," it said. "Today I drew a picture of you. You were in a car driving and there were mountains in back. I hope you call or send another post card. I miss you. Come home soon. Love, Toby xxxoo"

Toby had been writing Ellie every day and Sean hadn't even known. He could barely breathe as he picked up another one. "Dear Mommy, I made up a song for you today during music. It's in my head and I can sing it for you next time I see you."

The heat rose up through his chest, onto his tongue and the roof of his mouth. Tears blurred his vision and inhuman moans slipped from his body between gasps for breath. Every inch of him ached with grief. When the crying jag subsided, he sat paralyzed, staring at nothing. He finally climbed into Toby's bed with his computer. He typed "Methylphenidate and . . ." he held his breath. "Fatalities."

He scrolled through the first twenty of 40,600 results. Each article was more depressing than the next. There was no hard evidence that methylphenidate caused heart problems, but there were too many pieces of anecdotal evidence to discount. He closed the computer when he got to a site that blasted parents for poisoning the still-developing brains of their children with mind-altering drugs. He breathed in the smell of Toby's pillow and closed his eyes.

Sean woke from a black hole of sleep to his ringing phone. He sat up, disoriented, and looked around the room. A moment later, the reality of why he was here flooded him with a new wave of sorrow. His phone was charging in the kitchen. He ran for it.

"Ellie?" he said, flipping open the phone.

"Um . . ." It was a man's voice. "Toby missed tutoring yesterday." Noah. "I couldn't get through on your phone, like, all night. Is everything okay?"

Sean caught his breath. His heart pounded against his ribcage.

"No. Actually nothing's okay." He told Noah about Toby—about the diagnosis, the drugs, the hospital.

"Whoa, wait a minute," Noah said. "You put Toby on medication? Why the hell would you do that?"

The bottom fell out of his stomach. Why the hell *would* he do that? "I guess you don't think he needed it." Why hadn't he told Noah, asked his advice? He felt like an idiot.

"I wish you'd asked me, man. That's all. I wish you'd talked to me."

"Why are you saying it that way?"

"Let's just say—and this is off the record, not to be repeated to anyone, you understand?" He had a serious, un-Noah tone. "Do you?"

"Yeah, okay." Sean was getting impatient. "What is it?"

"Look, it's not my field of expertise or anything. But he seemed fine to me, perfectly fine."

Sean didn't need anyone else to tell him what a douche bag he'd been. He knew. "What's off the record?"

"I've seen this happen before. With Bradley. Other schools, too, but Bradley in particular. They do this. They make *suggestions*. They make threats. They don't leave parents much of a choice. Parents of boys, mostly."

Sean's heart rate sped up. "You're saying this happens . . . a lot?"

"I'm not saying anything. Because if a tutor in this city were to say anything about Bradley, that tutor would never get another referral from any private school ever again. But if I *were* to say something, I'd say that instead of changing the way they teach, schools go for the easy fix. What happened to Toby—it's not the first time this drugging-the-healthy-kid thing has backfired for them. I'd say they have a magic Bradley way of making their problems disappear."

"But why would they want to drug healthy kids?"

Silence. "Noah? Hello?"

"I'm here."

"Why?" The phone shook in his hand. "For better test scores?"

"I hope Toby gets better, man. He's an excellent kid." Noah paused. "I don't pray often. But I'll be praying for him."

CHAPTER TWENTY-ONE

Traffic clogged the Ninety-sixth Street transverse. Total standstill. Sean was trapped in the no-man's-land between Central Park West and Fifth Avenue with no forward motion, as some perky fake newscaster jabbered at him about the best cannoli in Staten Island. He stabbed at the power button on the TV screen until it went black. The quiet was almost worse. He tapped his thumb nervously on his thigh and clenched and unclenched his toes inside his shoes. He bit the inside of his lip and felt his blood pressure rise.

"Stop," he ordered, though the cab wasn't moving. "Here. I'll get out here." Sean rifled through his wallet, but it was empty.

"But," the driver protested. "We're not through the park yet. A few more minutes and we'll be—"

"Now," he said, desperately. "I need to get out."

The driver cut the meter and Sean poked at the screen to pay by credit card. Each time his fingers hit the wrong button his chest clenched a little more. When the Verifone machine couldn't read the strip on his card, he thought he might have a coronary. Somehow, he managed to execute the transaction and escape onto the narrow sidewalk that bordered the traffic.

Scenic paths threaded the snowy park above him. No one walked down here with the cars. He took a deep breath and coughed out a lung full of exhaust, then ran to Fifth Avenue, clutching the Spiderman suitcase to his chest. When he arrived at the hospital, he was out of breath and covered in sweat. While he waited for the elevator, he called Nicole to tell her what Noah had said. He needed legal advice and he wasn't going to talk to Ellie about any of this.

He and Ellie would have to talk at some point; there was no way around it. He would put it off as long as possible, obviously. Avoidance was not an adult choice, but it was all he could manage at the moment.

A few minutes later, he was pulling the Spiderman suitcase along the speckled linoleum floors of the PICU. The image of Toby's smiling face flicked through his mind. He knew he shouldn't wish it, shouldn't even think it. He'd jinx the whole thing. But it was too late. Even though he knew Ellie would have called if there'd been any change, he half believed that when he walked into the sterile hospital room, Toby would be propped up on pillows, sipping juice, telling knock-knock jokes. He wiped his palms on his pants.

He stopped just outside the door and listened. He waited to make sure it wasn't simply a lull between knock-knock jokes. Minutes passed. No jokes. No laughter. Nothing but the robotic beeps of machines telling him Toby was still hanging on.

When he walked in the room, Ellie was curled up against Toby, breathing him in. He knew it then: if anything was going to help Toby pull through this, it was that she was here. And if she could do that, well, who cared about the rest of it?

"There's something you need to see," he said to Ellie, and unzipped the suitcase. She looked at him skeptically, then climbed off Toby's bed to look.

Ellie read through the letters, stopping only to sob quietly until she could find the strength to read some more. Sean sketched Toby's hand, his cheek, the sheet draping over his chest. He and Ellie didn't speak for hours.

Finally, Ellie said, "I blame you for this. If he dies, I'll never get past it."

He clenched and unclenched his jaw. He would not take the bait. He was not going to fight with his estranged wife at Mount Sinai in front of their comatose son. She blamed him. So join the club.

"For the record," he said, "I'll never get past what you did to Toby, either."

A vertical crease materialized between her eyebrows and she screwed up her features, as if she had no idea what he was talking about. It took five full seconds before her face went slack. She bowed her head almost imperceptibly and nodded.

Neither said anything for a long time. "Oh my God, Sean. What if he dies?" He'd been so careful not to say the words. She started to shake, then put her head in her hands. As she sobbed, she rocked miserably back and forth. He hesitated. Just how mad was he? Could he really fight the Pavlovian response to comfort her? He just wasn't that much of a jerk. He put his arm around her. She was smaller, frailer than he'd remembered. They sat that way, watching Toby for a long time. When she'd cried herself out, she was exhausted and didn't seem to have any fight left in her. She blew her nose. "I don't know what I'll do if he . . ."

Sean cut her off. "Don't say it again, okay? Don't ever say it."

She nodded and wiped her nose as delicately as she could with the back of her hand. For the first time since she'd left, he actually felt sorry for her. No one on earth could understand what this was like for him. Except possibly Ellie. No matter what other shit had gone on between them, they were Toby's parents. They'd become Toby's parents in this very hospital eight years ago. He and Ellie had vowed to protect him, to love each other, to be a family.

"I've got to tell you something," he said, and forced himself to tell her about how the school had pressured him to give Toby the medication. He told her what Noah had said on the phone.

Ellie's nostrils flared and the tendons in her neck bulged. "The school didn't give him the drugs. You did." She let out a disgusted sigh. "This isn't the Grassy Knoll. It's a top-tier school—my alma mater, for God's sake. Half a dozen supreme court justices went there."

It was close to the speech he'd expected. "Forget it." Her condescension was the last thing he needed right now. "You're right and I'm always wrong."

He looked at her and tried to see the woman he'd married, but all he could see was an enemy.

"This is all your fault." She glared at him so hard it hurt.

"I'm not the one who wanted him at that fucking school," he yelled.

"Jesus Christ, you're such an infant."

"Fuck you, Ellie." It felt great to finally be able to yell at her. "Fuck you if you don't care why this happened and who did it to him."

"The only thing I want—and the only thing you should want," she hissed in a loud whisper, "is for Toby to come out of this fucking nightmare alive and healthy."

That's when he heard it. It was barely a murmur.

Ellie was too busy yelling at him to hear. She'd stopped only to suck in more breath. "And if you think that I'm—"

"Shh," he cut her off, and stared at Toby. It hadn't even been a sound. It was the start of a sound, combined with the faintest rustle of hospital sheets. Sean had almost missed it, with all the accusations they were hurling at each other. But in that room, where there had been no jumping on beds, no throwing of pillows, no noise or movement of any kind for almost four days, that rustle and beginning of a sound screamed of hope. He held his breath and listened harder.

Ellie, still animated from the fight, turned too. It may have been the only thing on earth that could make her drop an argument midstream. They stayed that way for a moment, frozen with anticipation and the terror that they hadn't heard what they'd wanted so badly to hear. Then they heard it again. The sound was a little louder this time. Toby was trying to say something, but it was as if his voice were stuck too far down in his throat.

Sean sprinted the four feet to Toby's side and grabbed his hand. Toby was moving, just a little, like he was disoriented after a deep sleep. Sean realized now that he'd been preparing himself for the real possibility that he might never see his son move again. He gasped out air as if he'd been holding his breath for days. Warm tears rushed from behind his eyes and blurred his vision. Ellie was there a heartbeat later, peppering Toby's head with kisses and thanking God. "The doctor," he said, hoping she'd volunteer to get him. He knew that nothing, not even the sensible idea of finding a doctor could force him to let Toby out of his sight right now. Ellie wasn't budging, so he reached for the buzzer and squeezed the button frantically.

The rest of the night was a blur of doctors, tests, and Toby's progressive recovery. By late morning, he was sitting up and drinking orange juice from a straw. Sean saw the color return to his cheeks. He finally saw the smile he'd been waiting for, filled with a hodgepodge of adult and baby teeth. Now that he looked so normal, it was hard to believe the last few days had ever happened.

"How do you feel?" the doctor asked.

Toby shrugged. "Good." It was so simple. So Toby. He was good. The doctors ordered endless diagnostic tests, which showed that Toby's brain was functioning normally. And he'd thought miracles were bullshit. They had him back. Still, there was something different about Toby. Every once in a while his son looked at him with the gaze of an old man, a look devoid of the sweetness and innocence of an eight-year-old. Toby napped throughout the day, and at dinnertime he asked for the Knicks scores. Sean climbed onto the bed and read him every sports page in every paper he could get his hands on. Halfway through the *Post's* game coverage, he noticed that Toby's eyes were closed.

He didn't know when it had happened, how it had happened, why it had happened. He should have been paying closer attention. How could he have had him and lost him again, just like that? His finger was on the call button before he realized Toby was only sleeping, his warm body curled next to Sean's, dreaming, resting, living. Nothing vegetative about him. Maybe when Toby woke up his eyes would be clear again and whatever he'd seen—whatever had happened to him over the past few days—would recede with time and be forgotten with the other devastating passages of his childhood, like toilet training and birth.

Over the course of the day, Toby's room filled with gifts. When Dick and Maureen returned from their cruise, they brought over a dozen silver balloons, and the school sent a huge basket of gourmet food from Dean and Deluca that Sean promptly deposited on the nurse's station. Cards, flowers, and stuffed animals arrived every half hour, it seemed. Sean wondered how the news had spread so fast. He'd snuck in a call to Jess, but other than Ellie's parents and Nicole, he hadn't told anybody. He hadn't wanted to waste time on the phone when he could be with his conscious, smiling son.

The doctor nodded as if he'd known all along that this was how it would turn out. "Children are resilient," he declared.

When he announced that Toby was going to be fine and could go home within the week, Ellie threw her arms around Sean's neck. "He's back," she sobbed. "He's going to be okay." Her wet cheek against his face, the feel of her hair, her smell—he'd wanted to forget those things, but there they were, as close as the breath on his neck. He squeezed her tightly. The near miss had left him weak, humbled, relieved. Clinging to her, he had the vivid realization that this was a second chance. He knew they should try to be a family again. He knew that if he didn't try, he would be fucking with some delicate balance of fate and luck and whatever powers existed beyond all that.

The fact that he didn't want to be with Ellie wasn't relevant at the moment. What was relevant—the only thing that mattered in fact—was that Toby was awake, alive, healthy.

"Mommy?" Toby had been watching them with a big smile on his face. "Are you coming home with us? To live?"

A smile melted onto Ellie's face. She turned to Sean. "Dad and I are going to have to talk about that."

CHAPTER TWENTY-TWO

TOBY STAYED AT THE HOSPITAL FOR FOUR MORE DAYS OF TESTS. When the doctors were satisfied that Toby was recovered, they discharged him with instructions to keep activity to a minimum. He'd been through the wringer and he was going to need lots of rest. No school, they said, until after spring break, and they wanted to monitor his heart for the next few months, just to make sure. They were being cautiously optimistic, but Sean could tell Toby was getting better every day.

On the cab ride home from the hospital, Toby sat between him and Ellie with a hand on each of their legs, oozing happiness.

"Toby needs someone to stay with him while you're at work," Ellie had whispered in the hallway outside Toby's room. "It should be me. Not some stranger."

"I don't want to get his hopes up," he said, though he knew Toby's hopes were already up.

"I don't want to leave him. I don't think I could do it."

"Okay", he said. "For a little while. Until he's stronger."

Ellie had reached for his hand and squeezed it. "Thank you."

When the taxi pulled up to their building, Sean lifted him onto his back. He knew Toby could walk into the building and up to their apartment. But why not give him a piggy back ride? Why not spoil him for the rest of his life?

"I'm taller than everybody," Toby announced. He felt lighter than Sean remembered, smaller. Ellie, who carried the balloons and flowers and cards from the hospital, smiled up at Toby dreamily, looking past Sean.

When they got out of the elevator, he dug into his pocket for the front door key, but Ellie beat him to it. "I've got mine." She jingled them and his throat constricted. Of course she had keys. She'd come back to shower and to leave her things. She opened the door—his door—and ushered them in. When she dumped all the stuff, she looked around and let out a satisfied sigh.

He let Toby slide down his back to the floor. "Good to be home?" Toby nodded happily and ran off toward his room. Which left Sean and Ellie alone. "So," he said.

"So." She smiled awkwardly. "I guess I'll—"

"What should we—" he said over her. "Oh. What were you—"

"Oh, nothing. I just . . ." She ran her eyes over the living room, lingering on the paintings. "I missed them. Especially the sunset."

It wasn't a sunset. It had started out as a sunset, but he'd worked over it fifteen times until it was an abstract expression of the moody internal landscape of their life together; dark and cloudy with deep, intense colors buried far beneath the surface.

"Whoa," Toby yelled from his room, and Sean froze.

A second later he was next to Toby. "Are you okay? Did something happen?"

"Look." Toby said, pointing up. The solar system—stars, planets, the whole thing—covered the ceiling.

Ellie peeked around the corner. "Like it?"

He nodded. "It's really cool."

"When did you . . . how . . . ?"

"Remember the night I came back to pick up some clothes for him? I just had the idea and went for it." She wrapped her arms around Toby. "Do you really like it?"

"It's perfect. Now the totem pole guys have something to look at when I'm asleep."

"I love you sweetie pie," she said. "I'm so glad you're home and well, and that we're here together."

It was pretty clear Toby was happy to have them all together, too. He took Monopoly off the shelf. "Can we?" he asked. "It's better with three people. I'll be the race car." He tried to stifle a yawn.

"We'll play tomorrow," Sean said. "Let's get you some food, then bedtime."

"Yeah, I'm hungry."

He loved the idea of feeding Toby. "Let's see what there is. Come on." But Ellie had beaten him to the kitchen.

"Can I have graham crackers?" Toby had already figured out Sean would never be able to say no to him again.

"Absolutely," he said. "For dessert."

"So what'll it be?" He clapped his hands together. "We can order. Anything you want. Ollie's? V & T's? Famiglia?"

Toby stared at the takeout menus Sean had fanned out on the counter and shrugged. "Can you make Arthur mac and cheese?"

"You sure?"

Toby nodded.

"Okay, coming up." He stepped toward the cabinet where Ellie was banging around reorganizing things. Ellie tried to move out of the way, but she must have thought he was going for the fridge and bumped him.

"Sorry," he said. He found a box of macaroni and cheese in the cupboard and held it up for approval.

Toby nodded vigorously.

Ellie was already filling up a pot with water. "I got it," she said with a smile.

He could get it. He'd gotten it without her for months. He *wanted* to get it. But making a scene over the mac and cheese would be infantile.

"Come on Tobe," he said. "I'll run you a bath."

"Can I have guys in the bath tonight?"

He wondered if all boys washed with their superhero collection or if this was unique to his comic-obsessed son. "As many as you want."

He didn't even yell at Toby when the warring defenders of truth and justice soaked the bathroom floor. Toby was home and happy. Nothing else mattered. He ate half his mac & cheese and announced he was tired.

Ellie tucked him into bed while Sean mopped up the bathwater.

Then it was Sean's turn. He pulled the covers tight around Toby and tucked them in just the way he liked. He focused on this happy scene, and tried not to dwell on how it would be when Toby was asleep and he and Ellie were alone.

"It's just like before." Toby closed his eyes, but the smile stayed.

Kids really couldn't tell. All you had to do was paste on a smile and they'd believe you were the happiest person alive. He wondered how long he and Ellie could keep it civil. He kissed Toby on the head. "Love you, Tobe," he said, and left the door ajar.

Ellie was trying to find room to unpack, but her old drawers were filled with brushes, charcoal and acrylic paint. One drawer was filled with sliced up photos of their life together.

"I'll go to the grocery store," she said.

"I can go."

"No, it's fine," she said. "I want to."

They were on their best behavior. It was nice. But he knew all that anger and resentment that had bubbled up at the hospital lay just beneath the surface. A scratch could set it free.

As soon as she was gone, he put on some music, lay on the couch, and checked his email. Not having to worry about being on his best behavior was a relief.

She was back half an hour later with bags of groceries containing what looked like a lifetime supply of lentils and tofu.

"I'm a vegan now," she said.

"Oh God, Ellie."

"I know you'll like it." She held up a steak. "But I got this for you, just in case."

"No, that's okay," he said. "I'll have whatever you're making."

As she cooked, the apartment filled with the unfamiliar smell of curry. It wasn't a bad smell, but his home no longer smelled or felt like his. "I know it's strange," she said, as she stirred enough lentils to feed a small Indian village. "We have to get used to each other again."

He'd just gotten used to being without her. To sleeping without her. He'd expected all out war, but she was more like the old Ellie than ever. He took a set of sheets from the linen closet and threw them on the coach. "You should take the bed."

"No, I'll sleep out here."

"I'm not going to let you sleep on the couch," he said. "I'm just not."

"Don't be silly, I'm fine on the—"

He shook his head. "I'm here."

"Okay," she said. "Thank you." She watched him throw the cushions on the floor. "You going back to work tomorrow?"

Small talk. It was brilliant. They could make small talk and ease into whatever it was they were doing. "I wish I didn't have to."

She stared at the cooking lentils like they were the most fascinating things in the universe. For two people who had everything to discuss, they seemed to have nothing to talk about.

"Staying home with Toby will be a treat," she said. "I really missed him."

Was she blaming *him* for that?

"And I'm glad I can help you out, too," she said. "I know this has all been hard on you."

Her lack of sarcasm was throwing him. "Um, thanks."

She grabbed the pot handle. "Fuck!" she yelled loudly, pulling her hand off the scalding pot. "Fuck! Fuck!" She ran her hand under cold water saying "Fuck."

As she cursed and yelled, his phone rang. He snatched it up and heard Cheryl's voice. She'd never called, and hearing the voice detached from the body was all wrong. "Jesus," she said. "Thank fucking Christ Toby is okay. How are you doing?"

"Good," he said. "Okay." Having Ellie in his kitchen cooking lentils was weird enough without Cheryl on the phone. He had to push the bathroom sex out of his head. "Thanks."

"I had no clue Toby was allergic," she went on. "Scary."

"Allergic?"

"I mean, it's a friggin' peanut—how can it poison so many kids? I can't even imagine what a hellish ordeal that must have been. God, I'm glad he's okay."

"What the hell are you talking about?"

"Shit, was that a secret? I thought—"

"Who said it was an allergy?" His voice rose unexpectedly.

"It went out in an email. Or maybe someone from the class told me. I can't remember. Why?"

While he was sitting in the hospital room wondering if Toby would live, the class parents were gossiping, speculating. It made his stomach turn. "Toby isn't allergic to nuts or anything else," he said. Ellie was watching him, trying to figure out who he was talking to.

"But—" Cheryl sounded confused. "So what happened?"

He inhaled deeply then let out a sigh. Why was he keeping this secret? Who was it helping? "I put him on Metattent Junior. For

ADD." Ellie glared. Obviously, this was not information she wanted spread around.

"Oh God," Cheryl said. "This was because of . . . that?"

"The school pushed me to have Toby evaluated. I don't think he even had ADD. I think this all happened for nothing."

Ellie was mouthing his name, pantomiming for him to put down the phone.

He turned his back to her. "Did they ever, you know, push you to evaluate Marcus?"

"Marcus is doing well in school. He's fine."

"So Shineman never, you know, suggested he might need to take medication."

"I told you, he's doing fine." Her tone was different. Tense. "Sorry, I just . . . I better help him with homework."

"I don't think I'm the only one they've pressured. I don't think Toby is the only non-ADD kid at Bradley on ADD medication."

He listened to the dead air. "But . . . most kids don't have that kind of reaction, right? It's unusual . . ."

"It's not a reaction. Or an allergy. The drugs affect the heart. It can happen to anyone. It happened to Toby and it's happened to other kids, too."

"Who? Who else did it happen to?"

"I don't know." He wished he could tell her what Noah had said. He wished he had more information. Most of all, he wished that he didn't sound paranoid and delusional. "But I have it from a good source."

"A doctor prescribed the drugs, right?"

"Yeah, but—"

"Don't blame yourself," she said. "You did what you thought was right."

"No, I didn't." She was missing the point. "I mean, the school pushed me. Hard."

"You wanted him to have every advantage," she said, then lowered her voice. "I get it."

"You put Marcus on it too, didn't you?"

She paused and he knew he was right. "I've got to help Marcus with—"

"I won't tell anyone," he sounded desperate. "Just tell me the truth."

"Coming sweetie," she yelled, ostensibly to Marcus. "Look, I've got to go. I'm here if you need me," she said, and hung up.

"Who was that?" Ellie asked. She'd set her mouth and was narrowing her eyes at him.

"Marcus's mom," he said, and shrugged. She'd wanted Marcus to have every advantage. And if everyone else in his class was on the stuff, he'd be at a disadvantage if he wasn't on it too. The cycle was vicious. And impossible to break.

"Cheryl?" Ellie practically recoiled when she said the name. "Why? Have Toby and Marcus become friends? Because that's hard to imagine."

"I don't know."

"And why are you telling her you put Toby on medication?" Ellie said, moving on to her real gripe. "That's none of her business. Or anyone's."

"She thought Toby had a peanut allergy."

"So?" She was incredulous.

"The school is trying to cover up what happened. I'm sure of it."

"What happened is that you put him on drugs that did this to him."

He imagined their future together as an endless loop of this same conversation. She wouldn't even contemplate the idea that Bradley had been the force behind all of this. He knew *he* was guilty. But so was Bradley. "So why is the school lying to parents about Toby?"

"Because, like I said before, it's nobody's fucking business what Toby was or wasn't on. Because everyone doesn't need to know." She shook her head tightly. "I'm sure Cheryl will have told everyone by tomorrow morning."

"Why are you so resistant to the idea that Bradley is trying to cover its own ass?"

"Do you really want to be *that* guy?" She looked deflated, disappointed, like he'd never learn. "You want to make this into a conspiracy? You want to accuse the most prestigious school in the country of some insane plot against children?" She took a breath, trying to defuse the last of her anger. Her hand found his chest. "I know this has been awful. Awful." She looked him in the eye. "We have him back now. Please Sean, let this go. Cheryl misunderstood. There's nothing malicious in that."

"But if the school is trying to cover it—"

"People make mistakes." She put her arms around him and lay her head on his chest. "I know I have."

This was as close to an apology as he was going to get from Ellie. He decided to take it. For Toby's sake. For his sanity over the next few weeks, or however long this temporary arrangement lasted. She was wrong about the school. But he didn't need to convince her of that right now.

CHAPTER TWENTY-THREE

On his first day back at *Buzz*, Sean was assigned a spread on cellulite of the stars. He'd posted paparazzi at every exclusive tropical resort he could think of with the singular assignment of snapping as many jiggling, puckering, dimpled A-list body parts as possible.

Rick was making his way toward Sean's desk holding two head-shots. "Nose and eyelids," he was saying like he'd discovered the secrets of the universe. He handed the photos to Sean.

"Mmm," he nodded, staring at Jessica Simpson's features. "Mmhmm." He knew Rick wanted to run a story about her "secret plastic surgery" that would quote doctors who had never treated Ms. Simpson, listing the numerous procedures she'd most likely had. They'd mark up the photos, circling the eyes and nose, and he was guessing the lips. They'd probably throw in liposuction for good measure. Their readers would lap it up.

Maybe if he sold enough work at the Burdot show he could finally quit *Buzz*. Start painting again for real. He'd spend his days at the studio. The turpentine and the heady smell of the oil paint were real for a moment. The fantasy was nice until he thought about what his life would look like now if he'd been uninsured when Toby collapsed. Even with insurance, he was swimming in hospital bills he couldn't pay. Of course he hated his job. Lots of people hated their jobs. That was just how life was.

He gave Rick a serious nod. "Let me see what I can come up with."

"Good to have you back." Rick clapped him on the bicep. "How's Toby doing?"

"He's great." Just being able to say it and mean it made all the other crap fall away.

He typed "Jessica Simpson and plastic surgery" into the Google search field and started his "research." When he thought he might crawl out of his skin, he typed "The Bradley School."

The conversation with Noah had been haunting him. He kept thinking about Shineman's hard sell and Dr. Altherra's certainty. And where were the Conners scales Altherra had promised to mail? Thousands of articles popped up on Google that called the school "elite" and "tony" and referred to the students as "privileged." He read about the exceptional education the children at Bradley received, the ever-increasing tuitions, the innovative teaching methods. But after forty-five minutes, he hadn't uncovered one incriminating piece of information. He was frustrated and disgusted with himself for wasting time.

As he was about to close Google, he noticed a story from the *Times* Science section that cited Calvin's death. "Deadly Allergies Responsible for Increasing Number of Fatalities in Children." Why hadn't he put this together before? His heart started to pound when he realized the Drakes might have answers. Either he was paranoid or he was right. Or both.

He tried to imagine what that visit would be like, the parent of the kid who lived sitting with the parents of the kid who died. It would be awful. But he sent an email anyway.

"Whatcha got?" For a big guy, Rick had an unsettling way of sneaking up behind you.

Sean hit a button on his computer and brought up the Jessica Simpson research. "I'm close," he said. "Give me another ten."

At five he hopped on the 6 train to the Upper East Side. When he got to the wood-paneled lobby of the Drakes' Park Avenue building, the doorman called upstairs and a moment later sent him to the private elevator that opened directly on to the penthouse. The Drake's Filipina housekeeper met him at the entrance. "Hello Mr. Sean. How is Toby?"

"Hi Divina. Toby's good. How are you doing?"

Divina twisted her mouth. "It's hard."

When Melanie saw him, she gave him a big smile before her face contorted into anguish. She covered her mouth with her hand. "I'm sorry, I'm . . ."

"No, don't be—" He hugged her tightly.

She held on to him until she pulled herself together, then stepped back and wiped her eyes. "I'm okay. I just get . . . you know."

Her emotions were so close to the surface he wasn't sure what to do with them. Or with himself. "Should I . . . do you want me to go?"

"No, I'm glad you're here. Come on," she said, leading him to the living room.

"Mr. Sean," Divina said. "May I hang your coat?"

"Oh . . ." He hesitated, then handed it to her. "Thanks."

He hadn't been here for years and found himself marveling at the skylights above the double-high ceilings. "The school told everyone to leave you alone." He sat in an upholstered armchair. "But I should have come sooner."

"You've had your share of shit recently," she said. Her eyes welled. "I'm so glad Toby is okay."

He nodded. "Me too." It came out barely a whisper.

"Can I get you some coffee?" He'd never thought of Melanie having a round face, but now, in comparison to just a few weeks before, her cheeks looked hollow, drawn. "I was just about to make some."

It was almost five-thirty. Coffee was the last thing he wanted. "Sure."

He watched Melanie disappear into the kitchen and his heart ached for her. The grief diet had left her frail and drawn. She was as wrecked from losing Calvin as he was overjoyed to have Toby back. How was she able to function at all, much less prepare coffee for him? He'd be curled up in a ball under the table if Toby had . . . he couldn't even think the word.

He looked around. The place was immaculate, a huge arrangement of fresh flowers at the entrance. He tried to imagine grieving in a place this tidy. The furniture, the lamps—even the knickknacks— were expensive and looked highly breakable. Nothing was out of place; there wasn't an errant newspaper or a stack of old *New Yorkers*, no sneakers by the door or pile of mail to sort through. Sitting still was too hard, so he took a tour of the Drakes' photos.

On the top shelf was a picture of baby Calvin buck naked on a sheepskin rug. It was only then that he realized Calvin had had those intense eyes from day one. In another, Calvin, maybe age six, smiled backstage with his sister and parents at *The Nutcracker* surrounded by sugarplum fairies. In another, Calvin shook hands with Mayor Bloomberg. He smiled proudly in a shot with his big sister at the Spring Fair. He recognized Calvin's Wolverine costume in a photo from Halloween just a few weeks before Sean found him on the stairs. Calvin's entire life was laid out in these photos. It was all in the past now, his history complete. He knew that someday he'd have photos of Toby at his prom, of Toby graduating from college, of Toby's wedding and of Toby playing with his own kids. Two weeks ago, none of that was a given. He could easily have been like the Drakes, stuck with the knowledge that there would never be any more photos, no more memories except for the ones already made. He had no doubt Melanie looked at these photos daily, agonizing over not having taken more, for not documenting every second of his life. He swallowed and tried to shake it off. Crying now was not an option.

He walked back to the bathroom to splash cold water on his face. The door to Calvin's room was shut. He wondered if they'd touched it since he died, if the bed was made, if the sheets had been washed. He guessed not. Next to it, Susannah's door was wide open. Her room jumped with polka dots of different sizes and colors. A stuffed gorilla rested on her pillow. Her Bradley soccer jersey hung on the wall above her bed. He turned to go but caught sight of a card on her desk. Written in crayon in careful eight-year-old handwriting: Happy Birthday to the Best Sister Ever.

"Cream or sugar?" Melanie called from the kitchen.

He rushed out of Susannah's room and into the living room. "Black's great," he said. He was nervous, guilty, and came in too close to the bookshelf. His arm brushed something heavy and, he was sure, expensive. He drew a sharp inhale as he heard the thing thud into a shiny trash can by his feet. He stooped to dig out a gold egg decorated with colorful enamel. He let out his breath slowly when he saw that it was in one piece, and placed it carefully back on the shelf.

Melanie emerged from the kitchen balancing a coffee pot and matching cups on a tray. As he sat opposite her, he could feel her misery hanging in the air. She put her coffee cup down without drinking and gave him a pained look. "How's Toby feeling?"

"Better. Much better." Chewing off his limbs would be more pleasant than this. "He misses Calvin. Lots."

Melanie pulled a tissue from her sleeve. "I know . . ." She blew her nose and wiped away some tears. "It's still so raw."

Divina emerged on cue from the kitchen and placed a new box of Kleenex on the side table next to Melanie and then slipped out again.

He took a sip of the coffee and put the cup next to a porcelain bowl filled with mixed nuts. He remembered the nuts from the last time he was here. They were a staple of the Drakes' décor. Did someone replenish the nuts, he wondered, or were these the same ones that had been here for years? The one thing he did know, however, was that if he'd had an ounce of doubt about his theory before, that was now gone.

"I have to ask you something."

She waited.

"Did Calvin really have a peanut allergy?"

She squeezed her eyes and nodded.

"Because Toby didn't have an allergy. His heart went haywire because of medication the school pushed me to give him. I thought . . . I thought maybe the same thing happened to Calvin."

Tears started to flow from her eyes. Melanie cried silently in her perfect living room. "Calvin had a peanut allergy." She shredded the tissue distractedly. "It only developed recently."

"If it was the medication, you can tell me."

"Susannah will be home soon," she said, standing. "I should . . ."

"Of course." He felt her close off abruptly, completely. She wasn't going to tell him anything. "Call me whenever you want." He meant it. He wanted to help her even though he knew he couldn't. "If there's anything I can do . . . if there's anything you want to talk about."

She nodded.

He left her in her beautiful apartment. When he got outside he felt a dismal rush of relief at being able to put some distance between himself and the oppressive sadness. Melanie would never be able to leave it behind. It would follow her wherever she went.

A couple of blocks later, he heard someone calling after him. It was a woman's voice. He stopped when he saw Divina running after him.

"Mr. Sean," she said, catching her breath.

"Did I leave something in the apartment?"

She shook her head quickly and glanced nervously behind her. "What? What's the matter?"

"For you," she said, pulling some crumpled papers from her pocket and putting them into his hand. He held two pieces of stationery that he realized were actually one piece that had been torn in half and balled up. "I found it in the trash. Maybe it will answer your questions."

He held the pieces next to each other, trying to read it, but it was difficult. ". . . I evaluated children in the private school system . . . His death worries me on many levels . . . evaluations often result in ADHD diagnoses . . . imperative that you get back to me . . ."

He looked at the return address. It was from someone named Hutch Garvey who lived at 203 Military Drive, Chesswick, Pennsylvania.

"She doesn't know I came after you," Divina said. "Okay?"

His heart pounded. "Thank you."

He hopped in the first taxi he saw and was home fifteen minutes later. He'd barely opened his front door when Toby ran at him, saying, "Dad, come see what I did!"

"How was work?" Ellie asked, in an uncharacteristic June Cleaver tone. "Good . . . okay," he said as Toby pulled him toward the bedroom.

Toby had created a tent by draping Buzz Lightyear sheets over the furniture. "Come into my fort," he said, and crawled in on his knees. Sean got down on all fours and crawled in, too. "We can look at comics," Toby said, propping himself on a pillow. He spread a pile over the rug and handed Sean a flashlight. "Or we could tell ghost stories."

"I love ghost stories," Sean said. "You sure you won't be too scared?"

"I'm not scared of anything."

He wondered if this were true after what Toby had gone through. He had no intention of finding out. "Let's read this one," he said, reaching for a *Green Hornet* special.

"Dinner's ready," Ellie called from the kitchen. "Veggie burger time!"

"Awww," Toby said. "Do we have to?"

"Wait here." He winked and crawled out.

Ellie had put the fake burgers at their places. Sean picked them up, pasting a smile over the grimace. "Let's all eat in the fort tonight."

"There's no food in the bedroom," she said. "It's the rule."

"Maybe it's time for a new rule." He forced another smile. "Toby will love it."

She was trying to go with it, but he could tell she was having a hard time. "Okay" she said. "Sure. You go ahead. I'll be there in a few minutes."

He crawled back into the fort carrying the burgers. "Dinner is served."

Toby looked skeptical. "We're not allowed to eat in the bedroom."

"New rule."

"Won't Mommy be mad?"

"She's coming too. In a minute."

A cloud of worry passed over his features. "You sure?"

Sean nodded and took a bite of the burger. It wasn't bad. "Mmm. Try it."

"I'm going to get Mommy first," he said, and darted out of the fort. He was back a moment later. "She's resting."

"She's asleep?"

Toby nodded.

Ellie had been napping a lot. It was all coming back to him, how she'd slept almost all the time last summer when she'd been depressed. "I don't think she slept well last night." He was good at making excuses for her.

They looked at comics while they ate in the fort, then Sean told a ghost story that ended up not being too scary, just in case. The icing on the cake was the Snickers bar he'd snuck in from the outside.

"Mom's been trying to give me this gross thing called scarab," Toby said, devouring the candy bar. "Why would she do that?"

"Carob," Sean said, gratified by Toby's smile, which was covered in chocolate. "And I have no idea."

When Toby fell asleep, Sean pulled a blanket over him, turned off his flashlight and crept out quietly. Ellie was asleep, fully clothed, on the bed, a trickle of drool at the corner of her mouth.

"Ellie," he whispered. "Ellie?" She was out cold.

I need to see you, he typed into his phone. *Can you meet me at the bar?*

When Jess wrote back saying she'd be there in ten, he scribbled a note on the back of an envelope, saying he was at the drug store. Ellie wouldn't wake up, but just in case. He grabbed his jacket and slipped out quietly.

The temperature outside had dropped. He sprinted through the whipping wind to Rite Aid for a tube of toothpaste he could use to provide an alibi. There was no reason he shouldn't be meeting Jess. Or maybe there was. It was a gray area he needed to think through. All he knew was that he missed Jess and she was the only person he could talk to.

She was grading math quizzes at the bar and when she saw him it was like a light switched on in her. He wondered if the bartender noticed that she was sort of glowing. But she caught herself and tamped it down.

"How's Toby?"

"Toby's good. He's great."

She smiled. "And everything else?"

Everything else had to mean Ellie. Him and Ellie. "Everything else is . . . complicated."

"Complicated." Her voice trailed off. "Back together?"

"No," he said. "Not back together." A smile twitched at the corners of her mouth. "We're together . . . as roommates," he said. "For now." He probably could have stopped, but he felt compelled to keep talking. "Toby needs his mom, and I have to work, so . . . it kind of made sense for everyone. On some level."

"That *is* complicated."

"I'm sleeping on the couch," he blurted out.

"As I recall, that couch is quite comfortable."

"It's much less comfortable without company."

He checked her ring finger. The miniscule thing was back on.

"What about you and the FedEx man?"

"Complicated."

"I guess it's none of my business."

"Not if you're a married man living with your wife."

"Come on, you're not really going to marry that guy," he said with a Tourette's-like lack of control.

She fixed him with her vapor-blue eyes and flashed him a half smile. "For the record, I've been looking for my own place."

"That's great," he said. "I mean, I'm sorry?" He had no idea what to make of the swarming bees ricocheting around his chest at the idea of Jess being unengaged. "You're still wearing the ring."

"Yeah," she said, tugging at it. "I have to tell Chris. He's going to be really pissed. So I've been kind of gathering my courage." She took another sip of her drink.

"Is that Scotch?"

"I thought that's what we drink here."

He flagged down the bartender and ordered one for himself.

He wondered if he'd figured into her decision to move out. "Have you found any apartments?"

"There's a place on 154th and Amsterdam that I can almost afford."

"That's kind of a sketchy neighborhood, isn't it?" He imagined her coming home late, getting ogled by the crack dealers. He didn't know if there actually were crack dealers, but there might be. And if there were, it would be dangerous.

"It seems okay." She shrugged. "Anything will be better than staying." She finished her drink, grimaced, then eyed the quizzes. "I should get back."

"Let me buy you another one."

"That would be one too many," she said. ""Besides, I should really . . ."

"Stay a little longer. I want to read you something." He'd taped the letter as best he could. "The Drakes received this in the mail."

She sat forward for a better view. "You were at the Drakes'?"

"Their cleaning lady gave it to me. Listen." He cleared his throat:

Dear Mr. and Mrs. Drake,

My name is Hutch Garvey. I'm a clinical psychiatrist who specializes in childhood ADHD. I evaluated children in the private school system for over twenty years and taught classes in early childhood development and the development of the adolescent mind at Teachers College. I've written several books on the subject of Attention Deficit.

I was terribly sorry when I heard about your son Calvin. His death worries me on many levels. For reasons I won't go into here, I am skeptical when I hear a student at a prestigious Manhattan school has died from a peanut allergy. Is it possible Calvin's death was a result of something else? In my years of experience, I know that Bradley wants the majority of its students to get evaluated and that those evaluations often result in ADHD diagnoses and medication. If this was the case, it's imperative that you get back to me as soon as possible. I will explain everything when we speak. Again, I'm sorry for your loss.

Sincerely, Hutch Garvey, M.D.

He looked up from the letter and Jess took it from him. She lingered over the return address. "Chesswick, Pennsylvania," she said. "When can we go?"

Saturday morning, he kissed Toby goodbye and slinked across the street to pick up his Zipcar. He'd told Ellie he was working on the Oscar edition. He couldn't recall ever having worked on a Saturday. Lying to Ellie made him queasy, but it was easier than having another fight about Bradley.

Sitting behind the wheel of the gray-blue Toyota Prius, he realized he hadn't been in a car in years, since he and Ellie used to drive up to Nantucket for the Fourth of July. He gripped the wheel firmly. It felt good. He could put his foot on the pedal and go anywhere, everywhere. A car was freedom. As he backed out he caught his reflection in the rearview mirror. His hair needed a trim and he noticed a few strands of gray at his temples. When had that happened?

He swung by D'Agostino where Jess was bouncing in place to keep warm. He pulled up, and she sprinted to the car and slid in next to him. She touched his leg. Kind of like a greeting. "Morning," she said. He could still feel her hand after she took it away. "So." Her gloves made a muffled sound as they clapped together. "Let's find Hutch Garvey."

The giddy energy of the treasure hunt pushed them forward through the tunnel and New Jersey and into Pennsylvania, but the mood turned somber when they arrived in Chesswick. They watched the post-industrial suburb of Philly slide by their windows. Each crappy, decrepit house was worse than the next.

Sean had researched Chesswick the night before: 20 percent unemployment with 25 percent of its residents living below the poverty level. He wasn't sure what he'd expected, but not this. He'd also Googled Garvey. It turned out Garvey hadn't just been a shrink, he was *the* kid shrink on the Upper West Side. Before he vanished a few years ago.

Soon, the neighborhood changed. Looking past the rust and rot, he realized the streets were wide and some of the houses were huge. Rich people had lived here once.

"Stop." Jess pointed to a sagging Victorian. "That's it."

They stared. The paint curled away from the wood and the second floor buckled. It looked unsafe. "That's his house?"

"That's what it says." She held up the envelope. "We should ring the bell."

They plodded down the path, which was covered in six inches of snow. When they reached the front door, he searched for the bell, but there wasn't one. No knocker either. He made a fist and pounded. When no one answered, he pounded again.

"I guess no one's home," Jess said.

He pounded one last time.

"Okay, okay." Whoever was inside did not sound happy about having visitors.

Jess stepped back and they both looked up and saw a figure staring down at them from a window. A minute later, the front door opened and a wiry middle-aged man stared out at them through intense eyes. A stubbly gray film coated his cheeks. "What?"

"Dr. Garvey? Hutch Garvey?" Sean asked. The guy wore khakis and a stretched out rugby shirt.

"I'm not buying anything," he said.

"I'm not selling anything."

Garvey squinted at him, then gave Jess a wary once-over.

"We'd like to talk to you," Sean said. "About Bradley."

Garvey licked his lips. "You're not screwing with me, are you? Because if you are, I'll have you arrested. I swear to—

"We're not screwing with you," Jess said.

A muscle pulsed over Garvey's right eye. "Who are you?"

"My son Toby is in the third grade at Bradley," Sean said. He touched Jess's shoulder. "This is his teacher." Garvey perked up. "Toby almost died because the school forced me to give him Metattent Junior. He didn't need it."

Garvey opened the door wider. "Come in."

Filing cabinets and accordian folders stuffed with newspaper clippings took the place of couches and chairs and coffee tables in the living room, making it look more like a storage facility than a home. Stacked at free wall space, piles of newspapers sat yellowing, waiting to be clipped. Sean caught a glimpse of an end table that had been pushed haphazardly into a corner. It was antique. Expensive looking. On it sat a framed photo of Garvey, a woman, and two kids on a big sailboat. They were smiling in the photo and Garvey looked healthy, not nervous and gray like he did now.

"I wasn't expecting company," Garvey mumbled, with a wave of his hand. "Come upstairs to my office."

They followed Garvey up the uneven steps of the old house. Crammed in among more filing cabinets in his office was a wide antique desk that he guessed had resided in a much larger room at some point in the past. "Sit, sit, please," Garvey said.

"That's quite a collection," Jess said, eyeing a shelf of Pez dispensers. Batman, Daffy, Spiderman, Fred Flintstone—he had them all. Dozens of them. Not only was it an impressive display, it was fun, colorful. The guy must have a sense of humor. One that wasn't in attendance today.

"It took me twenty-five years to find all those," he said. "The kids love it. *Loved* it." He clapped his hands. "So," Garvey said. "How did you find out about me?"

"The Drakes," Sean said. "Their cleaning lady found your note in their trash."

He sighed. "I'm afraid that's where the majority of my correspondence ends up. No one wants to listen to what I have to say."

"We do," Jess said. "What did you mean in your letter, about peanut allergies?"

Garvey blew air out his mouth, disgusted. "It's code, obviously. Think about it. When I was a kid, no one had peanut allergies. Okay, some kids did, obviously. Of course. But the numbers reported today? Come on."

"Code for what?"

He turned to Sean. "You came here because your child got sick from medicine he was taking. Unnecessary medicine. I agree. But it's much bigger than one or two children. It's happening all the time at these schools. I've been trying to expose this thing for years."

Sean swallowed, reminding himself to breathe.

"But every time a kid goes down, it's a peanut allergy, a bee sting, something, anything other than a reaction to the amphetamines or methylphenidates they've been given to make them zombies at school. And for some reason parents aren't coming forward." He scooted his chair closer, fixing Sean with a grateful expression. "Until now."

"Why not?"

"Stigma? Embarrassment? Fear?" Garvey shrugged. "Who knows?" He paused, gathering himself. "So Mr . . ."

"Call me Sean."

"Sean, tell me what happened to your son. And don't leave anything out."

Garvey scribbled in his notebook as Sean told him what had happened to Toby and what he suspected had happened to Calvin. He included what Noah had said, how the school had pressured him to get Toby evaluated and also about Dr. Altherra. He told Garvey how Melanie Drake had reacted when he asked about the medication.

"Okay," he said, finishing his notes. "Okay. I'm going to get you up to speed on the big picture."

"There's a big picture?" Jess asked.

"You have to know the background before you can understand any of what's going on now. I read everything," he said, making a sweeping gesture to all the cabinets and newspapers and clippings surrounding them, *"everything* written about it."

"Why haven't you called the police if you know Bradley's doing this?"

"Been there, done that," he said. "It's not that easy. These schools, Bradley especially, have an uncanny way of making you look like an escapee from the loony bin if you say anything negative about them. Look at me. My family wants nothing to do with me. My practice, my reputation—all ruined. I'm banished to fucking Chesswick, PA." He shook his head. "Hard evidence. That's what I'm working on. You can help me with this."

"But," Sean said, suddenly worried about what he was getting into. "What do you mean?"

"First, you have to listen. I'm going to give you the background, the history, the numbers. Numbers never lie."

"I don't need to know the history. I know my son didn't have ADHD. If you're telling me this has happened before, that's enough for me."

"Sean, please. Pay attention." Garvey raised his eyebrows in warning. "Attention Deficit and hyperactivity are serious problems from which fewer than 2 percent of the population suffers." He snorted. "The ADHD being diagnosed today is a disorder fabricated by big pharmaceutical companies to make big, and I mean *huge* money on drug sales."

"It's not *fabricated*," Jess said. "I've taught kids who've literally jumped off walls and bitten other students."

"That's right," Garvey said. "Two percent of the population will benefit from being medicated. No doubt about it. Don't believe me. Go read the *Journal of Attention Disorders* from June. Penn State psychologists tested 1,473 children and concluded children are no more or less inattentive and impulsive today than in 1983. And yet ADD is spreading across the country like a virus with diagnoses increasing 5.5 percent every single year. There's no more actual ADD now than there was thirty years ago, but doctors wrote 51.5 million prescriptions for attention drugs in 2010, up 83 percent from 2006." He sat back, as if exhausted, and let his hands fall into his lap. "Boys are not docile, easily-controllable, or easily teachable like some girls. It takes more energy, more creativity, more patience to teach boys."

"True," Jess said. "It's harder."

"And when teachers aren't interested in teaching, that shows up on the report cards and in conferences. Parents get scared their kids are going to fail out of school. Cue the school psychologist, psycho-pharmacologist, pharmacist, and the problem is solved. Easy, right?" The guy was amped up, but he seemed to know his facts. "It's why 13.2 percent of all boys have been diagnosed at some point with ADHD as opposed to 5.6 percent of girls."

The numbers were staggering. He didn't know what to ask first. "So that's what Bradley does?" Sean asked. "That's what happened to Toby?"

"That would be my theory," he said. "Even with what you've just told me, I don't know all the particulars of what happened to Toby, but I do know the history."

He cleared his throat and sat back in his chair professorially. "Ritalin has been around for half a century. In 1957, the Ciba Pharmaceutical Company started marketing it to people with chronic fatigue and psychosis associated with depression and narcolepsy. Sure, why not? It's speed! It'll pep up anyone, right?" He let out a bitter laugh. "They've marketed it over the years for a host of other problems. Starting in the sixties, they used it on kids with hyperkinetic syndrome, which later became ADD. Now there's ADHD, Attention Deficit Hyperactivity Disorder. Pretty much the same thing, just add some hyperness to the mix. You get the idea. In the seventies and eighties, drug companies developed a handful of other stimulants to treat it. But medicating children back then was still unusual, except in extreme cases where children were a danger to themselves and others." Garvey's eyes widened in anticipation of his next point. "But then, suddenly—and no one knows why—between 1991 and 1999, sales of Ritalin and other ADD medications increased five hundred percent in the U.S. alone." He paused for emphasis. "Five *hundred* percent. The United States, land of the free, consumes 85 percent of the world's production of Ritalin. The numbers are insane. In 2010, attention drugs were a 7.42 billion-dollar industry." Garvey opened a medical journal to a flagged page and read aloud: "Shire Pharmaceuticals sold 759 million dollar's worth of Adderall XR, that's extended release, in 2004 alone." He snapped the journal closed. "And that's not even mentioning Concerta, Strattera, Provigil, or the original Metattent—which, by the way never did much business until the Junior version came out."

"That's what Toby was taking," Sean confirmed.

"Ah yes." Garvey shook his head to convey something between awe and disgust. "The kiddie pill. Right. Other than some food coloring to make them look more like Flintstones vitamins, the active ingredients are virtually the same as in Ritalin."

"But . . ." What was the right question? "Then why did . . . Didn't the FDA have to . . ."

"Puh-leese," Garvey spat out. "The FDA. I'm talking about the medication wars, Sean. Have you heard anything I've said? Do you think a little obstacle like the Federal Drug Administration is going to get in the way of big pharma?"

"Isn't that the point?" Jess said.

Garvey sighed. "Listen carefully. I'm only going to do this once." He settled into the leather chair and continued the lecture. "When the original Metattent hit the market in 1980, sales never even came close to Ritalin's. The public had no reason to choose it over Ritalin, since it was—for all intents and purposes—the same drug. Plus, don't forget, Ritalin had the name recognition and the decades of quote-unquote *evidence* of its safety. Klovis, the company that made Metattent, they knew they had to get a gimmick, and fast. They got the gimmick, all right. But it wasn't fast. It took twenty years to get Metattent Junior approved. And by 2004, when it hit the market, there were more children taking ADD medication than ever. Parents were now on the Internet reading all sorts of horror stories about Ritalin, talking to each other online about it. And voilà. Suddenly, their doctors present them with a new drug specifically designed to put all those fears to rest. Supply and demand. It's basic economics. And with roughly two million children a *month* taking drugs for ADD in this country, there was plenty of demand. The first year Metattent Junior was on the market, it outsold Ritalin for the pre-teen set two to one. The second year, it made $980 million, three times what it cost to develop the drug."

"Jesus," Jess said.

"Jesus is right. The number of kids taking these drugs is growing every year. It was up to 5.1 percent of all children—*all children*—in 2008." Garvey formed a prayer with his fingers, which poked into his lips as he thought. "Okay, look. I had a patient a few years back. Like your son, he was also a Bradley student who had been pressured into getting a psychiatric evaluation. The child is diagnosed with ADD. Of course he is. The school knows exactly what to put on those forms to get back the diagnosis. Hard for parents to argue with an inattentive-type ADD diagnosis when the symptoms only surface at school. Brilliant, right?"

A wave of shame passed through Sean. He fidgeted in his seat.

"My patient's parents were uncomfortable with the idea of medication. They didn't believe the ten-minute session with the therapist could possibly have led to such a serious diagnosis. Especially since their son had behaved beautifully with the shrink. Ultimately, they were willing to accept the diagnosis, but not the medication. They'd done their research and decided they wanted to try a more holistic approach, adding more iron and fish oil to his diet. They wanted to try behavior modification and biofeedback. But Bradley refused to forgo the meds. The child could have all the fish oil he wanted, they said, but he'd already fallen too far behind and the holistic treatment would take too long. They gave this family an ultimatum: drugs or another school."

Sean was afraid to ask. "What'd they choose?"

"The child is still at Bradley is all I'll say. Great kid, too. Smart."

"I should talk to them," he said, reaching for a pen on the desk. "What's their name?"

Garvey slammed his palm on a stack of papers, causing them to slide to the ground. "Can't do it. Wish I could. Doctor-patient stuff."

He swiveled his chair and plucked a report from a pile. It was bound in a plastic cover, like a school report. He handed it to Sean. "My book." It was titled *ADHD: Focus on the Lie.*

Sean thumbed through it.

"It's eighteen dollars."

He laughed, but it turned out Garvey was dead serious. He dug into his pockets and held out a twenty.

Garvey snatched it, opened his wallet, and handed him back two dollars. "I've seen half-a-dozen kids from Bradley," he said. "All pretty much the same story. I'm determined to nail that godforsaken school. I brought three lawsuits against them. Lack of evidence," he spat out. "And then they made sure I'd never be able to speak up again."

"What do you mean?"

"I had a two-book deal with Simon & Schuster. Signed the contract and everything. Then all of a sudden they pulled out. Seems they got a mysterious phone call from a VIP who didn't like what the book implied."

"How do you know it was Bradley?"

"Because I mentioned them in chapter two," he said. "And they made it clear they weren't happy about it. No other house will touch me. I've been bound and gagged. Silenced."

"I guess you can do that when you have a hundred million dollar endowment," Jess said.

"And alumni who run the world," Sean added.

"Exactly." Garvey sighed. "Look what they did to that nice Bradley teacher who wrote an Op-Ed about boys in the classroom and the use of medication. The Op-Ed never ran, and now she's blacklisted."

"What?" Jess asked.

"She wasn't *really* a sexual offender, you know," Garvey said. "But if a school accuses a teacher of *being* a sexual offender, well, it'll appear on every background check that's done on her. That would just about ruin a career, wouldn't you say?"

"Sexual offender?" he asked. "Who?"

"Debbie Martin. Nice lady. Excellent teacher." Garvey shook his head sadly. "She tried to fight them, but that only made it worse. Her life is in the toilet right now. She's living under an assumed name somewhere outside of Baltimore, I believe. Copyediting electronics manuals."

"Debbie Martin was Toby's teacher." He looked at Jess. "The one you replaced."

"Well be careful, young lady. The last thing you want is to have a Bradley bull's-eye on your forehead. Trust me."

He watched Jess chew the inside of her lip. She looked paler than when they'd walked in, and he knew it was time to get her out of there. He stood and held out his hand to Garvey. "Thanks for your time," he said. "I'll be in touch."

"For your own sake I wouldn't recommend it." Garvey followed them down the stairs and opened the front door. "Sean," he said, as they turned to walk down the snowy path. "I don't know what your plans are for your son, but I would get him out of that school as soon as humanly possible."

They drove in silence. He pictured all the ways Bradley could ruin Toby's life if Sean tried to press charges against the school. How they could take it out on Jess.

"That was . . . not what I was expecting." She eyed the Blue Moon Diner coming up on their left. Checked curtains hung in the windows and it had a breakfast-all-day look.

"Hungry?"

"Starving."

He pulled the car into the parking lot.

"Grilled cheese with bacon may be the only thing that will get me through the rest of this day," she said.

His stomach growled thinking about bacon. He wondered if Ellie would smell it on his breath. He turned off the car, but neither made a move to get out. She stared out the window at the chipped lettering on the front of the Blue Moon motel that joined the diner.

"That teacher," she said, staring at her hands. "Debbie Martin. Do you think the school really did that to her?"

"He was pretty convincing."

"He was, wasn't he?" Her chest rose and fell.

"Did you tell anyone about coming here?"

She shook her head.

"Good." He rested his hand on hers. She grabbed it and held on. He slid his free hand up her arm and pulled her toward him, wrapping both his arms around her. "They won't find out." Her hair smelled faintly of apricots.

He felt her breath change, felt her hands in his hair. All he could think about was her naked body, how it would look, how it would feel. The car was way too cramped for what needed to happen next. "Screw the bacon," he said, catching his breath. "Let's get a room."

Inside, the front desk was abandoned. A sign directed them to ring the buzzer. While he waited for the ancient man to shuffle out from the back, he thought about what kind of men checked into cheap motel rooms with women who weren't their wives. It sounded awful when he thought of it that way. He wasn't some cheating husband and this wasn't some woman who wasn't his wife.

"We'd like a room."

"Cash or credit?" the man asked.

He hadn't thought this through. "Cash," he said, guiltily. He handed the man five twenties he'd taken out of the bank the night before for gas and emergencies. Jess shook her head subtly, like she couldn't believe they were doing this.

The man handed him a single key that dangled from a gouged rectangle of blue plastic. "Number 14."

Jess squeezed his hand as they walked down the narrow hallway in silence. He jiggled the lock until it unlatched. The room was small and the stain on the carpet looked like Texas.

"You take me to the nicest places," she said, examining a plastic cup sealed in plastic wrap.

"I wouldn't touch anything if I were you."

She folded her arms around him. "Nothing?"

"Let me rephrase that." He kissed her. "Don't touch anything but me." Soon he didn't even notice the cheesy posters of the beach at sunset or the weird chemical smell. It was just him and Jess in the queen-size bed, the polyester comforter thrown across the room and the sheets tangled around their feet.

The room was no longer cold. The windows were fogged over and he couldn't tell whose sweat was whose. When Jess caught her breath she spoke, but not directly to him. "Why doesn't this feel wrong? You're married. I seem to keep forgetting that fact."

"It sounds so lurid when you say it that way."

"Isn't it?"

"No." He kissed her. "Not to me."

She rolled onto her side to face him. "We could be biased." He traced the curve from her shoulder down to the valley of her waist and up again. The line was smooth and sloping. Perfect.

She opened her eyes and looked into his. "I keep hearing my mother's voice," she said, "saying not to get involved with a married man."

He nodded. It was good advice. "I don't know if you want to hear this, but I think you should know that Ellie and I," he winced—it was awful saying Ellie's name while he was in bed with Jess. "We haven't been together, like this, since before she left. Way before."

She nodded, thinking.

"Too much information?"

"I'm trying to decide whether that fact makes this more or less lurid."

"Can we pick a different word?"

"Sleazy?"

He rested his hand on her thigh. It was warm and smooth. "If your mother knew how I felt about you, she might be okay with it."

She allowed a half smile. "Okay, let's hear it."

His palm tingled where it came in contact with her skin. "When I touch you everything makes sense. I don't want to be with anyone else. Just you."

"But . . . you're living with your wife."

There was no arguing with this fact, even though it was a fact he desperately wanted to change. "Yeah."

"It's not good."

"I guess you need to hear about what's going on, or not going on, between me and . . . Toby's mom."

"Talk."

"I don't even like thinking about her when I'm with you, much less talking . . ."

She laid her hand on his cheek, which had the effect of making him want to tell her anything, everything. "Talk."

"When I go home now and Ellie's there I can't breathe. Everything about it is wrong. I told you this before, and it's still true. The arrangement is all about Toby." He thought about how much the divorce was going to hurt Toby, about how hard it was going to be to tear their family apart. It would be painful and expensive and worth every cent when his life was his again.

"Maybe you should try to work it out. For Toby."

"You'd be more convincing if you were wearing clothes."

"True," she shrugged. "Still . . ."

"I don't want to try." He wanted to put the Ellie chapter far behind him. "She's not who I want." As he said it, he wanted Jess again.

She reached for him, like she knew. "So what's the plan? What's going to make my mother stop nagging me from the Other Side?"

"Tell her Ellie is my roommate. That it won't be this way for much longer."

"Hmm," she said. "The old 'I'll leave my wife for you' line. This is exactly the kind of thing my mother's voice is talking about."

"Tell her I've never been as happy as I am right now. With you. Never."

The smile stayed on her lips as they found his. She scooted her body closer until their skin was touching. "I bet you say that to all the women you take to sleazy motel rooms in the middle of the afternoon."

"Actually, that's true."

When he thought about it later, he couldn't remember how they started making love again or when they fell asleep. When they woke up to Sean's phone, the room had gone dark. By the time he found the phone, Ellie's call had gone to voice mail. He didn't need to listen to it, and there was no way he was going to call back from here.

Jess rolled toward him, curling her front along the length of his back. "Shower time," she said. He turned to watch her silhouette walk away from him.

He could have slept another hour at least, but he followed her, the idea of a steamy shower leading him on. Inside the bright green bathroom, those thoughts evaporated. Jess watched water trickle from the showerhead that was clogged with rust and gook. A permanent brown ring tattooed the tub.

"I don't think I can do it," she said.

"Plan B," he said, grabbing a washcloth from the plastic bar. "Sponge bath." He filled the sink and plunged it in. He twisted out the water, then ran the hot cloth around her neck, down her shoulders, under her breasts.

"There's nothing wrong with Plan B," she said, turning so he could get her back. When she had been thoroughly wiped down, she took the cloth from him and immersed it in the hot water. "Your turn." She covered his face with it, swept it around his shoulders and down his stomach. She circled around and swept up his back with her face inches from his.

"Plan B." He kissed her, since her mouth was right there. "Works for me."

Later, he watched her pull on her panties, then step into her jeans and button them. He helped her fasten her bra and ran his hands along her back and down her hips. It was impossible not to touch her. For a moment, he forgot about his real life, where Ellie would be waiting for him.

He usually hated traffic, but not tonight. Tonight it meant more time with Jess. It wasn't guilt exactly, that he was feeling. Or maybe it was. Lying was never good. He wasn't a liar. He wasn't good at it, for one thing. In his head, he played out scenarios where he told Ellie she had to leave. Would she be surprised or did she already know? And how would they tell Toby? He predicted crying. Lots of it. From all of them.

Three hours later, he stood in front of his apartment door trying to force his pulse to slow down. He couldn't help feeling like a cheating husband coming home to his wife. But he wasn't cheating, he reminded himself. He was in love. Ellie had left *him* and this marriage was all just pretend. At least he hadn't picked up flowers. According to every movie he'd seen, cheating husbands brought home flowers. She would have known instantly where he'd been and what he'd been doing.

Inside, Ellie was scurrying around clearing surfaces. Anger usually accompanied her manic cleaning episodes and he felt it radiating

ACCELERATED

off her now. He thought he might vomit. If he did, maybe he could claim illness and go to bed.

"Hi," he said, trying to sound cheerful. "What's going on?"

"Did you get my message?" Ellie's tone was clipped, tight. Like it got when her parents came over. Then he remembered: her parents were coming over. They'd invited themselves for dinner, complaining they'd only seen Toby once since he'd been released from the hospital. They required "quality time with the family." Which meant he wouldn't have to confront Ellie. At least not right away. He relaxed a little.

"I . . . bad reception."

"You're so late," she said, continuing to straighten.

"Minor disaster at the office," he said, feeling the lie catch in his throat. "We lost a story and I had to pull something together quickly."

She looked at him and frowned. "Where are the flowers?"

"What?"

"The flowers. For the table."

He couldn't win. "I can get some now."

"No, never mind," she said. He could tell she was trying not to be annoyed. "It doesn't matter. Why don't you put out some cheese and crackers?"

He emptied some Triscuits and cheddar onto a plate and examined two decent bottles of wine Ellie had left on the counter. Through the open kitchen wall he watched her like he had for years. He recognized the dress, which she must have dug out of the closet. It was cut lower than he remembered and it actually showed a lot of cleavage. The pile of magazines she'd just made slid off the table and she let out a frustrated groan. She sunk onto the couch, defeated. "I am so not in the mood for this."

He let out the breath he'd been holding. "Tell me about it. Let's keep it short."

She was nodding. "They just want to see that Toby's okay. That we're okay."

He swallowed. Should he remind her they were not okay? That this was all for show?

"After they spend some time with Toby, we can say we're meeting friends for dinner."

"We're not meeting friends for dinner," Toby said, walking into the living room.

"Just don't mention that, okay?" he said, scooping up Toby. "I missed you today."

"Where were you?"

"I had lots of work to do." He felt lightheaded from all the lying. How did people live this way?

When the doorbell rang, Toby hopped up, opened the door, and gave Maureen and Dick a genuine smile. "Hi Grandma. Hi Grandpa."

Their faces melted. "Oh my lovely boy," Maureen exclaimed. "You look wonderful. Healthy." She wrapped her arms around him and hugged him gently, like she was afraid he might break.

"What a handsome young man," Dick agreed, shaking his hand. "Very impressive." For Ellie's parents this was an outpouring of emotion.

Toby smiled self-consciously. "We have snacks."

Maureen was easily charmed by her grandson. "For us? You shouldn't have."

"Hi Mom and Dad." Ellie hugged her parents. "Come on in."

Sean grabbed a wine bottle from the kitchen and twirled it nervously. "Hey." Sean gave a wave. "Great to see you. How about some wine?"

"Here." Dick plucked the corkscrew from the coffee table. "Let me." He popped the cork and poured. Sean handed the glasses around.

"Ellie, honey," Maureen said examining her glass. "Didn't you get a nice set of crystal for your wedding?"

Ellie ignored the comment. "We're glad you could come over," she said and put a hand on Sean's leg, like they were a real We. She took a sip of wine. He saw her recoil ever so slightly and put down the glass. He wondered if the wine had turned or if it had been crappy to begin with. Either way, bad wine wasn't going to go over well with Ellie's parents. He took a sip to see how bad it was. He took another. He didn't know much about wine, but it tasted fine to him. He checked Dick's glass, which was almost empty.

"You don't like it?" he whispered to Ellie.

She shook her head. "You can have mine." It was not like Ellie to pass up wine or anything that might numb her to a visit with her parents.

"Next time we'll cook for you," she went on. "But we're seeing old friends tonight for dinner." She was good. He almost believed her. He almost believed they were a We.

Dick poured himself another. Maybe Ellie wasn't drinking because of the health kick or maybe she was coming down with something. She'd been sleeping so much. He found himself staring at her chest. It wasn't just the dress. Ellie's boobs were bigger, he was sure of it.

Panic flashed through him when he put it together. His eyes went to her belly. She didn't look pregnant. But she was breaking out. She always had perfect skin. Except when she was pregnant.

Maureen was saying something, but he couldn't focus. He was doing math. Forget the fact the doctors said it wasn't possible. She had to be pregnant. But they hadn't even had sex since she'd come back. How long had it been since she left?

"Dick and I are planning a golf vacation in Palm Springs," Maureen repeated cheerfully. "We'll be going for ten days at the end of the month."

Dick smiled.

"You should all come with us!" Maureen said. "We'll have a family vacation!" She was excited as the idea formed. "Remember when we went to Bermuda when you were a teenager and we swam with the dolphins?" she asked Ellie.

Ellie smiled and reached for the wine, but then reconsidered. "The doctors want to make sure Toby is okay to travel. As soon as we get the go-ahead, we might go on our own vacation," she vamped. "Just the three of us."

He counted on his fingers: September, October, November, December, January. Could she be almost six months pregnant? He couldn't think straight. He began to sweat, but made sure to keep Ellie in his peripheral vision, looking for evidence to prove he was wrong. He tried to get a better view of her stomach.

"Oh, that sounds lovely." Maureen smiled at the idea of their happy family. "Doesn't it Dick?"

"I've got to hand it to you," Dick said, shaking his head like he couldn't believe it. "You two really came back from the edge of the abyss. Most people can't do that." He raised his glass and drank to them.

Ellie reached for Sean's hand and his entire life flashed before his eyes.

"Toby, I'm going to teach you how to play golf this summer," Dick announced.

"Okay," Toby said. "That sounds cool."

"I'll get you some clubs and we'll go out to Wapatuck. This summer it's you and me on the course."

Another baby would mean he'd be trapped with Ellie, with a baby, with a life he didn't want. His pulse quickened. Didn't anybody else notice the room was stultifying?

"Why don't we all play Sorry?" Toby said, carrying over the box.

"What a wonderful idea," Maureen said.

Dick raised his empty glass. "Is there more wine?"

Ellie hopped up to get it, and Toby slid into her seat.

"Move over, Grandma." Maureen scooted over and shifted uncomfortably. She reached behind the pillow and pulled out the foreign object that had been bothering her: a balled-up sheet.

Maureen raised her eyebrows accusingly.

"Sorry 'bout that." Sean took the sheet and shoved it under his chair.

Ellie was back with the wine. "So," she said, nervously. "Who wants more?"

"That's a funny place for a sheet."

"This is like my dad's bed." Toby rolled the dice. "I go first."

Maureen turned to Ellie. "He's sleeping on the couch?"

"Mom," Ellie said. "It's really not a big deal."

She pressed her lips. Toby handed her the dice and she rolled them without another word.

After the game, Ellie said they had to get going.

"Oh," Maureen said, disappointed.

"Let's do it again soon," Dick said. He looked more than ready to go.

"Next time I'm sure it'll be longer," Maureen said.

"Dad, can I ring the bell for Grandma and Grandpa?" Toby was shoving his feet into his slippers.

"Sure, I'll come with you."

"I'll start cleaning up," Ellie said, and kissed her mother and father. "See you soon."

When they'd successfully deposited Dick and Maureen in the elevator and returned to the apartment, the cheese plate and wine glasses hadn't been touched. Ellie was nowhere to be found. The bedroom door was closed. He peeked in and saw Ellie napping. Again.

She used to nap all the time when she'd been pregnant with Toby. He began to pace the length of the living room. On his second or fifth or tenth lap, he stopped. The baby wasn't his. Obviously. He was sleeping with someone else; why wouldn't she be? A jolt of something like jealousy shot unexpectedly through him.

Toby looked up from the floor where he was playing with a rubber band he'd found down there. "Why are you doing that, Dad?"

"Doing what?"

Toby rolled his eyes. "Never mind." He sat up. "What's for dinner? I'm hungry."

There was no way he could cook now. He wasn't sure he was even capable of boiling water for pasta. "Chicken fingers?"

"Yes!" Toby exclaimed.

Sean dialed the Metro Diner. When the food arrived twenty minutes later, he took the top off the plastic container and brought it to the table.

"Can I have one?" he asked, lifting one from the box.

"Okay," Toby said, grudgingly. "One."

Ellie was not waking up. It was the longest nap ever. A pregnancy nap. He gnawed on the chicken finger. Maybe the baby was his after all. It was possible. And if it was, what would that mean for them? For *him*? He didn't remember what to do with a baby. It would be years before a baby could talk or walk or even eat real food. There would be years of changing diapers.

"Dad, leave some for me." Toby moved the last three pieces onto his napkin.

"What?"

"You're eating them all," he said, accusingly. "And they're my favorite."

"I know," he said, ashamed that he'd scarfed his child's dinner. "They were your first favorite food."

"Can we watch me in the movie?"

In her Super Mom phase, Ellie had burned their home movies onto discs that stayed in a file box on a high shelf in the kitchen. "Why not?" It would give him something to focus on other than the end of life as he knew it. He climbed on the counter to reach the box, then flipped through the volumes of their life until he found the one Toby wanted to see.

He opened the disc on his computer. The first entry showed Toby, wailing at his third birthday party.

"Why am I crying?"

"You got a blue balloon." Sean smiled, remembering the crisis. "You wanted the pink one."

Toby's eyes widened and then pinched into a frown. "But pink is a girl color."

Sean shrugged. "You wanted pink." He fast-forwarded to Toby in water wings, held afloat in the ocean by Ellie in a bikini he hadn't seen in years. He wondered when she'd stopped wearing bikinis. She was smiling, encouraging Toby to kick. He wondered when she'd stopped being happy.

Finally, he found Toby's favorite part, his moment at the Metro Diner. The Toby on the screen had rounder, less defined features. His limbs hadn't unfurled yet. In only a matter of years, Toby had changed dramatically. "Chicken fingers are my first favorite food," three-year-old Toby announced to the camera, with a hint of a lisp he'd lost long ago. He took a bite. "Delectable."

"You and Mommy look different," he said, watching.

Younger, was what Sean had been thinking. They looked open, happy, in sync. They looked like they were in love. He tried, but couldn't remember who had filmed them that day.

Ellie finally emerged from the bedroom in sweats, squinting at the light.

"That was a long nap." Sean checked obsessively for signs of pregnancy through the sweats.

She nodded groggily and sat next to Toby to watch the familiar clip, a wan smile on her face. "Look at you." She kissed the side of Toby's head. "You were so little!"

Toby rested his head against Ellie's shoulder.

"Come on, sweetie," she said. "Let's get you to bed."

He followed Ellie toward his room, then twisted back around. "After Mom puts me to bed, can you read to me?"

"You bet," Sean said, wondering if Ellie had been hurt that he'd been chosen as designated reader.

A few minutes later, he settled in next to Toby to read, but Ellie didn't leave. Instead, she curled up at the bottom of the bed and listened. He couldn't remember the last time the three of them had been on a bed together like this, and it felt familiar, warm, confusing.

After Toby had been tucked in and kissed and tucked in again, Sean followed Ellie into his bedroom.

"Ellie." He sat on his bed.

The fact that he'd come in the bedroom wasn't lost on Ellie. She looked worried. "What's wrong?"

There was really no leading into it well. "Are you pregnant?"

"I knew I shouldn't have worn that dress. It made my boobs look huge."

He could hardly breathe. "So you are?"

She sat next to him heavily. "I'm not," she said. "I gained some weight. It always goes straight to my boobs. You know that."

He wasn't sure if he did know that. Or if he believed her. "But you're tired, you didn't like the wine. Your skin . . ."

She touched her chin where she was breaking out. Her eyes flitted away from his to the other side of the room. "I took a test yesterday."

"A pregnancy test?"

"No, a driving test." The sarcasm was fleeting. "Yes, a pregnancy test."

"And . . ." He held his breath.

She shook her head, a little sadly. "Not pregnant."

"But . . . the naps. The wine . . ."

She looked him in the eye now. "Definitely not pregnant." She paused, as if deciding whether to add more. "I was . . . I was late so I thought maybe . . . but a few hours after I took the test I got my period. So I'm definitely, you know, not . . . pregnant."

A rush of relief was quickly followed by the realization that she was testing to see if she was pregnant with some other guy's baby. His initial reaction had been knee-jerk jealousy, but now all he felt was a current of sorrow somewhere deep inside him. None of it was reasonable. But there it was.

She smiled but not because she was happy. "That would be pretty ironic, wouldn't it? If I were pregnant?"

"That's not the word I would have picked."

"Yeah, more like tragic."

There was nothing to say for what felt like a long time. "I remember that day in the Metro Diner like it was yesterday," she said, her face softening at the memory. "We always did make the best of naptime."

At the mention of naptime, it all came back to him: They'd had two hours of hot afternoon sex before taking Toby to the diner that day. "We certainly did."

She reached out and rested her hand on his chest. "I think about you," she said. "About us."

"Me too," he said, but instantly regretted it.

In slow motion, she took his face in her hands and kissed him on the mouth. Gently, testing the waters, seeing how he would react. He thought about pulling away, telling her to stop, but his body was switching on and he wanted her, suddenly and completely. He reached for the side of her waist and pulled her toward him.

She was pulling his shirt over his head, kissing his shoulders, his chest. His body surprised him by responding the way it always had. Her mouth tasted familiar—sweet and salty at the same time. He tugged her hair away from her face the way she liked and she moaned a little. Her neck was warm and she smelled like the ocean, which brought back Ellie in the bikini. He wanted that Ellie again and held on tightly. She was holding on tightly, too. When he pulled off her sweatshirt, he took a moment to admire his wife. He knew her body inside and out. He couldn't have imagined that she could still excite him this way. He pulled off her sweatpants and she glowed in the moonlight. He leaned in to kiss her again, but Ellie had another idea.

She pushed him back on the bed and ran her hands down his stomach, then unbuttoned his fly and worked off his jeans and his boxers. Before launching into her trademark move, she gave him a look that could have preceded jumping out of an airplane.

When he'd first encountered it, the move had seemed impossible. It was nothing short of awe-inspiring. And after more than a decade, he still wasn't sure exactly how she created the swirling effect. He peeked from his prone position and watched her head bob up and down and from side to side between his legs. Watching her used to excite him. Now he studied her with the interest of an academic researching a paper. He lay back and stared at the ceiling, wondering what the hell he was doing.

The excitement from a few minutes before had drained away. His body was on autopilot. He knew all the steps by heart. After she completed the virtuoso performance, she'd expect him to return the favor before they'd be allowed to move on to the main event. He wondered if all couples who'd been together a long time had checklist sex. He tried to imagine checklist sex with Jess but it was impossible. He kept drifting back to the Blue Moon motel. There had been nothing rote about what had happened there. He needed to stop comparing the two separate events, which, unfortunately, were separated by a very small window. It was a mess he'd single-handedly created. One more to add to his growing collection.

He decided he had to see it through, now that they'd made it this far. The truth was, he could do this in his sleep. He had on many occasions.

He was close, though he knew there were more steps to check off. Before the next sixty seconds were up, she'd pull back and it would be his turn. But he didn't want to go down on her. He'd made the commitment to have sex, but hadn't agreed to follow the steps. He wouldn't do it. He couldn't. She traveled back up on cue and he reached between her legs and found the spot. She moaned and gripped his arms the way she always had. Desire, love, intimacy—those things had nothing to do with what was happening, he realized now. He had to end this sooner rather than later. Ellie lay back, ready for him to follow protocol. She pulled him toward her, but the last thing he wanted to do now was kiss her. How could she not know that?

Instead, he rolled her over on her stomach and pulled up her hips, figuring he could get the job done most quickly this way. She let out a groan. He knew she didn't like this position. *I like looking you in the eye,* she used to say. He tried to remove himself from the reality of what his body was doing. This was just a dream, one he wanted to wake up from soon. When she grabbed his balls, he knew she wanted it over too. All it took was a few strategic yanks for the whole God-awful experiment to be over. The results were conclusive.

Ellie pulled the covers over herself and they lay awkwardly next to each other. He wanted to explain, but there was no good way to do it. "I . . . ," he started. "We need to . . ."

"You don't have to say anything," Ellie offered.

"I do. I have to say something." He took a deep breath and let it out slowly. "Ellie . . ." He propped himself up to look at her. "We can't be married anymore. I don't want to be married anymore."

She nodded and tears welled behind her eyes.

He thought about putting his arm around her, but didn't. "It'll be better for both of us."

"I just . . . I wanted us to be okay. For Toby."

"He'll be fine," Sean said. He would make sure of it.

"Toby would have been the happiest kid in the world." She wiped her eyes with the heel of her hand. "If we could have stayed together."

"He can still be happy," he said, quietly. "He has two parents who love him." The unspoken truth was that they no longer loved *each other.* He felt a deep, unshakable sadness at the finality of it.

"Poor Toby," she said, her voice cracking.

It was unbearable to think about the pain he was about to inflict on his son. "Kids get through these things," he said, knowing this had to be true. "We'll be there for him."

The words hung between them in the quiet room.

"So . . ." She was trying to pull herself together. "What do we do now?"

CHAPTER TWENTY-FOUR

SHE PACKED A BAG THAT NIGHT AND IN THE MORNING SHE KNELT in front of Toby. He'd grown since the last time she perched in front of him like this, and now she was eye level with his shoulder. "I'm going away for a while," she said. "To Montauk."

"No!" Toby threw his arms around her. "Don't go, Mommy." He held on tightly. "Stay."

Tears filled Ellie's eyes. "I promise I won't leave again like I did last time. Not ever. Your dad and I have to figure out how it's going to work. But I'm going to see you very soon. Promise. And I'll call you tonight." She kissed him on the head. "Love you forever."

After she disappeared down the hallway, Toby kicked around the apartment morosely for half an hour.

"It's going to be better this time," Sean said. "Way better. You'll see."

"I miss her."

"I know." All Sean had wanted was to be free from Ellie, but now that she was gone, he and Toby had to remember how to be here without her. They'd done it once. They could do it again. "Want to go to the park?"

Toby shrugged. "Nah."

"Monopoly?"

He shook his head.

"Ice skating?"

Toby must have smelled his desperation. "Video arcade?" A smile spread across his formerly glum face. How could Sean refuse that smile? The kid was a born negotiator.

"Get your shoes." Toby jumped up before Sean could change his mind.

By that night, they were back in a groove. Just the two of them. He reclaimed his bedroom and lay back on the bed where he'd been with Ellie the night before. A younger version of himself would have considered last night a conquest, or at least a release. But now he only felt sad, guilty, and a little dirty. He changed the sheets and pillow cases—anything that still smelled like Ellie. Finally, he climbed into his bed alone and realized it was even more comfortable than he'd remembered. The only thing that would make it perfect would be to have Jess next to him. Or underneath. No, on top. He opened his laptop. *Tell your mother's voice she can stop worrying now.*

After he sent the email, he tried to figure out logistics for the next day. Maureen had said she wanted quality time with Toby. It looked like she was going to get it. On the phone, he explained that Ellie had to go out of town for a few days. She could tell her mother what she wanted. He wasn't going to be the bearer of this news.

When she came over the next morning, Maureen brought baking pans and flour. Did she really think he didn't have any at the apartment? "We're going to have a fun day," she told Toby. "I'm so glad your dad called me."

"Thanks for being here, Maureen," Sean said, meaning it. He scooped up Toby, suddenly hating the idea of leaving him. "Love you Tobe. I miss you already."

Toby rolled his eyes but continued to smile. "Have a good day at work, Dad."

Toby was fine. Things were good. So why did leaving for work make his heart ache?

In the lobby, Manny was pointing madly at the mailboxes. "Mail!" he said. "Lots of mail!"

He hadn't checked his mail in days. Maybe a week. Mail had sunk to the bottom of his priority list. "Here you go." Manny handed him a thick stack that had been rubber banded together.

He plopped down on one of the red leather chairs no one ever sat on and pulled over the trashcan. He dumped every catalog and flyer and coupon packet and made a stack of bills. When he saw the envelope from Dr. Altherra, he froze. Time rewound to the moment he found her last envelope in the mail. The moment that had set the whole awful chain of events in motion. The moment he wished he could delete from his life. A sick feeling spread through him.

He ripped it open and read the note, which was scrawled in loopy handwriting.

> *Dear Sean,*
>
> *Please find two sets of Conners scales. One from before we administered medication, and one from the week before Toby went to the hospital. I hope this helps give you some peace as to the decision you made. I'm so glad Toby has pulled through this ordeal. He is such a lovely child.*
> *Warmly,*
> *Dr. Angela Altherra*

He scanned the pages, but none of it made sense. He forced himself to slow down and read every word. His head spun with the wrongness of it. The pages described another child, a boisterous troublemaker who couldn't follow directions or give coherent answers to questions because he was so distracted. Worst of all, the most damning report had been written by Jess. Even Shineman wouldn't write something as boldly false as this. Jess was just like the rest of them after all. She'd been lying to him this whole time. *She'd* done this to Toby. Less than twenty-four hours ago he'd been sponging off her breasts, thinking that he wanted to do this every day of his life. He was an idiot. She was a traitor, out for herself, her job.

He fumbled for his phone and left a desperate message for Angela Altherra. She called him back less than a minute later.

"This isn't Toby," he screamed at her, holding the pages lamely up to the phone. "It's all untrue."

"It's always a shock for parents of ADHD children to read a report by the child's teachers," she said. "I can't tell you how many times I get that reaction. I always make sure to get at least three separate teachers to fill out the forms, just to make sure I'm getting the full picture."

"Jess Harper, his teacher, told me she thought Toby was fine. That he might not have needed the drugs at all," he said.

"Well that's not what her report says."

"What if the report is wrong?"

"Sean, you have to stop thinking this way. It's not helpful."

"If these reports are wrong, the diagnosis is wrong," he was practically shouting. Manny raised his eyebrows from across the room. "True or false?"

"Sean, the Conners scales are only part of the—"

"Will you answer the goddamn question? If these reports didn't show ADD behavior you would never have prescribed those drugs."

She hesitated. "In this case, I guess I'd say that was true, but—"

He snapped the phone shut and ran to Broadway to hail a cab.

CHAPTER TWENTY-FIVE

IF HE HADN'T BEEN SO FURIOUS WITH JESS, WALKING INTO BRADLEY again might have been more emotionally fraught. But now his vision blurred with rage. Why had he trusted her? She was a Bradley teacher. He should have known better. The more he knew about this place, the more he believed it was pure evil.

He sprinted up the curved staircase two steps at a time until he reached Toby's old classroom. He watched Jess for a moment through a rectangle of glass in the door. He barged in as she was writing equations on the board. "I need to talk to you."

Jess and the kids all turned to stare at him. Shock was the first thing he saw in her eyes. Then annoyance. "I'm teaching class," she said, stating the obvious, but he didn't budge. Then he saw fear. "Is everything okay? Did something happen?"

"I need to talk to you. Now." She tensed at the coldness in his voice.

She turned to the kids. "Miss Bix will finish the lesson." The assistant teacher took her place at the board and Jess came into the hallway, shutting the door behind her.

"What happened? Is Toby okay?"

"You tell me." He shoved the papers in her face and she backed away from the force of it. "Did you really think I wasn't going to find out?"

"Shh. They can hear everything." She led him to a dark class-room, flicked on the light and closed the door after them. "Find out what?" She was trying to keep her voice down, even in here. "Why are you acting so weird?"

He shook the papers in front of her until she took them and started to read. "What is this?" She scanned the page and her eyes landed on her signature. "This is not . . ." She read on. "I never . . ." She flipped through to the end. "What is this? Where'd you get it?"

Fear twisted through him. "From the doctor."

"I didn't write this," she said. The color had gone out of her face.

"But . . . what do you mean? It's your signature."

"Why would I lie to you?"

She wouldn't lie to him. He knew it then. "Oh God," he said. The wall of anger inside him cracked and the room started to reel.

"Look, I'll prove it." She grabbed a pencil from a découpaged coffee can on the desk.

"No, you don't need to—"

But she was already signing her name on a scrap of red construc-tion paper. She held it up against the signature on the bottom of the Conners scale.

The one on the form was too careful, too studied. She hadn't rec-ommended medication for Toby. "So who signed this? And why?"

"This is a nightmare," she said, "Do I need a lawyer? I think I need a lawyer."

"I don't know," he said, trying to imagine all the ways something like this could implicate Jess. "Yeah, probably."

She clenched the forged document and raced out of the room. "Come on." He ran to keep up as she sped down the stairs to the basement level. They passed the art room, the nurse's office, and the gym.

"Where are we going?" he asked. But she was already knocking on Shineman's door.

"Bev," she said, banging. "Aunt Bev." When there was no answer, she looked at her watch. "Everyone's in assembly."

"So we'll wait."

She shook her head. "No, you should go." She pushed at his chest, but not hard. "It'll be better."

"No way." He wanted to see Shineman, wanted to shake her. Make her explain.

"If I talk to her alone, she might tell me what's going on. If you're there . . ." She grimaced. "It's not going to work."

He imagined seeing Shineman and his chest tightened. "Maybe you're right," he said. He let Jess walk him toward the staircase. "Call me as soon as you talk to her."

"Promise," she said. "And then you can tell me why I should tell my mother's voice to stop worrying. I got your email."

"A lot has changed in the past two days. Come over tonight and I'll tell you everything."

But Jess was looking past him and he could see her wheels turning. "What's the matter?" He turned and realized they were standing in front of the nurse's office. The door was open.

"The nurse," she said, holding up the Conners scale. "I wonder if she keeps copies of these in her office."

"We have all the proof we need. It's in your hand."

"But what if my signature is forged on other Conners scales, too? What if other parents put their kids on drugs because they thought I told them to?" She wrung her hands, then moved around him toward the nurse's office. He followed her into the tidy room where Jess was already behind the desk opening and closing drawers.

He looked around and saw an exam table, a few chairs, a desk— but no filing cabinets. "What about in there?" He gestured to the walk-in closet.

She pushed open the door, peered in, and looked from left to right with a puzzled expression. As it hit her, her eyes and mouth opened in horror.

"What," he said. "What is it?" Standing next to her a moment later, he stared into the room, which was lined floor to ceiling with dozens and dozens of shelves filled with prescription bottles. He'd never seen so many pills. He reached for the light switch.

Jess grabbed his hand and shook her head. She opened her cell phone and shined the blue light on the pill bottles. He opened his phone, too, for more light, and started reading the labels. "Ritalin 10 mg. Take two pills by mouth every four hours as needed." He picked up another: "Metattent Junior, 10 mg." He grabbed another handful. Almost every vial contained medication for Attention Deficit—Metattent Junior, but also Ritalin and Adderall, Adderall XR, generic methylphenidate and dexadrine. He even found a few bottles of Wellbutrin. "Jesus Christ," he said. He did a rough count: ten, twenty, thirty, forty per shelf. "There are hundreds of bottles here."

"It's way too many," she said, staring. "I've been paying attention, looking for signs that my kids are on this stuff. And they're there. In a few kids. But this . . . this makes it look like the entire student body is taking pills."

He thought he'd feel better knowing he'd been right about Bradley. But he felt sick. His hand trembled as he reached for the bottles on the shelf reserved for Jess's class. He grabbed a handful and read the labels: they were prescribed for Dylan, Alexis, and Marcus, each by a different doctor. Cheryl had lied to him, but he knew that already. Like so many other parents here, she'd been pressured into giving her child an edge in the competitive arena of the Bradley lower school.

Giving your child Ritalin wasn't like signing him or her up for tutoring or occupational therapy or sight training. Of course parents would talk to their close friends about it, but for the most part, the topic was still taboo, something Bradley mothers were not going to chitchat about over soy lattes at Le Pain Quotidien. The school had counted on that. He was sure of it. He leaned against the door frame, hit by the enormity of what he was staring at. He reached for more bottles to see who else had been diagnosed.

Jess was reading labels, too, as many as she could grab. "Oh my God," she gasped. "This is a nightmare. All these kids . . . all their parents. And if they're being diagnosed by forged question-naires . . ." She had a wild look in her eyes as she started dialing her phone.

"Whoa, wait," he said. "What are you doing?"

"The police. I'm calling the police."

"Wait," he said. "Let me think."

She glared at him. "Think about what? The school is . . . this is . . ." She was shaking, trying to find the words.

"Let's be smart," he said. "Think about Debbie Martin. We need evidence."

"Evidence?" She held her arms open and took it all in again. "What do you call this?"

"Do you know what kind of lawyers a place like Bradley has?"

"We can take the bottles," she said. "For proof."

He wondered how many bottles he could shove in his jeans pockets. It wasn't an efficient plan. "Even if we take some of the pills, it's still not going to—I'm not sure that will prove . . ." His mind raced. "The really creepy thing, the thing that will get people's attention is the pharmacy we're staring at right now." He looked at the phone in his hand, switched it to camera mode and snapped a series of photos of the closet. When Jess caught on, she held a few of the bottles up close, so the labels would be legible.

After they'd documented the discovery, she slumped against the wall. "What am I going to do? I can't . . . I can't keep working here."

"Get out of your contract. Come up with an excuse. Anything— a family crisis, an illness. And I'll call Nicole, see if there's anyone she trusts in Child Services. We'll go through channels. We'll do this right."

Footsteps clattered in the hallway and they swiveled toward the sound.

"Assembly's over," Jess said, shoving the pills back on the shelf clumsily. He tried to straighten them as best he could. "Let's get out of here."

His heart was pounding so loudly he wondered if Jess could hear it. They ducked out of the closet and Sean left the door slightly ajar, hoping it was close to the way they'd found it. Before they had a chance to escape, Astrid lumbered into the room and glared at them. "What are you doing in here?"

Jess froze for what seemed like an eternity. There had to be a believable excuse. His mind was blank. He swallowed hard.

Then he realized that not only was he still a parent at the school, he was the parent of a kid who'd been sick. Very sick. It suddenly occurred to him that it was weird that he hadn't been in before. He turned to Jess as casually as he could. "Thanks for bringing me down here," he said. "I always get lost in the basement."

Jess tried to smile. "Sure," she said stiffly.

"I know you probably need to get back to the kids."

"Right, I . . ." Jess turned to leave. "I hope . . . Toby feels better," she said, and darted down the hall.

He focused his attention on Astrid again. Her face was stone. "I wanted to talk to you about Toby," he started. "You know, about his condition. And what I should do."

If Astrid was buying any of this, her expression wasn't showing it. All he could do was keep going. "So . . . the doctors say Toby should rest," he said. "For now. They . . . they want to monitor his heart periodically." He swallowed. He was not doing well. "I . . . value your professional opinion. I mean, you know kids . . . and the school . . . better than anyone at that hospital. You might know better . . . about, you know, when would be right for him to come back." He would never in a million years let Toby set foot in this place again. He hoped she couldn't see it in his eyes. He looked away.

She looked him up and down suspiciously, and then, miraculously, softened. She nodded slowly, which made her chins jiggle. "You were smart to come by," she said. "Parents don't usually talk to me, and I do have insights to this place that the doctors don't have." She gestured for him to sit. He sat on a wooden chair and she waddled around behind her desk. "Here's what I'd tell you. Give Toby some time. Don't rush it. Once he comes back, it's hard to take it easy. He'll be swept up into the daily routine and he won't want to slow down. I'd keep him home until after spring break, at the very least."

He pretended to listen, to care what this crazy drug-pushing nurse had to say.

"Just make sure his teacher sends the homework home every week so he doesn't fall behind."

"Okay," he said, getting up. "Thanks. Thanks for your suggestion. I think it's a good one." He looked at his watch. "Wow, it's late. I better . . . I better get to work." He waved and made a quick exit.

Outside, he raced down the street, his mind reeling, when his foot slid on a patch of ice. He flailed, frictionless, for what seemed like an eternity, before he finally, miraculously, regained his footing. Being out of control for a few moments had been terrifying, but, he realized, not at all unfamiliar. He startled at his phone vibrating in his back pocket.

"Where the hell are you?" Rick shouted in his ear a moment later.

"I'm . . . I had an emergency."

"Jesus," he said, losing the bluster. "Is it Toby? What happened?

"No, it's . . . Toby's okay. I'm just getting in the subway. I'll be there in—"

"I'm in a meeting," Rick bellowed. "One you're supposed to be running."

"Ten minutes," he said, hanging up and waving down a taxi. As he hopped inside, his phone rang again and he flipped it open. "I'm in a cab now."

"Sean." He knew the voice, but it took a second to register. Walt. "Did I catch you at a bad time?"

"I'm just on my way to work."

"Go, go. I was just calling to tell you I heard about what happened to Toby. I'm glad he's okay. You must be . . . Jesus, I can't even imagine."

"Thanks. Thanks a lot."

"Hey," he said. "If you're free Sunday we could use you in the game."

Basketball was the last thing he wanted to think about. "Yeah," he said. "I'm probably not going to make it this week."

"I know you've got a lot on your plate. I bet you'll be happy when your son's back at school."

The sound that came out of his mouth started as a laugh but ended up more of an accusatory groan.

"What?" Walt sounded legitimately baffled.

"Nothing," he said. He was furious, but there was no reason to be taking it out on Walt. "I should . . . I've got to go."

"Sure. Don't want to keep you."

"Hold on—" he said, realizing that he had a Bradley Board member—and probably soon-to-be Chairman of the Board of Trustees—on the phone. "Walt?"

"Holding on," he said.

"I just came from Bradley," he blurted. "The nurse's office." He didn't know how to start. "It's filled with prescription bottles. Tons of kids at Bradley are taking drugs for ADD."

"Whoa, slow down. Start from the beginning and tell me what happened."

"Okay." He tried to slow down. Walt didn't know any of this, he reminded himself. He needed to walk him through. "I ended up giving Toby Metattent," he said. "It gave him an arrhythmia, which sent him into the coma." The more clinically he described it, the easier it was to say out loud, as if he were talking about someone else's horror story.

"Jesus, Sean." Walt exhaled into the receiver. "Jesus."

"I was just in the nurse's office at school. She has a closet packed with bottles of ADD medication."

Walt was listening, waiting. "That's where it would be, I'm assuming."

"Walt, Toby's teacher questionnaire was forged; the one that helped diagnose him."

"Forged?" Walt sounded dubious. "Sean, my heart goes out to you. But who would do that? Really. Who?"

"That's where I thought you could help. If the school is trying to get parents to put their kids on these drugs . . . I mean if it happened to Toby, then why wouldn't it have happened with other kids too?"

"If what you're saying is true . . ." He stopped. "Well, we need to find out if it's true. That's the first step. I hope you're wrong, Sean—that it's just a misunderstanding. Because if you're not . . ."

"What would your first step be? If you were me?"

He listened to Walt thinking. "Come to lunch today at the Yale Club," he said, finally. "I'm meeting Bruce Daniels there at one. I can give him the basics of what you told me, if you're okay with that. Maybe he can do some digging this morning and the three of us can sit down and figure out what the hell is going on."

He took a minute to try to imagine Headmaster Daniels eating lunch anywhere other than the Bradley dining room. He considered Walt's proposal. The headmaster ran the school. He could push Bradley to stop medicating kids. Unless he was the one who pushed *for* medication. Unless he was the one forging the documents. "I don't know."

"We've got to nail this thing head-on," Walt said. "I've known Bruce twenty years. He's a good guy. He'll know better than anyone what's going on over there—and if he doesn't, he's in the best position to figure it out."

The Yale Club wasn't far from the *Buzz* offices, and Sean slipped out at lunch unnoticed. He'd passed the blue and white banner countless times, but he'd never given the Yale Club any thought until the moment he turned into the revolving door and stood in the lobby, face to face with two uniformed doormen.

"Sir, may I help you?" one of them asked from behind a podium.

"I'm meeting someone, thanks," he said, checking out the somber portraits of old white men in academic robes.

"The Yale Club has a no-jeans policy." He said. "I'm sorry."

"Seriously?" He couldn't help the smirk. "They're just pants."

"House rule." The apologetic tone meant he wasn't budging. "There's nothing I can do."

"I have an important meeting." A few captains of industry seated in upholstered armchairs pulled their heads out of their *Wall Street Journals* to see what the ruckus was about. "I don't see what my pants have to do with anything."

"Please keep your voice down, sir," scolded the first doorman. "We didn't make the rule."

Walt jogged down the staircase, his slate blue suit pants rising and falling, exposing tactful black socks and dress shoes. It was the first time he'd seen Walt in anything but jeans.

"It's all right, Alberto. We can make an exception this time." He flashed his winning smile. "Won't happen again."

Alberto cowed. "Yes Mr. Renard," he said and stepped down.

Walt placed a hand on Sean's back and led him up to the fifth floor dining room. They navigated a sea of more white men with white hair sitting at tables covered with white tablecloths. Bruce Daniels was already seated at a table and stood when he saw them. He shook Sean's hand and held his gaze to show he understood this was serious. "I'm glad you brought me in on this."

Walt gestured to a buffet at the far end of the room. "Why don't we grab some food, then we can get down to business."

Food was the last thing on Sean's mind, but he trailed Walt, piling lamb chops and asparagus and fettucini carbonara onto his plate.

When they were seated again, an ancient waiter teetered over. "We have a lovely new Bordeaux in the cellar. Should I have Marco bring it up?"

"Not today," Walt said. "Thanks Bobby."

When the waiter had moved on, Daniels put down his knife and wiped his mouth. "Walt's filled me in," he started. "And I can imagine how upset you must be. Especially after everything you've been through the past few months." He placed his napkin back in his lap. "How is Toby? I've heard he's making excellent progress."

"He is. Thanks." Thanking Daniels was the opposite of what he wanted to do. "Bruce, I saw the pill bottles in the nurse's office."

"When you say pill bottles—"

"Hundreds of them. And the kids are being diagnosed by forged teacher evaluations. Why would the school want all their students on speed?"

"Obviously that's the last thing any school would want. Medication is an extremely serious thing and needs to be treated as such. I understand why you're upset. What you saw . . ." Daniels nodded, like he really did understand. "And bottom line is, you're right. There are a lot of kids at Bradley who are taking medication. First, you have to realize that the national average is up to—"

He felt his blood pressure rising. "Do not try to explain this away with national statistics. I know the statistics. And I know what I saw."

"Look, all I'm saying is 10 percent is a big number," Daniels said. "Not necessarily because more children have ADD than they used to—although you do know that television, advertising, and video games have all been proven to lower the attention span of children— but because doctors have better tools to diagnose them."

"And I'm telling you in Toby's case, and probably in the case of a lot of the other kids, those *tools* are forged," Sean said. "It looked like every kid in the school was on something."

"Let me give you everything I've got, Sean, then we can have this conversation." He tapped the table with both hands at once, to make a point. "I brought some reports I think you'll find interesting." He reached into his bag, which sat on the floor next to him and pulled out a packet. "There have been a number of studies done in Switzerland on the correlation between gifted children and Attention Deficit. Which would explain why Toby—and a high percentage of our students—suffer from it."

Daniels was the first person at Bradley to ever refer to Toby as gifted. *Struggling, challenged, behind,* but never *gifted.* Unless gifted was taken for granted for all Bradley students. "I've never heard about that study."

Daniels shrugged. "I don't know what to tell you. It's all out there for public consumption. This one's for you." Sean read out the title on the report: *"The Correlation between ADD and Giftedness,* Geneva, January, 2008."

Daniels sorted through some more papers until he found what he was looking for. "This is another interesting one that looks at how stress can trigger ADD symptoms. A death in the family, separation, or divorce." He paused for a guilt-inducing moment. "All kinds of factors figure in."

Sean took a copy of that report as well. He would read them front to back later, but simply holding them in his hand calmed him. Then he remembered Jess's signature. "So what about the signature on the Conners scale?"

"I have to ask why you believe the signature on that document didn't belong to Toby's teacher."

"I've . . . I've seen the teacher's signature," he said, lamely. "It was obviously not hers."

"And which of the three teacher signatures looked wrong to you?"

"You know, I'd rather not say."

He considered this and thankfully let it go. "I agree that if the signature does not belong to Toby's teacher, then we have a serious problem to deal with. Or, I should say, *I* have a serious problem to deal with." He rubbed his eyes. "I'll begin an investigation. Today. You have my word."

"You've been through the ringer this year," Walt said.

"How are Toby's spirits?" Daniels asked. "Is his teacher sending work home?"

"Honestly," Sean said, "it's been the last thing on my mind."

"The last thing *I* want is for Toby to fall behind because of this," Daniels stated. "What about a tutor? Is there someone who can work with him while he's home?"

"I—" He'd thought about having Noah come by the apartment, but he was already hemorrhaging money. "I'll work with him a little, help him along."

"I hope you'll allow Bradley to provide a tutor—or at least cover those expenses. We're behind Toby. Behind you. We want to make this as easy for you as possible."

"You don't have to do that," he said. "We're fine."

"Take me up on it." He leaned in with an expression of empathy on his face, his voice barely a whisper. "I insist."

CHAPTER TWENTY-SIX

"You really believe Bruce Daniels is trying to help you?" Jess's bicep flexed as she shook the salad dressing. "After everything—Dr. Garvey, Toby's tutor, my signature?"

"I don't know," he said, and watched her twist her hair into a knot. He wanted to pull it loose, run his fingers through it. "He said he was going to take action, find out who signed your name. He sounded like he meant it."

She poured the dressing on the greens and frowned. "So I'm the skeptic in the relationship. Interesting."

"I'll admit that's usually my role," he said. Were they in a relationship? It had a nice sound to it. "But I'm happy to give it up this time." He turned down the flame under the sauce and drained the tortellini in the sink. "You should look at the reports."

She took them to the couch, tucked her legs under her, and started reading. "I've never seen statistics like this."

"Maybe you should hold off on quitting." He sat down beside her and handed her a beer. "Until Daniels gets some answers."

"I really don't want to be the next Debbie Martin." She sighed. "I tried to talk to Bev, but she's in Minneapolis at some conference." She sniffed the air. "Is something—"

The sauce. He'd turned it down, but not far enough. The apartment was starting to fill with smoke. She followed him into the kitchen where he took the pot off the stove and cursed it.

"I'm willing to see what Bruce Daniels comes back with, but when something feels this wrong . . ."

"What's burning?" Toby asked, emerging from his room, nose wrinkled.

"Dinner." He put a new pot on the stove. "Give me a few minutes."

"Are you staying?" he asked Jess, a sweet, hopeful expression on his face.

"Only if we can do some more math after dinner," Jess said with a wink.

He nodded vigorously. "I think I'm getting good at word problems."

"I think so too."

"We have brownies for dessert." He fanned away the smoke. "And they're not even burned."

"How can I resist an invitation like that?" She smiled a smile that must have made more than a few eight-year-old boys fall madly in love. Can you show me where everything is and I can help set the table?"

Toby led her to the cabinet as if she were the student, giving her detailed instructions about which plates to use and which to avoid. He took extra time with her, the way a teacher might.

While Sean improvised new pasta sauce, he watched them setting the table. They had an easy rapport. For a moment everything made sense, the three of them here together. He realized the clenching in his chest he'd had with Ellie was a mere memory.

"Okay," he called from the kitchen. "Non-burnt sauce is ready. Let's eat."

"Yes!" Toby ran to the kitchen to get his plate. "I'm starving."

"Me too," Jess said, serving them all big portions.

"Where did you grow up?" Toby asked, when they were sitting at the dining room table.

"A town called Westerly," she said. "It's in Rhode Island."

"That's the smallest state." Toby smiled.

"You were paying attention in social studies."

Toby tried to hide his joy at the praise. "What's Westerly like?"

"I loved growing up there. In the summer I used to go to the water slide for hours. Or my parents would take me to the carousel— the old-fashioned kind with the flying horses. Sometimes we'd go to paint-your-own pottery and make cool stuff. Plus, they make amazing ice cream there."

"I love ice cream."

"Do you know how long it takes to drive from the south end of the state to the north end?" she asked.

"Five hours?" Toby guessed.

"Only an hour."

"That's how long it took to go to Coney Island on the subway." He considered this a moment. "Do your mom and dad live there?"

"My dad does." Sean saw a sad smile flicker across her face. "My mom . . . she died last year."

Toby looked at Sean, not sure what to say, then turned back to Jess. "How'd she die?"

"Tobe . . ."

"What?"

"Maybe Jess doesn't want to talk about it."

"It's okay," she said. "She was sick for a long time. Her heart wasn't strong . . ."

"I'd be so sad if my mom died," Toby said.

"You don't have to worry about that for a long time," she said.

"You can remember your mom," Toby offered. "That way it's like she's with you. Kind of."

"You're pretty smart."

"I think of all the fun things I did with Calvin." He shrugged. "But it still makes me kind of sad when I remember I can't see him."

"Yeah . . . I know how that is."

When the phone rang, Toby jumped up and ran into the kitchen to answer it. "Mommy!" he said. Ellie was right on cue for once, thank God. "Nothing . . . eating dinner. My teacher is here."

Toby's account of making brownies with Maureen went into great detail and soon became happy white noise in the background.

"Sorry," Jess said. "Maybe I didn't need to tell him about my dead mother."

"I'll throw a few extra dollars in the therapy jar."

"I've got to get a grip." She held her head with her hands.

"He'll be fine."

"I keep thinking my mom would know what I should do. Between what Dr. Garvey told us and all the school crap, my head is spinning."

"And your breakup," he said. "Don't forget the breakup."

She smiled. "I haven't forgotten. Trust me."

"You going to give me details, or am I going to have to beat it out of you?"

Her laugh was sudden and full. An unexpected gift. "I didn't know you were so interested in the gory details."

"Clearly you've forgotten where I work."

"*Reader's Digest* version: He called me every disgusting name you could think of and threatened me by saying I'd used up my last chance with him. Which came as a huge relief, honestly. I shoved some clothes in a duffel bag and went to Bev's."

"You should not be staying with Bev."

"She's my godmother."

"You should stay with me." He glanced at Toby who was still having an animated conversation with Ellie. "With us."

"I'm okay over there."

"Let's go get your stuff." He couldn't believe he was saying it, but he loved the idea.

"But . . ."

"I hear we're in a relationship," he whispered. "So it's fine."

"I don't think everyone here needs to know that."

"We'll be discreet." Was he pleading? And was that wrong? "I'll sleep on the couch. Or it'll appear that way." He reached for her hand under the table. "Move in with us."

"What if we get on each others' nerves?" she asked. "What if I snore? What if you leave goop on the toothpaste tube? That could kill a budding . . . relationship."

"Impossible." He took both her hands now. "I want to be with you. As much as humanly possible."

"Me too," she said, though she didn't have to because her eyes said it for her. "But Toby . . ."

"I saw the way he was looking at you. Trust me, he'll be with me on this." She still looked like she was on the fence. "Besides, he needs all the tutoring he can stand. Headmaster's orders."

She considered this for a moment. "Okay," she agreed. "For now."

All he heard was yes and it made him so happy he thought he might float out of his seat. "So Bev's out of town?"

"Til tomorrow night."

"After I put Toby to bed I'll call Gloria from upstairs. We can go get your stuff."

"Tonight?"

He didn't want to let a day go by, now that it had been decided. "Absolutely."

When Toby was asleep and Gloria was zoned out in front of *Project Runway*, he and Jess snuck off to Shineman's apartment.

The boxy two bedroom was depressing, bland, uninspired. Jess had been staying in the second bedroom, which Shineman had turned into a home office. The open futon banged up against the desk chair, making it impossible to sit at the small desk. There was a foot of space on either side of the mattress, a bookshelf on one side, and a small closet on the other.

"I don't have much here," she said, pulling clothes from hangers and shelves and shoving them in a duffle bag. "I'll grab my toothbrush and we can get out of here."

She ducked into the bathroom and came back a moment later, toothbrush in hand. "Ready."

He reached out and touched her hair. She relaxed, stepped closer to him until their faces were millimeters apart. It was the first kiss since they'd decided to move in together, and it was charged with possibility. How could he be in a room with her that was mostly bed and not pull her down onto it?

She'd unzipped his pants and he was fumbling with her bra when they heard the key turn in the lock. "Shit," she yelped, feeling around on the floor for her shirt. He zipped up and crammed himself in the corner between the computer desk and the bed.

Jess smoothed back her hair just as the front door opened.

"Aunt Bev!" Jess said, trying not to sound like she'd been moments from getting laid.

"Hi Jessie." Sean couldn't see her from his hiding place, but Shineman sounded tired.

"I didn't think you'd be home 'til tomorrow."

"I came back early," Shineman said. "I hate those things. Do you want some food? I can order something."

Sean pulled his legs in tight, the way he did when he played hide and seek with Toby.

"Have you . . . have you been drinking?" he heard Jess ask her godmother.

"Of course not."

"I can smell it."

"Oh for God's sake, Jessie. I have not been drinking."

He could hear it clearly now: Bev was slurring.

"Okay." Jess's tone said she didn't believe a word of it. "Okay."

He knew he'd smelled it on Shineman's breath. This was the woman responsible for the psychological well-being of hundreds of children—for *his* child. He wanted to strangle her.

"Can I talk to you?" Jess was saying.

"Can it wait until tomorrow?" Shineman yawned. "I was thinking of taking a bath and getting into bed."

"It's pretty important."

"It's been a long day."

"Someone signed my name on Toby Benning's Conners scale," Jess said.

"I don't know where you get this stuff," Shineman said. "I'm going to run a bath."

He heard Bev take a few steps toward her bedroom.

"It was your handwriting." Jess hadn't mentioned this damning piece of news to him and he wondered if she was bluffing.

The footsteps stopped and Shineman groaned. "Okay. Sit." He heard them walk to the living room. Shineman sighed and collapsed on the couch. "You know you're making something out of nothing, right?"

"Did you sign it or not?"

"Sweetie," she started. "Why do you think you were hired?"

"What do you mean?"

"I mean we both know you don't technically have the experience to be a head teacher at Bradley. I knew you could do it, Jessie. I vouched for you. But I knew there would be hurdles. I said so your first day. I also said I'd help you out."

He wondered if Jess would take the bait.

"I didn't give you permission to forge my name." She was saying the right words but her voice was suddenly smaller.

"Had you ever filled out a Conners scale?" Shineman pressed. He strained to hear.

"Answer me, Jessica."

"No." Jess answered.

"I've done several hundred," Shineman said. "That was something I could help you with. I've been observing Toby for years. My filling it out was the responsible thing to do. So don't go painting this as some malicious deed."

His legs were cramping up. He stretched them out carefully, but there wasn't enough room. He bumped the chair and it skidded three inches on the wood floor and thudded against the leg of the table. He froze.

"Why did you want Toby Benning on medication?" Jess raised her voice, possibly to cover up the racket he was making. "He didn't need it."

"Whoa," Shineman said dramatically. "Who says Toby Benning didn't need medication? He was diagnosed with Attention Deficit."

"Because of you."

Shineman chuckled condescendingly. "That's quite a theory."

Sean exhaled slowly, his heart hammering away against his ribs.

"And it doesn't paint me in a very flattering light," Shineman complained. "I am—and always have been—an advocate for children. I think medication helps most of the children who take it. And I think it helped Toby." She paused. "Occasionally one of them has a bad reaction and we take them off it. It's that simple."

He squeezed the leg of the desk hard, imagining Shineman's neck instead. There was nothing simple about having almost killed Toby.

"Look," Shineman was saying. "About a third of Bradley students excel there. Another third get by. With help. But the others . . . the school moves quickly."

"But—" Jess tried.

"The curriculum is *accelerated*. We have to help these kids feel good about themselves, allow them to focus on the work so they can succeed." She paused. "Don't you think they deserve that chance?"

"A chance to learn that drugs will solve all their problems?" Her anger was escalating and so was her register. "A chance to die from taking a drug they don't need?"

"Here's the thing about Bradley." Shineman was getting calmer as Jess became more agitated. "Some of these kids would be fine going without the meds at other schools. They'd be *fine*. But at Bradley . . . they need help."

His tongue tasted metallic and he had too much saliva in his mouth. He tried to breathe, but it came out as a rumble.

"We have the best SAT scores, the best college acceptance rates," she went on. "Our chess team has won the national championship ten years in a row. Our debate team rips all the others apart. We have the newest and best technology of any school anywhere and kids who know how to use it. A Broadway show could go up in our theater it's so well—"

"I don't give a shit about the theater or any of that other crap."

"Barack Obama spoke at the Bradley commencement last year, for God's sake," Shineman spat out. "We are the best of the best. I'm doing what I can to keep the standards of the school high."

"Stop it," shouted Jess. "Stop justifying it."

"Boys are put on ADD medication every day all over the country," she said. "This is no different. So please, stop making it sound so sordid. I'm just helping to insure that no child falls through the cracks. The health of the school depends on an ultra-high level of achievement. Our kids can do it. It's inspiring."

"So why the hell are you drugging them?"

He strained to hear, but all he could hear was Shineman breathing angrily.

"Kids are fidgety," she said sharply. "They can't sit still long enough to learn everything they need to learn every day. I'm just helping to make sure that down the road a huge, and I mean huge, percentage of our students will end up at Ivy League schools and go on to lead exciting, rewarding lives."

The pause drew out for a full fifteen seconds, which felt like hours from his cramped corner.

"Who else knows about this?"

Shineman pushed air heavily out her nostrils. "You're not paying attention to what I'm—"

"I'm paying closer attention than anyone else at Bradley. Who is making you do this?"

"No one's making me *do* anything," she said. "I'm just supposed to guide parents toward the right decision. That's all."

He was so furious, he hardly noticed the pins and needles pricking his dead legs.

"But . . . why?"

She let out a heavy, defeated sigh. "It's not like I have a choice."

"That's bullshit. Of course you have a choice."

"No. I don't. Jessie, I've had a hard time . . . your mom . . . she was my best friend."

"My mom?"

Another sigh from Shineman. "When she died I slipped a little." A foghorn sounded as she blew her nose. "I just needed something to get me through." She sniffed miserably. "I loved her too."

Sean rolled his eyes.

"Don't use Mom as an excuse for falling off the wagon. She'd despise that."

"Bruce found out, and . . ."

"Found out? You were drinking at school?"

"I don't need a lecture. I'm just giving you the facts. I need to do everything I can to keep my job."

"Is that the most important thing? What if Toby had died?"

"I don't see Toby's parents complaining," she snipped. "I wasn't the one who gave him the medication. They did."

It took every ounce of self-restraint he had not to storm out of the guest bedroom and rip Shineman's head off.

"And what about Calvin?" Jess was yelling. "You killed Calvin."

"Shut your mouth," Shineman hissed. "You have no idea what you're talking about. I don't kill children." He heard a quiver in her voice. "I help them."

He wondered if she'd convinced herself this was true or if she was simply so deep into the lie she couldn't get out. She'd just confirmed that Bruce Daniels was involved. Not only wasn't Bruce looking into the forgery, he'd set it up. His stomach twisted.

"You have to stop," he heard Jess say.

"Jessie, I won't sign your name anymore, okay? I promise. Just don't mention this again. Ever."

"Are you kidding me?"

"Trust me," her voice was desperate. "I'm not kidding."

"But you just told me . . . you admitted—"

"You know what?" Shineman's pleading tone had changed. "I don't think this is going to work out after all."

"What?"

"I'm giving you two week's notice," she said. "Effective immediately."

"You're firing me?"

"I made a mistake. You're not a good fit with the school."

"But, what—you can't just—"

"I can. And I am. I'll tell Bruce you had a family emergency. It'll get you out of your contract—a clean break—so you can get another teaching job."

"But—"

"This is your out—an out most of them don't get." Her use of "most of them" filled the room with the ghosts of past teachers. Good teachers like Debbie Martin. "You should take it. Let me protect you."

Jess was silent. "Okay," she said, finally. "Two weeks. That will give me time to tie up loose ends, say goodbye to the children."

"This is no joke." Shineman's tone sent a chill through him. "Go and don't look back. Leave town. You can still get out of this without becoming a casualty if you do what I'm telling you."

Shineman went to bed and Jess found Sean in the guest bedroom. "Could you hear?" Her eyes were huge and her whisper was charged.

"Every word."

"Go home, call your sister. Find a lawyer."

"But you just told her you wouldn't talk about any of that."

"I can't," she said. "But *you* can."

As soon as he was out of the building, the air bit into his skin. He replayed Bruce Daniels's lies and dialed Nicole.

"Hello?" Her voice was groggy. He checked his watch.

"Sorry."

"What's wrong?"

"I need a lawyer," he said, and told her why.

"Jesus fucking Christ," she said. "You need Nina Goldsmith. She does crimes against children, and she's a bulldog."

"Nicole . . ." The word *bulldog* ricocheted around inside his head. "I don't really feel like being reamed by Bradley."

"So what, you want to sit around stroking blue blankie?"

She hadn't teased him about the blankie in decades. He had a flash of how mad it used to make him. Now, instead, he smiled. "Nah, that's why I called you."

"Nina's good. I'll ask her to keep your name out of it if she can."

CHAPTER TWENTY-SEVEN

ON THE PHONE, NINA GOLDSMITH AGREED TO MEET AT A DELI near the courthouse. He ordered a coffee to go since there weren't any tables. He waited. When a petite blonde about his age blew in, he didn't think much of it until she marched up to him. "Sean Benning." It was more of a statement than a question.

"Nice to meet you." He extended his hand and Nina Goldsmith locked it in a fierce grip.

She led him to a narrow shelf that must have been the coffee bar and they leaned against it. "I've been looking into the allegations you're making. I can't lie to you. This is going to be hard. The Bradley School is . . . powerful. They've got some extremely well-placed alumni, including some people in my office. That's not to say we can't move on this. But we need to be careful. Meticulous. Did you do your homework?"

He handed her the pages he'd written, explaining everything he knew, everything he suspected, and the little proof he had. He also gave her the list of everyone he knew who was involved, and everyone he thought could help with the case, divided into those who would talk (Garvey), those who might talk (Debbie Martin), and those he was pretty sure wouldn't talk—the Drakes, Walt, Cheryl, Noah, Bev Shineman and just about everyone else.

She read through the list shaking her head. "Didn't you say something about photos?"

"Oh, right." He'd almost forgotten. He handed her the printouts of the pictures he'd taken with his cell phone, which were far darker and blurrier than he'd remembered.

She squinted hard at them. "What is this?"

"Those are pictures of the nurse's closet at Bradley." He pointed to a close-up of one of the bottles. "They're all ADD medication. It shows how many of the kids are taking it."

She let out an exasperated sigh. "Without proof of the forged signature, this doesn't show that the school is doing anything illegal."

"I think that's doable," he said. "As long as you can protect the teacher."

"I told you I'll do everything I can."

"I can get you Dr. Hutch Garvey. He evaluated hundreds of Manhattan kids for years and *he* believes the schools are forcing parents to medicate their kids."

"Yeah, Hutch . . . Look, Dr. Garvey has been trying to open a case for years. He has no hard evidence because none of the parents will come forward to back up his claims." She squinted at him. Her eyes were so dark you couldn't tell where the pupils ended and the irises began. "I believe you, if that means anything. People wouldn't be this scared to come forward if it weren't true. But if you want me to have a chance in hell of seeing any real results, you're going to have to get me more than

Hutch Garvey. Get the teacher. Find another parent who'll talk. Find a high-profile parent who'll talk. Any of those things will get us a step closer to where we want to be, which is in front of a judge who will give us permission to search the school."

"How am I supposed to make people talk to you?"

She shrugged sarcastically. "You're an attractive man. I'm sure some of the mothers have noticed."

"What?"

"I'm not going in there without the backup I need. Use what God gave you. I don't have a professional death wish." She tossed her coffee cup in the trash as she turned to leave. "Let me know when you get something I can use."

HE STOOD IN FRONT OF THE BROOKLYN BRIDGE STATION AND dialed Melanie Drake.

"Sean, hi," she said. She either sounded flustered or out of breath. Or both.

"Is this a bad time?"

"No . . . well, sort of. I'm in D.C., chaperoning Susannah's field trip to the National Archives.

"When do you get back?"

"Tomorrow afternoon. What's up?"

"I know it's hard to talk about, but I know Bev Shineman pressured you to put Calvin on Metattent—or Ritalin—or something."

"I really don't know what you're—"

"You need to say something. I just met with a lawyer who wants to help. But she needs—"

"Did you give her my name?" Melanie sounded panicked. "You had no right to mention Calvin or—"

"I didn't. But—"

"Good. Okay." Teenagers were screeching and sirens howled in the background. "Look, I have to go. Don't ask me again, okay?"

CHAPTER TWENTY-EIGHT

"She's terrified," Jess said as she tugged Toby's hat over his ears and then pulled her own jacket tight.

"She should be terrified," Sean said. "She should still talk to Nina Goldsmith."

"What are you guys talking about?" Toby asked from under many layers as they walked west along Twenty-third Street.

"Nothing Tobe," he said. "You warm enough?"

"When are we going to be there?"

"A few more blocks," he said. "Hang in there."

"I love when it snows," Toby said, running his hand over the hood of a parked car and packing another snowball. "There's ammo everywhere." He hurled it against the façade of a brownstone and smiled.

"I'll talk to the lawyer," Jess said. "I want to."

They'd had this conversation already. A few times. "Wait until we get more parents. Be patient."

"It's not my best thing."

He watched her trying to be patient.

"There must be someone else who'll talk."

"But why would they? I mean, if their kid is okay."

"Ethics? The desire to do the right thing?" She slumped her shoulders. "You're right. No one's going to do it."

Then he remembered there was someone who owed him a favor. He didn't know if Shineman had pushed Billy Horn to dope up his son, but if she had . . . "I have an idea," he said, and put his arms around Jess and Toby. "It's the only one I have, so it better work."

Toby pointed at the Burdot sign. "Is that it, Dad?"

"That's it. Let's go up."

Toby took the steps two at a time, and when he got into the space he froze. "It's so empty," he said. "There's nothing here."

"On the walls," Sean said. "Look at the art."

"Oh," he said, realizing what was surrounding him. "Cool."

"Sean!" Camille appeared as if out of nowhere and kissed him on both cheeks. "Parfait!" She took in Jess and Toby with a glance. "And who do we have here?"

"This is my friend Jess Harper and my son Toby." He patted Toby on the back. "Say hi."

"Hi," he said, shyly.

"You have a beautiful gallery," Jess said, even though Camille was still staring at Toby. She looked vaguely repelled, or at least worried he might touch something.

"Thank you," she said with a practiced smile, then turned her attention back on him. "Did you bring the headshots?"

Zee ed-shots.

He handed her the envelope, which she opened eagerly. She studied all three, settling on his favorite, a full-on shot that captured something he'd never seen before in his own eyes. "Very handsome. Excellent. We'll need a photo credit for these. You can send it over tomorrow."

"The photographer is right here."

Jess smiled uncomfortably. "I can write my name on the envelope."

"Oh." Camille seemed flustered, but handed her a pen. "Yes, good. Wonderful."

"Where's your artwork going to be, Dad?" Toby was asking from across the room.

"They will be the first pieces you see upon entering. They will set the tone for the entire show." Camille winked at him. "I'm already getting calls from my regulars about you. I think you're going to be very happy . . ."

"I'm starving, Dad."

Camille eyed Toby suspiciously, apparently unused to children's needs or filling them.

"I'm already happy," he said, shaking Camille's hand. "Thanks again . . . for everything."

"See you next week," she called after them as they descended the stairs.

HE DECIDED NOT TO LEAVE THE REASON FOR HIS CALL ON BILLY'S voice mail, only that he needed to talk to him as soon as possible. The return message from the Knicks' publicist said there would be two tickets waiting at the Garden box office that night and that he should stop by the team locker room at halftime.

THAT NIGHT, WALKING THROUGH THE CROWDS AT THE GARDEN, he reveled in the feeling of taking his son to a game. "This is great. You having fun?"

Toby nodded and eyed stand after stand. "Can we get a hot dog?"

He looked at the prices and tried to think of all the cash he'd have after his show. "Why not?" He shelled out twenty bucks for two hotdogs and a soda.

Toby followed him into prime third-row seats. "We should do this all the time," Toby said.

"Deal." He wondered how people could afford tickets like this *all the time*. "Hey, how are you feeling? Are you tired? Because if you get tired, we can go."

"I'm fine, Dad."

"Because you didn't take a nap today."

He rolled his eyes. "Only little kids take naps."

"Okay. But let me know if you get tired."

The game started and they watched for a while in silence.

"Why doesn't Zack's dad start?"

"He used to. The younger guys start now."

He watched for a while. "You and Mommy were mad at each other about my school. Is that why she left?"

The question came out of nowhere, but that's how it always was. When you least expect it . . . "No," he assured Toby. "It had nothing to do with that." He imagined Toby listening to him and Ellie fighting and his heart broke.

"So are you mad at my school?"

"I'm trying to make sure your school is going to be safe for all your friends, for everyone who goes there."

Toby nodded. "Okay."

"Mommy loves you. The reason she left had nothing to do with you."

"I know," he said, and went back to watching the game.

He wondered if Toby really knew it or if he was just saying it.

At halftime, the Knicks were miraculously up 50-46. He and Toby made their way to the team locker room. "Not a lot of people get to do this, you know," he said. "Isn't it cool?"

"I guess," Toby said, twisting back to watch the girls in midriff-baring outfits prance and thrust around the court. "But I kind of wanted to watch the show."

The locker room was damp and stunk like a dozen sweating men.

"Come in!" Horn extended his extra-long arm in greeting. "Toby, my man," he said, giving him a high-five. "Good to see you. Zack's been missing you."

Toby looked around hopefully. "Is he here?" Toby was stronger now, of course he was missing his friends.

"Not tonight, sport. But let's get you two together." Billy grabbed a ball, signed it and handed it to Toby. "You can go around and ask all the players to write their names on it, if you want."

Toby's eyes lit up. "Cool. Thanks." He took the ball and started around the room.

"So what's up?" Billy wiped a towel across his forehead. The sweat resurfaced instantly but he didn't seem to notice. "I've only got a few minutes."

Sean gave him a fast but uncut version of what had happened to Toby, what he knew about the school and the drugs. He told him about Calvin.

Billy shook his head and watched Toby across the room. "You are one lucky son of a bitch," he said. "The school shrink pushed me, too. Pushed and pushed." He wiped his forehead with his bicep. "She threatened to kick out Zack if he couldn't 'keep up,' like he's slow or something. Like he isn't up to the schoolwork. And that's bullshit. Zack is fine. He's *fine*. I told them no way in hell was I putting Zack on that shit. Bottom line, they could show me a million tests that proved it was *safe*." He mimicked Shineman when he said the word *safe*. "That stuff stunts kids' growth, man. I told her I wasn't risking a millimeter. Zack goes pro, he's gonna need all the height he can get." He grimaced. "If I wasn't who I am, I don't know if I could've gotten away with it. She finally left me alone, but that woman's a pain in the ass."

He knew he'd always liked Billy Horn. "There's a lawyer who's trying to open an investigation, but she needs parents to come forward."

Billy nodded at whatever internal dialogue he was having. "Have her call me tomorrow. And anyway," he winked, "I owe you one."

He suppressed the urge to reach out and hug the basketball legend. "Thanks man," he said.

Toby ran back with the ball, which was covered in signatures. "Look dad!"

He tried to calculate how much Toby could get for it on eBay. "Nice, Tobe. That's going to be worth a lot someday."

Toby smiled and shrugged like it was just a ball his friend's dad had signed. "Can I dribble it?"

"Go for it." Billy winked at Toby and slapped Sean on the back. "Tell her to call me . . . about that *thing*."

Toby dribbled out of the locker room. By the time they'd gotten back to their seats, he was exhausted. He rested his head on Sean's arm. "Dad," he said, yawning, "can we go home?"

CHAPTER TWENTY-NINE

SEAN CLAMPED THE PHONE BETWEEN HIS SHOULDER AND HIS EAR listening to Nina Goldsmtih as he poured a bowl of Cheerios for Toby. "It's no good," she was saying.

"He's as high-profile as they come."

"But he said no to them. The school pressured him, he said no and nothing came of it. They didn't kick out his kid. This disproves your theory."

Why was she convoluting everything? "It shows the school psychologist tried to get Billy Horn to put his child on ADD medication. Like she does with most of the kids."

"No, it shows that she's doing her job and accepting that he has a right *as a parent* to make his own decisions. Sorry, you're going to have to do better than this if you want me to get any leverage. Keep working on it." He recalled what Shineman slurred that night with

Jess—she'd put on the pressure, but it had been *his* call to put Toby on medication. That's what they would fling at him each and every time. He could have said no.

He slammed the phone. "Fuck!"

"Dad!" Toby walked into the kitchen pulling on his T-shirt. "That's the really bad word."

"Yeah." He tousled Toby's hair. "Never say that." The feel of Toby's head under his hand drained away some of the frustration. He wasn't going to let Nina Goldsmith wreck his weekend. "Want to come to the studio with me today?"

"I want to go sledding."

"I have an extra canvas. You can paint."

"Actually, I kind of want Jess to take me sledding."

"You do?"

He nodded. "She said she'd teach me her special ramp tricks."

SEAN WAS ALMOST JEALOUS AS HE WATCHED THEM PULL THEIR sleds down Riverside toward the park, deep in conversation.

Back in the apartment that afternoon, Toby and Jess had matching red faces.

"Remember that time I was going so fast over the ramp I almost flipped over?" Toby jumped a little, reliving the moment.

"You were in the air for almost five seconds. But you landed it perfectly."

"Thanks to the crouch technique."

"Crouch technique?" Sean stirred a pot of hot chocolate, breathing in the vapors.

"My dad's crouch technique." Jess ripped open the bag of mini marshmallows and popped one in her mouth. "You have to pull yourself into an egg shape, get as small as possible. You'll never flip."

"It works, Dad. Really."

Jess lined up three mugs and they drank the first round quickly.

"Can we have seconds?" Toby licked his chocolate mustache.

"I got extra milk at the store," Sean announced proudly. Soon, they were lounging comfortably around the living room, Toby looking at comics, he and Jess reading the papers.

"Let's play Clue," Toby said.

"No Clue," Sean whined. "Please?"

"Stratego."

"How about Scrabble?" Jess looked at Toby. "You're a good speller. And it's my favorite."

It was Jess's favorite because she had a knack for getting triple word scores on every word. And she knew a lot of words that included *x* and *z*.

"Are you hustling us?" Sean asked, when she spelled zephyr for a triple letter score over the *z*.

"I played a lot with my grandmother the summer I lived with her. She never let me win." It was Toby's turn. "Do you have an s? You could turn *weeps* into *sweeps*."

Toby slid his S onto the word and smiled proudly. "Thanks."

"My grandmother used to cheat, though. She used to spell all kinds of curse words and insist they were allowed."

"No way," Toby said. "My grandma doesn't do that."

"How old were you?"

"About Toby's age. I went back to school loaded with new vocabulary. Only I wasn't allowed to use any of it."

When Toby started yawning, Sean called the game. "It's been a long day."

"Jess," Toby said, pouring his tiles into the drawstring bag. "What's your emergency?"

"What emergency?"

"I talked to Zack last night on the phone. He said you have a family emergency."

"Oh," she said. "I . . . my dad . . . he needs me to come home."

"Because Zack really doesn't want you to go. Neither do I."

"I know." She smiled sadly. "But I have to."

"What are you going to do?" Toby asked. "For a job?"

"I got a job teaching. At my old school."

"You did?" The news hit Sean hard and low. "Really?"

She nodded and looked him in the eye. "I was going to tell you. I start next month."

"But . . ." He imagined her moving away and a queasy panic washed over him. "You can't go."

"Dad, she has a family emergency," Toby said.

"But—"

"Come on," she said, taking Toby's hand. "Let's get you to bed."

Sean sat, stunned. The hours he couldn't see her during the day were agony. It was impossible to imagine her leaving. When she came back into the living room, he couldn't control himself. "Don't go," he blurted.

"I have to."

"Why?" He sounded like he was eight, except that the eight-year-old had taken it better. "You can stay here, with us. You can find another job. I'll help you." Pleading was the only strategy he had. "Don't go."

She was giving him a funny look. "Come with me."

"What?"

"You should both come with me."

He'd never considered moving. Not really. Until this second.

"I wouldn't be Toby's teacher, we'd be far away from Bradley. We could just . . . live our life."

Living his life sounded good. He wondered what he'd been doing all these years. "But my job . . ."

"You hate your job."

"Of course I do. But it's . . . a job." He imagined not working for *Buzz*. It was terrifying. Freeing. Amazing. After the Burdot thing maybe he wouldn't need a nine-to-five job.

"There are tons of galleries in Providence. And Newport. Boston is close."

"I could quit *Buzz*," he said, liking the sound of it. "That would be fucking amazing."

"It would be fucking amazing," she said, laughing.

"Toby could enroll in school." As he said it, he could imagine the whole thing. "We could get a place. All three of us."

"Do you think Toby's ready? That's a big deal."

"He likes you so much."

"Do you think *you're* ready?"

"I love you," he said, fully aware this was the first time he'd said it. "I love you. So yeah, I'm definitely ready."

"Me too," she said, kissing him through a smile. "On both counts."

By the time Toby woke up, Sean had slipped out of bed next to Jess and was back on the couch.

"Dad, why are you sleeping here?" Toby asked, as he climbed on top of him, turning on cartoons.

"Jess stayed over and I let her sleep in my bed."

"Yay!" Toby bounced up and down. "Can she have pancakes with us?"

"Let's let her sleep," he said. "Then we can ask her when she gets up."

"Ask her what?" Jess emerged from the bedroom, pulling her hair into a ponytail. She looked like a kid, rubbing the sleep out of her eyes.

"If you can have breakfast with us."

"You know my specialty is chocolate chip pancakes, right?" she said. "Do you have any chocolate chips?"

Sean shook his head. "We don't really bake."

"No problem. Do you have any leftover Halloween candy?"

Toby ran to his room and returned with his stash.

"Great," Jess said, separating out the Hershey's Kisses and Nestlé Crunch bars. "We can chop and practice fractions at the same time."

She asked Toby to cut the candy bars in half, then in quarters. Then in eighths. He executed the tasks on cue, relishing every moment of praise.

"Where'd you learn to make these?" Toby was smitten, and Sean was in trouble, because he would now have to make chocolate pancakes every weekend.

"Tony's Kitchen. It's a diner near where I grew up. We used to go there Sunday mornings," she said. "Tony taught me how to make them. I think I was about your age."

"Is it still open? I want to go."

"Sure, we can go. And I'll take you sledding on the golf course, too." Jess smiled at Sean. "Westerly was a great place to grow up."

It was too cold to go outside, so they stayed in, reading the paper, watching movies, drinking hot chocolate. Sitting by her on the couch, his laptop propped on her legs, he brushed her arm because he couldn't stand not touching her. The buzzing in his chest hadn't stopped since they decided to move away together.

"Oh my God," she said, turning the computer screen to face him. "Read this."

The report Daniels had given him about the correlation between giftedness and ADD filled the screen. "Yeah, I have that, remember?"

"No," she said. "You have *part* of this." She scrolled to the bottom. "Look." This report contained an additional section, a conclusion that wasn't attached to the one he had.

"It contradicts everything else in the report." She read: "Despite the hypothesis put forward here, there is no proof that would uphold any theory that a correlation exists between giftedness and Attention Deficit Disorder. In fact, research has shown that giftedness and ADD overlap far less frequently than for those who are not gifted."

When he called Nina Goldsmith, she wasn't as ecstatic as he'd hoped. "It's something," she said. "But a judge won't—"

"Is it enough for the *Times*? What if I leak some of this stuff to a reporter?"

"*The New York Times*? The paper of record?" The snort was over the top, he thought. "Do you know how much evidence they need to make accusations like this? Do you know how many sources they need? Trust me, *The New York Times* is not the way to go here."

"She's going to sit on it," he said when he hung up. "She's going to sit on it until it dies."

"Maybe your sister can do something?" Jess picked up his phone and handed it to him.

He dialed her number. Nicole would be able to do something. She didn't sit on anything when she could pounce. "Nina Goldsmith is useless," he said, and regaled his sister with Nina's uselessness.

But Nicole didn't pounce. She didn't say a word, just let out a low growl. "She's right," Nicole said finally.

The words sounded foreign coming out of her mouth. "What?"

"That school has some juice. The resources, the alumni, the lawyers . . . You've got to come at them with an arsenal. Shoot to kill, baby brother. I want them dead as much as you do, trust me."

"But . . ." His mind was spinning. He wanted to trust her. "What about the *Times*? What if I go to a reporter there who can dig up some—"

"Not yet," she said. "Last thing you want is to come off as a delusional, paranoid New York parent. You need sources, documentation, evidence, for anyone at the *Times* to take you seriously."

"So what am I supposed to do?"

"We've got to build our arsenal."

Jess, who'd been hanging on every word, slumped back on the couch.

"I'll do some more digging," Nicole said. "I'll call you tomorrow. Don't worry. We'll get them."

As soon as he hung up, the phone rang in his hand. It was Rick, and he was slurring. Yelling and slurring. "Fucking Oscars."

"Rick," he said. "What's up?"

"We're supposed to have a Q&A with Natalie Portman. A ten-minute phoner."

"To go with the dress-shopping photos. Yeah, I've got it all laid out." He hated when Rick called him on Sundays and it always happened around the Oscars. Every issue through the end of February would spend pages and pages analyzing the getups, the hair, and the bling of anyone who walked down the red carpet. His days were spent looking for the most revealing, embarrassing, hideous, inappropriate, see-through, ripped, or otherwise flawed, fashion choices of Hollywood's A-list.

"Yeah, well she bagged us. Gave the interview to *Us*." He let out a long belch.

"So you need filler?"

"The intern's writing something about pre-Oscar boob jobs."

"Is anyone having boob jobs before the Oscars?"

Jess mouthed, *boob jobs?*

"She's got leads," Rick said, but he was lying. "Of course she does. Look, story'll be on your desk tomorrow. Just get me some images before the close."

After he killed the call, he threw the phone across the room. "My life," he pulled two fistfuls of hair, "sucks."

"Your former life," she corrected him. "I heard you're moving soon."

"That's right. I'm moving north." He relaxed as soon as he said it. "To the smallest state in the Union."

"We prefer *intimate*."

"Even better." He smoothed her hair, allowed his hand to trace the side of her face.

"So how come *Buzz* can run anything it wants, even if it's not true?"

"Because *Buzz* has no standards, not a shred of journalistic integrity."

"No named sources?"

"Named, unnamed—we don't need sources at all."

Her eyebrows perched high on her forehead in anticipation, waiting for him to put it together. When he did, he couldn't believe he hadn't thought of it himself. "You are brilliant."

He put on a pot of coffee and they worked on the story late into the night. The layout he would hijack the next day could accommodate about five hundred words, which was enough to do the job. It was enough space to get in all the facts, some history and the photos from the nurse's closet. The only way to make a splash with the article was to tell Toby's story. He wasn't a writer, but he'd read enough *Buzz* stories to know how it was done:

"The best school in Manhattan almost killed my son. Earlier in the year, they succeeded in killing his best friend by insisting that he take ADD medication to improve his focus. Both children were diagnosed as a result of teacher evaluations that had been forged by school officials." Without naming names, he recounted Bev's admission. He wrote about how the school had covered up Calvin's death—though he didn't name Calvin—by attributing it to peanut allergies. He wrote about how a sky-high percentage of Bradley students were on prescription ADD medication that Garvey said was unnecessary. Billy Horn said to go ahead and quote him about Bradley's "full-court press" to get him to put Zack on medication. Sean also stuck in the fact that Daniels had given him only part of the "Giftedness" report, and he quoted Noah as an unnamed source saying that schools "did this." Without naming names, he told Debbie Martin's story. In keeping with *Buzz* style, he threw in a lot of "allegedlies," "sources say," and "according to those involved."

For graphics, he enlarged an image he found online of a Metattent Junior capsule and downloaded the best of his cell phone photos. He smiled. It was his best work for *Buzz* to date.

The next day, he laid out the boob job story. A salacious smile twisted Rick's lips. "Now *that's* a story."

By the end of the day, the intern was still waiting on a quote from a plastic surgeon who had never treated any of the celebrities mentioned. "I can stay late," Sean told Rick. "Go home. I got this one." It was the first time he'd ever wanted to stay late at *Buzz*.

Rick slapped him on the back. "I owe you one."

After the intern had gone home, Sean pulled her story and replaced it with his Bradley article. It fit perfectly. The image of the pill cabinet wasn't the strongest, but it did the trick. At the last minute, he found a photo of Bradley's entrance, which helped place the story visually. He fooled around with some headlines. "Top School in Country Drugging its Students" was a good one. He also liked "Number One School in Nation Drugs Its Kids." He finally settled on, "Rx Academy," which he decided packed the biggest punch.

At midnight, he sent the files and it was done. He'd have to wait until the end of the week when the magazine hit the stands to know if anyone would even bother reading a *Buzz* story that featured no boobs, fashion gaffes, or celebrity gossip. Even if no one read it, that was okay. He'd have done something when no one else would. He could move on.

CHAPTER THIRTY

"ONE, TWO, THREE, AND GO." HE AND JESS HOISTED THE FRAME from the ground and walked it to the center of the Sean Benning wall of the gallery. Martin Vols had already hung a series of gory photographs of a decapitation, and Tina Crowe was setting up what looked like an electric chair and camcorder for a performance piece she had tried to describe to them earlier.

"You got it?" he asked as Jess slid her arm behind the frame.

"Almost, wait." Pieces of hair slipped from her ponytail. "Got it," she said, releasing the wire onto the hook. She let go of the frame and brushed the hair out of her face with the back of her hand. "Take a look."

He stepped back and admired her. Her jeans were splattered with the same paint that covered his. "Good. Very good."

"The frame," she said. "How's the frame?"

"Oh, that's crooked." He estimated an inch with his fingers. "Up on the left." She nudged the corner up with acute concentration he found both amusing and touching.

"I think I've found my second career," she said, standing back to appraise her work. "Picture hanger."

"I'm all for it, if it means you'll wear those jeans every day."

She draped her arms around his neck. "I don't think you're focusing."

"You don't?"

"On the right thing." She kissed him in the middle of the gallery. "We're almost done."

They'd been working all afternoon and it was finally coming together. Snow fell outside, but inside, the room was warm and bright and humming with creative energy. "I've got something for you."

She looked skeptical. "For me?"

He reached into the pocket of his down jacket, which was heaped in the middle of the room, and presented her with a gold mesh pouch cinched with a gold ribbon.

"What's this for?"

"I missed Christmas, so I guess this is for your birthday."

"My birthday's in May."

"Happy early birthday." He paused, watching her. "Open it."

She shook the necklace from its pouch and held it in her hand, smiling. "It's beautiful. I love it," she said, pressing it against her chest. "But I'm supposed to get *you* something for your opening. Not the other way around."

"I've never heard that rule." He took the necklace and stepped behind her to fasten it. When he'd seen it in the store window, he'd had no choice. The owner who'd made the necklace told him it was one-of-a-kind, made from something called blue topaz. When Jess turned to face him, touching the glittering stone, he knew he'd been right. It matched the vapor blue of her eyes. "There was no way I couldn't get that for you."

She leaned in and gave him an awesome thank you kiss that made him want to shower her with gifts. She took his hand and said, "have you ever noticed your skin is exactly the same temperature as mine?"

"I have."

"You've got to dance to this song," Vols announced, as the first atonal crash of "Here Comes Your Man" escaped from the mini speakers hooked up to his iPod. He started bobbing his head to the unmistakably catchy baseline. "The Pixies make such happy fucking music."

Crowe started to do a chicken dance around the electric chair. Martin Vols's entire body shook like he was having an epileptic seizure.

"I love this song," Jess said, and started shimmying around the room and swinging her hips.

He pumped his arms in the air and jumped up and down to the music. Soon, the baseline had them all bobbing around flubbing lyrics at the top of their lungs. They must have looked ridiculous, but no one gave a shit. They had their own show, who cared about anything else?

When the song ended, he and Jess turned, breathless, to his wall, and stared. "Wow," she said. "It's spectacular."

He looked at the collection. Mounted on the wall together, the individual pieces became something he couldn't have imagined. He thought about the love that had gone into each one of those sketches. He remembered how they'd changed for him when he started weighing down Ellie's form with the colorful shapes. From a distance, it looked like a mosaic. But as you came closer, peered inside, the whole effect changed and became dark, heavy. A smile crept onto his face. He'd done something. Something good.

Vols turned to look, too. "Those are kickass, man. Jesus, I want to buy one."

That got Crowe's attention. She looked up from what she was doing and took in his work. "Fuck me," she said. "Beautiful. *And* disturbing." She gave a slow, affirmative nod.

He could pretty much die a happy man. He looked at the room and at his work alongside two of the most interesting new artists around. Not only did he have a real show, he was moving out of the city to live with Jess. Everything was perfect, which made it that much worse that the *Buzz* story would go out to subscribers in the next few days, just in time for the opening. He prayed Rick would wait until Monday to fire him.

THE NEXT THREE DAYS WERE INTERMINABLE AS HE WAITED FOR the shit to hit the fan. When he wasn't making plans with Jess about the move, he buried himself in Oscar research and tried to avoid Rick. He tried to do normal things, like reading and painting. But sustaining concentration was as hopeless as trying to sleep or eat.

"Dad, you're doing the thing again," Toby said.

"What thing?" He stared at his fingers thrumming the dining room table. He balled up a fist and gave the table a thud. "Sorry."

"Are you going to leave your tortellini?"

Sean pushed his plate across the table. "Go ahead." He was sure the mixture of excitement and dread was going to give him a heart attack, or at least an ulcer.

That night, Ellie called after Toby had gone to bed. Instead of a greeting, she launched right in. "You're moving to Rhode Island?"

"I was going to tell you," he said, though he hadn't exactly decided when. "It's just been so—"

"With Toby's teacher?" He could tell Ellie was gearing up for a battle.

But there was nothing to battle over. "Yes."

"Sean, I don't even know her. I'm not just going to let my son move to a different state . . . with a stranger."

He decided not to point out that she had no say in the matter, that she'd set the tone for leaving months ago. "Jess is amazing and Toby loves her. I love her." The dead air may have meant he'd hurt her. It wasn't what he'd intended, but he was glad he'd said it, glad it was out in the open. "I know you don't know her. But you have to trust me on this one. Jess cares about Toby more than you could imagine. He will be loved."

"But . . ."

"I get to have a life too."

The line went silent again. "I promised Toby I'd see him, that it wouldn't be like it was before." Her voice had changed. It was smaller, more fragile. "I won't break that promise."

"You better not," he said, and meant it. "He needs us both."

HE TOOK A BOTTLE OF TUMS TO *BUZZ* THE NEXT DAY AND TRIED TO focus on an Oscar hook-up spread. The mouse shook in his hand as he worked.

"Jesus fucking Christ!" Rick shouted from across the office. Something heavy—a piece of furniture or a volume of the Encyclopedia Brittanica—crashed against a wall. "Benning!"

GETTING FIRED WASN'T AS BAD AS HE THOUGHT IT WOULD BE. Though he didn't feel good about screwing Rick, who would certainly be next on the chopping block.

Clearing out his stuff took exactly a minute and a half. He grabbed the only two photos on his desk, one of a tanned Toby from the beach last summer and another of their first hiking trip, with Toby on his shoulders after he'd realized that hiking really meant walking. He shoved three packs of multi-colored Post-its and a handful of pens into his jacket pocket and took the elevator to freedom.

He went directly to the Burdot Gallery to check on the last-minute details and to remind himself that getting canned by his crappy job didn't matter. He would devote his free time to making art. A day job would only slow him down after the show.

He climbed the stairs to the gallery and saw instantly that it was all wrong. Instead of putting the finishing touches on the show, there were people taking his art *off* the Sean Benning wall. He rushed at them. "Whoa, stop! What are you doing?"

"Taking this stuff down," said one of the workers, who wore paint-splattered coveralls.

"Why? What?" His heart was racing and the room seemed too bright. "Can you stop that?" he said to the one taking down his last piece. His head hurt. "Where's Camille?"

He heard the agitated click of her heels before he saw her. The unflappable Camille Burdot looked like she was about to implode. "Take them down, already," she yelled at the workers. "Move faster!" When she saw Sean, she clutched her chest and shrieked. "You terrified me. Where did you come from?"

"Why are you taking them down?" His hands were trembling. "Camille, what's going on?"

"What's going on," she said, bitterly, "is that I have to cut you from the show." She took a breath, then looked him in the eye. "I'm sorry. Very sorry."

"But," he stammered, "but it's all set to go. I've invited everyone I know." His heart pounded in his ears. "It's *tomorrow*."

"Trust me, this is a major blow to me, too."

"So why . . . what's . . . how come?"

She sighed. "One of our biggest investors fell in love with a new artist. When he gets this way, he is a big crybaby until he gets what he wants." She paused. "I had to pull you to include her."

"But . . ." His eyes darted around the room. "Why don't you pull someone else? You promised that I—"

"It's decided."

"Camille . . . I can . . . look . . . if I hang my work closer together, I can free up half the wall." This was a good idea. Constructive.

She was shaking her head tightly.

"Three quarters of the wall. I can figure it out. Just . . . just don't cut me."

"It's out of my control."

"But . . . it's . . . Who is it? Who's the artist?"

"You would not have heard of her," Camille said. "Like you, she is a newcomer."

"Camille, please, it's not fair. I—"

"Tell me about it," she snapped. "I'm having some nobody shoved down my throat. At my own gallery!" She exhaled sharply through her nose.

"What about one piece? Can I show just one piece?"

"No."

"No?" The word ricocheted inside his head, infuriating him. "No!? Who the hell are you to tell me *no*?" Everything in the room was blurring, spinning. He wheeled around, looking for something to help make his point. The stepladder by pregnant Ellie was the only prop around. He lunged for it and wound up aiming for an open piece of wall that used to house his work. He would smash the wall, make a hole, crack the whole gallery apart.

"Don't do it," Camille warned. "Just don't."

He tried to take a deep breath but the adrenaline was too strong and it came out as a grunt.

"You're talented." He noticed that Camille looked pale. "You'll get a show. Just not here. Not now."

He hurled the stepladder across the room where it landed with a loud crash. "Screw you, Camille," he said. "You just ruined my fucking life." He left without looking back. He was reeling when he hit the sidewalk. His cell phone vibrated in his pocket. He checked caller ID, then picked up.

"What the hell are you doing, Sean?" Walt was working the disappointed older brother tone. "You knew Bruce was looking into this for you."

"No," he spat back. "Bruce was trying to cover his own ass."

"This is your solution?" Walt's voice was loud. Behind him, Sean heard whooping and cheering. "You write an unsubstantiated story in a gossip rag? What did you think would happen?

That you'd bring down the most prestigious private school in the country?"

"My facts are accurate." Sean heard a whistle screech from Walt's side of the phone.

"Bradley will be fine. You, however, have dug your own grave."

"Screw you, Walt." He watched his breath freeze on contact with the air.

"I feel bad about the show. I do."

"The show . . ." He repeated the words slowly as he put it together. Walt knew about the show. He'd ratted him out to appease the Bradley dieties. "Prick. You fucking prick."

"I know it's tough. I like you, Sean. But this goes way beyond me now. You have officially pissed off the powers that be."

"I'm not scared of Bradley," he said, seething.

"Well maybe that's your fatal flaw." Sean heard a buzzer in the background. "If I were you I'd try to figure out a way to take it all back. But hey, it's your life to ruin."

Before Sean had even hung up the phone, he broke into an all out sprint. Chelsea Piers was only two blocks away.

He stormed through the glass doors to the gym, scanned the courts, and found Walt practicing free throws from the line. A couple of the other players were just arriving, unzipping their gym bags. The orthopedist was stretching. The whole thing happened in slow motion. Walt's eyes widened as he saw Sean run onto the court and rebound his bad shot. Sean must have looked as out of his mind as he felt, because every eye in the place was on him. He gathered his rage and threw a hard pass that drilled Walt in the gut and doubled him over. Walt was still hunched over gasping for air when Sean pulled him up by the T-shirt, wound up, and cracked him in the side of the face with his fist. It hurt like hell, and he thought he'd broken his hand. *It's worth it*, he thought, as he left Walt writhing on the ground. He felt the eyes of all of Walt's influential teammates on him as he stormed back out of the gym.

By the time he'd walked the ninety blocks uptown, the moment of victory was far behind him and the despair was back. The afternoon crowd at the bar oozed self-loathing. These were his people: washed up men wasting their lives. Their guts stretched over their belts, their red noses shoved into their drinks. It was only a matter of time for him. He pushed his glass toward the bartender, who refilled it without a word. With no job, no gallery show, and no chance of convincing anyone that Bradley was doing anything wrong, he sat glued to the TV above the bar, which he'd forced the bartender to leave on CNN. He drank another Scotch as he watched the talking heads tear apart his story. The talking head of the moment was Greg Clark, the President of the Board of Trustees of Bradley. His white hair, angry white eyebrows, and soft, saggy skin made it impossible not to trust the words coming out of his mouth.

"The unsupported accusations in the weekly gossip magazine are figments of a disgruntled parent's wild imagination," he said dismissively, as a picture of Sean's face appeared on the screen.

The bartender looked from the TV to Sean and back again. Twice. "That you?"

He shot the bartender a glance that insured he wouldn't ask any more questions, then turned back to CNN.

"This wouldn't be the first time a parent has blamed the school because his child couldn't keep up with the rigorous academics at Bradley. Mr. Benning's son was having problems at school. And the ... *article*," at this the guy made quotation marks in the air with his fingers, "contains no documentation or even evidence of any kind. Why?" he asked rhetorically. Condescendingly. "Because Bradley has done absolutely nothing wrong." He said it with a shake of his head, like he felt sorry for Sean's inability to distinguish fact from fiction.

Jess rushed in and spotted him. He'd left a message during his hourlong trek uptown, telling her where to meet him, but now he just wanted to drink himself into oblivion. "Are you okay?" She took the hand that wasn't wrapped around the glass.

"Bradley got to Burdot. I don't know how, but they made her pull me from the show."

"But—it's tomorrow. She can't . . . how can she . . . ?"

"Walt did it. You were right." A surge of renewed vitriol took hold of him and he batted the bowl of peanuts to the floor where they scattered. "I should have just walked away."

"Come on," Jess said, nudging him up from the barstool. "We'll get some coffee on the way home."

After Gloria went back to her own apartment and Toby was showering, he and Jess flipped through the channels, surveying the damage.

His *Buzz* article had gone viral. Not only had it been viewed half a million times on both The Huffington Post and the Drudge Report, it was all over the seven o'clock news. On NBC, a child psychologist was talking about the pressures on kids today. He kept referring to what he called "the overscheduled child," insisting parents didn't give their children enough downtime. On CBS, a representative from a group called Parents of Attention Deficit Disorder, or PADD, was ranting about how video games and high fructose corn syrup were responsible for the rise in ADD. ABC featured a pediatrician who outlined the dangers of methylphenidate-type drugs and reported that one in four college students now relied on ADD medication to help them study. He and Jess watched for a while. When he couldn't take it anymore, he left her with the remote and sat on Toby's bed.

"Can we read more *Prince Caspian*?" Toby asked.

Reading *Prince Caspian* was the last thing he wanted to do. "Sure," he said. He was still drunk but the hangover had already started. How was that possible? He lay on the bed and tried to get comfortable on the pillows next to Toby. He tried to focus on the page.

"Everyone except your Majesty knows that Miraz is a usurper," he read, thinking about how he could get back at Clark for saying those things about Toby on national television. "When he first began to rule he did not even pretend to be the King . . ." His mind flew to Toby's future, to the community college he'd be lucky to get into, to his job as a grocery bagger. "He called himself Lord Protector. But then your royal mother died, the good Queen and the only Telmarine who was ever kind to me. And then, one by one, all the great lords, who had known your father, died or disappeared. Not by accident, either. Bradley weeded them out."

"What?" Toby pried the book from his hands and studied the page. "Dad, *Miraz* weeded them out. Not Bradley."

"What?"

"You said Bradley."

"No I didn't."

"Dad, you seem tired."

"I am. I'm tired. Let's stop for the night."

"Aw, come on Dad. Please?"

"I'm beat, Tobe. I've got to go to bed."

"Can I read by myself for a while?"

"It's late. You need to—" Then he realized: Toby had just asked to read. By himself. For fun. The world could be falling down around them, which in a way it was. But if Toby wanted to read, everything was going to be okay. "You know what?" he said, casually, so he didn't kill the delicate moment. "Why not? It can be a special treat."

"Yay!" He snuggled against his pillow, holding the book up awkwardly and started to read.

Sean floated into the living room, unable to contain the smile. "He's reading," he said, sliding next to Jess on the couch. "He *asked* to read."

"Yesss," she said, throwing her head back and clenching the remote above her head in victory.

He squinted at the TV. "What are they saying now?"

"It just goes on and on. It's impossible to look away." She turned up the volume. On MSNBC, a twenty-four-year-old kid who had been diagnosed with ADD while he was at private school in Washington, D.C. was talking about his heroin addiction. "As a kid, my parents gave me Ritalin to fix my problems," he said. "Heroin didn't seem like a huge stretch to me. I'm trying to get clean now. My parents won't talk to me until I do, but, like, if you think about it, I'm really here because of them."

She flipped to CNN. A man in a suit, about Sean's age, was talking. "I never did well in school as a kid. I just thought I was stupid. Nothing the teachers said ever stuck. I couldn't focus long enough to finish a book or write a paper," he told the interviewer. "I was thirty when my doctor diagnosed me with ADD. I took that first pill and this noise in my head I'd never even noticed turned off and everything changed. Things made sense. I read books now. I can finish projects. I'm not saying methylphenidates are for everyone. But ADD isn't a pretend affliction. It's very real. And for someone who truly suffers from it, medication can make all the difference in the world."

"Thank you Duncan," the interviewer said, and turned to the camera. "That was Duncan Canton. His book, *The Medication Maze: How to Treat Your Child's Attention Deficit Disorder*, spent fifty-two weeks on the *New York Times* best-seller list. And now we're going to hear from the prestigious Bradley School, which is at the center of the *Buzz* magazine story that's got everyone talking."

A moment later, Bev Shineman was on TV. "Oh shit," Jess said, and turned up the volume.

"Our hearts go out to Toby Benning," Shineman was saying. She looked more pasty than usual. Fresh flowers filled the frame, though Sean had never seen flowers in her tiny office before. "We are thrilled with his complete recovery. But as you know, schools don't put children on medication. Parents do. It's not our place to even suggest it."

"Is there any truth at all to Mr. Benning's accusations that the school counsels parents toward medication?"

"Together with families, The Bradley School works to serve the students' best interests, so they may thrive and be successful."

"What about his accusations of forged signatures?"

"I think Mr. Benning has been watching too many movies. It's not like he has any proof whatsoever to back up his claims. The Bradley School is a top-notch institution with top-notch faculty. We've always put children first. It's why we've earned the reputation we have."

"So why would Mr. Benning be blaming the school so publicly?" the interviewer asked.

"It's perfectly normal for a parent to blame the school, the teachers, the doctors. It helps alleviate the guilt. But *as* the parent, he is ultimately responsible."

Sean snorted. He wondered if Daniels had given her a script.

"Am I right to assume the school will be pressing libel charges?"

"Absolutely," she said.

A quick cut and Billy Horn was on the screen. "The school psychologist pushed hard to make me put my son on that stuff. No way was I going to do it. But I know for a fact that article was right on. You don't want to believe Bradley could be doing that. But I'll tell you and anyone else who'll listen, you're wrong. In fact, I'm taking my son out of Bradley as soon as possible."

"Whoa," Jess said. "Did you know he was . . ." The sharp buzz of the intercom cut her off and they both flinched.

He hadn't ordered takeout and he definitely wasn't expecting company. Maybe if he ignored it, whoever it was would just go away. The intercom sounded again.

Jess looked scared. Sean stared at the house phone for a moment before picking up. "Yes?"

"I have a Meralee Drake down here for you," Manny announced.

Minutes later, Melanie was at the door, red-eyed and exhausted. When she saw Jess, she froze.

"It's okay," Sean said. "Jess is on the right side of this."

Melanie relaxed a little, but still looked confused. He thought about explaining, but quickly abandoned the idea.

"I can't believe you wrote that article," she said. "That was so ballsy."

Ballsy meant stupid where he came from. He wondered if Bradley would sue him directly or if they'd go after *Buzz* instead.

"I'm sorry I've been so . . ." She trailed off, shaking her head guiltily.

"Can I get you something? Tea or . . ."

"A drink would be great. Anything strong."

He cracked open a bottle of vodka that had been sitting in the freezer for years and poured three glasses.

"Cal is a private person," she said, accepting the drink. Sean wondered if someone who made the papers four times a week could really be described as "private." "At first, he was outraged that people wanted to know details. The peanut allergy seemed like such a simple way to make all the questions stop." She took a sip, grimaced, then took another.

"That makes sense," Jess said. "You wanted privacy."

"Exactly. That was all it was. At first."

He sat on the edge of his seat, waiting for the rest of it, listening to his pulse pound in his temples.

"I always wondered about the Metattent, whether Calvin really needed it. The school had pushed so hard, you were right about that. But the doctor's diagnosis was . . . and so many kids take it now I didn't think . . ." Her exhale was filled with grief. "Then that psychiatrist—the one from your story—wrote to me. He said the school had done this before. And then you came to the apartment and told me about Toby . . ." She cried silently. "Sean, I killed him. I killed my son."

"*They* killed him," Jess said, rubbing Melanie's back.

"You were trying to help him." He could only imagine how guilty she felt and would feel for the rest of her life. But she was here. She wanted to talk, and he had so many questions. "When I asked you if Calvin was taking medication, why did you lie?"

She wiped her eyes with a tissue Jess handed her. "I signed something."

"What do you mean?"

"I signed something that said I would stick with the peanut allergy story. It seemed like a good deal. We didn't want people gossiping about Calvin. And Susannah's—you know she's still at Bradley—she's looking at colleges this summer. They made it worth our while."

"Bradley bribed you?"

"They called it a settlement."

"How much?"

She looked him dead in the eye. "Lots."

"But . . ." He assumed the Drakes had more money than God.

"The last few years have been rough. We were in no position to turn down that much cash." Her fingers pulled through her hair. "Jesus, we sound like monsters . . . At first it all seemed reasonable. Our privacy was preserved. It all made sense. Nothing was going to bring him back, maybe we should just move on. But now I can't sleep. I can't eat, knowing I'm responsible for the next kid." She closed her eyes but he could tell it wasn't keeping away the demons. "Knowing that Susannah is going to that school every day . . . I can't bear it."

"What could Bradley do to you if you talked to the lawyer now?"

"I don't know." She wrung her hands. "Cal forbade me to talk about this with you, with anyone."

He buried his head in his hands. "What a mess."

No one noticed Toby padding out of his bedroom. "Done reading," he said.

"Toby." Melanie brightened briefly. "How are you? Look how tall you've gotten."

"I'm good." Toby looked at the three of them, trying to figure out what was going on. "When did you come?"

"I just stopped by to talk to your dad." She tilted her head to get a better look at the book.

"It's *Prince Caspian*." Toby offered it to her. "Did Calvin ever read it?"

She shook her head sadly. "No, he never got to read that one."

"Because I think he'd like it."

Melanie nodded silently as tears gathered in her eyes.

Sean hopped up and redirected Toby. "Wow it's late. Brush teeth and I'll be in to say goodnight."

When Toby had disappeared down the hallway, Melanie's expression changed. It was now steely. "I'm going to . . ." She cleared her throat. "I'm going to talk to the lawyer you told me about."

"But—" He was trying to keep up. "You just said . . . so you're . . ."

"I'm going to talk to the lawyer." She said it slowly, clearly. Possibly to convince herself.

He nodded because he was afraid words might break the spell.

"Let's call her now," she said. "Before I change my mind." Her son was dead and now she was about to kill her marriage and life as she knew it. He picked up the phone and dialed Nina. This could unfold in countless ways, but one thing was certain: Nina wasn't going to be able to sit on this one.

CHAPTER THIRTY-ONE

ON HIS LAST DAY IN HIS APARTMENT, SEAN STRETCHED THE packing tape over the last box and looked around the living room. Ellie had come to say goodbye to Toby. In the end, he'd left most of the furniture for her. Either she'd chosen it or it was crap, not worth lugging. His eyes settled on the tea kettle. He couldn't remember ever having used it, but it had been his mother's, so he grabbed it.

Looking around the apartment, he flashed back to when he was ten years old, moving out of his childhood house. The idea of leaving everything he knew had been terrifying. Now, he watched Ellie pick up Toby's backpack in one hand. Her other rested possessively, lovingly, on his shoulder. Either Toby was fine or he was hiding it well.

"Locked and loaded," Toby announced, pulling the Spiderman suitcase behind him. He held up a plastic bag bulging with five-month-old Halloween candy. "For the road."

"Toothbrush?" Sean asked.

Toby stopped in his tracks, dropped his suitcase and ran back to the bathroom.

"So," Ellie said with a sad smile, "this is it."

"I guess it is." He'd always hated endings, but this was different.

She pondered her feet uncomfortably. "I didn't believe you. About Bradley." Her boobs heaved when she sighed. He noticed they were a little smaller than they'd been.

"Ellie, you don't have to—"

"You were right," she cut him off. "I was so angry. At you—" She shrugged. "At myself. I couldn't see past it, but I should have trusted you."

"It's okay," he said, and meant it.

"Okay," Toby said, running back to them. "Ready."

Ellie crouched down and rested her hands on his shoulders. "So it'll look different when you come back," she said. "But your room will be just the same."

Anywhere else in the country, the arrangement would be absurd. But in New York people did insane things for rent-controlled apartments. Ellie would keep the place in Montauk and also live part-time here, in the home she and Sean couldn't live in together. She'd said she wanted continuity for Toby when he came back to visit every two weekends. She was also thinking about work again.

Toby's entire world was about to change, and Sean realized that giving him a minute wouldn't be a bad idea.

"Come on." Toby bounced impatiently. "Let's hit the road."

Sean hoisted the last box onto his shoulder and followed Toby out the door. Ellie locked it and they rode the elevator downstairs in silence.

For some reason, shaking Manny's hand was the thing that choked him up. "Thanks man," Sean said, his throat thick with emotion.

Nicole was reading the paper in the front seat of the rented Ford station wagon he'd double parked in front of the building. He jiggled the box down from his shoulder, caught it with both hands, and wedged it in the back. Before slamming the hatch, he surveyed the contents of the trunk. Except for his artwork, which would be shipped the next week, this was the evidence of his life to this point. When he'd moved to New York, he was sure he would be here forever. In a few minutes it would be his past.

He kept waiting for the regret, but it wasn't coming. After the past six months, he couldn't help thinking of New York as a trap, an amped-up bubble where everything had to be better, faster, more impressive. Cheryl felt the need to look twenty years younger with a perfect ass and toned everything. Ellie hadn't been able to conceive, and in a world where failure wasn't an option, she'd lost her ability to function at all. And he'd somehow let himself be convinced that his eight-year-old had a *deficit*—not because he was behind, but because he wasn't ahead. It was a unique brand of insanity that thrived in Manhattan. He swore he'd never fall into it again.

Suddenly, all Sean wanted to do was hop in the Ford and watch the city recede in the rearview mirror.

Manny emerged from the lobby waving a stack of mail. "Last mail before the post office forwards to the new place." He presented the mail to Sean with a solemnity appropriate to the final transaction as doorman and tenant.

Sean nodded in gratitude and flipped through the pile. He shoved the Time Warner bill into his pocket and handed the catalogs to Ellie. Then he noticed an envelope made of heavy paper the color of vanilla ice cream. He stared at the return address on the back before tearing it open.

Dear Sean,

Again I am so very sorry for the way things were left between us. I can imagine how angry you were when I pulled you from the show. Understand I had no choice in the matter.

I hope you don't mind, but I took the liberty of sending images of your work to a friend of mine who owns the Kennedy-Tufts gallery in Boston. Like me, he fell in love with them. If you have no objections, I'd like to send the work to Jacques. He'd like to talk to you about setting up a show. He's curating something at the Met he thinks you will be perfect for. I'm enclosing his card so you can be in touch with him directly.

I wish you all the best in your career, Sean. I will be following it with great interest.

Sincerely,

Camille Burdot

Camille had come through. Even after the shitty things he'd said to her. After throwing the stepladder. Over the past year, he'd amassed incontrovertible proof that people did horrible things. Camille's act of kindness leveled him. He wished he could apologize, thank her for this.

He watched Ellie pick up Toby and hug him tight, trying to keep it together. "Love you sweetie."

"Promise you'll be here when I get back," Toby said, bursting into tears. In all the excitement, he'd forgotten to be terrified he was going to lose her again.

She squeezed him. "Swear to God," she said. Then they were all crying. "I'm going to drive up to see you in your new house on Saturday, okay?"

Toby wiped his tears and nodded. Sean flicked away his own as inconspicuously as possible.

Nicole got out of the car, sidled up to Sean, and whacked him with a rolled-up paper.

"What was that for?" Sean said, slipping Jacques' business card into his wallet.

"It's for you." She held out the *Times*. "Your new best friend, Ben Shapiro, has been busy."

Ben Shapiro had broken the Bradley story for the *Times*. After Melanie and Jess talked to Nina Goldsmith about Calvin and the forged signature, it had all happened quickly. Bruce Daniels was fired the next afternoon, escorted from the school by policemen. Also canned immediately were the school nurse and Bev Shineman. With Garvey's help, Ben Shapiro dug up a half dozen other cases, one of which involved a former classmate of Toby's, a kid named Patrick who'd been hospitalized last year. The members of the Board of Trustees were under investigation and Walt was being looked at for brokering the Drake bribe. There was talk of a class action suit.

Today's story was broader. It led with Bradley, but delved deep into the trend across the country. Manhattan wasn't the only city with a Ritalin problem. Kids all over the country were being dosed for school. Ben Shapiro had even dug up statistics that showed how the different states fared: Nevada reported only 5.6 percent of its children had been diagnosed with ADHD while North Carolina came in with a high of 15.6 percent. Dr. Altherra told the paper that the practice of diagnosing children based on teacher evaluations needed to be re-evaluated. Experts from prestigious institutions debated which behaviors needed to be medicated and which were normal on the spectrum of childhood development. The article even went on to suggest there was evidence that a handful of the country's elite schools were in bed with the drug companies. In his wildest dreams, Sean hadn't imagined this kind of attention.

"You kicked their ass," Nicole said. "I'm proud of you."

She didn't say it often and when she did, it was powerful. "If a five hundred-word story in a trashy celebrity rag set off this kind of wildfire," Sean countered, "it must have been smoldering for a long time. All I did was give it some oxygen."

"You rule, baby brother. Don't you dare play that down."

He wasn't sure what to do with all this blatant praise from his sister. "At least the lawsuits are being dropped," he said. When the *Times* stories started to run, proving that everything he'd written had been true, Bradley was forced to drop the libel suit against *Buzz*. And when *Buzz* was hailed in every media outlet around the world for breaking the story, Crandall dropped the lawsuit against Sean. It was all falling into place, which was the last thing he'd expected a few weeks earlier. Much of that was due to Ben Shapiro and Nina Goldsmith, who had done serious damage. But it was impossible to know what kind of lasting effect any of it would have.

"And my task force was approved this morning." Nicole smiled smugly.

"Task force?"

"To look into the practice of prescribing ADD medication for children in New York City public schools."

"So you got a promotion?"

"And a raise," she said in the same way she used to come home to report an A+ on a paper. A rush of warmth for his sister caught him off guard. Luckily he didn't have to say goodbye. He would see her every couple of weeks while Toby was in the city with Ellie.

"Let's hit the road," Toby said. He'd pushed through the tears and was now revved for the journey.

Sean flashed an open-handed salute to Nicole and then to Ellie. "See you soon."

They pulled away from the curb and headed up Broadway to Jess's old apartment on 123rd Street where she'd retrieved the last of her things. She waved when she saw them coming, and hoisted her bags into the back seat.

"Hey guys," she said, letting in a blast of cold air.

"How was it?" He hated thinking of her in there with the old boyfriend, even if it had only been for a few hours.

"Fabulous," she said, meaning the opposite. She turned to face Toby in the back seat. "Ready for a road trip?"

"Road trip, road trip," Toby chanted.

Jess squinted at the *Times* sitting on the seat between them, picked it up, and started reading. It took a moment to register, then she let out a loud whooping sound. "A national trend story? Ben Shapiro is a *god*."

"Then you're a goddess. None of this would have happened if you hadn't come forward."

"We are a carful of deities," she proclaimed. "Let's hit the highway."

Sean smiled and pulled the car away from the curb. "Okay everyone, say goodbye to New York. For a while anyway."

"Um, Dad?"

Sean knew that tone. "Tobe, you should've gone before we left."

"No, it's just . . ." Toby hesitated. "Can I say goodbye to my school before we go?"

"Really?" The idea of seeing it again made Sean's stomach turn.

Toby nodded. "Really."

Sean made a right turn onto 125th. "Of course we can." They were chatty as they drove down Fifth Avenue, but when the car pulled up in front of Bradley, they were silent.

"If it's so bad," Toby said, not taking his eyes off it, "what about my friends? Why don't their parents make them go someplace else, too?"

"Bradley's not bad," Jess said, carefully. "There were some bad people there who did some bad things. But they're gone now."

"They are?"

Jess nodded. "Your friends will be okay."

Toby looked at Bradley wistfully. There was no denying it was a beautiful building—as long as you didn't look too closely.

"Okay," Toby said.

"Ready?"

"Ready."

Speeding north on the FDR, Sean felt the anxiety Bradley had created in his life drain away.

"What's a road trip without snacks?" Jess said, reaching into her duffel and producing a box of donuts.

"I call chocolate," Toby said. "Do they have good donuts in Westerly?" he asked, as soon as his mouth was full.

"*Good* donuts?" Jess said, handing him a napkin. "They're the best. There's a place called Donut Heaven and if you get there early enough you can watch them make the donuts. They've got a Boston Cream that might be the best thing I've ever had."

"Let's go there tomorrow," Toby said. "I want to see how they make donuts."

"Me too," Sean said, thinking about tomorrow and what it would be like for the three of them to wake up together in Westerly. It had all happened so fast—getting their jobs, the place, deciding to live together. From a distance it seemed impulsive, crazy. But he didn't have any doubt in his mind. In fact, he'd never been so sure of anything.

"Can I be in your class at my new school?" Toby asked Jess.

She smiled at him. It was bright, almost blinding. "I'll be teaching sixth grade this year," she said. "You're going to have Miss Moore." Toby looked skeptical. "I hear she uses candy to teach math."

Toby's eyes widened. "She does sound good."

"And I'm going to teach you art," Sean said.

"I know, Dad. You told me."

Jess stifled a laugh. "Maybe your dad will use candy, too."

"Stranger things have happened," Sean said. "Much stranger."

Rhode Island seemed as good a place as any for a fresh start, plus it would be easy for Ellie to visit Toby. Easy to bring Toby into the city. Toby would have two cities, two apartments, two parents. That was the most important thing.

"Will our apartment have two bedrooms?"

"We're going to have a whole house. Remember?"

"With a basement?" Toby asked. "And an attic?"

"And a room for making art." He loved the sound of it. "For both of us."

"Cool," Toby said. "And I can get a Formica bunk bed in my room? For when my friends come to visit?"

"Formica?"

"Yeah, you said we were going to get our new furniture in Formica."

Sean and Jess looked at each other, baffled. Jess figured it out first. "From Ikea."

"Right. That's what I said."

"From Ikea," he repeated, and smiled to himself. "Yes. You can absolutely get a bunk bed from Ikea. We'll go together—all three of us—and pick out furniture for our new house."

"But not all at once," Jess said.

"That's right, we're going to take our time, pick things we really like."

They'd decided the night before not to rush any of it, to let it unfold on its own. Their home, their relationship, their careers would evolve and they'd take life as it came. And he knew it would all work out because everything that mattered was within arm's reach.

He eased off the accelerator and settled in for the ride. He had plenty of time to get where he was going.

ACKNOWLEDGMENTS

A special thanks to those who helped this book see the light of day. I owe you big time:

To my earliest readers, Dean Hicks and Karen Palmer, thank you for not mentioning how crappy the first draft was, and for just telling me to keep going. Jennifer Belle, Michael Sears, Desiree Rhine, Jon Reiss and Juliann Garey, your brutal honesty and kind encouragement helped me stay the course through a long re-write (and a half). Thanks especially to Juris Jurjevics for his inability to sugarcoat and for helping me find the heart of this book (a moment of silence please, for the bloody scraps left on the cutting room floor).

I might never have started this book if it hadn't been for Nicole Bokat's class and an assignment to write the entire outline for the second session. That seemed insane, but it got me started. Phil Neal, Kara Unterberg, Jim Delisle, Jon Spurney, Mick Herron, Abby

Wasserman, Nancy Jaffe, and Steve Kettmann, thank you for your intelligent insights that simply made the book better. Thanks also to Jeff Gordinier for being my personal cheering section as well as a sobering source of inspiration.

To my brothers, Andrew and Matthew, and their exceptional wives, Rebecca and Flossie, and to Graham, for believing in me and in this book and for helping with the kids on so many days, to give me time to get a few more words down.

Thanks to The Vermont Studio Center for the residencies that allowed me to spend time in your beautiful space and write and write and write, and to "Colt" Barrows for his support through all of this, even though he hasn't read a novel in years.

But most of all, thanks to my wonderful agent, Stéphanie Abou and to my amazing editor Jessica Case and publisher Claiborne Hancock, who saw the potential and gave this book a life. I am forever indebted to you (and also to Juliet Grames, who pointed me in Stéphanie's direction in the first place.)

Of course, none of this would have happened without the love and support and creative spirit of my parents. I will be forever grateful to my immensely talented father, Alan Hruska, who encouraged me every step of the way, and to my mother, Laura Hruska, my first, last, and perennial editor. I miss her every day.

And finally, thanks to Will and Nick, to whom this book is dedicated. You've been there through the ups and downs and the never-ending revisions. You are not only the inspiration for this book, you gave me the time I needed to finish. You are, without question, the best kids, ever. I love you with everything I've got.